THE SCENT
OF SECRETS

DOUBLEDAY CANADA

THE
SCENT
OF
SECRETS

A NOVEL

JANE
THYNNE

Doubleday Canada and colophon are registered trademarks of Random House of
Canada Limited

Originally published in the United Kingdom by Simon & Schuster UK Ltd, London, in
2014 in a different form.

This book contains an excerpt from the forthcoming book *The Pursuit of Pearls*
(originally published in the United Kingdom as *The Winter Garden* in a different form
in 2014) by Jane Thynne. This excerpt has been set for this edition only and may not
reflect the final content of the forthcoming edition.

Library and Archives Canada Cataloguing in Publication

Thynne, Jane, author
The scent of secrets / Jane Thynne.

Issued in print and electronic formats.
ISBN 978-0-385-68291-6 (deluxe trade pbk.).--ISBN 978-0-385-68292-3 (epub)

I. Title.

PR6070.H96S24 2015   823'.914   C2015-901949-4
                                              C2015-901950-8

The Scent of Secrets is a work of historical fiction. Apart from the well-known actual
people, events, and locales that figure in the narrative, all names, characters, places, and
incidents are the products of the author's imagination or are used fictitiously. Any re-
semblance to current events or locales, or to living persons, is entirely coincidental.

Book design by Barbara M. Bachman

Printed and bound in the USA

Published in Canada by Doubleday Canada,
a division of Random House of Canada Limited,
a Penguin Random House Company

www.penguinrandomhouse.ca

10 9 8 7 6 5 4 3 2 1

Penguin
Random House
DOUBLEDAY CANADA

For
Joanna Coles

How horrible, fantastic, incredible it is that we should be digging trenches and trying on gas masks here because of a quarrel in a faraway country between people of whom we know nothing.

—NEVILLE CHAMBERLAIN,
SEPTEMBER 1938

Our displacement of women from public life occurs solely to restore their essential dignity to them.

—JOSEPH GOEBBELS

In my state, the Mother is the most important citizen.

—ADOLF HITLER

AUGUST 1938

I T WAS ANOTHER FINE SUMMER'S DAY AND THE MS *WILHELM Gustloff* cruise liner was making its leisurely way across the Atlantic Ocean. The 25,000-ton ship rose like a sheer white cliff from the water, eight stories high, gracefully transporting a cargo of more than a thousand citizens of the German Reich. The sun was already dazzling, bouncing back from a sea of hammered cobalt as the ship's prow carved a confident line past the spectacular coastline of Madeira. The island, with its black volcanic sand, its coves fringed with laurel trees, and red-roofed houses clambering up the mountain slopes, glittered in the sapphire morning light. Birds with iridescent necks and little dashes of blood at their throats fluttered through the wooded mountains, which were swathed at their peaks with a light garland of cloud. A fine spray, thick with the tang of salt, pearled the faces of the people watching from the deck, many of whom had never set foot outside the Reich and had never seen the sea. The liner was the first dedicated ship of the National Socialist Strength Through Joy movement, the Kraft durch Freude, organized by the German Labor Front, and it was the only way an ordinary German was able to leave the country now. The fact that the passengers were getting a glimpse of the world that lay beyond the borders of the Reich— for now at any rate—and that they were seeing it on a two-week cruise costing less than a fortnight's wages, was yet another reason to be grateful for the Führer's reforms.

ADA FREITAG HAD NEVER seen the sea before either, but that didn't mean she wanted to hang over the deck, waving a swastika flag at it. Smearing a little more Elizabeth Arden suncream on her freckles and over the skin on her shoulders, already turning a rich caramel, she anchored her bag more firmly beneath one arm, lay back in her deck chair, and tried unsuccessfully to relax.

Relaxing was not, Ada had quickly realized, a priority on a Strength Through Joy holiday. Even when at sea, any citizen enjoying a KdF tour had a packed schedule of daily activity, requiring daunting levels of enthusiasm and stamina. The day began in the main dining room with a ceremony of dedication to the Führer (compulsory), presided over by a portrait of the man himself, regulation scowl in place, tar-black hair slicing diagonally across his brow. The ship had originally been named the *Adolf Hitler*, until the assassination of Gustloff, Party leader in Switzerland, by a Jewish upstart had provided a Nazi martyr made for the bow of a ship. But even without his name on the side, Hitler's image was everywhere: in the cocktail lounge, above the swimming pool, even glowering out at passengers when they took a bath. There was no such thing as a holiday from the Führer.

The morning's dedication ceremony was followed by a strenuous series of PE workouts on deck, gym sessions, fencing, table tennis, dancing lessons, piano recitals, swimming galas, and bridge parties, all of which were not so much obligatory as strongly recommended by the ship's holiday reps, who didn't leave you alone until you gave in.

Just walking round the ship was a major expedition. There was the Führer suite on B deck, kept for VIPs, the walnut-paneled Folk Costume Lounge, and the Winter Garden. The German Hall, the Music Salon, the Ballroom, and seven different bars. There was an indoor swimming pool, bouncing with echoes from excited Bund Deutscher Mädel girls bathed in dazzling, refracted light. And then there were meals, meals, and more meals, which you had to dress up for and which were served with napkins folded into swastika shapes, beneath banners sewn with the KdF slogan ENJOY YOUR LIVES! The coffee tables had ashtrays with pictures of the ship on their plastic bases and matchbooks, with WILHELM GUSTLOFF printed in gold lettering, alongside them. Someone had put the Hitler Jugend in charge of the ship's radio, which meant that in between the dance music and regular broadcasts from Joseph Goebbels, random exhortations were bellowed over the Tannoy, mostly concerning military excitements. The most recent one had come when the *Wilhelm Gustloff* passed a couple of German warships idling off the coast of France, and passengers were urged to "think of the man who has given the German people their reputation and their position of power in the world: our Führer." The HJ boys had also instituted a daily quiz—sample question "What is Adolf Hitler's favorite flower?"—to which the passengers roared the answers in unison.

In her chair on the sundeck, a silk scarf round her head, Ada kept her eyes shut and sighed. Looking at the sea made her feel sick, what with the glare of the sun off its writhing currents and the stink of fish. The vast expanse of water only reminded her how far from home she was, and the proximity of so many others made her feel nervous. Far better to lie back and pretend to be asleep even if there was no chance of relaxing.

Yesterday, to break the tedium, she had taken a trip ashore, but even on dry land the pace did not relent. It was an outing to Funchal to view the flora. The group had wended their way past jacarandas thrusting fiery purple blossoms in their faces, giant ferns and dragon trees, yellow frangipani and tremulous orchids. Above them the mountain slopes were tumbling with verdant growth, and in the market old women in shawls attempted to sell them lace, wicker baskets, and painted gourds. One woman had a fruit Ada had never seen, pomegranate it was called, a fruit like a cup full of jewels, but as she stretched out her hand, the tour guide leapt forward and advised her not to touch it on account of disease. The guides were exactly like schoolteachers. While everyone was marveling at the banana trees and the birds-of-paradise and flamingo flowers, the tour guide kept pointing out the poverty of the local inhabitants, their ramshackle homes and gutters flowing with waste, saying these things proved how other cultures were inferior to the Germans'. It was lucky the locals didn't understand. The peasant women kept on smiling their toothless smiles while the group ignored them and hurried on. Bringing up the rear were a couple of SS surveillance staff, employed to prevent the German women striking up holiday romances with foreign men. The guards were a burly pair, who saw everything and wouldn't hesitate to rough up any locals who tried as much as a friendly greeting.

Avoiding men had become a full-time occupation for Ada. She couldn't help having good legs, a nice dress, and a suntan, but the ship was full of lads who had qualified for their tickets in groups from the factories where they worked and were delighted to find any unattached women, let alone a pretty twenty-three-year-old with a voluptuous figure, a snub nose, full lips, and eyes of bright Aryan blue. Ada's creamy blond plaits framed a face as delicate as that of a porcelain doll, and her red and yellow halter-neck sundress emphasized her generous curves. Men hung around her like wasps, offering to buy her a beer and asking for a dance. Even when she picked up one of her stack of film magazines they didn't let up, making idiotic comments about movie stars or suggesting, predictably, she should be on screen herself.

But Ada had not the slightest interest in men just then, or in Madeira and its flowers. She was far too nervous for that. Her entire attention was fixed on the ship's next stop, Lisbon. There the *Wilhelm Gustloff* would dock and she would complete the business she had come for. Then there would be plenty of time to enjoy herself and she might even take one of the young men up on his offer. In the meantime, to stop being bothered, she had come up with a pretty good deterrent.

At first, when the teenager from the neighboring cabin had begun stealing glances at her, Ada had sighed. He couldn't be more than fifteen, with a wiry boy's frame just beginning to fill out and the faintest dusting of hair on his upper lip. Actually his lean, dark-eyed face reminded Ada of her little brother. The lad was on holiday with his grandmother, who had qualified for the tickets through her job at Berlin's Charité hospital, and they had been assigned to Ada's table at breakfast. As she tried to eat her eggs, Ada found herself machine-gunned with questions. Where did she come from? Berlin? They did too! Weren't they lucky to have tickets on the best ship of the fleet? And only its second cruise! How had she qualified for hers? Then the boy noticed the film magazines and an album of movie star cards she had—the kind you sent off for with coupons from your cigarette packets—and he became even more excited. Did she know his own godmother was a film actress? Her name was Clara Vine and she was featured on a cigarette card herself. Perhaps Ada had her picture?

Emboldened by this shared enthusiasm, the boy had skipped his post-breakfast gym session and offered to carry Ada's coffee up to the sundeck. She could tell from the puppyish way he followed her that he was in the grip of a serious teenage infatuation. Ada groaned inwardly, until she suddenly realized the boy's devotion might actually be an advantage. His name was Erich Schmidt, and he wanted to tell her all about his plans to join the Luftwaffe. That was fine by Ada. She closed her eyes and instructed Erich to keep talking.

The thing was, it wasn't just the factory workers who had set Ada's nerves on edge. Yesterday, she had been lying in the same spot on her lounger when she caught a brief snatch of scent that made her sit up in alarm. She couldn't understand why she had reacted the way she did. It was inexplicable. But there was some prickle of danger in that harsh, citrus-edged cologne, some quality in its musky base notes that left an ominous imprint on the air. It was the kind of perfume that hung on a person, like garlic on the breath. For a second the perfume formed itself into something mistily substantial—a wraith with an arrogant face, eyes black as olive pits, and a smile sharp as a knife—but the image was gone as swiftly as it had come, like a puff of breath misting a mirror, wiped away to reveal nothing. Ada tried to conceal her alarm, yet she must have looked worried because a girl in a deck chair near to hers, with pasty skin, lank braids, and thick spectacles, noticed her distraction.

"Is anything the matter?"

Ada was tempted to ask whether the girl herself had seen anyone, but realized instinctively that this was a matter she needed to keep to herself, so she turned a dismissive, suntanned shoulder and said rudely, "No. Why should it be?"

That morning, after Erich had gone off happily to fetch the coffee, Ada caught a trace of the cologne again. There was definitely a memory floating there, amid the mix of lemon, amber, and moss. Though the day was perfectly warm, a chill crept over her. She clutched her cardigan and sat up, her filmy scarf snapping in the breeze. She looked around at the women, wedged in their deck chairs with their copies of *Stern* and *Die Dame,* and their husbands with their trousers rolled up, but she could see nothing to account for it. Yet like an animal hearing a sound much higher than human ears can hear, Ada detected in that perfume a note of danger, a high, ringing register of alarm with a low undertone of fear. Attempting to rationalize the feeling, she reminded herself how very many people used the same scent. Kölnisch Wasser eau de cologne, for instance, Germany's oldest scent, was used by millions. It was said to be the Führer's favorite. There was no reason why this one particular scent should mean anything at all. It reminded her of something, though, and it was something that made her afraid. It was a male scent, so it must be a man she was reminded of, but which man?

Was it someone back home? Ada frowned and gnawed her lip as she tried to place it, but all she knew was that the scent made her heart race and the hairs rise on the back of her neck. She needed to know where that perfume came from, if only for her peace of mind.

Thank goodness for the boy, balancing two cups and two pastries on a tray, which he must have bought with his own cash.

"What a darling you are, Erich! Now I have to go somewhere, just for a minute. Could you look after my things? Make sure you keep an eye on them. And don't let anyone take this deck chair."

The boy looked dismayed at having his coffee spurned, and she felt a pang of guilt, but there was nothing for it.

Decisively Ada put down her magazine, rose from the deck chair, and strode off.

ERICH WAITED AN HOUR, watching Ada's coffee grow cold and eating both pastries himself, before he realized that she was not coming back. The awful suspicion arose that she did not have an important appointment at all. Maybe she had just been trying to get rid of him. A humiliated flush stained his cheeks as he imagined all the fat women—friends of his grandmother's sitting around in their deck chairs—secretly laughing at him while they pretended to read their magazines. They must assume he had an adolescent crush, but it wasn't like that; there had been a real connection between Ada and himself, despite the age difference, and it wasn't just because she was so beautiful. It was to do with the way her eyes sparkled when she looked at him over her sunglasses and the interest she took in his future with the Luftwaffe. The way they seemed to share the same taste in movies. He couldn't have made a mistake, could he?

He sensed the sly glances of the other holidaymakers and felt a twist of anger. He had never wanted to take a summer holiday with his grandmother, what boy would? Oma kept going on about what a privilege it was to go on a KdF trip and how the ship would be luxurious beyond their wildest dreams. There was even a library on board. But what boy in his right mind wanted a library on holiday?

A little after four o'clock a squall blew in from the east, pitting the watered silk of the sea and driving everyone from the sundecks inside to play skat or table tennis and watch the spray lashing the portholes from the warmth of the recreation areas. Only one hardy passenger, shivering in the spitting rain, remained on deck to witness what followed.

The first thing she noticed was a commotion at the port side of the ship, where a gaggle of sailors were shouting and hauling an object onto the rain-lashed deck. She thought it was a fish, a shark perhaps, or a porpoise, but wiping the spray from her glasses and looking closer, she saw it was a young woman's body, beached like some delicate, exotic mermaid from a child's fairy story. The dead girl lay on her back, curly hair plastered across her face like seaweed and skin as white as a fish, her flesh already turning to ice. Water gushed from her mouth and nostrils, and ran in rivulets down her face, pooling around her body as it lay defenselessly still. For a second the sailors stood gaping at her until the youngest of them, the one who had first glimpsed the white shape rolling on the waves and raised the alarm, grabbed a tarpaulin to wrap her up. So the woman watching caught only a glimpse of the girl's face, just enough to see that it was extraordinarily pretty in the conventional Germanic model, with high, arched eyebrows and blue eyes now fixed and empty, as if their color had already been washed out by the sea. The dead girl wore a halter-neck sundress that clung to every voluptuous curve, leaving nothing to the imagination except, perhaps, the method of her death. For the back of her head was a great bloody mess of hair and bone, the kind of wound that might have been sustained by hitting the side of the ship as she fell or even, perhaps, suffering a blow from a heavy instrument, if such a thing were possible.

THE HORRIFIED PASSENGER WAS shooed swiftly away from the scene and later that day received a personal visit in her cabin from Heinrich Bertram, the ship's captain, who was most solicitous about her shock. He suggested that she try to forget it as much as possible and enjoy the rest of her holiday. It would be wrong to allow a tragedy like this to mar such a special voyage, let alone spoil the enjoyment of others by talking about it. Captain Bertram had to warn the gnädiges Fräulein that any mention of the incident anywhere else at all would have serious repercussions for her, both at home and in the workplace, and put at risk the chance of any future trips she or her family might hope to make with the KdF.

THE SCENT
OF SECRETS

1

PARIS

P ARIS IN LATE AUGUST 1938 WAS A CITY LIVING ON ITS NERVES.
Rumors swarmed around the streets like rats, refugees
from every corner of Europe brushed shoulders on the bou-
levards, and the cafés were a babel of foreign languages—
Spanish, Italian, Czech, Polish, and of course, German,
rising and falling in anxious disputation. In the city center
the clatter of cream-topped buses, the blare of taxi horns,
and the shouts of traffic gendarmes were overlaid with the
distant sound of reservists, in hastily assembled khaki,
marching along the Champs-Élysées. German, Austrian,
Polish, and Hungarian Jews congregated in the Marais
quarter in anxious exile, scraping a living by day, and drinking it by night. Morsels of foreign news were picked up and
ravenously chewed on, then discarded as propaganda or lies.
Refugees choked the railway stations. Native Parisians were
packing up and moving their families to the country. Others
lingered longer than usual in the churches. A dry summer

wind blew around the city, chivvying along the gutters a vortex of leaves and litter and scraps of newspaper alarm. Hitler was claiming that the German-speaking population of Czechoslovakia's Sudetenland, just south of the German border, desired reunion with the Reich. If the Czech government did not agree, he would march in and take it. France and England seemed certain to reject Germany's demands. Hitler had set the date of October 1 for military action. The threat of war hung like a distant thunderstorm on a sunny day.

CLARA VINE THREW OPEN the tall shutters, leaned over the narrow balcony, and gazed down at the Boulevard de Sébastopol below. She had only three days on location in Paris; the last two of them had been spent shooting scenes for her latest film, an adaptation of Maupassant's *Bel Ami*, but the third, today, was entirely, gloriously, free. A whole day ahead of her and only an engagement that evening before catching a train at the Gare du Nord early the next morning and heading back home to the Babelsberg studio in Berlin. She could visit the Louvre, go shopping, see a concert, or maybe just sit in a square beneath the dusty trees and drink a café crème. An entire day to herself in Paris! No lines to learn, no character to assume. No takes or retakes, no director's temper or costume fittings. No delays or disputes. After filming almost nonstop for months, a day off in a foreign location felt like a fantasy. And despite the mood of the city, Clara was determined to make the most of it.

The Bellevue, where the cast was staying, was not everyone's idea of Parisian chic. Its forty rooms were squeezed into a narrow, five-story building, and Clara's bedroom on the top floor was sweltering. The paint on the wrought-iron balconies was flaking, the plaster decayed, and the entire building reeked of drains. But who cared about that when there was all of Paris to look at?

The city seemed impossibly beautiful, the elegant precision of its buildings and the classical uniformity of its blocks and streets bathed in a golden light that appeared to saturate the pale stone. Even now, in high summer, when most Parisians were on their vacations, the pavements were thronged with people. Immediately below Clara's window, between the patchy trunks of the plane trees, a cart bulged with red, yellow, and pink blooms, like a bright shout of color in the morning air. Vans making deliveries and a porter hauling a crate of baguettes collided with a man bearing a box of oranges on his head. In the fishmonger's window a chorus line of doomed lobsters waved their limbs helplessly on a tray. Young women with crimson lips and kohl-lined eyes clipped past wearing Breton-necked tops with wide scarves slung diagonally across them, in keeping with the latest fashion, and little felt hats studded with flowers or feathers. Some wore printed summer dresses in ice-cream colors, and they even managed to make their heavy wooden-soled shoes look stylish. Men in open-necked shirts and berets swaggered past. Despite the undercurrent of nerves that rippled through the city, the citizens on the Boulevard de Sébastopol were doing their best impression of elegant nonchalance.

What a contrast with Berlin! In Clara's home city the daily roundups of Jews and the sporadic Gestapo cruelties had worsened throughout the year. That spring Hitler had marched into Austria and found himself greeted not with hostilities but with a carpet of roses; *Blumenkreig,* he called it, a war of flowers. The lack of international outcry over the Anschluss had only emboldened him. Hitler was, everyone realized, more confident than ever.

Unlike Clara herself.

Clara Vine had made a successful career for herself since arriving in Berlin five years earlier. She had seven films to her name, and by sheer chance had forged connections with many people in Berlin's high society, including the wives of several politicians. Yet despite her acquaintance with his own wife, Joseph Goebbels, the minister for propaganda and public enlightenment, had become increasingly suspicious of Clara's motives. It was as though he was determined to prove what he suspected— that even though her father was a British aristocrat and Nazi sympathizer, and she herself was working full-time in the Babelsberg film studio, Clara was an agent of British intelligence. That she was passing snippets of information and gossip to her contacts in the British embassy. That she deliberately mingled in Nazi society to observe the private life of the Third Reich.

It would have been absurd, if it hadn't also been true.

What made Clara's position more perilous was the discovery she made when she arrived in Germany, that her own grandmother was a Jew. The document of Aryan heritage Clara carried everywhere was as much a fabrication as the russet highlights in her hair, but infinitely more dangerous.

Every day she asked herself why she stayed in Berlin. Every day she came up with the same answer. She would stay in Berlin as long as she could because it meant seeing her godson, Erich. He was the only man in her life right now, and for his sake most of all she prayed that war could somehow be averted.

A PASSING BARROW BOY aimed an admiring whistle up at her balcony, forcing Clara's mind back to the present. Paris had always been one of those big statement places, like a famous perfume that everyone knows, burdened with the weight of expectation. The Parisian air was a complex fragrance of baking and drains, a whisper of flowers, undercut with something acrid and rotten. The leavings of vegetables from the market stalls mingled with the enticing aroma of garlic and coffee. Berlin's own air, by contrast, carried the gray, metallic edge of wet stone and steel offset by the tang of pine from the Grunewald.

Much as she relished the prospect of a day in Paris, suddenly Clara felt herself wishing she had someone to share it with. Most of the time she liked her solitude; at the age of thirty-one, she considered it part of her identity. Her self-sufficiency was a carapace toughened against the barbs of loneliness, and safer too. But solitude seemed wrong in the city of romance. This was Paris after all, whose streets murmured with the promises of lovers through the ages, and she was alone. As she leaned back against the casement, a whirlwind of memories assailed her, like leaves thrown around in a storm.

There were only two men she had ever cared for, and both had disappeared from her life. She had not seen Ralph Sommers, the man she had met in Berlin the previous year, since the day he left for London. Since then, his work as a British agent had been exposed. Now it was too dangerous for him to return to Germany. Ralph had sent Clara a message saying that so long as she stayed there, she must do her best to forget him. It hurt, but she was trying her hardest.

Then there was Leo Quinn. Leo, her first love, who had returned to England after she turned down his proposal of marriage. In her darkest moments Clara questioned if there was something within her that destroyed her deepest relationships. Did she shy away from intimacy or deliberately reject it? Did she emit some invisible signal that warned, "Leave me alone"?

The previous evening her film's director, Willi Forst, had hosted a dinner at Maxim's for the cast. Maxim's, just off the

Place de la Concorde, was the restaurant of choice for German visitors to Paris, and Willi Forst thought its Art Nouveau opulence perfectly suited to celebrating Maupassant's story. The group had the best table in the house, the one usually reserved for the Aga Khan, spread with snowy linen tablecloths and silver cutlery, and they were served platters of oysters with vinegar and shallots, *quenelles de brochet* floating in a rich cream sauce, and crème brûlée to finish. Ice buckets cradling bottles of vintage Krug rested to one side, furred with frost. The actors indulged themselves loudly, jokes and stories flowing, impressions being performed, anecdotes related. The sheer relief of being away from Berlin inspired a feverish jollity, a holiday atmosphere that had already prompted a couple of romantic liaisons among cast members and promised more nights of passion ahead. But none of the actors had propositioned Clara. It was as though they divined something in her that told them their approaches would be rebuffed. As they reveled in the unaccustomed fine food and called loudly for more wine, Clara felt the restaurant's other clientele eyeing the Germans, in their expensive suits and scented furs, with wariness and resentment.

"To my magnificent cast!"

Willi Forst raised a glass and beamed. Sitting there, Clara thought back to the newspaper pictures in March, when Hitler had entered Vienna in his six-wheeled bulletproof Mercedes, striking his familiar pose, upright, gripping the windscreen with his left hand while raising the right in the Nazi salute. The crowd had erupted in a volcano of feeling, and flowers rained down on him like ash. Would these Paris streets too be overtaken by tramping boots and thumping drums? Might France go the way of Austria? Austria wasn't even Austria anymore; it was part of Greater Germany. It seemed countries could end, just as much as relationships.

———

A KNOCK AT HER DOOR made her turn. It was the bellboy, wearing a little navy cap and holding out a manila envelope. "Pour vous, mademoiselle."

"Merci." She fished for a coin, then opened the envelope. Inside was a heavy cream notecard with the logo of Big Ben and a company name at the top. Beneath was spiky, academic handwriting.

Dear Miss Vine,

Please forgive me for approaching you directly, but I noticed from an article in France Soir that you were in Paris and felt compelled to get in touch. We would be very interested in discussing a proposal with you. Would you be free to meet at the café Chez André in the Rue Marbeuf, today at 12:00 noon? If you are able to come I shall be looking out for you,

> *Sincerely, Guy Hamilton,*
> *Representative, London Films*

London Films? Clara frowned. She had heard of it. From what she remembered, London Films had been started by the Hungarian émigré Alexander Korda. The company was based at Denham in Buckinghamshire and had hired Winston Churchill as a screenwriter. Hadn't they made *The Private Life of Henry VIII* and *Things to Come* and last year's *Fire over England*, with Laurence Olivier and Vivien Leigh? Clara had taken a special interest in that one because a director had once casually referred to her as "the German Vivien Leigh," so she had attended the first night at the Ufa Palast, closely studying the actress's classic porcelain beauty, before concluding that the director, unfortunately, was exaggerating. Clara might have the same heart-shaped face, clear brow, and dark eyebrows, but her cheeks were fuller than Vivien Leigh's, her skin more olive, and her mouth had a rebellious purse to it that gave her looks a distinctive, less classic edge.

She read the note again, then checked her watch. It was already eleven. She was suddenly, unaccountably excited. This proposal would almost certainly be the offer of a part—she was becoming better known, and as many of the German Jewish actors and directors who had been forced to leave Berlin had now relocated to England, it was likely that one of them had mentioned her name. And maybe, if this company was offering her a job, she should take it. What might it be like returning to London, picking up the threads of a life she had abandoned five years ago, and doing an ordinary job without risk or subterfuge? Seeing her father, sister, and brother, and other people who had been consigned firmly to the past. That was a prospect both consoling and daunting.

After clanging the shutters closed, she grabbed a short jacket to slip over her dress. Peering in the mirror, she applied a thin layer of Elizabeth Arden's Velvet Red—always her first weapon of concealment—and gave her reflection an encouraging smile. Dabbing a trace of powder over the freckles that the sun had brought out, she pulled a brush through her hair and pinned it loosely at the nape of her neck with a diamanté clip. Then she donned her sunglasses.

Clearly the idea of a day without business was just a fantasy after all.

THE CAFÉ CHEZ ANDRÉ WAS A TWENTY-MINUTE WALK AWAY, situated on the other side of the Champs-Élysées. Past the Rue de Rivoli, Clara entered the Tuileries Garden, relishing the perfect mathematical precision of its gravel and greenery. She had always loved patterns. Her father had noticed— when he still noticed his children—that Clara possessed an unusually retentive memory, and he had done his best to develop it with memory techniques and card games and mathematical exercises. For a short while Clara, the cleverest of the three Vine children, had been an experiment for him, a project almost, to be developed and tested before, as abruptly as he began, her father lost interest. Yet for Clara, puzzles remained a lasting passion. She loved word games and riddles of any kind. She learned how to memorize a deck of cards using images of their old home in Surrey. She liked to work out crosswords in her head, with a stock of the esoteric words—*triptych, orris, eidetic*—that compilers tended to favor. Her mind organized the world into patterns quite unconsciously: the number of tiles on a floor, biscuits in a box, the repetition of trees or flags or lampposts, or, as here, the mirrorlike symmetry of the flower beds and paths. She noticed anomalies too. Without even knowing she was doing it, her brain sought out anything that was wrong, any asymmetry or deviation from the norm. Difference leapt out at her. The knots in a piece of wood, the fleck in the glass, the flaw in a Turkish carpet that spoiled the line.

But that morning everything was normal, or as normal as a city could be perched on the edge of war.

The Champs-Élysées was planted with geraniums and begonias, and bees, like a hundred seamstresses, nipped and dipped through the blooms. Clara threaded her way through elegant women pulling along children in smocked dresses and dogs on plaited leather leashes. Parisians always made other nationalities feel worse dressed, she decided, even though her own dress flattered her, with its delicate leaf-green cotton cinched at the waist and setting off the color of her eyes.

FROM ITS SCARLET AWNING to its basket-weave chairs and pavement tables, Chez André in the Rue Marbeuf conformed in every respect to an idealized vision of a Parisian café. Inside, nicotine-stained walls enclosed globe lamps and vinyl banquettes. A poster warned customers to beware of pickpockets. Potted palms and a glass partition separated the smarter part of the restaurant from the café area, and at the zinc counter the owner was polishing glasses while a waitress in white collar and apron deposited cups of coffee on a table.

As she was early, Clara decided to walk to the end of the street and dawdle, loitering in front of the storefronts, making the most of the shopping trip she had been obliged to forgo. She lingered outside a chocolatier whose window was decked with jewel-colored jellied fruits, sugar almonds, rich chocolate, and cakes with labels that made them sound like perfect works of art, *soleil levant, opéra, criollo, charlotte aux fruits exotiques, religieuse.* Her mouth watered and her stomach clenched as the dark waft of chocolate emerged from the shop.

As she gazed in the window, something curious reflected behind her made Clara's senses quicken. On the other side of the road, a man stood slouched, a wide flat cap rammed onto his head, customary cigarette perched to one side of his mouth, and his hands thrust into his pockets. The archetypal Parisian flâneur. He was leaning against the peeling green paint of an advertisement column, apparently loitering the day away; yet suddenly, this air of profound relaxation was interrupted by a swift, instinctive look from right to left down the road, before he slumped back into his previous position. Even in the hazy grain of a shop window's reflection, Clara recognized that look. It was not the glance of a casual bystander. Something was wrong about this situation. The man was a watcher. A tail.

Was she really being followed, here, in Paris? Could she not manage a brief respite from the all-encompassing surveillance of the Gestapo? Being in France had encouraged her to let her guard down. How could she have forgotten that foreigners, and Germans in particular, were conspicuous just now?

If the shadow was looking down the road, he must be waiting for someone, probably a colleague, which meant there were two people on her tail. A team. A swift glance confirmed that she was right. A second man, with dark, brilliantined hair, a copy of *Paris-Soir* under his arm, and a smart, velvet-napped felt hat tipped over his face, was strolling towards her. Unlike his accomplice, something about this man was adamantly not French. For one thing he was wearing a trench coat, even in the height of summer, over a well-cut suit, and for another, his bearing, the determined nature of his strut, and the touch of arrogance in the tilt of his head, told her in a single glance that he was German.

Even as she registered this information, Clara's brain began to formulate a plan. Watching her own ghost in the window, apparently choosing chocolates, she quickly decided her best option would be to enter the shop and spend a long time deliberating between montelimar and noisettes, before slipping out. Instead of returning to her hotel, she would head back to the Boulevard Haussmann for one of the large department stores, Galeries Lafayette or Printemps, and give her followers the slip from the ladies' changing rooms. Either that or disappear into the nearest Métro station and lead them on a dance round the whole of Paris. She had done it before. It was a part she played well.

In the few seconds it took for these thoughts to form in Clara's mind, the man in the felt hat passed her and she saw the flâneur swivel and follow him. Glancing to her right, she realized that she had made a mistake. The watchers had no interest in her. Instead, their attention was fixed on a middle-aged man in horn-rimmed spectacles and a herringbone suit, who had entered Chez André and was making his way to a seat at the back. The flâneur took up residence in a doorway opposite, and the felt-hat man kept walking. The pair were shadows, but Clara was not the target of their surveillance. That target was, startlingly, the person she had come to meet.

The man Clara assumed to be Guy Hamilton was sitting on a red vinyl banquette with a glass of beer to one side, extracting a pen from his inside pocket, and applying himself to a postcard of the Eiffel Tower. As she approached, she noted that he was in his mid-forties and above average height, with tightly cropped sandy hair, a tawny mustache, and a face as mild and forgettable as an English summer's day. If she was forced to memorize him, she would have focused on the dusting of freckles across his sallow complexion or the receding hairline, which gave him a faintly donnish air. As it was, there was no time for analysis. She needed to alert him as soon as she could without compromising herself. But how?

She walked straight past him. Dangling carelessly from her arm, her handbag swung across, knocking the big sugar shaker on his table onto its side and unleashing a sticky white tide over the tabletop.

"Oh, I'm so sorry! How clumsy of me."

Hearing an English voice, he looked up immediately. Recognition dawned in his eyes.

Clara bent over the table, her back to the window.

"Here. Let me."

The sugar coated the table like sand. With one finger, Clara wrote in the granular tide: NO. She waited until Hamilton had blinked through his horn-rims and nodded. Then she grabbed a napkin and quickly wiped the spillage away. "Awfully clumsy of me."

"Not at all."

A waitress armed with a napkin bore down on them. Hamilton rose and brushed a few specks of sugar from his jacket with a fastidious flick. "I hope you don't mind me guessing, but I'd say you're a visitor here," he told Clara, in an educated English accent. "Have you ever seen Paris from the top of Notre Dame?"

"Afraid not."

"You should, you know. It's quite a sight. Gives you the big picture of the place. The best time to go is in the afternoon, while the crowds are still having lunch." He rolled his newspaper and tapped it in her direction like a lecturer's baton. "Around two o'clock is ideal. I recommend it."

"Well, thank you. I might try it."

"I hope you do."

Tipping his hat, Hamilton strolled across to the bar, paid the owner, and left. Glancing through the window, Clara saw the flâneur thrust his cigarette butt away and drift languidly on down the street in his wake.

She found a table at the back of the café and made herself linger for a further thirty minutes, which was not much of a hardship as it involved ordering an *omelette aux champignons,* as light as a pale yellow cloud and sizzling with butter and herbs. She ate slowly, savoring every last scrap. Eggs were in short supply in Berlin, and it was rare to find any butter that was not rancid. She followed the omelet with a café crème that was deep and mellow, with none of the chicory or hazelnut coffee substitute one found in Germany. She passed the time riffling through *The Times,* trying and failing to concentrate on news that Len Hutton had scored a triple century in the fifth test match against Australia; the government was leading an allotment drive called Keep Calm and Dig; and the queen was heading a new charity for disabled ex-servicemen. Occasionally Clara glanced outside, her mind working furiously.

What kind of film producer had a surveillance team on his tail? Was Guy Hamilton really a representative of London Films, and if so, what kind of role was he proposing for Clara? However much she might project the picture of a relaxed tourist enjoying a day in Paris, Clara had never felt more wary, or more alone. Surely it was madness to involve herself with a man who was being tailed by German agents. Briefly she contemplated forgetting Guy Hamilton and whatever proposal he had for her, but even as she considered it, she knew perfectly well that curiosity would overcome her.

3

THE BROODING GARGOYLES ON THE PARAPETS OF NOTRE
Dame Cathedral looked out over Paris like stony invaders
from some Gothic land intent on the city's conquest. From
the tower, tourists who were prepared to climb the four
hundred–odd steps up the spiral staircase could gaze far
across the russet rooftops to the bone-white Byzantine domes
of Sacré-Coeur on the heights of Montmartre. Beyond the
crenellations of Notre Dame, the skyline, pierced by the
Eiffel Tower and the gold-leafed dome of Les Invalides, wa-
vered in the heat. Far below, people the size of insects crossed
the square and *bateaux mouches* plowed the thick emerald
stripe of the Seine.

At two o'clock, in the heat of the day, the place was almost deserted. Ranks of pigeons clustered in the shade,
shuffling mutilated feet, like war-wounded soldiers. A pair
of priests in long dark coats flapped past. And at the far
western corner of the parapet Guy Hamilton, in his well-cut
herringbone suit and brown felt hat, leaned his elbows on
the stone, staring down at the scene below. Her heart thud-
ding with exertion, prickling with sweat, and trying not to
appear out of breath, Clara approached, keeping her sunglasses on. She disliked heights and tried not to look down.

Hamilton removed his hat and gave a little bow.

"I'm told Herr Hitler detests Gothic architecture. He thinks it's strange and unnatural and fosters Christian mysticism." He made a little gesture, like a tour guide. "All these grotesque gargoyles."

"Some might say he has a taste for the grotesque."

"Indeed. Perhaps he recognizes himself. At any rate, let's hope he never makes a visit." He nodded. "Thank you for your warning, Miss Vine, and forgive my choice of venue. I couldn't resist mixing business with pleasure."

Hamilton's manner was pleasantly self-effacing in a way that suggested a talent for anonymity. He seemed more like a civil servant than a film producer. He might have been one of thousands of men who streamed across London Bridge every morning, clutching an umbrella and a briefcase. Perhaps with a weekend hobby of studying church architecture, judging by the way he was assessing the construction of the flying buttresses.

"Is this the pleasure then?"

"Absolutely. I've always wanted to see the view from up here. And I must admit, it's worth it. Takes the breath away, doesn't it?"

It certainly did for Clara. She felt an instant rush of vertigo as she looked down and the continuous dim rush of the city, punctured by car horns, rose up towards them.

"That's assuming you've managed to get your breath back to begin with. I have to say, Mr. Hamilton, these seem rather elaborate efforts just to have a conversation. Couldn't you have contacted my agent in Berlin? Or explained things in your letter? This is to do with a film, I assume?"

"In a manner of speaking."

He swiveled towards her, smiled impeccably, and extended a hand. His grasp was surprisingly firm.

"I should have introduced myself properly, Miss Vine. I'm afraid I neglected my courtesies when I met you this morning."

"It rather looked like someone wanted to meet *you*."

"Indeed. I discovered last night that I had company, but I thought I'd shaken them off. Unfortunately it means I'll have to leave Paris very shortly, and I'm afraid my wife will miss out on her face cream. Anything French, Diana likes, but there's no time now. I daresay it can wait." Hamilton smiled cheerfully. "What's that motto? 'Good manners and a fine disposition are the best beauty treatments.'"

"Not one I know."

"It's a Latin tag. Ovid, I think."

For a second Clara thought she had misheard him, or that the wind had lifted and twisted his words. Her throat tightened.

"Ovid, did you say?"

The name rang through her like a depth charge, but it was not the Latin poet whose face rose to the surface of her mind, or an enthusiasm for the classics that made her catch her breath. She was thinking of her former lover, the man who had first persuaded her to pass information to British intelligence. Leo Quinn, who translated Ovid in his spare time to relieve the pressure of work in a British consulate besieged by German Jews desperate to emigrate. The image of Leo naked, reading the *Metamorphoses* aloud in bed, was a memory Clara cherished; and here was another Englishman standing in front of her making a casual reference to the same poet.

"Are you very familiar with Ovid?" she asked carefully.

He laughed. "Heavens no! Don't ask me to quote any more.

I can't imagine how that line stuck in my mind. The remnants of a classical education, I suppose."

With supreme effort Clara stopped herself probing further. If Guy Hamilton did know Leo, she would only want to ask if he was settled or married, or still in England, and Hamilton wouldn't tell her. And what difference would it make to know? The past was a foreign country you revisited at your peril.

Nonetheless the quote decided her. She was going to trust Guy Hamilton.

"I take it you're not a film producer?"

He blinked. "But of course. I've seen a lot of your work, Miss Vine. I'm an admirer."

"Thank you."

"You're right, though. It's not filmmaking I wanted to discuss. Not exactly." He hesitated and looked about him. They were entirely alone on the windswept parapet. "Ever heard of Colonel Claude Dansey?"

Clara shook her head.

"Dansey was, until recently, the British chief of station in Rome," he explained. "Code name Z. He's spent his life in the intelligence service. He's a good fellow, a little irascible, but he inspires tremendous loyalty. Unfortunately Dansey has become disillusioned over the state of our intelligence network in Europe. He thinks it is badly compromised and could collapse entirely. Which I don't need to tell you would leave us in a parlous position. Dansey's view is that one mistake could leave us without any proper contacts in the event of war."

"The entire European network?"

"Precisely. As a result of which, he's established a shadow intelligence network. They call it Z, after him. It runs parallel to the existing European operation. Its operatives are businessmen mostly. People helping out for the principle of it. There's over two hundred of them now."

He paused. "Care for a smoke?"

Freeing a cigarette pack from his jacket pocket, he lit one for her, then one for himself, and turned his back, leaning against the parapet to prevent the curls of smoke being blown back into their faces.

"Anyhow, that's where I come in. Let me explain."

Alexander Korda's London Films, Hamilton told her, was all aboveboard and a thriving enterprise, but the company had a second, more secret endeavor. In the course of establishing a Europe-wide network of offices, Korda and his employees were also undertaking espionage and reconnaissance.

"Reconnaissance?"

"Their cover is foreign sales or talent scout or location search, but the true job is to check out locations, photograph coastlines, and make connections. What better excuse could there be for having a camera to hand than hunting out locations for your forthcoming travel movie? When the inevitable comes, we'll need to be prepared. But I don't have to tell you this, Miss Vine."

He didn't. It seemed half the world was making preparations for war and the other half resolving to ignore them. The copy of *The Times* Clara had bought that morning featured a front-page photograph of men digging trenches in Hyde Park. Two long trenches had been gouged into the ground, with four shorter ones at right angles to them, like a ladder descending into the bowels of the earth. On a bench in the foreground a man in a bowler hat sat quite unconcerned, as if the great gaping hole behind him simply did not exist. A lot of people in Britain preferred to think that way.

"Not everyone assumes war's inevitable," she remarked.

"That's true. Prime Minister Daladier here has no illusions, nor do men like Churchill and Vansittart at home, but Halifax and Chamberlain seem to be far more sanguine about Herr Hitler's intentions. An awful lot of people seem hell-bent on appeasing him."

Fastidiously he removed a strand of tobacco from his tongue.

"Our prime minister believes all Herr Hitler wants is a little territorial readjustment for the benefit of the German minority in the Sudetenland. Whereas it's clear to us that he wants to wipe the whole of Czechoslovakia off the map. If not Poland and Romania. We run the risk of everything we won in the war being thrown away because Chamberlain fatally misreads Hitler's intentions."

"You sound entirely pessimistic."

"Not entirely. Though time's getting tight. It's not an exaggeration to say that the future of the continent hinges on what happens in the next month. We're hearing that Hitler intends to enter Czechoslovakia in October. France is Czechoslovakia's ally and will be duty-bound to respond. They've already mobilized a million men. War could be just weeks away. But there's still a chance to avert it."

Clara shrugged. "You mean if Chamberlain and the others agree to stand by while Hitler goes ahead and takes what he wants?"

"No. That's not what I meant. But if the British stand firm, and Daladier comes in alongside them and denounces any incursion into Czechoslovakia, that will enable certain highly placed people in Berlin to paint Hitler as a warmonger who is about to drag his unwilling people into another European conflict."

"I appreciate that. But why are you telling *me* this?"

Hamilton lowered his voice, as if there was any possibility of being heard on those windblown ramparts, high above Paris. A breeze lifted his sparse hair and buffeted his jacket.

"It's Dansey's view that it will help our side very much if we can gain an insight into Hitler's thinking. The dictator's mood could make the difference between peace and immediate war. The fellow is immensely mercurial. It's incredible how enormous actions can turn on the whim of a single man."

He waited until a family with two children had passed out of earshot, then said, "That, Miss Vine, is where you come in."

Startled, Clara took off her sunglasses. "Me?"

"Indeed. If you're willing. You know who I mean by Eva Braun?"

"The Führer's girlfriend? Only because Magda Goebbels told me about her. The rest of Germany has no idea who she is."

"And it's likely to stay that way, particularly if . . ." Hamilton paused.

"If what?"

"If someone decides to remove her. Apparently the top brass—Goebbels and Goering, and to an extent Hess—are concerned at Miss Braun's hysterical moods. She's attempted suicide twice. The one thing worse than people knowing Hitler has a relationship with a little blond secretary would be people knowing that he makes the girl so desperately unhappy she's tried to do herself in. As it is she remains Germany's best-kept secret. It's easier to breach the operational security of the Wehrmacht than to discover anything about Miss Eva Braun."

"I'm sorry, but I can't see what Eva Braun or her happiness has to do with me."

"Ah." He stubbed out his cigarette, tossed it into the air, and watched as it was snatched away by the Parisian breeze.

"There's the thing. The fact is, we'd rather like you to get to know her."

Clara gasped. "Eva Braun? If she's Germany's best-kept secret, how on earth would I go about even meeting her?"

"She admires your work, doesn't she?"

Clara paused, remembering a postcard with a scrap of neat, curly handwriting on it that had arrived at the Babelsberg studio the previous year. "Just wanted to tell you how much I enjoyed *Black Roses*."

"You're talking about that fan letter."

"Exactly."

"She sends dozens of actors fan letters. She sees all our films, several times over. None of us know who she is, of course. She doesn't mention the fact that she's seen our films sitting next to Hitler at the Berghof. Anyhow, how ever did you hear about that postcard? I didn't exactly pin it up in my dressing room."

He shrugged. "All her mail is monitored. They keep an extremely close eye on her, as you can imagine. So I'm sure your postcard was genuine. Eva adores Ufa movies, as you say. Appears to be somewhat fanatical about the cinema. She's even going to the Venice Film Festival next year."

Clara looked out at the city beneath her, but in her mind's eye she had already traveled far beyond it, across Europe to the distant alps of Bavaria, towards the slight, blond figure of the Führer's girlfriend watching movie after movie in the Great Hall of Hitler's impregnable mountain retreat.

"I don't see how ... just because she sent me a letter ... I mean, Hitler keeps her out of sight, doesn't he? Magda Goebbels says Eva Braun wasn't even allowed to meet the Duke of Windsor when he was in Berlin last year. Hitler made her hide in her room. Not even the top brass are supposed to know Eva

Braun's exact status. She can have anything she wants, except to be known as Hitler's girlfriend."

"And one of the things she wants is to meet some famous actors. Celebrities, you know. Perhaps have a look around a film set. You could offer to show her round."

Clara laughed out loud. "I think you're rather overestimating my powers of persuasion. How could I possibly do that?"

"We've thought of that. There's a film being shot in Munich. *Good King George*, it's called. About the Hanoverian monarch, I hasten to add, rather than our present king. All entirely aboveboard. It's directed by a chap called Mr. Fritz Guttmann, whom we understand would like to make his career in England very soon. Mr. Guttmann will be getting in touch with you about an audition for the role of Sophia, the unfaithful wife. She falls in love with a Swedish count, but their affair is destined to be tragically unrequited." He squinted pensively. "It goes without saying we're hoping you get the part."

Clara looked across the rooftops. Another wave of vertigo hit her in a panicky rush, making her stomach heave and her head swirl. Guy Hamilton's proposition seemed an equally dizzying prospect.

"Why would you expect this of me? I mean . . . to go to another city and attempt something that is almost certainly going to be entirely unfeasible. It's an impossible task!"

He glanced at her, puzzled. "It's what you do, isn't it?"

Clara had a sudden vision of a great web of people, strung out across Europe, all assembled by this man Dansey and responding to his requests. All like her, carrying on with their ordinary lives, and living an entirely different life in the shadows. Holding their secrets and their loyalties close. Waking each day not knowing what it might bring. Despite herself, she was already laying plans, already calculating the task in hand.

"If I do . . . manage to meet her . . . what would you want to know?"

"Any detail that might be relevant. 'Pillow talk,' I think they call it. We believe Miss Braun could be the chink in Hitler's armor. We're hoping she will provide that crucial 'back door' into the Führer's thinking."

"I can't imagine he would confide military detail to her!"

"Who knows what he would confide? The man's an enigma. He's extremely careful with his top people. Plays them off against one another. Miss Braun may be the only person he's completely straight with."

He leaned further towards her, so that she caught his scent of warm wool and starched linen.

"On the subject of which, there's something else. Something that could be quite significant. We understand she keeps a diary."

"That's not unusual."

"We'd rather like a look at it."

Clara's eyes widened.

"You want me to obtain Eva Braun's diary? You don't ask much, Mr. Hamilton, do you?"

If he noticed her sarcasm, he didn't betray it.

"When you have something to communicate, put a classified advertisement in the Situations Wanted column of one of the British newspapers." He reflected a moment. "Include the word *Latin*. That should stand out. We'll set up a meeting at the Siegessäule in the Tiergarten the Wednesday after the message appears. Let us know the time and so on. We'll keep a lookout."

"What if it's urgent?"

"There's always a DLB we have in Berlin. It's checked regularly."

"A DLB?"

"A dead letter box."

That was one of the espionage terms Leo Quinn had tried to teach her. It belonged to the world of "brush contacts" and "switches" and "box surveillance." A world where people passed messages rolled up inside cigarettes or secreted inside tubes of toothpaste. A shadow world that she could barely believe she had entered, and where she still trod apprehensively.

"Do you know the Volkspark in Friedrichshain?" continued Hamilton. "There's a fountain there. The fairy-tale fountain, I think it's called."

"The Märchenbrunnen." It was an elaborate fountain surrounded by sculptures of fairy-tale characters that had been created for the children of Berlin in the nineteenth century. Cinderella, Hansel and Gretel, and the Frog Prince were all there; but despite the theme, the serried ranks of stone figures with their frozen limbs and vacant eyes had very little magic about them. "I know it well."

"Excellent. Look for the stone bench on the left-hand side closest to the pillar. There's a cavity underneath."

"That's a little public, isn't it?"

"It needs to be somewhere people congregate so one doesn't arouse suspicion. But time, as I said, is of the essence."

A gabble of voices rose from the entrance to the stairwell behind her, and Hamilton glanced over her shoulder. A party of schoolboys had emerged and were making their way along the walkway, giggling and play-fighting, pretending to throw one another off the side.

"It's getting a little crowded up here. Shall we go down?"

They descended the stairway into the chilly, flickering gloom of the cathedral itself, and Clara slipped on her jacket. The place felt like the sanctuary it still was, resounding with hushed murmuring, heavy with the odor of incense, its glimmering shadows pierced by great shafts of light. Hamilton went over to light a candle at one of the side chapels, dropped to his knees, and gazed fixedly at the countenance of the Madonna in an attitude of pious contemplation. Clara knelt beside him.

"About those men this morning," she murmured. "They were Germans, weren't they? I thought at first they were following me."

"Has that happened recently? You being followed?"

"Not here, as far as I know."

"I apologize. I changed hotels and I thought I'd thrown them off. I was warned about them last night by a chap we have here, a fellow called Steinbrecher. Steinbrecher says the Gestapo's pretty well entrenched in Paris now. Heydrich has an extensive network of informers in place, and Steinbrecher thinks they've been watching me for a couple of days. I'm glad you've been free of them, but if I were you, I'd be very careful all the same. Check your hotel room for bugs. All the usual things. Watch out for any gifts. I'm sure there's nothing I need tell you."

He rose, brushed the knees of his trousers, and smiled down at her warmly. "Have a pleasant journey, Miss Vine. And very good luck. Forgive me if I don't shake hands."

He strode off into the dim interior, transforming instantly into the amateur enthusiast, guidebook in pocket, contemplating the splintered ruby and violet majesty of the famous south rose window.

CLARA WALKED SLOWLY BACK through the winding, cobbled streets of the Île de la Cité, onto the Île Saint-Louis. She watched the fishermen at the water's edge throwing out their lines, fracturing the Seine into a thousand choppy diamonds. The meeting with Hamilton had unsettled her profoundly. Partly because his mild, unassuming Englishness had provoked a sharp nostalgia for her homeland, yet also because his request took her breath away. The mention of the mysterious Dansey reminded her that there was an entire realm of people in England whom she had never met yet who knew of her existence. Uniformed men in Whitehall, perhaps even well-known politicians like Winston Churchill and Sir Robert Vansittart, as well as others sitting behind desks in shabby, anonymous London offices, posing as civil servants or accountants or film producers while they ran vast, shadowy intelligence networks. People who were aware of her activities and whose confidence in her was seemingly far greater than her own.

She thought of the task they were asking of her now and shivered. Getting close to Eva Braun and taking a look at her diary, all in the space of a month? How was she possibly going to manage that?

Before she could begin to answer that question she had one more errand to run.

4

THE PLACE VENDÔME HAD, IN MEDIEVAL TIMES, BEEN A cloister for Capuchin nuns, but now the exclusive octagonal arena at the heart of the Right Bank was the shrine to another form of female devotion. The spectacular adornments of Van Cleef & Arpels, Chaumet, and Cartier were showcased in opulent shopfronts clustered around the chief attraction of the place, the Ritz Hotel. And the star occupant of the Ritz was Coco Chanel, who had been given the use of an entire third-floor suite and decided to make it her home. The couturier had redesigned every aspect of the suite to reflect her personal style, and now the room seemed to float with color and light, a mirrored cocoon of cream, black, and gold. Around the lavish sitting room with its white satin armchairs, lacquered Ming dynasty screens were grouped, silver cranes and dragons glinting beneath crystal chandeliers. Banks of sofas were piled with velvet cushions, and heavy gold drapes framed the windows. Long, smoky Venetian mirrors turned the guests into Mondrians; Oriental tables were clustered with glinting vermeil boxes, bronze animals, and a gold-plated frog. The guests at Chanel's salons—international socialites, playwrights, poets, politicians, and artists, members of the haut monde—were just as gilded. Jean Cocteau was a regular. Salvador Dalí came frequently. Winston Churchill was known to drop by.

Clara caught sight of her elongated image and repressed a smile. How easy it was to change a perspective! Being here, in this looking-glass world, had a transformative effect on the guests. Just like certain actresses who, on the street, seemed as unremarkable as any waitress or shop assistant yet were transformed into astonishing beauties once they stepped in front of the camera, these elegant people might have existed in a different universe from the uneasy crowd outside. They even smelled different. Most of the people you passed on the street, or pressed up close against on the Métro, smelled of old clothes, sweat-stained at worst, mothballed at best, but patched and mended and made good. Here there was a mingled aroma of fur, cigars, champagne, and perfume. The haze of opulence was dominated by the complex undertow of Chanel's own No. 5, which the hostess liked to spritz on the coals in the fireplace.

Good manners and a fine disposition are the best beauty treatments. It might have seemed that way to Ovid, but that view wouldn't pass muster here. The women, lean and etiolated in sumptuous confections of lace and tulle, with hair as polished as the pelts of the animals they wore, were made up to the nines. They held flutes of sparkling champagne, and their antique Russian necklaces, star medallions, and enamel cuffs were studded with glass stones according to Chanel's own fashion for costume jewelry that mixed actual gems with glass and paste, so one couldn't tell the real from the fake. As far as the guests' clothes went, however, they were all genuine. Every dress was by Chanel; no one would have dared to wear a Schiaparelli suit or a frock by Patou, Lanvin, or Mainbocher. The only fake in the room was Clara herself, who had always admired the sleek dresses and narrow jersey tailored suits that made Chanel's name, but could never afford her prices. That evening she was wearing a green silk dress with a matching short jacket with pearl buttons made by her friend Steffi Schaeffer, a Berlin dressmaker who tailored costumes for the Ufa studios and ran up clothes for Clara at bargain rates. Her hair was fastened at the back and fell to her shoulders in loose curls.

Sipping her champagne, she wondered if there was any way Chanel would be able to detect that Clara's lipstick was by her archrival Elizabeth Arden. The manager of the Elizabeth Arden salon on the Kurfürstendamm, Sabine Friedmann, was another friend and often gave Clara samples of lipstick, mascara, and the fabulous Eight Hour cream. Indeed Sabine had sent a couple of messages recently asking her to drop by. Clara hoped it was for something nice.

Across the room the mellifluous flow of French conversation was intercut with the jagged, polysyllabic growl of German. There was no need for Nazi uniforms here; the men in their impeccable Hugo Boss suits and mandatory swastika pins were identifiably Nazi government officials, yet in Chanel's salon they were spared the looks of hostility or trepidation they met elsewhere in Paris. That must account for their boisterous good humor, Clara decided. The leader of the group was a handsome man with sandy hair swept off a high brow whom she recognized as Chanel's lover, Baron Hans Günther von Dincklage, better known as Spatz.

Though Chanel was famous for loving black and white, the designer's love life was a distinctly gray area. Most of her relationships were with married men, including a long-running affair with the Duke of Westminster, but the scandal that had recently leaked into the French newspapers concerned her liaison with Spatz, the special attaché at the German embassy in Paris. Sections of the French press had waged war on Spatz, accusing him of building up a spy network throughout Paris reporting directly to the Gestapo, monitoring German exiles in the city, and passing on their addresses to Reinhard Heydrich. Watching Spatz now, possessed of the brash, confident demeanor of a German abroad, Clara could understand just what Chanel must see in him. The couturier was known for liking winners, and Spatz, with his suave playboy's manners, blond hair, and distinguished looks, fitted precisely that template, not to mention the fact that he was more than a decade younger than Chanel.

Spatz's companion was his equal in good looks, with a broad, intelligent forehead and neatly parted thick hair above eyes set widely apart. In his well-cut gray flannel suit the man looked vaguely familiar, and Clara racked her brains to place him. A studio executive? Or a politician perhaps? She hoped very much that she would not be obliged to talk to him.

A waiter approached with a bottle of champagne, and, unthinkingly, Clara held out her glass. The events of the day, and Guy Hamilton's request, had set her nerves on edge. It was not only the thought of what she was being asked to do but the time involved—mere weeks perhaps—that alarmed her. She took a sip of crisp bubbles and tuned in to the conversation of the women beside her, who were arguing about the secret of Chanel's success.

"It's all down to tailoring," drawled an exquisite blonde, wearing the gold lamé evening dress and short jacket that Chanel had showed in that year's collections. "Chanel can make a woman look like a princess just through tailoring."

"Except when she's a real princess," said another.

There was a ripple of laughter. Everyone knew this was a reference to Elizabeth, the frumpy new queen of England, elevated as a result of Edward VIII's liaison with Wallis Simpson.

"In London, Wallis and Elizabeth both used the Elizabeth Arden salon in Bond Street," murmured another woman. "The staff had a terrible time trying to keep them apart. Sometimes they had to pretend they were closed for redecoration when there was a clash. Anything rather than have that pair end up side by side."

"Wallis can be most awfully amusing," said a petite figure with a bob as black as a bird's wing sweeping across her cheekbones. "When she was asked what Queen Elizabeth could do to boost British fashion, Wallis said, 'She could stay at home'!"

"The Duchess of Windsor is a loyal customer," came an imperious voice. "I won't have any gossip about her."

Coco Chanel had materialized among the women as silently as a cat, accompanied by a gust of Camel cigarettes. She had a hard face and taut neck, from which several ropes of pearls were hanging. Her skinny legs were bowed like those of a grasshopper, and her intelligent, feline glance traveled across Clara's moss-green dress as though calculating to the last pfennig its provenance and likely cost.

"Good evening, Mademoiselle Vine," she said softly, resting a silken claw briefly on Clara's arm. Then, more loudly, she addressed the women around her.

"I have always been a great admirer of the duchess. When the duke was courting Wallis, Winston Churchill came to dine here with me at the Ritz and begged me to exert my influence. He implored me to persuade the King of England not to marry an American divorcée." She gave a laugh, like the snort of an aggressive little bull. "Winston burst into tears and said, 'A king should never abdicate! David should do his duty.' Could I

not persuade him to think again? I said, 'Winston, are you asking me to stand in the path of true love?'

"What would you have done, Mademoiselle Vine?" She
switched to English, with a glance of cool scrutiny. "Do you
believe anyone should stand in the way of true love?"

"I think love has its place, but Churchill's right. There are
times when duty is more important."

"Ah, a realist then! I think you, Mademoiselle Vine, are like
me. Passion fades. Only work remains. You need to be a realist
when your work is peddling dreams. Because that's what we
both do, isn't it? We peddle dreams. We put romance in people's
lives, even when there's none in our own."

"I suppose that's true."

Chanel's feline smile was shot through with spite. "I'm sorry
I don't know your work. Perhaps you think me rude, but since
my time in Hollywood I never go to the movies. I find them
insufferably dull."

Though Chanel had made the trek to America, her hopes of
a new life designing costumes for Hollywood had fallen flat.
She had returned to France with a lasting grudge against a film
industry too philistine and shallow to appreciate her talents.

"As it happens, my new film is based on a novel," Clara replied mildly. "And a French novel at that. *Bel Ami.*"

"Ha! Well, I approve of that, certainly. I like to think in my
salon we are all of us, French, German, and English, meilleurs
amis. Like Herr Brandt here."

Clara looked round to see a man watching her. She had noticed him earlier, in the thicket of guests, because he stood out
from the polished and manicured crowd. Though as smartly
dressed as the other men, in an impeccably cut dark blue suit
and tie, his powerful build and glowing tan made her think
instantly of the countryside and vigorous exercise, rather than

the refined air of this couturier's perfumed parlor. He must have been in his late forties, with golden brown eyes, dark hair that was receding and graying around the temples, and a deeply cleft chin. Now, he advanced and held out a hand.

"Max Brandt." Little arrows of laughter crinkled his eyes.

"Clara Vine."

"Herr Brandt is a cultural attaché at the German embassy," Chanel explained.

"How interesting," said Clara politely. "I imagine that means an awful lot of opera."

Brandt chuckled and swept a lock of hair from his brow. "Indeed. But we must all perform our duty for the Fatherland, no matter how arduous. Besides, sometimes only opera can make our German language sound as lovely as French."

Clara, who often thought that sounds had their own colors, imagined Brandt's voice as a rich, chocolate brown. He had the languid, easy demeanor of a man secure in his own attractiveness and well used to the company of women. His expression had a subtle sparkle to it, as though he'd known, even before Chanel's introduction, who she was. Perhaps he had seen one of her films, she decided. Detecting her schoolgirl French, he switched to German and raised his voice against the dance music that had started up in the background.

"Can I ask what brings you here?"

"I'm making a film. With Willi Forst. It's called *Bel Ami*."

"Maupassant, eh? Do you have official clearance for that? It's hard to imagine our propaganda minister favoring a film whose hero is a lying, cheating womanizer."

Laughter danced in his eyes, but Clara dipped her head. Jokes about the notoriously womanizing minister were dangerous.

"Perhaps Doktor Goebbels hasn't read the script," she said.

"Don't all scripts have to gain his approval? Besides, I thought nothing escaped his eyes."

"Maybe he admires Maupassant."

"Possible." Brandt nodded, pretending to consider this. "And of course, romance is a keen interest of his."

"I'm sorry?"

"Romanticism. Goebbels's doctoral thesis was on the German Romantics, I recall."

Brandt smiled, and Chanel chose the moment to intervene sinuously. "Mademoiselle Vine is here this evening on the recommendation of *Madame* Goebbels."

A frisson of surprise passed across Max Brandt's face. He had just made fun of Goebbels's womanizing, only to discover that the woman in front of him was on friendly terms with the propaganda minister's wife.

Chanel, however, seemed to delight in his faux pas.

"Magda has entrusted Mademoiselle Vine to collect a special package of my perfume. If you wait here, mademoiselle, I'll go and fetch it."

Brandt took a deep drag of his cigarette and smiled. "So our culture minister's wife prefers a French scent? I thought the minister was most strict about a perfume's provenance?"

That much was true. Goebbels frequently delivered radio diatribes about how buying foreign cosmetics meant robbing the German Volk. He himself was generally preceded by a blast of Scherk's Tarr pomade, a citrusy blend made by one of Berlin's biggest perfumiers, whose smell always provoked in Clara a Pavlovian shudder.

Clara surveyed Max Brandt warily. "I would have thought perfume, of all things, was free of nationality."

"You're right, of course, Miss Vine. It's a holy thing. Comes from the Latin actually. *Per fumus,* by means of smoke." He exhaled, as if to illustrate his point. "*Perfume* once meant the sacred incense in temples, but it's rather more debased now, I fear. Did you know they make civet out of the musk of a wild cat? It's pretty disgusting, isn't it? Strange how something so rank can be transformed into something so alluring."

Clara focused on his swastika tiepin. "But people do sometimes find the most repugnant things appealing."

"I suppose you're right. And perfume's power has nothing to do with sweetness. Apparently, it works on the brain in the most extraordinary way—it stimulates olfactory memory. That's the part which lies in the deepest part of the brain and connects with our primal drives. So you see, perfume unleashes our most primitive desires."

"How funny. Perfume always seems so sophisticated to me. I love the words they use. *Ambergris, attar, wormwood. Wormwood*, especially."

"Yes! I've always thought that too. But those words don't work so well in German—you have to say them in French. Like your own perfume. Soir de Paris."

Clara regarded him, astonished.

"You can tell?"

"But of course."

Then he laughed. "Don't look like that. I can't really tell a thing. The only reason I recognized Soir de Paris is that someone I know used to wear it. It's sweet. It suits you. And it's somewhat appropriate, in the circumstances."

Responding to the gramophone music, some of the couples had cleared a space on the parquet floor and begun an impromptu dance. Brandt looked round. "I wonder, would you permit me?"

Without waiting for an answer, he reached for her waist and drew her towards him. The imprint of his hand was firm against the flimsy silk of her dress, the music was hypnotic, and her body fitted perfectly into the rhythm of his own, the more easily because he was a natural dancer. As she moved beside him, Clara felt the champagne spreading like a warm tide through all the veins of her body, relaxing her and softening the edges of the world. Normally she refrained from drinking; it only let down her guard, and in most situations it was far too dangerous to lower her defenses. But the mere fact of being in Paris had induced a certain recklessness, and she had already downed two glasses of Chanel's Pol Roger. She pressed closer to Max Brandt. His hand rested on her back in a way that would have seemed erotically possessive if it wasn't merely customary. Not for the first time, Clara wondered how dancing ever came to be seen as an empty convention of polite society, rather than the tantalizing, sensual experience it was.

"Perhaps I spoke a little hastily earlier," he murmured. "About our culture minister."

"Don't worry. If you can't relax at a party . . ."

"Quite so. And our hostess is good at getting people to relax. She likes us to shed our defenses so we render up better gossip. She sees it as a challenge. Whenever I come here I go away wondering what indiscretions I've committed."

"A few glasses of Pol Roger must help that."

"It's true. Perfume's not the only expensive substance Chanel understands. She's an expert practitioner in the use of champagne. She has a saying, 'I drink champagne on only two occasions—when I'm in love, and when I'm not.' "

Clara laughed. "I wonder which it is tonight?"

Brandt nodded his head in the direction of Spatz, whose head was bent close to Chanel's, in intimate conversation. "Can't you guess?"

"Your fellow attaché, I presume."

"We both work at the embassy, but our paths don't often cross. I'm not sure Spatz shares my tastes."

"Your tastes?"

"In opera and so on."

"Who's that other man he was talking to?"

Clara nodded at the man in the gray pinstripe, the one who had seemed vaguely familiar.

"That's Schellenberg. SS Hauptsturmführer Walter Schellenberg, to be precise. Ever heard of him?"

Clara shook her head.

"That's good. You don't want to have heard of him."

"Why's that?"

Brandt smiled. "It doesn't matter. I'd rather talk about you. So you're a friend of Frau Doktor Goebbels?"

Clara sensed him trying to place her, to gauge her status in the Nazis' social hierarchy. It was unusual for actresses to befriend the propaganda minister's wife. Usually they were too busy trying to escape the clutches of her husband.

"More of an acquaintance. I modeled for her Fashion Bureau when I first came to Germany from London. My father's English, you see, and I grew up there."

"You're English?"

Surprise hardened his voice. His eyes held a flicker of suspicion at discovering she was not what he thought.

"Half English, half German," she clarified. "My mother was born in Hamburg, but she left for England at the age of twenty-two. She was a concert pianist. My father went to Germany on holiday and fell in love with her when he saw her playing Brahms."

"What a romantic story."

"I suppose so," she replied. It wasn't in fact. Though it had started well, her parents' marriage had been far from happy-

ever-after. Arguments and silences had punctuated their relationship for years as her father's need to control clashed like a
harsh bow against her mother's highly strung nature. "What
about you, Herr Brandt? Is your wife here?"

She sensed him stiffen.

"A less romantic story, I'm afraid. My wife is no longer with
me."

"I'm sorry."

"You needn't be. She's certainly not. Gisela found the appeal
of an instructor at the Grunewald Riding School an infinitely
more exciting prospect than traveling the capitals of Europe as
the wife of a cultural attaché."

He shrugged and smiled down at her, swaying closely to the
music. Clasped in his arms, Clara felt at once soothed and intensely alive.

"But you, Miss Clara Vine, agree with Chanel." His voice
was a teasing murmur in her ear. "You're a realist, like Coco.
You think we should all put love firmly on one side when duty
calls."

Clara laughed. "That's hardly what I said!"

"Don't be ashamed, it's an admirable thought. In these difficult times, duty must drive us. Although as Paris is the city of
lovers, I don't think you'd find it a popular sentiment here."

"What I said was, there were times when duty is more important than love."

He steered her round the floor with the lightest of touches.
Was he aware that with every movement of his body, a current
of heat ran through her, making the blood rush to her face?
That he was provoking in her the most unseemly tide of excitement? Clara guessed that he was. She looked away, hoping he
didn't see the blush suffuse her cheeks.

"And," he whispered, "is this one of those times?"

Hamilton's comment ran through her mind. *War could be just weeks away.*

"I suppose it is."

"Some might say people must seize their pleasures where they find them. Carpe diem."

She looked up at him and tried to keep herself from smiling.

"Some might. But at the moment my duty is to catch a train tomorrow for Berlin."

"You're leaving Paris?" He seemed dismayed. "Surely not. Stay awhile, won't you? There's so much to see."

"I'd like to, but I can't."

"It would be a crime to leave Paris without seeing the Louvre! You have to walk in the Left Bank and take coffee at the Dôme. Visit Fouquet's on the Champs-Élysées. See the zoo at the Jardin des Plantes. There's an ape there who can make a charcoal drawing as well as a human. Surely you can't leave without seeing him?"

"I'm certain I'll come back some time."

The music finished. The couples began picking up their glasses and lighting cigarettes, but Brandt's hand remained on the small of her back. Clara felt the pulse of his body against her and could tell the dance had stirred him too.

"I wonder . . ." he began.

Clara glanced across the room to see Chanel watching them fixedly, a trace of irritation creasing her brow. She was holding a black and white package with an intertwined double C, tied with a lavish amount of black ribbon.

Hastily, Clara stepped back. "Actually, I should leave now."

"So soon?"

"I'm sorry. It's been a long day and I've a bit of a headache . . ."

"Where are you staying?"

"The Hotel Bellevue. It's not far."

"Perhaps I could walk with you?"

"No. Really, thank you, Herr Brandt, but I'm quite all right. The fresh air will clear my head."

He kept hold of her hand for a moment, as if unwilling to let her go, or unable to believe she was going, and she had to give a little tug before he freed her fingers from his grasp.

Chanel crossed the room and proffered the package with a perfunctory smile. "Tell Madame Goebbels this comes with my compliments. I'm flattered that she wants to try my No. 5. Please let her know that my perfume always tells a personal story, as well as a public one, so although my perfume is popular, for every woman it is unique."

After accepting the package, Clara clattered down the stairs and nodded when the reception manager in his long cutaway coat bowed solemnly to her as she passed through the Ritz's gilded doors. She walked swiftly to the north of the Place Vendôme, making her way towards the fourth arrondissement. The mingled fragrance of garlic and roasting meat blew across her path, and the cobbles beneath her feet, wet from a brief shower, were sequined with light. She peered into courtyards behind high wrought-iron gates, past tall doors illuminated by iron lanterns with elaborate stone scrolling above them.

The poignant refrain of *"J'Attendrai,"* the hit song of the moment, snaked up from a basement bar.

"J'attendrai, le jour et la nuit, j'attendrai toujours ton retour."

I will wait, every day and night, for your return. How perfectly Jean Sablon's melancholy lilt suited the mood of the time, Clara decided. Waiting was what everyone was doing now. There was a sense of time suspended and breath bated as Europe's leaders, like invisible chess players, bided their next moves.

———

IN THE DESERTED MARKETPLACE of Les Halles the cleaners were sweeping the vestiges of cabbage leaves and rotten fruit left over from the day's trading and hosing down the floor. Clara loved this louche aspect to Paris, the blast of petrol and urine from the Métro entrance and the slick of oil on the pavement that reminded you how closely earthiness and glamour coexisted here. Huge wheels of cheese were being rolled onto a cart, the last traders were stacking boxes, and a litter of dead chrysanthemums withered in a heap.

As she picked her way through the remnants of vegetation, a flock of starlings whirred balletically up into the glass-and-iron vault, and, turning to watch them, she noticed out of the corner of her eye the figure of Max Brandt rounding the corner about two hundred yards behind her, his shadow under the streetlamp stalking boldly ahead of him. At once, a bubble of laughter rose in her throat. Brandt was actually in pursuit of her! He was evidently a man who couldn't take no for an answer. He couldn't possibly have known that he was following a woman expertly versed in the arts of evasion. She could lose him in an instant if she wanted. But did she want to?

Quickening her step, Clara wove through the streets, doubling back on herself, choosing side streets and alleys. A current of exhilaration spurred her on as she walked away up the Rue Quincampoix and ducked into a tiny cul-de-sac containing a couple of shops and the back door of a bar. Easing herself into a doorway, she saw Brandt stride past, heard him hesitate, grunting with frustration as he looked from right to left, wondering how she could have disappeared. The heat made her skin prickle with sweat, and she shifted a little in the darkness, stifling a laugh.

Suddenly, behind her, a door swung open and a ribbon of noise billowed out. A man was emerging from the bar, maneuvering a crate of empty bottles towards her. A blade of light, as sharp as any Gestapo lamp, sliced across Clara's face, and, at that moment, Brandt glanced down the alley and saw her.

He smiled, and she couldn't help smiling too.

"Fräulein Vine." He came slowly towards her, ambling now that he had his prey in his sights. "When you wanted to clear your head, I hadn't imagined you intended to walk halfway around the city."

"I enjoy a long walk."

"It is refreshing, isn't it?"

He smiled and leaned a hand on the wall beside her head, imprisoning her in the circle of his arms. "In fact, I have an even more refreshing idea. Why don't you and I go for a cognac at my apartment?"

"You forget. I need an early night."

"Of course. What if I promise not to detain you too long?"

His hand brushed lightly along her arm. An electric thrill ran the length of her body, and again her pulse quickened. Brandt was right; she did find him attractive and he knew it. Perhaps a man like him assumed that women would fall at his feet. Or maybe he thought that an actress on her own in a foreign city for a single evening would be an easy target. He couldn't know that Clara would not dream of succumbing to the approaches of a Nazi bureaucrat. If indeed a bureaucrat was what he was. She thought again of Hamilton's comment. *Steinbrecher says the Gestapo's pretty well entrenched in Paris now. Heydrich has an extensive network of informers in place.*

"I don't think my boyfriend would like that very much."

Brandt recoiled visibly. "A boyfriend? You didn't mention him. Is he here or back in Berlin?"

"He's in Berlin."

"Of course. Is he an actor too? Perhaps I know him. Can I ask his name?"

Clara's mind went blank. The only two men she had ever cared for—Ralph Sommers and Leo Quinn—were both English. In the heat of the moment, she conjured the first name that entered her head and gave him a rank for good measure.

"He's not an actor. His name is Sturmbannführer Hans Steinbrecher."

It worked. The seductive nonchalance of Brandt's face vanished. He lit a cigarette and inhaled, continuing to scrutinize her all the while.

"Is that so? Well, if you won't come to bed with me, Clara Vine, perhaps you'll come to dinner?"

Clara wanted to. She had an urge so deep it surprised her. It had been a year since she'd had a dinner date with a man. There were always actors, of course, at the studios, who would meet up at one of the popular restaurants in town, the Café Einstein or Borchardt or Lutter und Wegner, but a dinner date, with a single man, who did not want to dissect his own film career or fret about his future in the Reich Chamber of Culture, was a rarity. Yet now was not the time, and besides . . . there was something about Brandt that felt not quite right. Clara had a sixth sense that there was more to him than met the eye. Chanel's salon was full of Nazi agents, and Clara feared a trap.

"I'd like to, Herr Brandt. Believe me, I would. But I leave at six in the morning and I don't want to miss my train."

"It wouldn't do to be stuck here in Paris, you mean?"

"I mean I do genuinely need to get some sleep."

"Perhaps we'll meet again in Berlin then."

"Maybe."

"Could I not tempt you to stay? Just a day? We could see the

Mona Lisa, the only woman in Paris more inscrutable than you."

She smiled.

"The Tour Eiffel? Montmartre?"

She shook her head. "Maybe another time."

"What about the artistic ape in the zoo? The one who makes beautiful drawings?"

"I'm sorry."

"Auf Wiedersehen, then."

Taking her hand, he raised it to his lips and kissed each knuckle in turn. The gesture caused a soft, melting sensation deep inside her, so that for a moment she impulsively longed to raise her own lips to his mouth in response. Instead, she steeled herself to keep her face down as Brandt lifted his hat to her and turned away.

CLARA TOOK THE LONG way back to the Hotel Bellevue, almost losing track of time as she wandered the streets, deep in thought. Partly, she wanted to savor the last vestiges of her time in Paris, and partly, after the encounter with Max Brandt, she was too full of nervous energy to sleep. There was no point denying she was attracted to Brandt. Yet she had learned never to take people at face value, no matter how handsome the face. Five years in Berlin had taught her that when a man followed you it was not always flattering. Instinct told her that suave façade was concealing something deeper, but what?

The moon hung over Paris like one of Chanel's own pearls, its soft brilliance blackening the sky around it. As Clara walked, Chanel's remark sounded in her mind. *I think you, Mademoiselle Vine, are like me.* Was Chanel suggesting that Clara, like her, was cynical and accustomed to using men for her own advantage? If so, then the accusation resonated uncomfortably. She had rejected an offer from the only man she had ever considered marrying, Leo Quinn, in order to commit herself to her life as an agent in Berlin. The last man she'd felt anything for had advised her to forget him. Was she destined to become one of those single women who rattled from affair to affair, finding nothing profound or lasting, searching for love the way an aging actress searches for roles, sleeping with whichever handsome Nazi diplomat came her way? Or did Chanel think being a "realist" meant forgetting your country and your loyalties and siding with whomever might be a winner?

And yet, Clara thought, perhaps you should take pleasure wherever you found it, in case it never came again. Sometimes you passed love like a blossoming tree, without properly noticing it, hurrying on to a future where you imagined that it would be in endless supply, not realizing that you had already bypassed your entire chance of happiness.

Clara stopped abruptly and gave herself a mental shake. Chanel was right about one thing. She was growing cynical about her chances of finding enduring love. But that didn't mean she was not prepared to defend everything else that she held dear.

THERE WAS A BOUQUET WAITING for her at the hotel reception desk. It was a lavish bunch of roses, papery white petals with a soft blush at their hearts. Clara closed the door of her room behind her and removed the note that was tucked in the tissue paper.

Dinner in Berlin

That was all. She rested the petals for a moment against her cheek and inhaled their sharp fragrance. It was intense and delicate, with an edge of dew-drenched gardens and freshly cut grass. Then she took the flowers over to the basin and stripped the petals methodically one by one, until a heap of bruised shapes littered the porcelain beneath. But there was no listening device inside. Nothing suspicious at all. Just roses.

5

BERLIN

"HE FIXES THE HOROSCOPES, YOU KNOW."

Steffi Schaeffer nodded towards Clara's copy of the *Berliner Tageblatt* and gave a sniff more robust than seemed possible for a woman of such refined appearance, in her pale gray linen skirt and jacket, with a silk flower in her lapel.

"Who does?" asked Clara.

"Goebbels," said Steffi, scornfully. "He tailors them. He likes people to think that everything's going well. He orders them to print lines like 'A successful and happy day. Germany is a land of smiles!' Ha! Has he looked at the faces in the streets recently? You don't notice many smiles there!"

Clara glanced out of the window at the street below. She was back in Berlin all right, and, just as Steffi said, a single glance at the citizens was better than any horoscope at predicting the general mood. The sultry heat had not broken, and worry whipped the streets like a dry summer wind. Most people darted along quickly, as if on urgent business, heads down, trying not to attract attention. Most likely those people were heading home because they were Jews served with a curfew and must perform all necessary tasks within daylight hours or risk arrest.

The two women were in a small studio with a scruffy, pock-marked façade, north of the Hackescher Markt in the Scheunenviertel. This quarter had been the center of Jewish life in Berlin for centuries. Its narrow streets were the first port of call for Ost Juden refugees fleeing from the east, and it was now the hub of Berlin's textile trade. Shafts of light from the high windows illuminated a room dominated by a massive wooden table, crowded with rolled bolts of vivid cloth, scissors, pins, and kaleidoscopic spools of cotton. Tailors' dummies stood around like ghostly guests in half-finished finery, and hatstands bore toques, turbans, pillboxes, and tip-brimmed hats in felt, flowers, feathers, and pastel braided straw. It was a place of disguise and concealment, which was fitting considering that Steffi Schaeffer's other role was as part of a resistance network helping Jews to leave Germany. Clara had never discussed this aspect of Steffi's secret life with her, but her friend Bruno Weiss, the painter, had secured a false passport and travel documents to Switzerland courtesy of this elegant and courageous woman.

Outside, a passage led from the street to a dingy courtyard containing a patchwork of work spaces and storage areas occupied by tailors and cloth sellers. Stalls on the pavement sold ribbons and buttons, and the shops were largely selling clothing, stockings, and shoes. On the street side many of the shopfronts were painted with a white *J*, as well as obscene cartoons, six-pointed stars, and pictures of Jews being hanged, decorations for which they had roving bands of storm troopers to thank, or sometimes brigades of Hitler Youth sent out on Saturday mornings with paint pots and brushes.

Clara turned away. "I thought Goebbels took horoscopes really seriously," she said. "He and Hitler often consult the horoscope of the Third Reich when they're planning policy."

"He does," said Steffi, who was at that moment darting around her dress with a mouthful of pins, adjusting the hem. "He even loves Nostradamus. He claims that Nostradamus predicted German troops would march to the Rhine and occupy Vienna, and now he's saying that Nostradamus predicts Hitler will triumph in the Sudetenland too. The destiny of the Third Reich is written in the stars, though that doesn't stop Goebbels from giving it a helping hand."

She pursed her mouth and jabbed the pins viciously into the cushion on the table. "But then I suppose none of us knows what's coming, so it may as well be Goebbels as anyone else."

A tough life and the loss of her husband five years ago, not to mention nights of sleepless anxiety since, had etched hard lines on Steffi's face, yet she was still a beautiful woman in her mid-thirties, petite, with dark blond hair, sharp, elegant cheekbones, and eyes of violet-blue. Her talents as a dressmaker had won her steady work from the costume department of the Ufa studios until the Aryanization measures introduced by Goebbels outlawed Jews from working there. As a Jew on her mother's side, Steffi was barred from working in any part of the Reich Chamber of Culture. And now the commissions she had from society women were drying up too.

She stretched the cornflower-blue cotton for Clara's dress between thumb and forefinger.

"It's hard enough to get the material with this textile shortage, so I can't think why you want to spoil it by making it look like a dirndl," she said, curling her lip at the square, low-cut neckline. "It's not your style at all. You always prefer something elegant."

"It's not a dirndl. It's just a little lace at the neck. Besides, I'm going to be working in Munich. They like things a little more traditional down there."

"Well, I've done my best to give this dress a Marlene Dietrich twist."

"Thank you, Steffi. And for the lovely green silk suit. You'll never guess—I meant to tell you—I wore it to the salon of Coco Chanel."

Steffi Schaeffer widened her eyes and laughed, displaying even white teeth. "Coco Chanel saw my work! I can't believe it! I would have loved to have been there. Perhaps she could give me some commissions!"

"I assume things are getting worse?"

Steffi shrugged. "Of course. Most of my regular customers are going elsewhere now. On the other hand, in the past few weeks I've found a new income stream."

Clara tilted an inquisitive head, and Steffi hesitated, obeying a deep, instinctive caution until their eyes met and she confessed, "It's a new type of tailoring I'm doing. Since the latest announcement."

"Which one is that?"

Since the introduction of the Nuremberg Laws, three years ago, the lives of Jews in Germany had grown ever more circumscribed. They were no longer allowed to marry gentiles or even call themselves citizens. In recent months, however, the stream of restrictions had turned into a crushing torrent. Almost every day there would be a fresh encroachment on Jewish freedom announced on the upper-right-hand side of the newspapers' front pages. Jews could no longer practice medicine or law. They could not hold bank accounts. Non-Aryan cars were issued Jewish license plates, and all too often Jews with cars were called to report to the police station, and, when they were released, their cars remained in custody. Just that week Jews had been told they would all be photographed and fingerprinted and issued with new ID cards.

"This month all non-Aryans had letters ordering them to give their jewelry to the state. They have to take everything to the nearest police station and hand it over. Can you believe it? The thieves! My friend asked for a receipt and the cop said, 'What do you want a receipt for? You won't be seeing these again in your lifetime!'"

"So what's this new tailoring you're doing?"

"Simple." Steffi walked across to a tailor's dummy on which hung a coat of checked tweed and drew it back to reveal the lining. "You know how we sometimes put pfennigs in the lining? So it hangs properly? Well, this time it's not pfennigs. It's something a little more valuable."

She ran her neat, painted fingernails down the navy satin and found an edge that had been left unsewn. Tucking her fingers inside, she withdrew a pearl necklace. From the lined flaps of the pockets, she picked out a pair of ruby and diamond earrings.

"If you need to leave the country, you're going to have to take your coat. Or your jacket, or your suit. This way, you can take your jewelry too."

Clara shook her head in admiration.

"But it has to be done by a professional so the seams lie flat. See? It's no good botching the job; the Gestapo aren't stupid. I do hats too." Steffi gestured at a hatstand on the table. "They're even better because, look." She ran her fingers along the intricate folds, where the raffia was stitched into rivulets. "They're stiffer. They have more detail. They're harder to unpick."

She pulled over a creation of plum velvet, with a scrap of veiling, and removed a rosette from the crown. In the cavity beneath glistened a gold ring.

"Everyone who leaves gets searched. The guards on the trains take the soles out of shoes; they even squeeze tubes of toothpaste looking for valuables. So it pays to be very careful if you're going to conceal something."

"It's so cleverly done."

Steffi shrugged. "Women don't mind leaving everything else, but they won't leave their jewelry. It's not just the value. It makes them feel beautiful, and we all need that now."

"I'm glad you've found some business."

"Business? I'm not sure I'd call it that. Sometimes they pay me with a bit of butter or a few eggs. Sometimes, I do it for nothing. What's the point of money if it's going to be taken away from you?"

"I'm sorry. That was thoughtless of me. I didn't mean . . ."

"Don't worry." The other woman smiled. "Besides, I'm not the only one with extra work. A friend of mine, Herr Feinmann, is a paper manufacturer, and he says the demand for blackout cardboard has soared. He can't keep up with it. You know what that means."

Clara did. Bomb shelters and blackout materials were on everyone's mind. Sandbags had begun appearing on the streets, and public buildings were being transformed into barracks.

Steffi looked at Clara intently. Though she knew no details of Clara's real life, their four-year friendship meant the two women trusted each other implicitly.

"Last month they told us we have to change our names. Did

you hear that? All Jewish passports will be stamped with a *J* and Jewish people who have names of 'non-Jewish' origin have to add Israel or Sara to their given names. Gentiles will be banned from giving their children Jewish names."

"What? Like Joseph, you mean?"

They laughed, despite themselves, at the monstrous absurdity of Goebbels.

"Joseph is exempted. It's been declared an honorary Aryan name."

Steffi's brave smile died and her voice hushed, even though there was no chance of them being overheard.

"It's dreadful, Clara. Every day people are being fetched from their homes and taken to Oranienburg or Buchenwald. They take away their belts and ties and shoelaces, and when they get there, they make them stand in the square all night with spotlights on them. A lot of the men round here spend the day dodging the Gestapo. They stay with friends and their wives pretend that they're traveling. Everyone's leaving. Why wouldn't they? It's that or stay here and take poison. A woman I know killed herself just the other day, up in the Westend. Everyone I know is trying to get to Palestine, or South Africa, or Italy. We're being forced to creep away from our homes like criminals."

Clara had the impression that Steffi was only just holding herself together. That every day the knocks and the fear carved the lines a little more cruelly into her face.

"First the Nazis want you to leave, then they make it impossible for you to get out. People spend all day going to different embassies, and all they do is learn the word *no* in twenty different languages. People turn up at the embassies with hundred-mark notes folded into their passports. They send baskets of fruit and flowers. But it never does any good. That's why I'm trying to help."

"What can you do?" Clara's voice sounded unnaturally loud in the quiet of the workshop.

"I do what I can. There are several of us." She bit her lip and frowned at Clara. "You must know."

Clara did. They were called U-boats, the escapees, because of the sudden descent they made into the vast Berlin underground.

"There are houses all over Berlin, and further out. Some people are going into hiding, you know, sleeping in friends' basements, or moving from house to house. We all contribute what we can. Look here."

Steffi walked across to a wardrobe built into the wall and pushed at the back. The wooden panel gave way to reveal a narrow space, in which a series of uniforms hung.

"I have a friend—not a Jew—who owns a clothing company that is now obliged to work for the Wehrmacht. My friend knows how the uniforms are made, and how to make them up. They check everything, you know. The way the cloth is cut, the precise location of the buttonholes. They leave nothing to chance."

"What about you, Steffi? Are you trying to leave?"

"I can't." Steffi looked at Clara resolutely. "There's my mother to think of. I couldn't leave her."

Clara had met Steffi's mother once, a smiling woman with snow-white hair and eyes clouded by cataracts, confined to a chair by a bout of polio.

"Even if I could go, what would happen to Mutti? There's no one to look after her. Except my brother of course, and he's hopeless. He says, 'We Jews made it through the Red Sea. We'll make it through the Brown shit.' Mutti can't even feed herself, so I'm staying put. But it's Nina I'm worried about."

"How old is she now?" Clara recalled Steffi's only child, an anemic-looking girl whom she had met when collecting a dress from Steffi's home. Like her mother, Nina had been dressed beautifully in a hand-stitched blouse and hand-made skirt, but unlike her blond mother, Nina was dark-haired, with her father's sallow skin and golden brown eyes. It was those eyes Clara remembered most, taking in every detail of Clara's face and clothes, hesitating before eating the cake that she had brought. Nina reminded Clara of herself at that age, observing the world, without intruding on it, creating an elaborate interior universe behind a self-effacing façade.

"She's ten. And she's different from other children. It's probably because she's an only child. Or because she lost her Vati. In some ways Nina's really advanced for her age, but in other ways she's . . . I don't know. Too naïve. Or rebellious." Steffi gave a quick, instinctive glance around her. "The other day she got in trouble. She defaced a news cabinet of *Der Stürmer* on her way home from school. They put the stands deliberately right outside the schools so the children have to walk past them every day, but Nina decided to kick an entire cabinet down."

Despite herself, Clara gasped. *Der Stürmer* was the Jew-hating Nazi newspaper whose lurid pages were dominated by stories of how criminal and defective the Jews were, and blistering editorials on how to resolve the Jewish question. The idea of any child—let alone a Jewish child—defacing one of its Stürmerstands was alarming.

"Fortunately, one of the kinder teachers saw, and the matter hasn't gone any further. But when I talk to Nina about it, she just looks at me. I can't tell what's going on behind those eyes. My daughter's unfathomable, even to me. In fact, most of all to me. What I would really like is to send her away, but lone children are not allowed to leave Germany unaccompanied. And that's not all . . ."

Steffi took Clara's hands in her own and lifted her face. Her normally calm hands were shaking, and her eyes glistened with unshed tears.

"I'm scared, Clara. I think they're planning something here. We've had bands of storm troopers walking around the streets for months, painting on the walls and kicking in the windows, but there's a man—one of the block wardens—who swears something bad is coming. He has contacts in the Gestapo, and he took me aside the other morning and said, 'They have something planned for the Jews. They're making up lists of names and properties. No one will be able to help you.' He was doing me a favor by warning me to go as soon as I could."

"Something planned?"

"That's what he said. Why doesn't anyone do something? Sometimes, I think, When all of us Jews have gone, what will the Nazis do? What will do they do with their hatred then?"

Steffi turned away to busy herself parceling up Clara's new summer dress.

"I'd better be off," Clara said softly. "I'm meeting my godson at the Lehrter Bahnhof."

There was no way Clara was going to tell Steffi that her godson had been on a KdF cruise. The idea of some Germans heading off on sunny foreign jaunts while others did everything in their power to escape the country only to be obstructed by bureaucracy at every level was simply too grotesque.

She touched Steffi lightly on the arm. It was hard to show the sympathy she felt or the gratitude that her friend had trusted her enough to confide her dangerous secret.

"I'm sure that block warden was just scaremongering. About something happening. It'll be fine."

But secretly she thought that was about as credible as the horoscopes in the *Berliner Tageblatt.*

———

SHE WAS LATE, OF COURSE. At the station, the train from Hamburg had already arrived, and the clatter of disembarking passengers rose high into the steel arches of the vaulted roof. Clara searched frantically for the two figures in the crowd.

Brown as a nut and bursting with health, Erich looked just as Clara expected him to look after two weeks in the sole company of his grandmother. Mutinous, grumpy, insolent. The interests of a widow in her seventies had little in common with those of a teenage boy. Old Frau Schmidt's desire to see her grandson avoid the kind of tragedy that had befallen his late mother tended to express itself in a perpetual low-level nagging. The nagging was born of love, of course, but that didn't make it any easier for Erich, and Clara knew that both of them would be longing to escape each other's company for a while. The pair lived in Neukölln, in an apartment at the end of a long corridor stinking of cabbage stew and drying nappies.

"Here, let me take that, Frau Schmidt." Clara heaved a couple of bags from the old lady and looked around for a porter. Frau Schmidt was stout, with swollen ankles and knuckles like walnuts. Whenever she looked at those hands, Clara remembered Helga talking of her mother returning from the hospital where she worked as a nurse each night, her apron dark with blood and her hands raw with scrubbing. "Why don't I take Erich off for a meal and let you get back home?"

The old woman's face lit up. "That would be kind, Fräulein Vine." Though she had known Clara since the death of her daughter five years ago, and accepted a monthly payment to help with Erich's costs, old Frau Schmidt still found it difficult to address Clara informally. "It will give me a chance to unpack, and Erich can tell you all about our excitements."

Clara saw the old lady into a taxi and, turning brightly to Erich, took the smaller of his bags from him.

"What would you say to tea at the Konditorei Schilling?"

The Konditorei Schilling on the corner of Kochstrasse and Friedrichstrasse was their new favorite place, largely because of its famous selection of excellent cakes, which were irresistible to Erich's sweet tooth. A long counter displaying baked goods and pastries led to a series of tables and chairs at the back. Erich would devote several minutes of intense scrutiny to the trays of cinnamon-speckled *Apfeltorte*, syrupy honey cakes, and towering chocolate cake layered with cream before making his choice. They were not as delicious as they used to be—sugar was in short supply and the chocolate cakes were layered with a peculiar artificial cream that tasted like petrol—but they still looked splendid, and it was a pleasure for Clara to have her godson to herself.

They established themselves with a hot chocolate and *Butterkuchen* for Erich and a glass of tea and *Apfelkuchen* for Clara, but Erich kept his eyes lowered and fiddled with his spoon, tapping it annoyingly on the side of his glass.

"So tell me everything," urged Clara, partly to stop the tapping.

"Not much to tell." He shrugged, continuing to tap his spoon.

"Tell me anyhow. I want to hear everything. You don't look like someone who's just had the holiday of a lifetime."

"It was all right."

"Just all right?"

"Okay, it wasn't then."

Erich scowled and squinted up at her. When she had first become involved in the boy's life, as a promise she made to his dead mother, Clara had seen Helga in him all the time. But now only the occasional flash of his skeptical, dark eyes reminded her of his mother, and when that happened Clara felt a pang of sorrow at what Helga had missed and a renewed resolve to look after Erich as well as his mother would have wanted. They talked about Helga less and less now, and Clara found herself hesitating to mention her name, in case Erich should be upset.

Erich paused, as if assessing whether to confide in her. "There was this woman—lady. She was very friendly. She had the cabin next to mine. We got talking because of you actually."

"Me?"

"She was interested in film. She had this collection of cigarette cards, like the one I have, only much better."

Cigarette cards were a craze that crossed all age-groups. All the tobacco companies did them, with subjects ranging from cars and airplanes to flowers or film actors. The idea was to acquire a complete set, and in the process to smoke a lot of cigarettes. One brand, Reemtsma, had recently produced a series of Ufa actors, and Clara's own photo had been included.

"She had the one you did for *The Pilot's Wife*, and I told her you were my godmother."

Clara smiled. "Sounds nice. What was her name?"

"Ada Freitag. But that's not the point." Erich traced a pattern on the table's linoleum surface, as if the path of its shiny tessellations might help him comprehend the puzzling sequence of events. "The thing is . . . she disappeared."

"Disappeared?" Clara cocked her head with curiosity. A lot of people were disappearing right now. But not from cruise ships in the middle of the Atlantic Ocean. "Where was the ship docked at the time? Do you think she just wandered off and didn't make it back?"

Tightly, he replied, "It wasn't in port. It was at sea. I think she fell overboard."

"Oh, Erich, that's terrible." Impulsively Clara reached a hand across to him. "That can't be true. Are you sure?"

Her godson shifted his arm slightly to detach her hand. "I don't know. One moment she was there talking to me, the next she said she had something to do and could I look after her things. But she never came back."

Clara's mind leapt to the obvious conclusion. The girl had formed a romantic attachment with another passenger and spent the remainder of the voyage in his bunk. It was a holiday, after all, though Erich might be too innocent to understand the concept of a holiday romance.

"I think," she said tentatively, "that perhaps Ada met a friend, and decided to spend the rest of the cruise with them."

"I'm not a baby, Clara. I thought that too. Of course I did. But she never came back to her cabin. And all her belongings in her cabin disappeared too."

"Perhaps she moved into another cabin."

"I wondered that. So I thought I'd go to the captain and ask him."

"Goodness." Clara quailed at the thought of her godson interrogating the ship's captain. It was entirely in character. Though small for his age, Erich possessed a stubborn inclination to stand up to authority. He had inherited it from his mother. In her case, it had proved fatal. "Are you sure you should have bothered the captain?"

"He's in charge of the ship, isn't he? He ought to be worried if one of his passengers just vanishes. Anyway, he was happy to help. He told me she had disembarked at Funchal. He even showed me the ship's log, with all the names and dates on it, and I could see that it was written there: Fräulein Ada Freitag. Disembarked Funchal, August twenty-third."

"So that's the explanation."

"No." Erich's scowl deepened. "Because I know that wasn't true. I talked to Ada *after* we left Madeira."

"Are you sure?"

He shot her a brief, withering look.

"I asked Oma about it, but she said the ship's captain knew best. And after I'd asked a couple of times, she got cross and refused to talk about it anymore. So I decided on a plan."

"Which is?"

"It involves you. Do you think, Clara, you could ask someone?"

"Me! Who could I ask?"

"I don't know. Journalists. You meet them. They interview you. You must know someone."

Clara wanted to ask Erich why the fate of a chance acquaintance, even if it was a pretty young woman, should matter so much to him, but the answer was staring her in the face. Or rather it was sitting before her, a bundle of tempestuous adolescent emotion, his boyish features sharper, and his body growing so swiftly that the HJ uniform she had so recently invested in would all too soon need to be replaced.

"I'll see what I can do."

His face softened in relief. "Thank you, Clara. I knew I could count on you. Especially as she was so interested in you. I know she was a fan."

CLARA SAW ERICH ONTO the U-Bahn back to his grandmother's apartment in Neukölln, and then headed down Friedrichstrasse, puzzling over the boy's story. The fact that the woman's departure was noted in the ship's log seemed pretty conclusive, but it was not like Erich to make such a mistake. He had an excellent memory and a sharp mind. Above all, Clara was sorry that the mix-up should have spoiled his first foreign trip. There was no telling when the boy would get another chance to travel abroad, and God forbid it should be in the cabin of a Luftwaffe plane. Erich chattered endlessly about his ambition to begin pilot training the moment he reached seventeen.

Sunk in thought, she received a sharp blow in the ribs as she collided with a man. She apologized instinctively, or at least the English half of her did, even though it was she who had been jostled.

"I'm sorry."

The man had a handsome face with a thin mustache. His lips twitched upwards in a ghost of a smile. "You want to watch yourself, Fräulein."

Clara frowned.

Why did no one have any manners these days? But then, wasn't it absurd to mind about Berliners losing their manners when you remembered everything else they were losing?

THERE WAS ALWAYS A SMALL CROWD OF SIGHTSEERS OUTSIDE
the Reich Chancellery in Wilhelmstrasse. Mostly they were
tourists from out of town, hoping to catch the glimpse of
the Führer that would form the highlight of their trip to
Berlin. Hitler knew this, and when he was in the city he
would often make an impromptu appearance on a first-floor
balcony that had been added to the building for precisely
this purpose. He would emerge like a god on Mount Olympus, albeit a putty-faced god in brown uniform with a swastika armband, accepting the salutes of the crowd before
ducking away again as the disembodied white gloves of SS
guards, like stage magicians, closed the curtains behind
him. That day, as the sky pressed down like a hard blue lid
and a blast of heat rose from the pavement, the crowd was
there as usual, but they looked clammy and less excitable.
The sentries, rigid in their steel helmets and gleaming black
boots, sweated through the seams of their uniforms as they
stood outside the newly refurbished bronze double doors.
The Chancellery was being extensively rebuilt by Hitler's
favorite architect, Albert Speer, and this week it had gained
a new, unexpected decoration. Like all the other public

buildings in the city, it had had slender antiaircraft guns installed on its roof, pointing menacingly up at the sky and, as if in response, a squadron of silver Luftwaffe planes soared directly overhead. Along with the bunkers and the bomb shelters now being dug, the belligerently billowing swastika flags and the detachments of soldiers clattering along the Unter den Linden in their high boots, these roof guns suggested a city preparing for war.

Clara strode along the road, saw the crowd, and crossed to the eastern side of the Wilhelmstrasse, where the buildings cast welcome blocks of shade. The windows of the Propaganda Ministry, known to everyone as the Promi, had been opened, and the faint clatter of typewriters could be heard, compiling the daily stream of orders and directives that reminded the nation's newspapers about the atrocities of the Czechs or reprimanded them for printing unhappy horoscopes. It was an oppressive, airless day. Not a whisper of breeze touched the leaves on the linden trees. It was the kind of day to be in Berlin's great park, the Tiergarten, or farther out, walking among the Grunewald lakes or sunbathing on the silver sand of the Strandbad Wannsee. But sunbathing was the last thing on Clara's mind as she made her way back towards her apartment, a few streets beyond Nollendorfplatz. She had more important things to contemplate.

The more Clara pondered Eva Braun, the more she realized how little she knew about her. No more than a handful of facts. Eva came from Munich, where Hitler had first encountered her working in the shop of Heinrich Hoffmann, his official photographer. She was much younger than he, no more than twenty-six, Clara thought, but still the Führer considered her a pleasant enough companion for the opera and excursions to the

Berghof, his retreat in the Obersalzberg Mountains. Eva Braun came to Berlin sometimes, but Clara had never even glimpsed her. Magda Goebbels had dismissed her as silly, ill-educated, and provincial, and Emmy Goering claimed she liked cheap jewelry and perfume. To Clara, the more astonishing question was what such a young, and apparently ordinary, girl could have in common with a man like Hitler. How could she bear to be erased from the public record because Hitler had proclaimed himself married to the nation? And now Clara had been asked to get close to her. She had no idea how she would even meet the girl or get to know her, let alone develop that acquaintance enough to steal a look at her diary! It was a mission that seemed as fraught and impossible as scaling the cliffs of the Obersalzberg itself.

Turning in to Winterfeldtstrasse, Clara quickly scanned the street. This scrutiny came as second nature to her now, one of a number of new habits, like memorizing the number plates of cars parked outside her apartment or counting the pedestrians she passed. Today the long, leafy street of residential blocks, including her own ocher-painted nineteenth-century building with its heavy wooden front door, looked the same as ever. The only changes she detected were an advertisement for Leni Riefenstahl's latest film, *Festival of Beauty*, featuring three young women in swimming costumes, that had been erected on a hoarding at the end of the road, and a poster next to it on which Berlin's top illusionist Alois Kassner posed menacingly over a nubile brunette with the slogan "Kassner makes a girl vanish!" Also there was a brand-new swastika flag hanging on the pole outside the apartment door.

Nothing out of the ordinary.

Entering the dim hallway, and skirting as always the single

missing tile in the chipped checkerboard floor, Clara heard the familiar greeting from the cubicle of Rudi, the block warden.

"Heil Hitler! Fräulein Vine!"

Rudi, a fanatical old Nazi with a leathery complexion and a clutch of brown teeth, was in charge of the building's maintenance and caretaking. His spine was severely bent from scoliosis, but somehow he was still able to dart swiftly from his cubicle like some barnacled sea creature scuttling from its hole. Despite his inauspicious appearance, Rudi was a perfect example of the way the Nazis managed to keep Berlin's 4 million residents under control even when they were behind closed doors. The old man maintained a relentless scrutiny of the residents of the block and reported the slightest deviation from proper behavior to the authorities. Even activities not in themselves illegal could suggest potential criminality to Rudi's luridly suspicious mind. Excessive typewriting might imply the production of resistance pamphlets. And tantalizing cooking smells could mean the resident had been benefiting from black market food. Recently, Clara suspected that the arrest of Herr Kaufmann, the shy bachelor who worked as a fiction reader at Ullstein publishers and occupied the apartment adjoining hers, had been prompted by a denunciation from Rudi about his visits from young men. The vast majority of arrests for homosexuality came from local informers. Herr Kaufmann might no longer be there, but the suspicion of his homosexuality lingered like a stain, and the other residents grew more cautious of Rudi's all-encompassing gaze.

Though Clara was rarely able to avoid Rudi, she always ensured that she was carrying something in both hands so she didn't have to return the *Führer Gruss.* That day she had a rolled-up magazine in one hand and her handbag in the other.

"Is that mail for me?"

She might just as well have asked what was in it too, given that Rudi had almost certainly had a look. If ever her letters escaped the attentions of the censors, which was unlikely, they faced a second censor in the person of Rudi. Clara knew he would not hesitate to steam her post open if he thought it contained anything incriminating.

"By the way, Fräulein Vine, we have a new resident in the block. A Herr Engel. A very pleasant gentleman. He has the apartment next to yours."

"So Herr Kaufmann's not expected back?"

Rudi gave her a look signaling that Herr Kaufmann would be as welcome as a case of typhoid if he ever made it out of the camp. Accepting her letters, Clara ascended in the rickety elevator to the top floor and closed the door of her apartment behind her. Only then did she feel her whole body relax.

This apartment was her refuge, the place where she tried to instill a sense of security that was so lacking in the city outside. She had laid thick rugs on the floors and painted the walls a soothing dove gray. Even in the heat of a stifling summer, the apartment was cool. The narrow hall opened into a wide space lined on one side with bookcases. On the other side a large mirror reflected back the light from the window, which looked over the crooked roofs towards Nollendorfplatz. There was a desk with a wobbly leg, a gramophone, and a red velvet armchair, with the new English novel that her sister had sent her, *Rebecca,* lying invitingly open beside a pile of scripts. On the mantelpiece a signed photograph of the entire cast of *Es leuchten die Sterne,* Clara's most recent film, stood beside a picture of her late mother, and one of Erich aged six. At the times she felt almost resigned to being alone, this place was her solace, as familiar to her as the face of an old friend. Even the air in the apartment seemed distilled with the fragrances that spelled comfort, from the row of herbs on the kitchen windowsill and the bowl of apples on the table to the tang of the tar melting on the asphalt outside.

After putting on the kettle and sitting at the kitchen table, she took out of her bag the identity cards she carried at all times. The first was a gray standard document certifying that she was Clara Vine, born 1907, with her fingerprint and photograph and the purple stamp of the Ministry of the Interior. The other was a red cardboard document with an eagle on the cover. Inside, an Aryan certificate, the *Ariernachweis,* confirmed that Fräulein Clara Vine was a member of the German race, possessing birth and baptismal records of her parents and grandparents and a genealogy table in which the Jewish ancestry of her mother and grandmother was replaced with Christian blood. It was a forgery, produced not by the government Race Office but by an underground printer in a basement in Wedding equipped with a variety of inks and papers, a knife, and a set of stamps, intricately carved from champagne corks. By day this man printed musical manuscripts, and by night he risked execution working for British intelligence. This document, which Clara carried with her everywhere, was the last communication she had received from Leo Quinn. It was tattered now, and dog-eared, but increasingly essential. Her entire life in Germany, and her whole film career, depended on it. No one with Jewish blood could work in any part of the Reich Chamber of Culture, be it film, radio, theater, or newspapers. Every time she handled this forged certificate she thought of Leo. His presence still lingered in her life, the image of him always at the edge of her thoughts. The document, like the pale blue volume of Rilke's poems he had left her, was yet another way that he had made her who she was.

But Leo was gone now, resettled in England, no doubt with a pretty wife. And Ralph Sommers, the man she had met the previous year, wanted her to forget him. "Your work matters more than personal happiness, Clara. It matters more than ever." By *work*, Sommers didn't mean acting. Clara felt a sudden, painful shaft of longing. Sifting through her wallet, she extracted two photographs, one of her brother, Kenneth, in school uniform—gray shorts, blazer, and cap—eyes squinting into the sun, grubby legs almost visibly twitching with his eagerness to escape, and the other of herself with her sister, Angela, three years older and far more beautiful. Where had it come from, the distance between them? They hadn't always been adversaries. As a child Clara had adored her, and Angela had taken her responsibilities in shepherding her younger sister seriously. She had taught her the piano and coaxed her at chess, giving up abruptly when Clara started to beat her. Angela directed Kenneth and Clara in the plays they staged for their parents, and it was Angela who taught her younger sister always to carry a handkerchief stuffed in her left knicker leg, instructed her on applying foundation and eye shadow long before Clara was old enough to wear it, and explained what happened on a girl's wedding night. Her sister's description, though vague and couched in terms of Kenneth's dogs, provided Clara with a lot more information than anyone else had.

She sighed and turned at last to the thick, vanilla-colored envelope, franked with the Big Ben logo of London Films, which had come with her mail. Her fingers trembled slightly as she opened it.

Inside was a card with a perfectly bland instruction.

Dear Fellow Member of the Reich Chamber of Film,

You are invited to audition with Herr Fritz Guttmann for the role of Sophia in Good King George, *to be made at the Bavaria Film studios at Geiselgasteig, Munich. Initial meetings will be held at the Artists' House on Lenbachplatz in Munich, September 8. Please report to reception at 3:00 p.m.*

Heil Hitler!

Three days away! Clara's heart sank. She had never expected it would be so soon.

She flicked rapidly through the rest of the mail. There was a postcard from Vienna with a photograph of the Ringstrasse and an invitation for a drink. The card carried no signature, but Clara instantly recognized the handwriting of her friend Rupert Allingham, a British journalist who always dropped her postcards from his travels and never signed them. The other letter was a reminder from her friend Sabine Friedmann, manager of the Elizabeth Arden salon on the Ku'damm, to pay a visit. Across the bottom of the card she had scrawled: *Please come soon, Fräulein Vine, it's important.*

What on earth could be important about a session at the beauty parlor? People in the world of fashion and beauty seemed incapable of getting their priorities right. As if the whole business of creams and potions was anything but utterly trivial at a time like this!

On the other hand, if she was attending an audition, it might be a good idea to arrive looking her best. And, as Clara never forgot, sexual allure was an essential weapon in her secret work. Lipstick, mascara, and perfume were all important items in the toolkit of a female spy, and her favorite lipstick, Elizabeth Arden's Velvet Red, in its prettily engraved gold tube, was right down to its stub. However much the Führer might hate cosmetics, the female citizens of the Reich liked them even more at a time when new clothes were hard to come by. Yet lipstick, like coffee and butter and oranges, was getting scarcer and fresh supplies were difficult to find. Clara decided to visit the salon that afternoon.

7

ROSA WINTER FLINCHED AND TRIED VALIANTLY TO SHUT her ears to the shrieking children in the adjacent room as she carried on with her typing. Secretarial duties were dull enough without children being brought into the office to disrupt everything. When their mother had arrived that morning for her interview, hands clamped on the shoulders of her offspring—two boys of around eight and ten years old—she had shrugged apologetically, and Rosa had smiled and nodded towards the empty office next door. The boys had brought a board game with them, the mother explained, which would keep them quiet for at least twenty minutes. Instead, it was having the opposite effect. The game was the current craze, Juden Raus, and it looked fairly normal—in that it involved dice and playing pieces in the shape of large pointed hats, with "Jewish" faces on them—but in terms of the aggression it aroused, it was more like a boxing match than a board game. Every few moments the boys punctuated the air with victory cries of "Jews Out!" or howls of dismay. Rosa was developing a splitting headache.

She sighed. She liked children, indeed she often identified with them, but she had no intention of having any of her own. Not yet, at any rate, or for a good long time. That was something she had never told anyone. It was not the sort of thing a twenty-five-year-old woman confessed in Germany in 1938, not out loud, not to friends, not even to her own parents. Not now, when children were the chief justification of a woman's existence and having more than four of them—being *kinderreich*—was every woman's ambition. Not when being voluntarily childless was deemed "deliberately harmful to the German nation," which sounded an awful lot like treason if you thought about it. And most of all not if your workplace, this drab office crammed with filing cabinets and smelling of carbolic and unwashed clothes, happened to be the very epicenter of the family in Germany, a veritable shrine to the role of women as housewives and mothers—the headquarters of the National Socialist Women's League, the NS Frauenschaft. Whose leader, installed within close barking distance in the office next to Rosa's, was Gertrud Scholtz-Klink, universally known as the Führerin, the most important woman in the entire Reich.

With six children of her own and 10 million German women at her polish-free fingertips, the female Führer was in charge of all National Socialist women's organizations, including the Women's League, the Reich Mother Service, and the German Women's Enterprise, and was described by Hitler as "the perfect Nazi woman." Frau Scholtz-Klink wore her hair snaked round her head in braids, a field-gray uniform shirt buttoned to the neck, and an expression like thunder, exacerbated by the fact that she was going through a divorce, because she deemed her country doctor husband insufficiently Nazified. Rosa sometimes wondered if Hitler himself was frightened of the Führerin, given that everyone else was. Rosa had met the Führer once. He had paid a visit to the office and talked about his mother and the importance of women to the future of the Fatherland. He was much less intimidating than the Führerin herself. He had a pudgy, pale face and strangely penetrating eyes that looked at you as though they were looking *through* you. He was so different from the shrieking figure on the platform she had seen on the newsreels, rattling away like a machine gun, that she could almost understand those women who were said to turn up at the Reich Chancellery, offering to carry his baby. But not quite.

The only person who was certainly not scared of the Führerin was SS Reichsführer Himmler, who had responsibility for coordinating the activities of the Woman's Bureau at ministerial level because no women were allowed in Hitler's cabinet. Rosa had answered the telephone once, and the sound of Himmler's soft, menacing rasp had almost caused her to drop the receiver. The idea that he too might pop in for a courtesy visit was frankly terrifying. She couldn't help imagining Himmler with his moon face and receding chin standing over her desk, peering at her like an owl eyeing its prey, interrogating her about why she, Rosa Winter, was actively weakening her nation by refusing to become *kinderreich*.

What Rosa did want, and had always wanted, was to become a journalist. She had no intention of following her elder sister, Suzi, into marriage and downtrodden motherhood, especially not marriage to a thuggish civil servant who was not averse to the occasional bout of wife beating. After leaving school Rosa had taken a typing course, quickly become a skilled and fluent typist, and readied herself for an exciting career. When she was growing up in Berlin there had been a hundred newspapers—it was a city that loved journalism, and Germany, her father often reminded her, had more newspapers than Britain, France, and Italy put together. But after Hitler came to power, in 1933, closing opposition papers and dragging the journalists off to concentration camps, the press grew cautious. The number of newspapers halved, and government directives on saving meat or mending socks had far more chance of getting into the news pages than murders or burglaries.

To Rosa's dismay, getting a break as a journalist turned out to be next to impossible. She traipsed around the newspaper district for months, but whenever she applied for a job, the editor, either apologetic or dismissive, would explain that male employees must now take priority. Each time she returned disheartened to the apartment she still shared with her parents, her mother would say, *Never mind. No one in our family has ever been a journalist....* But it didn't mean Rosa's typing skills need go to waste, her mother soothed. There were always secretarial positions to be filled. Journalism could wait. *But I don't want to be a secretary!* Rosa screamed inside. Yet sure enough, eight years after leaving school, here she was in front of a typewriter, with a stack of letters on one side and a dictation pad on the other. The Führerin had taken one look at the skinny girl, mousy hair parted dead down the middle, bitten nails, and gray, blinking eyes behind thick glasses, and hired Fräulein Winter on the spot. The fact was, Rosa looked infinitely more convincing as a secretary than as a journalist.

Even then, despite her role, the first time Rosa had sat behind this typewriter her fingers had flitted over it with a visceral thrill, as though perhaps on this machine she might still get the chance to type dispatches, personal reports, maybe a newsletter for her new employers. That was until she had received her first letter to type—a report on the marriage allowance scheme to the Interior Ministry—and she felt the excitement in her fingers drain away. Instead, she had taken to feeding her passion by keeping a notebook of what she called her "Observations"—articles based on the kinds of essays she

used to read in the newspapers by famous writers like Joseph
Roth, made up of eyewitness observations of Berlin. Not earth-
shattering events, but little things about life in the city; people
she noticed, small incidents in the streets. She liked to watch
strangers and work out what she could tell about them from the
trivial details they gave away. The fact that Rosa was shy and
self-effacing meant no one gave her a second look. Who took
any notice of a drab young woman in a head scarf, peering at
them through meek, secretarial spectacles? Rosa wrote up her
Observations at night, letting her imagination run wild. Writing was where her soul revealed itself.

The boys let out another volley of shouts, and Rosa shot a
quick glance at the closed door, behind which the Führerin was
interviewing their mother. Perhaps it was punishment for her
unnatural desire to forgo children that she should now get to
spend her days with a portrait of the flaxen-haired Goebbels
family staring down at her desk. It was the standard, Party-
issue photograph, and whenever Rosa looked up from her typewriter, or ate her sandwiches during busy lunch hours, or
paused to wonder whether she might actually spend her entire
life here, the Goebbels family would return her gaze. Being the
model family, they had produced an entire marching squad of
children for the Führer, little girls in pigtails and the boy in
lederhosen, flanked by their mother, Magda, with a jaw
clenched like an industrial vise, and the minister himself, with
a smile as sharp as a broken bottle.

Rosa squinted across to the opposite wall, to a map of Germany bristling with flags bearing tiny swastikas. Each one signaled the presence of an office of the NS Frauenschaft. It
looked like something a general might use, charting the progress of Panzer divisions across hostile terrain. The hostile terrain in this case being anyone who attempted to frustrate the

aim of providing ever bigger families for the Reich. Occasionally the Führerin would enter the office and stab a fresh flag in the map, proving that the doctrine of increasing the birth rate was being carried to the farthest corners of the Reich.

The door opened. The job candidate walked dejectedly past Rosa's desk to retrieve her children, yanking both boys up by their arms in a practiced gesture that provoked howls of protest. As Rosa understood it, her husband had recently been killed in Spain and she was keen to return to work, but Rosa didn't fancy her chances here. Rosa's predecessor had been obliged to leave when she got engaged. It wouldn't do for the head of the entire Nazi women's service to contravene all Party doctrine by employing a married woman, let alone one with children.

Rosa, on the other hand, gave no impression of having a boyfriend, which obviously suited the Führerin quite well. After all, hadn't she just given Rosa the trip of a lifetime—two weeks in the sun, with negligible duties and no typing at all? The Kraft durch Freude organization was hosting a National Congress of Women's Fitness next month that would welcome delegations from thirty-two countries, and top guests, including Heinrich Himmler himself, were to be accommodated on the KdF flagship vessel, the *Wilhelm Gustloff*. Therefore it had been deemed useful for Rosa to undertake a little reconnaissance. She'd been ordered to sample the ship's amenities and provide a report to the Führerin that would avert any potential embarrassments and ensure that nothing would compromise the smooth running of their event. Rosa's colleagues had been jealous, especially when she put on her desk a framed photograph of herself standing in front of the ship with windblown hair, wearing a new peach-colored sundress and straw hat and a most unlikely tan on her skin. Smiling, as much as Rosa ever smiled, with her lip bitten in one corner and an elusive look in her eye. All the girls at work stopped at her desk and marveled. She must have had the time of her life, they cooed.

How astonished they would have been to learn that Rosa Winter bitterly wished she had never set foot on that ship.

CHAPTER

8

THE GOEBBELS FAMILY HAD A NEW ADDRESS. ONLY TECHNI-
cally though; they still resided in the same imposing villa
on the corner of Behrenstrasse and Hermann-Goering-
Strasse that they had occupied for the past five years, but
having undergone a 3.5-million-mark refurbishment, the
residence was now officially designated a palace. The
grounds running down to the Tiergarten were clipped and
pruned, the lawns laid with graveled paths and statuary, and
the interior had been ruthlessly updated. The parquet floors
and ornate ceilings were still there, but in keeping with the
house's elevated status, carpets had been imported from
Berlin's Art History Museum to match the National Gallery
Old Masters on the walls, and marquetry tables and Louis
XIV furniture had been acquired from the villa of a Jewish
banker in return for his passage out of the country. In front
of a glass display case of antique china, recently liberated
from the Schloss Charlottenburg, a vase of lilies and roses
scented the air. But it was going to take more than flowers,
plush furniture, and rich tapestries to warm the frigid atmosphere of the Goebbels family home.

Magda Goebbels didn't seem especially grateful to receive her gift of Chanel No. 5. She untied the packaging

listlessly, drawing aside the black ribbons as though unwrapping a parcel of socks sent in for the Winterhilfswerk, the Party charity, rather than a hundred marks' worth of rare perfume. After a glance at the opulent glass bottle reeking of wealth and luxury, she gave it a brief squirt, and put it aside.

"Thank you for fetching this. It's kind of you to spare the time." She spoke with a martyred sigh. "I suppose I'll be buying all my own perfume from now on."

"It's a good choice," replied Clara politely, deciding not to point out that the perfume had cost Frau Doktor Goebbels precisely nothing.

"Yes. It's a new one for me. And at least it's not Drachenfutter."

Clara grimaced despite herself. *Drachenfutter,* "dragon fodder," was slang for presents given by men to pacify their wives. From what Clara had heard of relations between the propaganda minister and his wife over the past summer, Magda must have received *Drachenfutter* by the kilo, but it was having little effect. Clara took a sip of the tea she had been offered and hunted for some small talk.

"Madame Chanel was flattered you'd chosen her perfume."

Magda shrugged. "Was she? I thought it would make a change. We all have to embrace change sometimes, don't we? At least, that's what I'm told. And I understand this perfume is very popular in certain quarters."

That seemed like a strange thing to say about the world's most famous perfume, but Clara had grown used to Magda's gnomic utterances, with their peculiar, bitter subtext, in the years that she had known the propaganda minister's wife. Back in 1933, Magda's request that Clara model for the Reich Fashion Bureau had given her unrivaled access to the gossip and feuds of the senior Nazi wives, not to mention an insight into the tortured relationship between Magda and her relentlessly unfaithful husband. Now, Clara guessed, Magda was ruminating on a new low in the relationship, wrought by Goebbels's fraught love affair with the Czech actress Lida Baarová.

Magda aside, there were enough comic aspects to the affair to keep everyone amused. It was on the set of the aptly named movie *Hour of Temptation* that the pair had met, and Goebbels had instantly succumbed. Unfortunately, Lida Baarová was living with another Ufa heartthrob, Gustav Fröhlich, at the time, in a house just a few doors down from the Goebbelses' country villa in Schwanenwerder. On finding the lovers together, Fröhlich had punched the propaganda minister in the face, blackening his eye and forcing Goebbels to pretend he had injured himself in a car accident. But Fröhlich's resistance had proved futile. The delicate brunette with high, Slavic cheekbones was referred to everywhere, with a liberal dose of Berliner humor, as Goebbels's "Czech conquest," and her latest film, *A Prussian Love Story,* provoked yet more laughter. While the Nazi hierarchy was plotting the Reich's entry into Czechoslovakia, Goebbels was fighting to keep hold of both his wife and his Czech mistress, and, according to recent rumors, it was a battle he was losing.

"I meant to say, congratulations, Frau Doktor, on your new daughter!"

"Thank you. She's sweet, little Hedda. She's four months already."

"So you have five children now!"

"Six," Magda replied tersely, as if correcting the asperities of an especially forward maid. "You forget the son of my first marriage, Harald."

Unlike the wives of other leading Nazis, Magda Goebbels had always been surrounded by a miasma of nerves, but now her complexion was cracked with anxiety, like paint, and there was a grim set to her mouth. She was beautifully attired in a cobalt-blue dress by Hilda Romatzki, one of Berlin's leading designers, but her eyes were hollow from lack of sleep and the latest baby had left another layer of flesh around her waist.

She stared at Clara without speaking; then, abruptly, she looked away.

"There's no point pretending, Fräulein Vine. I've confided in you before, after all. Things are very bad here."

"I'm sorry to hear that, Frau Doktor."

"Oh, I know people think it's always bad, but they have no idea! First, my husband insisted on building an annex at Schwanenwerder where he could take his actresses 'to play records for them.' That was awkward enough, but I didn't object. I know a man in Joseph's position, under a lot of pressure, sometimes falls victim to predatory women and imagines himself infatuated. I thought the best thing I could do was try to contain it until it wore itself out. Keep them away from the children, but otherwise try to put up with it. That was until his latest request." She cast Clara a savage glance. "You've heard about this woman, I'm sure. I daresay it's the talk of the studios."

It was, of course. Clara guessed the best response was to remain impassive.

"Joseph takes her everywhere, out on his yacht, on little trips in his car. He has no shame, but his latest proposition really astonished me. He asked me to have her over for a meeting where we would all agree to live in a ménage à trois. He's a heartless devil! Can you believe such a thing?"

Clara could, but she was not about to say so. She confined herself to a sympathetic frown of assent.

"I was so miserable I said yes, and he came back with this

big diamond ring for me. What a fool I was. The moment she moved in, I discovered he'd given her one too. Exactly the same! He loves her more than any woman he has ever met."

"I'm sure, Frau Doktor, that . . ."

"Oh yes he does! I read it in his infernal diary. It's that diary he loves most of all, actually. He shuts himself away every night, scribbling down his thoughts, and then he has them preserved on photographic plates to be stored in the vaults of the Deutsche Bank. I never hear the end of that damn diary. It's his testament for posterity. Well, posterity's welcome to it." Magda stopped and gave a sniff. As when many women unburdened marital unhappiness, her misery, once unleashed, became a bitter torrent that showed no sign of slackening.

"Anyway, the ménage à trois was intolerable. I couldn't stop crying—I even thought of killing myself and the children. I did, honestly. When we accompanied the Führer to Bayreuth in July, I sobbed all the way through *Tristan und Isolde*." Red patches had formed on the bands of her neck, as they always did when Magda was overwrought. "Then do you know what I did?"

Clara dreaded to think.

"I got up the courage to go down to Berchtesgaden and ask the Führer for permission to divorce."

"Divorce?" echoed Clara, instinctively wishing Magda would speak more softly. Even if all this was true, she doubted that the propaganda minister wanted his love life discussed in detail with casual callers, and everything she knew about Goebbels convinced her he was paranoid enough to bug his own home.

"Exactly. And the Führer listened to me so kindly and was quite horrified to hear everything Joseph had done, but it was no good. The Führer was furious, of course, with my husband.

He summoned Joseph and banged his desk so hard all the pencils jumped in the air." At the idea of this, Magda's voice hushed and she seemed to pale. Even if you were the favorite of the senior wives, even if Hitler called you the First Lady of the Reich, there was no doubt that an interview with an enraged Führer would be traumatic.

"But he wouldn't hear of a divorce. He adamantly instructed us to reconcile. He said it would never do for the first family in the Reich to separate; in fact, quite the opposite. Joseph must increase the press focus on the importance of the family and run more photographs in the newspapers of our children. And the newspapers must be made to print articles about the home life of the Goebbelses. Ha! We're a model family, after all. The whole of the Reich looks up to us."

Bitterly she dragged a moist handkerchief from her sleeve. "Joseph is to institute more cultural emphasis on large families and the importance of childbearing."

"I thought that was SS Reichsführer Himmler's domain."

"It is. But the Führer wants Joseph to find ways of encouraging women who have yet to have children. Addresses on film and radio and so on. What do I care? It's of no concern to me."

Magda stalked over to the mirror and pretended to adjust a lock of hair that had escaped from the stiff ranks of curls on her forehead.

"Joseph's livid with me, of course." She frowned at her reflection. "He hates me for blackening his name to the Führer. He actually cried. He said Hitler will only speak to him on official business and will only receive him in an outer room. He's in deep disgrace. He sits there every night confiding his misery to his wretched diary, and now he's planning some eye-catching event to rehabilitate himself in Hitler's eyes."

"You mean like a parade?"

A contemptuous shrug. "God knows what he'll dream up. He's been plotting it with his police chief friend, von Helldorf."

"Count von Helldorf?"

The chief of the Berlin police was a notorious gambler and anti-Semite, who hosted sex parties on his yacht involving brigades of HJ boys.

"Yes. Joseph said it would make headlines, but that doesn't bother me. Anyhow"—she turned back to Clara defiantly— "some good did come out of it. The Führer barred that marriage wrecker from appearing in any films or plays or attending any social functions. Her current effort is to be her last. She's to be completely blacklisted."

She smiled, grimly, at this triumph.

"I'm so sorry, Frau Doktor . . ."

"Oh, don't imagine I'm looking for your sympathy, Fräulein," Magda snapped, her eyes flashing and her misery transformed to naked hostility. "I'm telling you all this for a reason. I want you to let all your little actress friends at Ufa know that the Führer has commanded my husband to remain faithful. If I'm to stay with him, they can keep that in their silly heads. If they're tempted to stray, they will be disobeying the orders of Adolf Hitler. It probably counts as treason. I will make sure the Führer knows their names, and the punishment will be a camp, at the very least. Can you manage that?"

In the background a car door slammed, and then there was the sound of the front door closing and steps proceeding along the narrow hallway. It was a tread so distinctive that everyone recognized it, one foot firm, the other slightly dragging. The steps hesitated outside the drawing room; then suddenly, the door was thrown open and the diminutive figure of Joseph Goebbels stared in.

As always when she encountered the Reich's most vicious

baiter of the Jews, an involuntary shudder ran through Clara. She had to work hard to control the tremble of her hands and paste a polite smile on her face. This was the man who had ordered her in for questioning only the previous year, suspecting her motives and her allegiances. When their paths first crossed, Goebbels had decided Clara might be useful to him; he had summoned her to his ministry and asked her to keep a confidential eye on his wife. But all that was long ago. Now Joseph Goebbels no longer treated her with anything but suspicious distance. He had put his agents on her tail in the past and would do so again in an instant. He was probably as familiar with the contents of Clara's underclothes drawer as she was herself.

Yet now his appearance shocked her. As a senior cabinet minister of a country on the precipice of war, Joseph Goebbels might be expected to look preoccupied, but beyond his natty white double-breasted suit and beige fedora, there was a wild air about the little man. His cadaverous face was pale, his eyes red-rimmed, and the limp from his crippled foot seemed more than usually pronounced. He was clearly in torment. But whether it was over the hostilities in the Sudetenland or those in his private life, Clara couldn't guess.

She smiled a greeting, but Goebbels didn't bother to return it. Indeed he barely acknowledged her. He stood frozen in the doorway, a clutch of manila files under one arm, surveying the room with a frantic gleam in his eye, as though it must contain more than just Clara and his wife.

For a second, Clara was bewildered, and a glance at Magda's face puzzled her yet further. Magda's expression was pure, malicious . . . *satisfaction.*

"Are you looking for someone, Joseph? It's just myself and Fräulein Vine here, I'm afraid. Did you expect anyone else?"

Clearly Goebbels had assumed someone else was there, but

why would he think that? There were no other voices but hers and Magda's, and no car in the drive. What did Goebbels imagine was going on?

Clara's eye fell on the golden gleam of Chanel No. 5 on the table beside Magda, and she suddenly understood. It must be Lida's perfume. Goebbels had smelled its distinctive rose-laden trail and had hoped, against all hope, that his lover was present. Following her glance, he saw his mistake.

"Fräulein Vine has brought me a delightful gift!" crowed Magda with hideous brightness.

Goebbels glowered. "So I see," he said tightly. "That's an interesting choice of perfume."

"We all have to make choices," said Magda, newly miserable now that her ploy had succeeded. "Isn't that what you said? And I seem to recall this perfume is one of your favorites."

Goebbels gave his wife a savage glance, and Clara cursed silently, hoping that the minister did not suspect her of a deliberate provocation. She couldn't afford to get on his wrong side, but neither could she point out Magda's machinations in this marital firefight.

"Actually, Herr Doktor, the perfume was a gift from Coco Chanel. I happened to see her in Paris."

"So you've been filming there?"

He knew already, Clara could tell that from the flatness of his eyes. Every movie schedule in the Ufa studios had to be submitted to Goebbels's office before filming began.

"Yes, I'm just back. I'm about to leave again for a job in Munich."

That did take him by surprise. Goebbels liked to think he knew everything that went on in the cultural life of the Reich, and that included the movements of actresses.

"Are you? What's the film?"

"It's called *Good King George.*"

Goebbels raised an eyebrow, so Clara elaborated.

"Not the current King of England, of course. George the First. The Hanoverian who took the English throne."

If England was ever to be represented in German film, Goebbels preferred a historical setting. He especially liked films about Britain that featured people in wigs. It was all part of his campaign to present England as old-fashioned and class-ridden, in contrast to a modern, dynamic Germany. With its setting of seventeenth-century Hanover coupled with the theme of a German succeeding to the English throne, *Good King George* might have been engineered specifically to appeal to the propaganda minister. Indeed, Clara reflected, it probably was.

"It's being directed by Fritz Guttmann. At the Bavaria Film studios at Geiselgasteig."

"Interesting. Sounds like an improvement on Guttmann's usual sub-Expressionist tripe. What's your role?"

"I play Sophia."

"The unfaithful wife. She dies, doesn't she, at the end?"

"I think so."

"Fitting," he remarked curtly, but already his mind was on other things. A calculating flicker ran across his face. "Report to me, would you, when you get back. I have a task for you."

"A task, Herr Doktor?"

"It's to do with a new documentary I'm planning. Fräulein Riefenstahl's *Triumph of the Will* has provoked a raging appetite around the world for German documentary—the Americans have been particularly complimentary. Our relationship with Hollywood is of great importance to the Reich, so it's extremely gratifying that they love our documentaries. These Hollywood producers are so much more impressive than their rather poor British counterparts."

Clara did not allow her smile to waver.

"Anyhow, I've decided our next international effort will focus on the role of German families. There's a new decoration for kinderreich mothers to be awarded by the National Socialist Frauenwerk—it's a fresh initiative of Reich domestic policy I'm announcing this week—and that would be a good place to start. I sense a global excitement about our plans for German womanhood, and this documentary will satisfy that hunger. I think you would be ideal to narrate it."

"I'm flattered."

"Don't be. I need an English speaker for the American version, and there aren't many of those around. I'll be in touch."

Without another glance at the *kinderreich* mother of his own children, who was staring stonily out the window, Joseph Goebbels left the room.

9

To all outward appearances, the Café Kottler on the leafy Motzstrasse in Schöneberg was a model restaurant of the Reich. Beneath the old-fashioned brass lamps, its paneled oak walls and generous chairs glowed with a sense of comfort and security. It purveyed Swabian cuisine, the starchy food of southern Germany beloved of the Nazi top brass, and, like many cafés, it took the opportunity of a captive audience to hand out some worthy advice about smoking, for example, or not wasting food. That month the proprietor had hung a sign over the bar reminding customers of the importance of the Führer salute.

DER DEUTSCHE GRÜSS HEISST "HEIL HITLER!"

The sign was, however, a disguise, as was the photograph of Hitler surrounded by adoring flower girls that sat next to the liquor stand on an adjacent wall. These outward manifestations of Nazi zeal only masked an establishment where the opponents of the Party felt unusually safe. Everything about the Café Kottler—from the layout of tables in discreet alcoves to the dim lighting and the enthusiasm of the zither player, whose music drowned out conversations—

made it the perfect place to congregate without fear of being overheard. The restaurant owner was a jokey, swaggering character, who was known to be sympathetic to anti-Nazis, or at the very least unlikely to bug their conversations and forward the tapes to the Gestapo. For precisely that reason it was the ideal setting for Clara to meet Rupert Allingham, Berlin bureau chief of the *Daily Chronicle* and the man who had first suggested she come to Germany.

Clara looked on with amused disgust as Rupert's meal arrived—two boiled Weissewurst coiled around a swamp of congealing vegetables, a dish of cabbage, and a jar of brown sauce.

"I don't know how you can eat that."

"It's a Proustian madeleine to me. Reminds me of boarding school. Especially the sawdust in the sausages."

Clara smiled affectionately at Rupert. Even now, when he was almost perpetually drunk, in a battered tweed suit that had seen better days and two days' growth of stubble, there was no disguising his aristocratic good looks. The chiseled, blue-blooded features were blurred by drink, like those of a decayed seraph, but there was a skeptical intelligence behind those sleepy eyes, and the rhetorical flourishes were undercut by the ironic slant of his smile. When she had first met him, at a grand London party given by a friend of her sister's, she had taken Rupert for exactly what he resembled—a well-born, Oxford-educated, cultural dilettante with absolutely no need to earn a living. The only son of Lady Allingham, heir to a thousand acres of Northumbria, and destined from birth to occupy the most comfortable of niches in the English establishment. Instead of which, Rupert Allingham had emerged as a passionate journalistic opponent of the Nazi regime who frequently came perilously close to being ejected from Germany. It was a difficult balancing act. Every bit of copy he filed had to get by a series of Nazi censors, so often he had to rely on a deep English sense of irony to convey the opposite of what his Nazi minders would read. He was an embodiment of upper-class charm, which simultaneously baffled his Nazi minders and pleased his interviewees.

She leaned over and flicked some crumbs from his jacket. "Had you ever thought of getting this cleaned?"

"No point. My laundry's run out of soap. They say it's harder to get soap than tobacco now."

He took another greedy bite of his sausage and chewed it. "I'll manage fine so long as Kottler's never runs out of sausage. This wurst may be an acquired taste, but once one has acquired it one can't get enough."

"I suppose you have to eat it to soak up the alcohol."

Rupert assumed a hangdog expression. "It was a rough night," he conceded. "But you should eat something too, Clara. You're getting thin. Those Nazis like their film stars with a bit of meat on them."

"I'm not a star. I don't even want to be. And I already ate with my godson, Erich. I'll just have a drink."

Rupert called the waiter for some coffee, then turned back to her. "How is that lad of yours?"

"He's just got back from a KdF cruise."

"A National Socialist holiday? I always think that sounds like a contradiction in terms."

"It was, rather. Not because Erich objects to the Nazis, of course. He's all in favor. He was upset because a woman fell overboard."

"I can understand wanting to get off one of those god-awful cruises, but that's a bit drastic."

"Don't joke. It was a young woman. I think Erich had taken a shine to her."

She recalled her godson's face as he'd told her about it. He was growing so fast. His round features, which she had known and loved since he was a child of ten, were now sharpened with incipient adulthood. The light in his eyes was becoming guarded— that was, when he didn't avoid her gaze altogether. Clara didn't blame him. She remembered all too well how secretive adolescence was. A time when excruciating self-consciousness made contact with other people intense, like rubbing on raw skin. The fact that Erich was an orphan, with only an elderly grandmother to fight in his corner, had made the naturally shy boy even more defensive.

"It's a strange story, from what I could get out of him. He was pretty awkward about telling me."

She recalled the nervous glances Erich had shot at her as he imparted little bits of information, leaving her to fill in the gaps.

"They were on the *Wilhelm Gustloff*."

Rupert's eyes widened. "The pride of the fleet. Last word in luxury, apparently. How did they get the tickets?"

"His grandmother's a nurse at the Charité hospital, and she qualified for them through work. From what I could gather, Erich became friendly with this woman who had the cabin next to his, and he got in the habit of fetching coffee for her each morning. One day she asked him to look after her bag and she never came back. Erich seems convinced she fell overboard."

"Sounds like a bit of a story. Is he the imaginative kind? You don't think he made it up, do you?"

That thought had occurred to Clara, yet it seemed so unlikely. Erich had a solid, scientific kind of mind. He loved quoting to Clara the number of planes in the Luftwaffe, or the specifications of every single model of Mercedes-Benz going back to the 1920s. He enjoyed hearing stories, certainly, but he'd never been one for making them up. And besides, why would he fabricate a tale like that?

"Why do you ask?"

Rupert shrugged. "Simply because I've not heard anything about a woman being lost overboard on a KdF cruise. An accident like that would make the papers, and I do read the German papers, as you know, courtesy of the Propaganda Ministry. They ensure that the Foreign Press Club is lavishly provided with Berlin's finest, and they like us correspondents to read them all. Which now that they've gone down so much in size, doesn't take long."

"The thing is, Erich was so worried about it, I promised him I'd find out about this woman. He seems to feel an obscure loyalty to her and"—Clara felt a surge of love at the thought of her godson's face, with its mixture of youthful bewilderment and hurt pride—"I'm determined to look into it."

"Clara . . ."

"I have to. Poor boy. It was his first foreign holiday too." She took a sip of the coffee the waiter had brought and put it down hastily. It tasted of acorns, or what she imagined acorns must taste like, a bitter mix of wood chippings and grit, with the consistency of sand scraped from the bottom of the Spree. "Anyhow, I said I'd ask you."

"Me?" Rupert paused mid-bite and frowned.

"No, not you specifically, of course, but a responsible journalist I happened to know through my work. You are that, aren't you?"

"I suppose."

"So as a favor to me would you ask around, see if you can find anything about a woman called Ada Freitag, lost on a cruise? You know policemen, don't you? You must have contacts."

He raised his eyebrows. "I don't know if you've noticed, darling girl, but there's a rather different kind of foreign travel at the top of the news list right now. Herr Hitler's packing his bags for Prague, by the look of it."

Clara leaned her arms across the table and plucked at his sleeve. "I do understand you're busy with far more important things, Rupert. I know this is trivial, but it broke my heart to see Erich so upset. I don't think he's ever had a crush on a girl before. You remember what it's like to be that age, don't you?"

"Every day."

At fifteen, she knew, Rupert had been immured in Winchester, spending his evenings taking sherry with a German master who liked to read Goethe to the more intelligent and appealing of his pupils. It was a time of intense adolescent ferment, but crushes on girls had not been part of the picture.

"Erich feels it's his duty to find out, and if he hadn't told me he would be pursuing it with the local police, which would lead to all sorts of attention he could do without. So I have to get him some answers one way or another."

Tears stung her eyes. Noticing them, Rupert mimed a little courtly bow, then reached for the notebook in his top pocket and scribbled a note.

"I'll do what I can, darling. Perhaps it's understandable it got hushed up. I suppose a tragedy like that's not exactly great publicity for the Reich. Can't compete with this, for example."

He gestured at the *Berliner Tageblatt* on the table beside him. From an inside page the face of little Hedda, the newest Goebbels daughter, stared out under the headline BABY JOY FOR THE REICH MINISTER'S FAMILY. Evidently, Goebbels was enthusiastically obeying his master's order to produce more copy about the home life of the Reich's model family.

Clara squinted at it. "Magda told me he's determined to increase coverage of German families. In fact he's asked me to present a documentary about the work of the Deutsches Frauenschaft."

"I never quite understand what that involves. Is it like the Women's Institute, but without jam and Jerusalem?"

"More like the WI run along military lines. It oversees everything to do with women in the Reich. It's headed by Gertrud Scholtz-Klink."

"That horror? I don't know why they don't put her in charge of the Wehrmacht. She's enough to scare any enemy."

"Apparently there's a new initiative for women that Goebbels wants publicized. Something to do with honoring German families."

"He is keen on family news at the moment, isn't he?" Rupert gestured to the facing page. IN THE SUDETENLAND, WOMEN AND CHILDREN MOWN DOWN BY CZECH ARMORED CARS. He looked from one headline to the other with bemusement. "It's hard to know what to believe. Goebbels invents these atrocities to arouse fury. All these riots and shootings by Czech bandits or Bolsheviks in the Sudetenland. Half of them never happened, or if they did, they were staged by German agents themselves."

"Is Prague next, do you think?"

"I think Hitler's caught between two sides. Goering and Goebbels urge caution, but Count von Ribbentrop wants him to act aggressively. Von Ribbentrop seems to be consumed by the thirst for war. The more I meet that man, the more I'm convinced that he has very little between his ears. He loathes the British in particular. He told Churchill that if Germany was allowed a free hand to take Lebensraum in the east, then he could guarantee Britain's security."

"What did Churchill say?"

"He said the Royal Navy had been guaranteeing Britain's

security for several centuries and didn't need Hitler's help, thank you."

Clara smiled. "It's a shame Hitler never really sees what the British think of him."

Rupert gave a delighted laugh. "That, my dear Clara, is where you're wrong. He does, and it drives him crazy! Ribbentrop held a special meeting with Lord Halifax this summer to complain about the *Evening Standard* cartoonist, Low. He said if Germany ever went to war with England, Low is one of the first people Hitler wants shot."

"He probably means it too."

"Undoubtedly. Ribbentrop doesn't understand humor. Goebbels does, though, and he even took me aside. It was after one of the morning briefings; he came over all confidential and made a play for sympathy. He said, 'Low makes the most offensive and lying cartoons, which I am obliged to show the Führer, and each time I do he blows up. It absolutely spoils his day.'"

"So that's something."

"That's what I thought. Nice to think the British press can provide a useful service. I only wish my articles had the same effect." Rupert's face darkened.

"Has something happened?" she asked impulsively.

He poured another glass. An alcoholic flush was beginning to develop on his face, and the laughter drained from his eyes.

"You could say that. There's a new editor at the *Chronicle*. Reginald Winstanley. He couldn't be more different from the previous chap. Winstanley hates anything critical of the regime here. Believes Herr Hitler is much misunderstood. Britain's place is on the sidelines, et cetera, et cetera, et cetera."

"Surely he must see what you write?"

"If so, he seems determined to ensure that no one else does. He thinks I should be more conciliatory to the regime. He says,

'Ward Price of the *Daily Mail* gets to visit Herr Hitler at the Berghof. Why are you never invited, Allingham?' "

"To the Berghof? I can't think of anything worse!"

"I've heard the view is spectacular."

"Oh, Rupert. What are you going to do?"

He wiped his mouth and cast the napkin carelessly aside. "God knows. Maybe I should follow up your story about the Reich Führerin. Perhaps she could find me a replacement for my office assistant. She's got married and insists the place of a German wife is in the home. Apparently keeping my office in order is incompatible with keeping her husband in hot meals. The place is a frightful mess."

"I'm surprised you can tell."

"I may never have maintained Nazi levels of order, dearest, but it's come to something when you need to mount a search and rescue operation for the telephone every time your editor rings."

He drained his drink and added, "Winstanley's a good friend of your father's, as it happens."

Clara flinched. She hated any mention of her father.

Sir Ronald Vine, a former Conservative MP, had formed a group of aristocrats and senior politicians active in the cause of Anglo-German friendship. But in recent years their cause had gone beyond friendship to appeasement of Hitler. Now their powerful, covert coterie did everything it could to advocate the National Socialist cause to the English government.

"I saw them together, actually, last time I went back. Winstanley was giving a talk to the Anglo-German Fellowship at the Grosvenor House hotel."

"So you want me to intercede with my father?"

"If the occasion arises."

"If that's what you'd like."

He caught the wistfulness in her eyes. "Ah, dearest girl. Do you miss England?"

Spending time with Rupert, speaking English, always awoke a stab of yearning for her birthplace. London in all its sooty glory, the museums, the National Gallery, Hyde Park, the Thames. The stucco terraces, cracked like brittle icing on a cake, the crowds on the underground. English gardens with their blowsy pink roses and tidy lawns. The BBC, her old theatrical friends, even her family. Though Clara was only half English, that Englishness was profound—the Vines had come over with the Conqueror, and they had been based in the West Country for hundreds of years—yet still, England felt forbidden to her. Was it because she had insisted to her family that she loved life in Berlin? Or was it because England contained a piece of her past that she could never revisit?

"A little."

"Nothing stopping you making a short trip."

There was nothing. But there was also everything. The thought of her mission in Munich rose vividly to her mind.

"I think we have company."

They had been talking in English, and Clara noticed that a party of men at the table next to them had dropped their voices and were eavesdropping. Rupert gave a quick, redundant dab of his mouth with his napkin and stood up.

"If I really can't tempt you to sample this delicious food, dearest, perhaps we should take a walk."

They strolled west along the street towards Viktoria-Luise-Platz, where a fountain provided a cooling mist in the sultry heat. It was a popular place for an evening drink, and the pavement was crowded with café customers, but these were no relaxed, late summer evening meetings, full of laughter and beer.

Instead, a subdued mood prevailed. People seemed jittery, exchanging information in whispers.

"You won't forget, will you, Rupert, to ask about that girl on the cruise?"

"Sure. I'll ask, of course. I can already imagine the moment in the press conference when I interrupt Doktor Goebbels's drone about Jewish affairs to ask about a girl falling into the sea. From a KdF ship too."

"Thank you, Rupert. I mean it."

"You didn't tell me about Paris. It's a while since I've been there. Is it lovely as ever? Did you enjoy yourself? Meet anyone nice?"

An image came irresistibly into her mind. A saturnine face growing slightly fleshy about the jaw, the smudges of gray beneath the mocking eyes. The receding hair and the air of impatient physicality about him, like a wild animal confined by convention and society. His unconcealed astonishment when she said she needed to leave; his slow, seductive smile when he cornered her in the alley. The extraordinary presumption of his remark.

If you won't come to bed with me, perhaps you'll come to dinner?

Did people really behave like that? Did the urgency of the times mean traditional conventions could be overlooked? Something about Max Brandt provoked images Clara had never thought about before, forbidden images of hotel beds with rumpled sheets and glasses of champagne on the bedside tables, and clothes cast carelessly on the floor.

Rupert laughed. "You *did* enjoy yourself! Tell me everything. Was it a seductive Frenchman? You want to watch out for those!"

Clara pushed him away playfully. "It wasn't anyone, Rupert. It was work."

"I'm not sure I believe you, but if so, what a tragic waste. Never mind, sweetheart. You'll have to make do with me. There's a party coming up for the foreign press. Perhaps you'd like to accompany me."

It was risky for her to be seen with an English journalist, so she said, "I may still be in Munich. I'm off tomorrow."

"Munich?"

Even though Rupert must have had some idea of her double life, Clara was careful never to share any more information than she needed to. Generally, he understood this and refrained from asking any questions, but he was a journalist all the same, and she knew too well that he had curiosity in his veins where other people had blood.

"I'm up for a part in a film at the Bavarian Film studios. It's called *Good King George*. It's a historical picture about the Hanoverian dynasty taking over the throne of England."

He gave a dry laugh. "Let's hope it's historical, darling. These days the idea of Germans seizing the throne of England might count as current affairs."

10

FOR A GOVERNMENT DEPARTMENT DEDICATED TO THE DOMES-
tic arts, the headquarters of the National Socialist Frauenschaft in Derfflingerstrasse, Tiergarten district, bore few
signs of homeliness. The entrance opened to a parquet hall
painted institutional green and scented with carbolic bleach
and the faint tang of infant vomit. Famous faces of the
regime—all men—hung along a corridor interspersed with
corkboards fluttering with instructions on infant care, hygiene, nursing the sick at home, children's education, cooking, and sewing. Glass-paneled doors led off to a series of
offices and conference rooms, and at the far end was the library, which was more like a vast collection of filing cabinets than a conventional library, containing every letter,
pronouncement, and pamphlet ever issued concerning the
NS Frauenschaft, sparsely leavened with volumes on mater-
nal health and child care and a few government-sanctioned
children's books. Needless to say, no one went in the library
looking for light entertainment.

Next to the library was the domestic science room, where
a couple of aproned women were that morning completing
a demonstration of nutritious national recipes—pig's cheek
broth and pickled herring rolled in bread crumbs—whose

unappetizing smells snaked out into the surrounding corridor and into the conference room, where an instructor from the Reichsmütterdienst, the Mother Service, could be heard holding forth. The subject of that morning's talk was Love and Marriage, and forty hausfraus were obediently ranked in semicircles to listen.

"What are the Ten Commandments for the German Woman?" barked the instructor.

The audience must have assumed the question was rhetorical because the instructor supplied the answers herself.

"Remember you are a German! Remain pure in mind and spirit! Keep your body pure! Do not remain single! Choose a spouse of similar blood! Hope for as many children as possible! Anyone else know one?"

The housewife representatives wore the official Frauenschaft uniform of blue-black jacket with matching pleated skirt and gray blouse buttoned to the neck. Their faces were unblemished by lipstick and their hair braided as precisely as steel cables. Most bore expressions of slavish interest as they listened, but a few had an air of absent anxiety, as though struggling to recall if they had left the cooker on.

When she had first heard the Love and Marriage talk, Rosa Winter had listened incredulously. Now, sitting in the adjacent office and hearing it for the tenth time, she merely tuned out and tried to focus on that morning's task—completing data on the names and addresses of mothers in Berlin who had not yet applied for membership in the network of schools run by the Reichsmütterdienst. Membership was not compulsory, but if a woman didn't join she would get a visit from a Nazi official wondering why, and if she still delayed joining she might find herself guilty of failing in her duty to the Reich, which was in itself illegal. The lessons of the four-month mother-training courses were pretty basic—thrifty shopping, mending, garden-ing, handicraft, avoiding foreign goods, making meals from leftovers—but all instruction was underpinned by the strict ra-tionale underlying the regime. A mother should avoid buying imported food, if possible, to support the national welfare, but if absolutely necessary she should select goods from a country friendly to the Reich. The shortages in the shops had provided the opportunity for another brilliant example of the Führerin's ingenuity. Disturbed by stories of fighting and unpatriotic squabbling between housewives as they queued for their daily groceries, she had decided to create a whole new division called the Market Police, a crack troop of women trained to serve on the shopping front lines, who would shepherd the queues and adjudicate disputes between shoppers and shopkeepers that might otherwise turn nasty. Rosa's job was to collate the names of those whom the Führerin had chosen to volunteer and orga-nize training sessions in cooperation with the Berlin traffic po-lice. You had to hand it to the Führerin. She really did think of everything.

The Love and Marriage session was ending. Rosa flinched as the roomful of women launched into the obligatory hymn to Hitler, bellowed with special passion because everyone knew the words.

> *Yet as once you loyally struggled for us,*
> *Now we are yours with every breath we draw.*
> *You suffered alone for us so long*
> *The strongest heart that ever was on earth!*

The only wedding Rosa had ever attended was her sister, Suzi's, and that union was as far from the Love and Marriage talk as was possible to imagine. Pauly Kramer was a middle-ranking official in the Deutsche Labor Front. A thickset man with a scalp like the pink, bristled skin of a pig, he regarded Rosa with a look that seemed to combine simultaneously lust and disgust. Suzi and Pauly's marriage was not so much a meeting of minds as a careful demarcation of duties, seemingly arranged so that the couple met as little as possible. They had one child, Hans-Otto, a slow boy who at the age of five had still not learned to button his coat or lisp his numbers from one to ten.

Rosa adored Hans-Otto. She loved his wide, dreamy eyes, and the way he sucked his thumb when she hauled him onto her lap to read to him. Her nephew barely spoke and knew far fewer words than most children his age, but emotions moved on his baby face like clouds passing across the sky as he listened to the stories of Hansel and Gretel or Cinderella or the king who turned everything to gold. Hans-Otto loved animals too, and there was nothing he liked better than to visit the zoo and watch the lion cubs pouncing and squealing in their cage or run his hands through the rough hair of the goats in the petting enclosure.

Hans-Otto's dreaminess, however, was not universally admired. Recently there had been letters from the headmaster at school concerning the child's inability to tie his shoelaces and demanding an improvement. More worryingly, in the past few weeks Hans-Otto had suffered a number of convulsions, which left his little face more washed out and vacant than ever.

No wonder Suzi showed little inclination to increase the Reich birth rate with a second child. Hans-Otto's inadequacies seemed to compound her general bitterness about her circumstances, which she never hesitated to express when she saw her sister. "We can't all spend our lives on luxury cruises," she had remarked resentfully when Rosa returned from her trip.

That comment had caused the memory to resurface in Rosa's mind, though in truth it had scarcely been out of her thoughts. She returned to it again and again, as though revisiting the scene of a crime.

The picture was frozen in her head like a still from a film. She was standing in the gloom of the rain-lashed deck, watching the thrilling progress of the storm. A mist of spray rolled across the sea, obscuring the middle distance, but she could just see the water boiling up beneath the prow of the ship every time it veered and listed in the wind, and a mountain of violet clouds banked on the horizon. Suddenly, away to her left, came the gleam of something white, sprawled at the feet of a group of sailors. Looking closer she saw it was a young woman, hauled clumsily onto the deck like a fish. Rosa felt again the shock of seeing that delicate face, its beautifully curved lips bleached of color like a marble Madonna, and the soaked tendrils of hair splayed across it like seaweed. The girl's sodden dress, flattened against her breasts, and the crumpled mess at the back of her skull. The sailors staring at her, agog.

Rosa couldn't get that image out of her mind. Why had the captain instructed her not to mention it? Why should such a tragic thing be hushed up? The fact that she had exchanged a few words with the girl gave her a sense of personal responsibility. It was as though she was actually involved in the death, which was plainly absurd. Surely just being a witness to a crime, if indeed it was a crime, didn't make you a participant? She, Rosa, was not responsible for what she had seen. Yet the disquiet lingered.

Her first thought was to confide in the Führerin—that would be the proper thing to do. After all, hadn't her entire purpose on the cruise been to assess the suitability of the *Wilhelm Gustloff* as a VIP venue? Details like passengers falling overboard and drowning must surely reflect on the ship's safety record. Not mentioning what she had seen was a direct violation of her duty, and yet . . . it was hard to imagine confiding anything to the Führerin. Besides, such a report would only spoil the glow of approval that Rosa was enjoying just then. The Führerin was already talking about sending her on another trip, this time to explore the Prora complex, a holiday camp on the Baltic coast that was being built by the KdF. The place was a hulking, blank-faced high-rise almost three miles long with ten thousand rooms. It looked like Rosa's idea of hell. But grandiose constructions were essential to convey the epic status of the Reich, and someone needed to reconnoiter the complex for the forthcoming conference on women and domesticity. If Rosa confided what had happened on board the *Wilhelm Gustloff* to the Führerin, it would only mar this pleasant glow of approbation. The Führerin would be bound to question why Rosa had left the incident out of her original report and would immediately take it up with the ship's captain, who would be likely to contradict Rosa directly. It would be the word of a secretary against that of a decorated captain of the German navy. Rosa might lose her job. Shuddering, she remembered the stern warning of Captain Bertram: any mention of the incident would mean neither she nor her family would ever again attend a KdF holiday. Her mother would be heartbroken if her daughter's actions meant she was barred from KdF cruises for life.

Yet at the heart of Rosa Winter was an unorthodox spirit. She knew there was something terribly wrong about what she had seen, and there must be somebody she should tell. The dead girl's face seemed to float before her, like a photographic negative developing in its solution, standing out sharp from its blurred surroundings. The bloodless face and the empty blue eyes that just a few hours earlier on the sundeck had been looking around with a panicky air. *Is anything the matter? No. Why should it be?* Other than the few words they had exchanged, Rosa had no idea who the girl was. Somebody's daughter or someone's mother even. Maybe the girl's own family had no idea what had become of her, and they never would, unless someone disobeyed the ship's captain and revealed what really happened.

11

THE ELIZABETH ARDEN RED DOOR SALON ON THE KURFÜRST-endamm was the haunt of Berlin's most fashionable women. Its perfumes and potions escaped the general disapproval of foreign cosmetics because Miss Arden herself, despite being American, was a personal friend of Reich Minister Hermann Goering, and the Nazis' favorite beautician. She was the only person who had ever been brave enough to offer the gargantuan minister some useful diet and exercise tips, and he had indeed gone so far as to buy an exercise horse on her recommendation, even if he never used it. Every Christmas, Goering would buy up dozens of boxed sets of Elizabeth Arden cosmetics to distribute to the wives of his officers, whose photographs hung on the salon walls, alongside those of famous clients like Leni Riefenstahl, Olga Chekhova, Zarah Leander, Marlene Dietrich, and, in their midst, Miss Arden herself, swathed in white mink and shot by Cecil Beaton. Also dotting the walls were pictures of the Arden spa, with its hooded sunloungers and Riviera striped canvas awnings, and a framed advertisement for the famous Eight Hour Cream with the slogan "Neither wind nor sunrays will alter the purity and brilliance of your complexion." It may have been the photographs of the actresses, or the expectation of glamorous transformation, but the whole salon had the air of a movie set, from its jade-gray walls and silver drapes to the gleaming marble floor and crystal chandeliers. There were French chairs, upholstered in rose velvet, and flatteringly lit mirrors surrounded by pink and blue bottles of Venetian Cream, cosmetics, oils, and treatments. Only the white leather treatment chairs added a slightly clinical touch, suggesting that beauty was essentially a science and its effects could be scientifically obtained.

At ten in the morning the salon was almost empty, except for a single elderly woman attempting in vain to stave off the ravages of time with a bottle of Ardena skin tonic and a cloud of scented steam. With the temperature already rising on the street, Clara pushed through the door, relishing the cool air tinged with the scent of pine and eucalyptus, and a faint trace of Blue Grass.

Sabine Friedmann had started out as a makeup assistant at the Ufa studios, where she and Clara had met, but her flair and personal charm had attracted the attention of Elizabeth Arden herself and Sabine had been offered a job at the salon, followed within a few years by a promotion to manager. Now she was a walking advertisement for the products she sold. Tall and striking with suitably Aryan blond hair, she made it her business to adopt the Arden Total Look, which entailed lip, cheek, and fingernail colors coordinated with military precision. That day her face was a porcelain mask and her mouth a cupid's bow of signature salmon pink. Her usual effusive greetings, however, were muted. Instead she gave Clara a swift kiss, then walked over to the door, turning the sign around to read GESCHLOSSEN, and with a quick glance round the salon ushered her to an alcove at the back, where a chair was spread with a spotless white towel. Beside it a tray was laid with a filigree lace napkin and bone china teacup containing hot water and lemon.

"We keep this seat for our special customers. They like a little privacy."

"I'm flattered."

"It's less obtrusive."

Clara cast the other woman a quizzical glance in the mirror. "I thought you had come by some new samples, Sabine. They must be pretty hush-hush!"

"It's not about that exactly." Sabine's china-blue eyes met Clara's soberly in the mirror. "It could be nothing, but I thought I should let you know. Why don't I give you a facial?"

Whatever Sabine wanted to discuss, it wasn't cosmetics. Leaning back obediently, Clara closed her eyes as her friend poured a few pearls of apricot-scented oil into the palm of her hand and began massaging her face with soothing, rhythmic strokes. Bending over Clara, she murmured softly in her ear.

"I tried several times to get hold of you."

"I've been in Paris."

"Perhaps you should have stayed there."

"What on earth do you mean by that?"

"I hope you don't mind me saying this, Clara."

"Please . . . tell me."

"It's very delicate. If anyone knew I had mentioned this . . ."

"Sabine, I know how to keep quiet."

"You see, they all come here, the top wives. Frau Heydrich, Frau Goering, Frau Goebbels, Frau Ley. I hear all the talk. Not deliberately, but I can't help it sometimes. They gossip, you know. What else are they to do when they're having treatments? When you're lying on your back having a massage or relaxing with a facial, your guard is down. You talk. They assume that the person who tends to them is a servant who simply won't hear. Or perhaps they think a servant can't understand." Sabine's fingers fluttered over Clara's brow, smoothing the apricot oil in relaxing circles.

"Anyhow, the other day, I overheard something Frau von Ribbentrop was saying. She knows you a little, I think."

Clara opened her eyes. "She does. I didn't know she was a client of yours."

Sabine made a grimace that suggested she knew of no beauty treatment that could soften the iron mask of Annelies von Ribbentrop.

"She comes often. And she's very happy at the moment. This spring the SS took over a castle called Fuschl near Salzburg, executed the owner, and handed it to her family. It's proving to be the perfect holiday place, apparently."

"I pray I never get invited! What was she saying?"

"She was talking to Frau Heydrich, the Obergruppenführer's wife." Sabine lowered her voice, though they could not possibly have been overheard. Merely the name of the man in charge of the Gestapo and the Sicherheitsdienst, the SS's own spy service, was enough to provoke people to an instinctive whisper. He was called Himmler's Hirn, Himmler's brain, because his severe, meticulous attention to detail was invaluable to his superior. His wife, Lina, a cool, Nordic beauty, was known to be a more ardent Nazi than her husband, if such a thing was possible.

"Both ladies were here to have a treatment before the Nuremberg rally. And they were gossiping about the propaganda minister. There's always so much gossip about him. It's their favorite topic."

"I think the same goes for everyone in Berlin."

"Annelies von Ribbentrop was telling Frau Heydrich that Joseph Goebbels is so blinded by love for this actress—you must have heard—that his judgment is quite askew. Otherwise he would notice that Berlin is infested with English spies."

"English spies?"

The soothing motions of Sabine's hands massaging Clara's face were in inverse proportion to the alarm that this remark engendered.

"Yes. Infested, Frau von Ribbentrop said."

"Strange thing to say."

"Perhaps not. You know better than I do that the von Ribbentrops hate England with a passion. Ever since he was ridiculed when he was ambassador there. His wife is worried that the Führer has been so blinded by those English women he hangs about with, the Mitford sisters and their crowd, that he will let them influence him in this Sudetenland business. He will refrain from action out of an unfounded respect for the English."

"If he refrains from action that's good, isn't it?"

"Maybe, but it's not that . . ."

"What are you getting at, Sabine?"

"That's just it, Clara. It's what surprised me. Frau von Ribbentrop mentioned you."

"*Me?*"

"She said you might have Goebbels fooled, but you don't fool her. It was about time someone checked up on you." Sabine lowered her voice yet further to a frightened whisper. "Frau von Ribbentrop said Heydrich should have one of his men keep an eye on you."

Clara sat up and caught Sabine's agonized expression in the mirror. Her own face, sleek with cream, had a ghostly, impenetrable glow. "Keep an eye on me?"

"That's all she said. To Frau Heydrich. I thought you should know."

"Thank you," said Clara, leaning back again in an attempt to suppress the panic that flared within her.

Sabine didn't bother with platitudes about trying not to worry. Nothing could be more worrying than the attention of Obergruppenführer Reinhard Heydrich. Lean and blond with a savage, watchful gaze, of all the Nazi leaders, Heydrich most conformed to the Aryan stereotype, which was ironic, given that when he was a child his school friends had called him Issy in reference to the rumors of Jewish blood in his veins. But no one dared make jokes about Heydrich now. In his immaculate black SS uniform, with the silver insignia of the SD on his arm and jackboots polished to a high gleam, the man who proclaimed himself "as hard as granite" was considered the most fearsome member of the Nazi elite. A shadowy army of fifty thousand men was under his command, and everyone in Germany lived in fear of them. They were based in an ominous cluster of buildings in Prinz-Albrecht-Strasse, but like a poison gas, Heydrich's men were seemingly everywhere. If the grocery had run short of eggs, or a military parade held up your car, and you made an unwise comment, the man next to you might show his Party badge, demand your papers, and request your appearance at the police station. It was worse when they didn't make themselves known. Heydrich's stool pigeons were always there, keeping an ear out for anyone who might betray a sympathy for Jews, Marxists, Social Democrats, or Freemasons, and, if they did, the details would be noted in a vast archive of files stored in the bowels of Prinz-Albrecht-Strasse for future reference.

As Sabine took up a warm flannel and massaged Clara's face, then set about perfecting her makeup, Clara anxiously calculated the effect that Frau von Ribbentrop's comments might have. Would Lina Heydrich actually bother to relay gossip about a half-English actress who had fallen foul of the foreign minister's wife? And even if she did, what was the chance that Heydrich would pay any attention, given that the Nazi hierarchy was in the midst of an international crisis? When the continent stood on the brink of war, who could be bothered with gossip about actresses? Politicians, maybe, merited scrutiny, and statesmen, even journalists. But who cared about actresses?

Somehow Clara managed to thank Sabine and leave the salon with a semblance of calm, but once outside she walked along the Kurfürstendamm without seeing it. The streets were sticky with melting tar, and the sun's glare bounced off the hot steel of postcard sellers' carts and reflected in the windows of the department stores. A snatch of music issued from a bar, and the cries of a newspaper seller on the corner of Joachimstaler Strasse competed with the sound of drilling on yet another new building. Yet despite the hustle of the street, Clara felt as though she was in a film with the sound off, cocooned in silence and her own panicked thoughts. Sabine's comment echoed in her mind.

Heydrich should have one of his men keep an eye on you.

While the threat of surveillance was always with Clara, in recent months it had become a more low-level fear, a theoretical possibility that led her to undertake routine precautions out of habit rather than immediate concern. She still, religiously, followed the lessons Leo had taught her. She must never carry with her the name of Archie Dyson, her contact at the British embassy, nor should she keep tickets to trams or cinemas. Tickets were tiny, valuable mines of information that pinpointed your location and left an unmistakable trace. The only tickets in Clara's pocket should be those she had deliberately placed there. She must always ensure her moves were accountable and have a valid reason for going anywhere she went. Last, and most important, she must assume she was being watched, day and night.

Despite these precautions, however, since questioning her the previous year the Gestapo seemed to have satisfied themselves that Clara was nothing more than she seemed: a moderately successful actress whose ambitions lay in securing better roles rather than in securing secrets for British intelligence. She had not dropped her guard, yet she had been able to breathe a sigh of relief. Now all that had changed. Fresh threat lurked all around her; more than ever she would need to be at her most alert.

She came to a halt in front of a green, octagonal, turreted news kiosk. The *B.Z. am Mittag* was displaying a photograph of the most famous baby in the Reich, Edda Goering, with her adoring parents. The fact that the child had been given the same name as Mussolini's daughter raised excitable gossip about her paternity, particularly since the Duce had been visiting Berlin at the time of her conception and Goering was widely assumed to be impotent. That was easy to believe, Clara thought, looking at his face like a ripening cheese, the fat wet lips, and slightly protruding eyes as he bent over the child in the arms of her mother, Emmy, who at forty-five might well be cradling the only baby she would ever have. The couple's joy was shared around the world, at least if you believed the six hundred thousand telegrams plus vanloads of artworks, Meissen porcelain sets, and other lavish presents that had poured in. In terms of kings bearing gifts, Edda's arrival made the original Nativity look like a yard sale.

Clara had encountered Frau Goering many times and knew that whenever they next met, Emmy would expect her to be entirely up-to-date about the baby and all her appearances in the press. Like any new mother, only a hundred times worse.

Blindly, she took a paper from the rack.

"Dreissig pfennig, bitte."

She fumbled in her purse for change and dropped the coins. Stooping to pick them up, she was beaten to it by the customer behind her and looked up to find herself staring at a familiar face. It was jovial and slightly fleshy, with beads of sweat on the forehead, crinkled lines around the eyes, and unruly, receding hair.

Cultural Attaché Max Brandt.

At once, the sounds on the street amplified as though an invisible volume had suddenly been turned up. The screech of tram wheels ripped through the cocoon of thought that enveloped Clara, and her every sense went on alert. She was suddenly intensely conscious of her freshly made-up face and the trail of apricot scent that radiated from her.

"Herr Brandt! You're in Berlin? What a surprise."

"Isn't it?" He took off his peaked cap and smiled down at her. "People tend not to like surprises nowadays, but I say this is a remarkably pleasant one."

"And you're in uniform."

"Unfortunately. These things are unbearably hot, you know. But it could be worse. This is just the day uniform; our full diplomatic uniform has a dark blue tailcoat embroidered with oak leaves and a silver sash and dagger."

"A dagger doesn't sound very diplomatic."

"Depends what kind of diplomacy you're engaged in. Diplomats with daggers seem to be in vogue right now." He ran a finger round his collar. "As a matter of fact, all these getups are a new thing. A few years ago we foreign service people wore plain suits. Then someone had the bright idea of dressing us up like eighteenth-century dandies. They're designed by some fellow called Benno von Arent."

"I know von Arent. He's a stage designer. He works at Babelsberg."

"That makes sense. We all look like we're performing in an operetta."

Even in his uniform there was something unruly about Max Brandt, something untamed, as though dark hair might curl mutinously from the neck of his shirt, or the buttons of his uniform burst apart. Unlike that of a lot of Party men, who liked to shave their heads so that only a single, brutal strip remained, his hair was wavy and only just controlled by brilliantine. Instead of the polished charm of a professional diplomat, he exuded a kind of insubordinate humor. Despite herself, Clara's anxiety lifted and she laughed. "So what brings you from Paris?"

"Just some work matters. But it looks like serendipity."

"Are you here long?"

"A few days, probably." Although he looked older in uniform, his eyes were still sleepy and teasing and his manner suggestive. "As I recall, we had an arrangement to meet for dinner. What would you say to making that a firm plan? That is, if Sturmbannführer Steinbrecher doesn't object."

Despite herself, Clara blushed at the memory of her made-up boyfriend. "I'm really sorry. I can't just now."

"Lunch then. It's not yet midday."

"Again, I can't."

"Can't today, or can't with me?"

"It's just not possible."

"That's a shame. I thought you gave me your word."

She hesitated. Though she felt again the intense gravitational pull of attraction, the appearance of Max Brandt redoubled her alarm. Moments earlier she had been warned that Heydrich might be watching her. And here was a Nazi officer on the street in front of her, claiming coincidence. How could it be coincidence that he should surface in Berlin, let alone contrive to turn up right by her side at this precise junction on the Ku'damm at exactly the same time? Coincidence troubled Clara. She had learned to see it for what it was, genuine but rare, and always meriting scrutiny. Where other people saw coincidence, she tended to see patterns. *Just some work matters,* Brandt had said carelessly, but how could the work of a cultural attaché have any importance at a time when the fate of nations hung in the balance? His business was opera and art, but which opera could merit his immediate return to the capital? What painting could require high-level attention in Berlin?

And yet . . . she yearned to accept his invitation.

Unbidden, her mind traveled ahead to the idea of a long lunch with Max Brandt, talking about theater and opera, and a slow walk afterwards, perhaps culminating in a hotel somewhere, silk sheets rumpled and curtains drawn against the world. A tangle of clothes on the floor. Her cheek against that tanned chest, her naked limbs entwined with his. The perfume of French cigarettes and his warm skin. The image was so scandalously real in her mind that she blushed, and in that flash she perceived that similar scenes were playing in Brandt's imagination too. For a fraction of a second, the possibility hung tantalizingly between them. A stolen afternoon of pleasure, cut off from the world and its troubles. Then she remembered how lonely she had felt in Paris and realized that Brandt, with his broken marriage, no doubt felt that way too. He would probably have gone with any girl who might, for a few days, staunch the isolation of a solitary existence, but Clara wasn't just anyone and she was not interested in a few days' pleasure, above all not when it came to sleeping with a Nazi officer whose motives were far from romantic.

"I don't have the time."

"Please."

There was no mistaking the note of appeal in his voice. For a second it was as though the suave mask had slipped to reveal a kind of desperation. A need for contact that went beyond the purely personal. Brandt reached a hand forward to her arm, and his touch seared her, but she kept her tone light.

"I have an audition in Munich tomorrow, you see, so I'm taking the night train down this evening. We'll have to postpone our dinner."

It did the trick. His mask was resumed, the languid smile back in place. "I note you say *postpone* and not *cancel*, Clara Vine. I shall take that to heart. I won't forget."

She rested her hand in his briefly.

"Nor will I."

Brandt remained, watching her thoughtfully, as she headed up the street.

12

I T WAS NEVER A GOOD IDEA TO BE TOO EARLY FOR AN AUDI-
tion. Standing in the gleaming marble hallway of the Munich Artists' House, beneath an ornate ceiling spattered
with gilded stars, Clara counted the minutes until three
o'clock and tried to relax. Despite the fact that *Good King
George* was merely a cover for another, more serious assign-
ment, she felt the nerves that came with any audition, even
now, when she was well established in her career.

When she had first come to Germany, five years ago, and
applied for work with the Ufa film company at Babelsberg,
she had needed to learn her craft all over again. Until that
point she had been a stage actress, but she soon discovered
that acting for the movies was an altogether subtler affair. It
required intense control over the tiniest nuance of gesture
and facial expression. A raised eyebrow could contain an
ocean of expression. A glance was enough to convey a heart
full of love or hate. You needed rigid self-discipline to por-
tray emotion in a camera close-up, and the effort Clara put
into her acting provided useful respite from her secret life.
It might seem perverse that in front of the camera should
be the place she felt most calm, but the spotlight was a refuge from the task she had willingly taken on. It also pro-

vided her with an authentic cover. Clara Vine was exactly what she said she was—an actress who devoted herself diligently to each role. Except that now, in Eva Braun's hometown, her other role suddenly felt more real and far more daunting.

Having consulted the receptionist and been told to wait, she wandered over to a chair at the foot of the stairs and looked around her.

When the Party had risen to power in Munich, the Führer had loved relaxing at the Artists' House on Lenbachplatz. He'd frequently hosted parties there, inviting actresses from whichever show he had seen to reprise their dances or songs in a more intimate setting. Even though international events now precluded such harmless diversions, Hitler, like Goering and Goebbels, still liked to think of himself as a tasteful sophisticate with a sacred regard for art, and the Artists' House, with its marbled halls and gilded ceilings, echoed that idea. To the casual visitor the place was like some exotic, pagan temple. On the outside caryatids supported ornate gables, Neptune and Bacchus adorned the walls, and the gateway was crowned by the statue of a centaur wielding a club. There was a lengthy waiting list for membership, and the centuries-old Munich synagogue next door had, on Hitler's orders, recently been razed to create more parking space for the club's patrons.

Clara took out a silver enamel compact from her bag and applied another coat of her rapidly dwindling Elizabeth Arden Velvet Red. Then she found her copy of *Rebecca* and attempted to lose herself in the landscape of the faraway south coast of Cornwall, where she had spent so many of her childhood holidays, tramping through damp rhododendrons and picking the sand out of snacks beside the icy sea.

"Clara Vine! Thank God. At least there's someone I've heard of here."

A statuesque blonde swept through the door as though pursued by a phantom horde of news reporters toting flashbulb cameras and notebooks. She was dressed as for a first night, complete with a hat featuring a little bird picked out in diamanté, a taut silk dress against which her breasts strained, and perfume that trailed luxuriously after her like a mink wrap. Her face was a flawless expanse of creamy foundation, and her bleached hair shone like a pale flame in the dim light. Perching on the chair beside Clara, she extracted a cigarette from her bag, lit it, took a disdainful drag, and peered loftily about the hall.

Clara tried to contain her astonishment. Ursula Schilling was an A-list star, one of the country's favorites. For years her lovely face had stared seductively out from billboards and film posters, and the gossip columns of innumerable newspapers and glossy magazines. It was a face simply made for the screen. Ursula Schilling could drown a man in the depths of her violet eyes and unleash a tide of contempt with a twitch of her arched brows. She possessed a kind of sulky grandeur that made men want to kiss her or slap her, usually both. Yet here she was auditioning for a potboiler that would barely get screened at the local Munich fleapit, never mind the Ufa-Palast am Zoo.

"Ursula! What a surprise to see you!"

"You can say that again, darling."

Ursula gave Clara a sidelong look and exhaled a stream of smoke sideways out of her mouth. On previous occasions, when they had passed in the corridors of the Ufa studios, or rubbed shoulders at parties, Ursula had barely deigned to speak to Clara, but now, it seemed, things had changed.

"God knows why I came! It's not my kind of film, and to top it all I'm being asked to play the wife's friend. A role with about three lines! Fritz Guttmann told me she was the girl-next-door type, and I had to tell him, 'Fritz, I'm a *movie star*. That's why people come to see me. If people wanted the girl-next-door look, they could just go next door.' "

"But you accepted?"

A faint shrug. "I'm thinking about it."

"So Herr Guttmann must have been thrilled to get you."

"If he was, he was keeping quiet about it." Ursula flicked her hair impatiently and out of sheer habit looked around for the crowd she would usually attract. "What about you? Which part are you up for?"

"Actually . . ."

Clara was saved from an immediate answer by a shout of greeting. A flamboyant man with a sweep of brown hair and a generous mouth was clipping down the stairs towards them. Though his SS uniform was personally tailored by Hugo Boss, he wore it like an evening dress accessorized with an invisible feather boa.

"Ladies! What a relief. At last we can expect some quality in this production!"

Hitler had often opined that if he had not been singled out by fate for the role of Führer and savior of his nation, he would have chosen to be a theatrical set designer, but as it was he would have to settle for patronizing the genius of Benno von Arent instead. The pair of them would linger late into the night, poring over the Führer's own designs for sets and revolving stages and lighting techniques. As well as designing blockbusters like *Viktor und Viktoria, Hitlerjunge Quex,* and Clara's most recent film, *Es leuchten die Sterne,* the Reich stage designer also had the immense job of transforming *Der Meistersinger* every year at the rally into a Nazi extravaganza, complete with massed crowds, flags, and banners.

He glanced curiously at Clara's book. "I always forget you're English."

"Half, Herr Sturmbannführer."

"You play the German half so well, sweetheart. Why don't we ever see you in the Kunstler Klub?"

The Kunstler Klub in Berlin was one of Goebbels's recent business enterprises, a private members' club with dancing, restaurant, and bar. It was full of actresses with plunging necklines and strutting Nazi officials, most notably Goebbels himself, who liked to take actresses there to discuss their work as a prelude to other matters. When he first had the idea of creating his own nightclub, Goebbels had seized on von Arent, as the Führer's favorite, and put him in charge. The choice had paid off handsomely.

Von Arent wagged a finger. "*No* excuses. I insist you come. In fact we're holding a reception for the Propaganda Ministry to honor the American-German artistic friendship. I think that's what they called it. Anyhow, everyone who is anyone will be there. I'll send you two ladies invitations when we're back in Berlin."

"Which can't come soon enough," added Ursula.

"Come, come, sweetheart, it's not that bad. This may not be Babelsberg, but I shall be making you the most magnificent costumes. Get the clothes right and the rest will follow, that's what I always say. They tell me the script is an absolute disaster, but if there is any way of saving us all from total humiliation . . ." He whirled round. "And here's our director now."

If it was true that Fritz Guttmann was preparing to flee to England, he was giving no sign of it, other than a complexion as gray and mottled as the ash from his own cigarettes and a frame as starved as a Giacometti sculpture. His green-shaded director's cap with tufts of hair sticking out reminded Clara of the ostriches at the Berlin zoo. Guttmann was not Jewish—or he would have been barred from working as a director by the

Reich Chamber of Culture—but his films were hardly noted for their ideological fidelity to the Reich and were routinely branded as turkeys in the press conferences of the Reich Chamber of Film. This latest production would, no doubt, suffer the same fate. When he shook hands, Clara noticed that his nails were bitten to the quick.

"Thank you so much for coming, everyone. Fräulein Vine, perhaps if we could talk first. Would you follow me?"

Guttmann led the way into a hall, shut the door firmly behind them, glanced around, and lowered his voice. "I appreciate you coming. It's not always easy to tempt actresses to Geiselgasteig anymore."

The Geiselgasteig studios, which occupied a leafy plot of land a short train ride south of Munich, had an illustrious history. During the silent era they had attracted prestigious foreign directors including Alfred Hitchcock, and people began to refer to the studios as "Los Angeles on the Isar." But all that had changed since the Reich Chamber of Culture took over the film industry and any movies that were daring or experimental, or strayed outside Goebbels's rigid parameters, were destined to be cast-iron flops.

"Have you found pleasant accommodation?"

Clara was staying just a few minutes' walk away in a small pension in Maximiliansplatz. It was a gloomy place with all the atmosphere of a funeral parlor. Her room had a bed of heavy, Bavarian fretted wood and a tiny desk covered with an embroidered cloth, but the furniture was polished, the sheets clean, and the window overlooked a leafy square, decorated with terraces and stone urns and a large bronze statue of Goethe.

"Thank you. Yes."

"You come highly recommended from London Films. I met

them first when they were scouting for locations in Munich. Are you familiar with their work?"

So there was to be no overt mention of Guy Hamilton's elaborate plan. Alexander Korda's film studios may have been engaged in a high-stakes espionage scheme, but Fritz Guttmann was not going to risk discussing it, and however impatient Clara was to broach the real purpose of her presence in Munich, she knew he was right.

"I am."

He tilted his head to one side. "Do you miss England?"

"Sometimes."

"I hope to see it myself someday."

A flicker of understanding passed between them.

"Soon, I hope," she said.

His face relaxed into a smile. "I hope so too. I should tell you, Fräulein Vine, that I have followed your career with some interest. I remember your first film for Ufa, *Schwarze Rosen,* wasn't it? That glance you gave when you said goodbye to Hans Albers—I've never forgotten it. It was only fleeting, but you managed to express so much. That's what I always tell my cast: a good actor should be able to compress a thousand words into a momentary glance. Anyone brought up with silent films understands that, but our modern actors, unfortunately, seem to believe that a bellowing voice or clever script will do the job for them."

Snapping out of this reverie, he continued, "Anyhow, about this part . . ."

Ushering her to the back of the hall, he continued with a rapid rundown of the film and the role of Sophia of Celle, George I's unfaithful wife.

"It's a marvelous story. A tale of unrequited love. You've done a few of those."

"My specialty."

"Indeed. Sophia spent decades in love with a Swedish count, even though she was thrown in prison by her husband on account of it. That's my only concern actually."

"Oh?"

"It's the issue of portraying an unfaithful wife. You know how it is. The last thing we want is the minister ordering a last-minute rewrite of history."

"He didn't seem to mind when I mentioned it to him."

Guttmann paled visibly. "You mentioned my film to Goebbels?"

"The minister asked me what I was doing in Munich. Obviously I had to tell him."

The director could not have looked more terrified if Clara had been wearing a Gestapo leather coat instead of a Jaeger jacket and carrying a search warrant in place of her crocodile clutch bag.

"Have I caused a problem?" she asked, gently.

"No, of course not. You did the right thing. And the script has been approved. We submitted it to the ministry for all the usual moral, political, and racial-purity checks. We've ensured there's no Jewish music in the score, and of course we had to observe the ban on images of political unrest, which will rule out our crowd scenes." Guttmann was ticking off the regulations on his fingers, as though terrified to have overlooked a rule. "But I didn't expect to attract the attention of Doktor Goebbels. Generally it's only the lowly officials who handle pre-censorship, unless something specifically catches the minister's eye."

"He seemed to think it was fine, as long as she dies at the end."

"Ha! It would probably help if she could turn out to be Jewish too. No matter. With my films . . ." Guttmann shrugged. "Let's just say, the Herr Doktor does not view my output with especial enthusiasm. But I thought I'd be safe with a historical theme."

"I'm sure it'll be a success."

"And I'm grateful for your confidence. But Goebbels is always a worry to me, to be honest. Film matters so much to him, and he notices everything. The only time I had the experience of meeting him, he told me that the entire Third Reich could be seen as a cinematic event . . ."

A bang behind them caused him to halt mid-flow. Clara whirled to see that another person had entered the room and was standing hesitantly beside the closed door. The newcomer was a woman in her mid-twenties. A stiff raffia hat was set jauntily to one side of her head, and soft curls reached her shoulders. She wore a green dress with a sweetheart neckline and carried a calfskin bag with a shiny enameled swastika for a clasp. Though she had never seen the woman before, Clara recognized her instantly.

Eva Braun.

She paused a moment before stepping forward decisively and extending a hand. "Fräulein Vine, I'm so pleased you agreed to see me. Sorry for butting in."

Clara allowed no inkling of surprise to cross her face. This was the person she had come to see. The object of her mission. The woman who, if Guy Hamilton was to be believed, might be the only person on earth privy to the Führer's true plans, motivations, and intentions. The girl who might hold the fate of the world in her white lace gloves.

Guttmann sprang forward as though propelled by an electric charge. "May I introduce Fräulein Braun?"

"I hope you didn't mind me writing to you last year." Eva

Braun's voice was softer than those of the senior Nazi wives, gentle and hesitant compared to the confident rasp of Frau von Ribbentrop, or the husky tones of Magda Goebbels. "I expect you get a lot of bother from fans . . ."

"Not at all. I was flattered to receive your letter."

Despite the girlish façade, a single glance at Eva Braun's face told Clara there was a core of steel behind the shy exterior. Everything about the girl's appearance was in direct contradiction of Hitler's cherished notions of feminine beauty. Her carefully styled hair was peroxided, despite his hatred of artificial colors, and her liberal use of foundation and lipstick made mockery of the Führer's famous ban on cosmetics. Clara was reminded suddenly of a character she had once played in Noël Coward's *Hay Fever*—Sorel Bliss—charming, brittle, and outwardly girlish, with a glimmer of steel beneath the surface.

"*Black Roses* is one of my favorite films. Wolf and I have seen it several times at the Obersalzberg."

The reference to Hitler's mountaintop fortress was deliberate. As was the use of her nickname for him—Wolf. It ensured that Clara knew beyond a shadow of a doubt that the topic of the Führer need not be taboo with Eva Braun. Indeed, it might be practically compulsory.

"We watch a movie every night at the Berghof. Sometimes two. Wolf loves movies. He says a great film has the power of a great speech."

At last Eva Braun seemed to notice Guttmann, quivering beside her.

"I do hope I'm not interrupting, Herr Guttmann."

"Not at all, gnädiges Fräulein," he stammered.

Clara's mind was whirling. She might have been exchanging pleasantries with the Führer's girlfriend, but there was no chance of forming any deeper acquaintance so long as Guttmann was quaking like a leaf alongside them. She needed to get Eva on her own.

"I wonder . . . Fräulein Braun. I'm longing for some tea. Would you like to join me?"

"That would be lovely. Herr Guttmann, are you coming too?"

Guttmann recoiled as though he had been asked to take tea with a rattlesnake. A shudder of horror ran through him, which he failed to disguise.

"So busy right now, gnädiges Fräulein, so many people to see . . ." he muttered. "In fact"—he turned to Clara—"why don't we dispense with the audition? I know you'd be perfect for the part. Filming begins next week. May I assume you are interested in the role?"

"I'm interested, yes."

"Very good then. We'll need to see you for costume fittings. Could you talk to my production manager about timing and so on?"

"Aren't you forgetting something?"

He started as Clara pointed at the script in his hand.

"Oh." Almost as an afterthought, he thrust out the wedge of paper. "Of course."

Before she could take the script, the tremor in his hand caused him to drop it, and the papers fluttered to the ground like the petals of a blown rose. Guttmann scrabbled to pick them up, losing his spectacles in the process. Eva Braun regarded him impassively, as if she were watching a waiter who had clumsily dropped his tray.

"I've an idea," she said brightly. "Why don't we go to my favorite café? If you've finished business for the day, of course, Fräulein Vine?"

"Please call me Clara."

"And you must call me Eva."

Clara picked up her bag and took the pages, wishing fervently that there was a script for the encounter to come.

THE TAXI DELIVERED THEM to the Hofgarten, Munich's beautiful central square, and they crossed the sun-dappled cloister to the Café Heck. The fine weather had brought out the crowds. Around the graveled paths men in typical Bavarian costume—short leather trousers and kneesocks, and small green hats planted on their shaven heads—strolled, accompanied by stout matrons in ankle-length dirndls and frothy lace at their bosoms. In the center of the square a brass band had set up, thumping out a medley of uplifting Bavarian songs.

As Clara and Eva Braun entered the café, heads swiveled, and the man opposite them blatantly lowered his newspaper to stare. Eva planted herself at a window table, clearly aware that all eyes were on her. Indeed she seemed to bask in the attention. Pursing her crimson lips, she blew a long stream of smoke towards the ceiling.

"Don't mind them gawping. You're lucky we're not with *him*," she quipped. "Then everyone stands and applauds."

They ordered glasses of orange pekoe tea, and Eva Braun's eyes roved greedily over a glass cabinet of cream cakes, Black Forest gâteaux, and puff pastries before she settled on *Kaiserschmarrn*, a mess of cream and cherry sauce enveloped in a pancake.

"I don't know why I eat this. It's terribly sweet, but it's Wolf's favorite. I suppose I order it out of habit. Bad habit!" She gave a little laugh and gestured at her waist.

"I'll need to keep my figure if I'm ever going to act, myself."

Clara almost choked on her cinnamon cake. "I didn't realize . . . Are you planning on an acting career?"

Eva fixed her with wide blue eyes.

"It's all I've ever wanted to do."

"And are you, I mean, do you have any plans?"

"I act already." She gave a modest smile. "Just putting on plays with friends. That probably sounds a bit amateurish to you, but at the moment it's all he'll allow me to do."

"You've got to start somewhere," said Clara encouragingly.

"Exactly! And I love making my own little films and getting my school friends to act in them. Wolf—the Führer—gave me a cine camera for my nineteenth birthday, and I never go anywhere without it. So you see, I'm as much at home behind the camera as in front of it. In fact, that's how I first met Wolf."

"How's that?" Clara prompted.

"I worked for his photographer, Heinrich Hoffmann, not far from here, in Schellingstrasse. I took the orders and supervised the framing and so on. I had a lot of time on my hands, so I used to spend it looking through Hoffmann's drawers at all the photographs of Wolf. Not very flattering, most of them! Then one day I was serving behind the counter, bored out of my mind, and I looked up to see him standing right in front of me. I was terribly flustered; I mean he wasn't the Führer then, but he was still incredibly famous, and he asked me to the opera. It was so romantic. And after that he started taking me regularly and sending flowers. He sent so many flowers to Hoffmann's the place smelled like a cemetery."

She wrinkled her nose.

"A shame it had to be the opera he loves. I'm always nagging him to go to the ballet, but he absolutely refuses. He hates it. He thinks men in tights are disgusting. He says it's a cultural

disgrace to see people hopping about and even ballroom dancing is a stupid waste of time and effeminate. He told me Vien-
nese dancing is the reason for the decline of the Austrian
empire."

Eva rolled her eyes in time-honored exasperation at the
waywardness of men, and Clara gave a sympathetic smile. Even
though she was acting on instructions from Guy Hamilton,
there was something endearing about Eva Braun's girlish demeanor and the way the chatter tumbled out of her as though
she was starved of social life. She had that in common with
other Nazi women Clara had met. They lived closeted exis-
tences, imprisoned by the dictates of their men and the suspicions of an increasingly paranoid regime.

"He's very stubborn when it comes to taking any interest in
my hobbies." Eva sighed. "Like perfume, for example. There's
a shop in Theaterinerstrasse that sells the most delicious French
perfumes; Worth's Je Reviens, that's my favorite—awful that
my favorite perfume should be French, isn't it? Anyhow, I used
to love going in and trying different scents, but he hates going
into women's shops. He'd just wait for me in the car. That was
ages ago, of course—he never comes shopping with me now
and you can't find French perfumes these days. Anyway"—she
smiled brightly—"it doesn't matter because I've started making my own."

"Your own perfume?"

Eva nodded. "Sounds awfully eccentric, doesn't it? But it's
true. I like creating my own concoctions. Taking two completely
different scents and mingling them and making something
unique. Don't you think that's how incredible things happen?
You pick the most unlikely ingredients and put them together
and somehow they make an impact?"

She laughed lightly, wiping cream off her mouth, and Clara

thought there was nothing more unlikely than the match between the gauche young woman in front of her and the monstrous German dictator. Yet where exactly did they go from here? How was she going to keep Eva talking? She needn't have worried. Eva's conversation flowed on, an unstoppable stream of chat and confidences.

"There was an industrialist at the Berghof the other day who was trying to explain it to me," added Eva. "He said they had discovered molecules that could also be used in perfume to make them last—aldehydes, I think they're called. When you put them in perfumes the particles collide and re-form into something quite different. You'd never guess that perfume would contain strange, synthetic molecules, would you?"

"It's amazing what chemistry can do."

"It is, but to tell the truth, I don't really like the idea of all these chemicals. I like things to be natural. Did you know Chanel No. 5 contains a thousand jasmine blooms and twelve roses in every bottle? It's true. I know someone who works at a perfume company, and they told me all about it. I decided I wanted to create a cologne for Wolf, so I needed some samples. I thought the first thing I had to do would be to find out all about the ingredients of the famous perfumes—myrrh, jasmine, iris, violet, narcissus, and so on—and how they fit together. I love the idea of observing someone's personality and creating a scent for them."

Clara lit two cigarettes and passed one to Eva. "You know, I've always secretly wanted a scent made especially for me."

Eva pursed her lips and tilted her head to one side. "Why don't I make one for you?"

"Make me a perfume? Really?"

"We'd need to meet again."

"In that case I'd love it."

Eva's eyes lingered on Clara's Velvet Red lipstick. "I'm glad you don't scrub all your makeup off like some of those wives. Most of them have faces as wrinkled as custard skin. More lines than the Berlin U-Bahn. I couldn't bear to let myself go like that." Her smile drooped. "Don't know why I bother though, now. No one's allowed to take any pictures of me. Wolf has banned Hoffmann from ever putting a photograph of me on the market. He says no one must know what I look like. The Russians might want to kidnap me."

"Are you scared?"

"Not a bit. How's any Russian going to get to me, surrounded by all this?" She waved her arm, and Clara followed her gaze, noting the way the other customers hastily averted their eyes, pretending to devote their entire attention to the coffee cups in front of them.

"Does it ever bother you? The attention?"

"A little. But I have my ways of keeping my own confidences." Eva's eyes sparkled secretively. "And besides, if I'm ever going to be an actress, I'll have to get used to people looking at me, won't I?"

Clara sipped her tea and took stock. Within a day of arriving in Munich she was taking tea with the Führer's girlfriend, who was entrusting her with a flood of intimate confidences. Already she had accomplished the first part of Guy Hamilton's request, and yet . . . what were these confidences worth? The Führer loathed ballet? Eva liked makeup and French perfume? Clara needed to focus on the Führer's intentions for war. But how?

"It must be hard for you, having to listen to him talking about politics, night after night."

"It is." Eva made a sulky pout at the thought of it. "He used to be so much more romantic—I'd slip little letters into his coat pocket, and he'd reply, but now it's all politics, politics, politics. The Czechs, the French, the English. Blah, blah. You know what he told me the other evening . . ."

She stopped abruptly as a figure entered the restaurant and seated himself at one of the tables near theirs. He was a hulk of a man in a leather coat, with a shaven scalp and a face as creased as a balled fist. He opened a copy of *Das Schwarze Korps*—the SS newspaper—and buried his nose in it, his little eyes flickering constantly in Eva's direction.

"Actually, shall we go? I don't like this place anymore." Eva jumped up, giving Clara only enough time to fold a bill under a saucer before following her out of the door and along the street, where the girl marched swiftly, her face set like stone.

"That man is paid to watch me." Eva's eyes glittered with tears. "I can't bear the way that ugly brute follows me everywhere, watching me in cafés and questioning my friends. I can't do anything without him on my tail. You have no idea what it's like to be under permanent surveillance!"

"It must be awful for you."

The tension of a life under surveillance was something Clara knew all too well.

"He doesn't even bother to hide the fact that he's following me!"

"Why don't we give him the slip?"

"Impossible," said Eva.

"It's worth a try. Remember what you said about the Führer hating women's shops? Well, that goes for most men. So let's go where most men fear to tread."

Taking her arm, Clara steered Hitler's mistress at an unhurried pace across Odeonsplatz towards the Feldherrnhalle, the city's military memorial, where the lavish monument to the putsch was flanked day and night by an SS guard of honor. The site had been co-opted by the Nazis as a memorial to the holiest day in their calendar, when marchers staged an unsuccessful clash with police resulting in sixteen Nazi deaths, and on solemn days the site resembled a Greek temple, complete with flaming urns. Even on ordinary days two enormous laurel wreaths were guarded round the clock by steel-helmeted sentries, requiring everyone who passed to make a right-armed salute.

The women's swift exit from the café had indeed taken the SS man by surprise. As they continued down to the central square of Marienplatz, Clara checked in car side mirrors to see him lumbering breathlessly in pursuit, his newspaper rolled up beneath one arm and his face scrunched with the effort of keeping them in sight. Threading through the crowds, Clara quickened her pace until she spotted what she was looking for, a department store.

SHOPPING WAS THE ULTIMATE antisurveillance technique for the female agent. Drifting through dress rails fingering the fashions, lingering at cosmetics displays, and sampling the odd perfume was a woman's natural habit but entirely anomalous to a male shadow. In a beauty hall, with its infinite mirrors, glistening reflections, and largely female clientele, an SS man in a leather coat would stand out a mile. Nowhere were men and women more different than in the way they shopped. Men were impatient and impulsive; browsing was anathema to them. Most could not spend two minutes in a shop without being bothered by a sales assistant, whereas women could loiter for hours, sniffing, sampling, and examining themselves in mirrors that afforded an excellent view of what lay behind.

"If he follows us"—Clara nodded towards the elevators—

"we'll just go up and down a few times until we lose him." Eva's face broke into a wide smile.

After several minutes of lingering at a cosmetics counter, trying, then rejecting, Palmolive soap, Pond's face cream, and a few Tosca powder compacts, there was no sign of the SS man, so Clara deemed it safe for them to make a last circuit of the shop before passing out of the large brass doors. Eva followed her, laughing.

"You saved me! I'll have to remember that trick," she giggled, hailing a taxi. "I suppose it comes in useful in your line of work."

Clara felt herself go cold. "My line of work?"

"Filmmaking. I guess you're always having to dodge fans." Eva pressed her hand into Clara's. "I've had the most wonderful afternoon. Thank you."

"Of course."

"I imagine you want to take a look around. Perhaps see the Bürgerbräukeller. Everyone wants to see the Bürgerbräukeller. It's where the putsch started in 1923. They should do one of those historic tours. The Führer's favorite beer hall, the Führer's office, the Führer's apartment block. In fact I could lead it myself. I could reveal a thing or two. That red sofa in his office, for example. That could tell a tale."

She gave a sardonic, tinkling laugh and pressed a card into Clara's hand. *Wasserburgstrasse 12, telephone 480844.*

"This is one place no one gets to see, though. If I'm going to create that perfume for you, you'll need to come to my home because it's where I keep all my ingredients. Might you be available tomorrow, Clara? Around noon?"

"I'm sure I am."

"Tomorrow then!"

13

HE FIRST THING ANYONE SAW WHEN THEY ENTERED THE
National Socialist Women's League headquarters was the
image of Gertrud Scholtz-Klink in gray worsted jacket and
tie, glaring from the wall like a leathery gorgon guarding
her lair. With her basilisk smile and face as scoured as a pan,
it was perfectly possible to believe that her gaze alone, like
that of her mythic doppelgänger, could turn onlookers to
stone. Certainly it appeared to have had that effect on the
blond Englishman in worn tweeds whom Rosa found standing in the lobby, staring up at it.

"Can I help you?"

He recoiled a little. "I was just thinking that looks awfully like an Old Etonian tie. I wonder if the Führerin is
entitled to wear one."

"I'm sorry?"

The man recovered himself with a brilliant smile. "Forgive me, I'm Rupert Allingham. How do you do?"

Rosa gave him her hand, baffled.

"I'm a journalist," he elaborated. "I'm here to interview
Frau Scholtz-Klink. Is she around?"

The Führerin answered this inquiry by bustling in at
speed and shooting out her hand like a Walther 6.35. After

greeting Rupert Allingham, she acknowledged Rosa's presence with the single barked command "Coffee!" and led the journalist into her office, talking as she went.

When Rosa rejoined them with a tray of coffee, the Führerin was still in full flow. From what Rosa knew of the Führerin's interview technique, there was little need for actual questions. At that moment she was boring Rupert Allingham with a rundown of her duties training German women in accordance with National Socialist ideology. She was elaborating on the Frauenschaft's culture, education, and training sections, and even the propaganda department, which produced leaflets for German women living abroad detailing the inferiority of foreign races.

Rosa set down the tray and settled on a chair in the corner. It was strangely thrilling to be in the presence of a real journalist. She hoped that, if she sat quietly, she could remain unnoticed and study his technique.

"I'm not sure if you were present at my talk to the annual rally, Herr Allingham," said the Führerin, sliding a sheaf of paper across the desk.

"Sadly not."

"Then you will have missed our exciting news on tax reductions. I've had some information printed out for you. No income tax at all for families with more than six children. So long as the children are racially pure and valuable."

"I see."

"You'll be wanting some statistics, I daresay."

She motioned to Rosa, who scurried over to a filing cabinet and withdrew the relevant papers.

"The figures are extremely encouraging. Marriages are up, there are only half as many divorces, and births have risen to"—she checked a sheet—"one point four million this year,

THE SCENT OF SECRETS   145

nineteen point two per thousand head of population." She rattled off the figures like a Lewis machine gun. "That's up from five hundred thousand births in 1932. So National Socialist ministers have tripled the number of babies being born."

Some National Socialist ministers more than others, if gossip was to be believed, Rosa thought.

"More cribs than coffins is my motto, and it seems the birth rate is exceeding all our expectations," the Führerin added with satisfaction.

Babies, Rosa realized, were just another crop in the new Reich, like potatoes or wheat, to be counted, monitored, improved, and lied about. Good one year, free of blight for the most part, a creditable reflection on the citizens of the Reich.

The journalist looked up at the poster of a woman and child beneath a sun in the shape of a swastika, emblazoned with the slogan "Warriors on the Battlefield of Childbirth" and then hastily down again at his notebook. Peering across, Rosa noticed with fascination that the page was filled with nothing but doodles.

"Could you remind me, please, what exactly the Reichsmütterdienst . . . ?"

A flicker of irritation crossed the Führerin's brow. "The Reichsmütterdienst is open to all racially pure women in the Reich. It prepares women for their role as housewives and mothers because the family is the germ cell of the nation."

Rupert Allingham stifled a yawn.

"We already have hundreds of mother schools all over Germany, and so far more than a million and a half women have attended fifty-six thousand courses. There are four million women in all the Frauenwork organizations. Not to mention the Reichsbund der Kinderreichen, the league for large families."

Now, Rosa observed, Rupert was doodling a cruel little sketch of the Führerin down one side of his notebook. Languidly, he inquired, "Are there any other recent developments you would like my readers to know about? I had heard there was to be a new initiative for German women?"

The Führerin frowned. "We have brought about new reforms to the divorce law, which allow divorce on the grounds of one partner's refusal to have children," she suggested. "We call voluntary childlessness a diseased mentality."

"Diseased?"

"A disease of the mind, rather than the body. But just as harmful to the health of the nation."

The journalist fixed Frau Scholtz-Klink with a look of undisguised distaste. "I always wonder, Frau Reich Führerin, how it is that a woman of your impressive stature can support the fact that one of the first ordinances of the Nazi Party was to exclude women from ever holding a position of leadership. As I understand it, you believe that women should no longer have the vote?"

Sarcasm was always wasted on the Führerin. It glanced off her like a bullet from a tank. She regarded him pityingly. "The Führer sees the emancipation of women as being on the same level of depravity as parliamentary democracy or"—she cast around—"jazz music."

"Jazz music?" echoed the journalist incredulously.

"I think that's what he said. Herr Hitler believes, and we agree with him, that there is no interest whatsoever in woman maintaining the vote."

"I wonder . . . are there large numbers of female politicians in your own country, Herr Allingham?"

He shrugged.

"Precisely. And I think you will find the reason is that

women themselves prefer to confine themselves to their own sphere. They don't want to be spending their time wrangling in parliamentary chambers with men who are equipped with law degrees. They would far rather occupy themselves in their own area of expertise. Which is producing children and ensuring that they are properly equipped to carry on the nation's culture to future generations."

The Englishman looked over to Rosa and raised his eyebrows, but Rosa ducked her head and gazed fixedly at her knees.

"As it happens," persisted the Führerin, "Herr Hitler *is* working on something very exciting. It's been under wraps, but it's felt that now is a useful time to reveal it. It's a mother's cross. To be given to *kinderreich* women with four or more children. Only live ones, of course, and not defectives. There will be three gradations. Bronze for four children, silver for six, and gold for eight or more. In fact, I think there may be plans for a diamond cross, featuring genuine diamonds, for mothers of twelve children. Anyone wearing a mother's honor cross must be saluted in the street and receive a range of deferences."

"Deferences?"

"She must be given the best seat on the bus, for example, go to the front of the queue in a shop, have the best seats at the theater, and so on."

"Now that's an interesting idea."

"I'm glad you think so. It's our women's equivalent of the Iron Cross. It is to be awarded every year on August twelfth, the birthday of the Führer's mother. Despite our excellent figures, we need to give women every encouragement we can to reproduce."

At this, a thought seemed to seize the Führerin and her eyes dwelled on Rupert Allingham speculatively.

"As our regime promises every unmarried girl a husband, we

are establishing a chain of marriage bureaus for eugenically eligible candidates. Everyone who signs up must declare themselves willing to establish a large family."

"Marriage bureaus, you say?" asked Rupert, making a note.

"That's right. It probably seems terrifically modern to you, Herr Allingham, but in Germany we have never been afraid to embrace change in the cause of national advantage. Are you married yourself?"

"Afraid not."

She gave a girlish smile. "Then we shall have to see if we can help you!"

That idea was enough to propel Rupert Allingham swiftly to his feet. He thanked the Führerin for her time and muttered something about a press conference beginning shortly at the Foreign Ministry.

The Führerin seemed disappointed. "If you must then. Please escort Herr Allingham, Rosa," she commanded with a brusque nod.

It was as they were making their way out that it happened. They were walking past Rosa's desk when the reporter halted suddenly and stared at the framed holiday snap she had placed there. In the picture Rosa was looking uncharacteristically relaxed, leaning against a railing with the cruise liner looming like an iceberg behind her.

"Isn't that the *Wilhelm Gustloff*?"

"Yes, Herr Allingham. I was sent on a cruise. For work."

"Nice work."

"It was important reconnaissance business," she added firmly. "We're staging the National Congress of Women's Fitness in Hamburg next month. The important guests will be housed on the ship."

"I see. Did you have a good time?"

Rosa hesitated, looked over to the Führerin's door, then back at the journalist. She felt a mixture of anguish and resolve. Rupert Allingham's piercing blue eyes were trained on her intently, and for the first time since the Englishman entered the Frauenschaft offices, he seemed genuinely interested in an answer. She realized the time had come to make an important decision.

"No, I did not, mein Herr. I did not have a good time at all."

"I'm sorry to hear that. Why?"

Rosa was on the brink of continuing, but at that moment there was the bang of a door along the corridor and the simultaneous ring of the telephone, which she picked up with alacrity. Rupert hesitated a second before taking a card out of his wallet and sliding it onto her desk. Rosa covered it with her hand. Then she transferred it silently to the very deepest region of her bag.

E VA BRAUN'S HOME WAS A SQUARE, RED-ROOFED VILLA IN Bogenhausen, an elegant suburb across the river Isar, with white shutters on the windows and a small green door at the side containing diamond-shaped panes of glass. The building was surrounded by a high stone wall and wooden gates, and its privacy was further enhanced by a cluster of apple trees in the front garden, bursting with bright fruit. When Clara rang the bell, frenzied yapping could be heard from deep within.

"Negus! Stasi! Be quiet!"

Eva Braun flung open the door with a little flourish, gesturing at the whirling dervish of fur that was circulating around her feet.

"I'm sorry. They're so protective. They think they're my bodyguards!" The black fur ball separated into two Scottish terriers. "Go on, you two, back into the garden."

Eva was dressed in a high-necked blouse with puffy sleeves and a full, flowery skirt, her blond hair rolled neatly away from her face. She raised a quick hand to touch Clara's teal-colored pencil dress, which Steffi Schaeffer had originally made for her as a costume.

"I love that dress! I have one just like it!"

She led Clara proudly into a small front room, stocked with heavy, Bavarian-style furniture: a bookcase, a desk, and two chintz armchairs. Turkish rugs lay in front of the fireplace. A stack of *Filmwoche* magazines was piled high beside a chair. Eva gestured to a telephone on the sideboard.

"It connects directly with the Berghof. Isn't that something? I only have to pick it up. The trouble is, the SS installed it, which means it connects directly to an awful lot of other people too."

Clara glanced politely at a couple of insipid watercolors hanging above the fireplace, one of a church and another a Bavarian street scene.

"Nice, aren't they? Wolf painted them. Not that he ever has time to paint anymore. He bought this house two years ago, but I had to furnish the entire place myself. He says if I want something for the house all I have to do is ask Martin Bormann." Eva gave a little theatrical moue. "Do you know Bormann?"

"Only by reputation."

"Well, let me give you some advice. Never discuss home decorating with Martin Bormann! In a bad mood he's terrible. And he's never in a good mood. He's a horrible man. Really. He hates his brother Albert so much they will only communicate through their adjutants, even when they're in the same room."

She studied Clara. "In fact, Bormann warned me against you."

Clara gave a start and tried to disguise it. "Me?"

"Not you in particular. Bormann said I should avoid making friends with people in case they were really interested not in me but in my relationship with the Führer."

"He might be right."

Eva giggled. "He might, but what do I care? I. Hate. Bormann. And I don't mind if he knows it."

She went over to an Anglepoise lamp, drew it towards her like a megaphone, and shouted into the bell, "I *hate* Martin Bormann!"

Clara tried to conceal her shudder. The special telephone line was almost certainly not the only device that the SS had installed in the house, but the thought didn't seem to trouble Eva Braun.

"Let's hope that gives someone an earache!" she said. "But I'm forgetting myself. Let me make tea."

As Eva bustled into a minute kitchen, barely large enough to contain a porcelain gas stove with two rings, Clara took a swift look around. She went quickly over to the desk and glanced through the stack of notepaper and the litter of receipts from dressmakers and shoe shops. There was a program from a performance of *The Merry Widow* at the Theater am Gärtnerplatz and a half-completed letter to someone called Herta proposing a trip to Italy. There was nothing that might resemble a diary. Somehow Clara would need to find a better opportunity to search—preferably when Eva was not in the next room.

She joined her hostess in the kitchen, which led onto a wide terrace covered with an ocher striped awning and edged with window boxes of scarlet geraniums.

"Would you like a chocolate?" Eva proffered a lavish silver box, tied with frilly ribbons, in which nestled a luxurious pound of chocolates. Despite herself, Clara's mouth watered. Luxuries like that were increasingly rare in the Reich.

"Wolf gets sent them all the time, but he won't eat them. He's convinced he's going to be poisoned. I say, 'Well, I'm not going to waste them! If it's my fate to be poisoned, then I accept it willingly!'"

Clara decided to pass on the chocolates.

"How about a smoke then?"

Eva poured hot water into the pot, placed it on a silver tray with two cups, and carried it out to the wide terrace off the kitchen, setting it on a rickety wooden table in the dappled shade of the trees. In the corner of the lawn the dogs had momentarily ceased their yapping to tussle over a dead mouse, worrying its tiny corpse in their jaws, then each grabbing one end and tugging it apart.

"Is this all right for you, Clara?" There was still an edge of shyness in Eva Braun's voice, as though she could not quite believe that an actress she had seen on the screen was in her own garden. Her moods reminded Clara of a spring day, one minute cheerful, the next downcast. It was as though the barometer of her temperament was in constant flux.

"It's lovely here. Your garden's charming."

"I know." She flipped open a packet of cigarettes and offered one to Clara. "I'm very lucky really. We have everything here, even an air-raid shelter in the cellar. It has an armored door leading to an underground passage with radio, telephone, cupboards with provisions, medical supplies. You wouldn't believe it! I have everything. Everything except Wolf."

"He must be incredibly busy."

"He is!" Eva looked up, as though Clara had made an impressive insight. "And just now he's in a terrible state."

"About the . . . international situation?"

"I think it's that. He's not sleeping and he's hardly eating. Just boiled vegetables now, mainly corn and beans and asparagus, and that can't help, can it? I tell him, Wolf, you have to eat something that gives you energy, but there's no changing him. He says that eating meat is a perversion of our human nature and when we reach a higher level of civilization, we'll overcome it. The other day at lunch he told everyone at the table that he's thinking of banning meat altogether." She laughed gaily at the memory. "You should have seen Himmler's face when he said that! It was so funny! Himmler was a chicken farmer, you know. I almost hope Wolf goes ahead, just to annoy him."

Clara was beginning to understand why this uncomplicated girl appealed to Hitler. Eva Braun was never going to uncover the ill-educated, provincial side of him, never going to mock the Führer's liking for operetta, or his taste in art. Unlike those of the other wives, her pretensions to sophistication ended at clothes and perfume. She was more likely to worry about his digestion than his dictatorship.

Unfortunately this spelled failure for Clara's own task. She thought of Guy Hamilton. *Pillow talk, I think they call it.* But pillow talk between the Führer of all Germany and his girl-friend was never going to involve the Treaty of Versailles. It was impossible to imagine Eva listening intelligently as Hitler confided his plans for European domination, and if he started talking about Lebensraum, she would probably interrupt with a reminder to take his tablets.

Clara took a draw on her cigarette. "It's impressive that the Führer has time to consider his diet given all the other affairs that must be preoccupying him."

Eva's face drooped. "I'm so sick of politics! I absolutely pine for the Berghof, but we hardly go there now. There's a cook there called Lily, who he hired from the Osteria because he loved her cheese noodles. He had her brought out from the kitchen at the end of a meal and said, 'Lily, I'm taking you to Obersalzberg.' It's not just the food though. Everything's so wonderful there. I swim in the Königsee, there's a bowling alley in the cellar, and you can ski, though he hates that. In fact, he's thinking of having skiing banned because of the number of accidents involved."

"He wants to ban skiing?"

"Oh yes," Eva giggled. "Along with meat eating and smoking and lipstick and all the other things on his list. It's a pretty long list."

Clara thought of Steffi Schaeffer and all the other people in Germany right then who were feeling the force of Hitler's loathing. Was this insouciant young woman even remotely aware of Hitler's other list—his persecution of the Jews, Communists, gypsies, and homosexuals, and anyone else who disagreed with his politics of hate?

Eva's face clouded. "The trouble is, even when I'm there, we're never alone because of all the guests. Some of them I don't mind. Herr Speer is nice. He talks to me when no one else does. Whenever all these actresses come to the Berghof flirting and comporting themselves like silly women—not like you, of course, Clara—Herr Speer sits with me. The wives, though, they all hate me. They call me the blond cow. Honestly, Clara, they do! Magda Goebbels even asked me to tie her shoelaces when she was pregnant. As if I was going to kneel in front of her! I rang for the maid and left the room. And Frau von Ribbentrop is worse. You'd think she was queen the way she insists that all the potatoes are the same size and she sends back a fried egg if the yolk isn't right in the middle. Can you imagine!"

Clara could. The anecdote fitted precisely with her experience of von Ribbentrop's wife.

"The others aren't so bad. I like Margarete Speer, and Wolf adores their children. And Gerda Bormann's all right, even if she is constantly pregnant." Eva giggled again. "Though I can't think how she manages it because he's always off. He runs after anything in a skirt."

"What do they talk about at lunch? Is it all politics?"

Eva burst out laughing. "As if they'd try! Himmler has some

idea about establishing a Women's Academy for Wisdom and Culture, where high-class women would learn the social graces and how to talk about art and politics, but I could tell him right off, that's never going to work. Wolf hates women talking about politics."

Clara's heart sank. The chances of Eva Braun having any political insights were dwindling by the second.

"What does he like then?"

"What he really likes is a woman who will sit with him and listen to him talk. He wants companionship, I suppose. But we never seem to get the chance to be alone anymore. It's even worse in Berlin! I have my own apartment at the Chancellery—it used to be Hindenburg's bedroom—but I have to have all my meals there and I never get to see *anyone*. The only place I ever visit is my dressmaker's, and I have to go in and out of the Chancellery through a private entrance, in case anyone sees me."

Whatever she may have thought about a woman who was prepared to love a man like Hitler, Clara felt an intense pang of sympathy for this girl, shunned, isolated, treated as an embarrassing secret, to be kept out of the public eye at all costs.

"I get so lonely here. He thinks I have everything I could want—my own Mercedes and a chauffeur and Negus and Stasi—but I don't have *him*. I don't understand why he never wants to come here."

Hearing their names, the terriers abandoned their fight and raced across the grass, clamoring for attention with incessant barks and jumping up at Clara's legs with their sharp little claws. Even for a man who loved dogs, it was hard to imagine Hitler tolerating these two without the help of the bullwhip he carried at all times.

A chill wind fluttered the leaves of the apple trees, stippling their skin with goose pimples, and Eva jumped up.

"Come," she said. "Let's go inside."

Following her upstairs, Clara caught a glimpse of a blue-tiled bathroom and a frilly bedroom, hung with the obligatory photograph of the Führer and an oil painting of Eva alongside it. On the dressing table a silver-backed vanity set engraved with the initials *EB*, stylized like a butterfly, lay alongside a jumble of bottles and creams. A pile of ribboned underwear lay on the bed. Clara gave a quick glance at the bedside table, but there was nothing there except a bottle of Vanodorm sleeping tablets.

"Excuse the mess." Eva ushered her in, folded her arms, and tipped her chin resolutely. "Now, Clara. You'll have to be honest. I need to know the truth about you."

For a split second, Clara was speechless. The house was no doubt bristling with listening devices, even here in the bedroom. Perhaps especially here.

"Whatever do you mean?" she asked carefully.

"If I'm to make a perfume for you! I need to know more about *you*. What you're like. All your secrets."

"Of course! I forgot."

"Well, I didn't. I have all my equipment."

Eva gestured across to a mahogany dresser crowded with tiny glass bottles. Even with their stoppers in, the bottles sent a pungent, intermingled aroma into the air—floral, citrus, woody and smoky, jasmine, tuberose, violet, and pine. Each flask had a label inked in a neat hand, and Clara was surprised to see that Eva's writing was so small and precise. Could there be a meticulous streak behind her girlish frivolity? A sense of discipline and control?

Eva reached for a larger bottle and took out the cork.

"I've prepared a few things based on what I think you're like"—she glanced shyly upwards—"sophisticated, of course, but with a soft heart. At first I came up with this." She waved the vial under Clara's nose. The fragrance was light and floral on top but undercut with a deep, sweet ghost of vanilla and violets.

"But then I thought, no. Perhaps too sugary." She picked up a second bottle. "What about something more like this?"

The second scent had the freshness of clean linen and windows opening to green orchards, with a trail of vetiver in the background.

"That seems more like you, but it's not perfect. I think I need to know more about you. Like one of those quizzes they have in *Stern*. Are you a city or a country girl?"

"City, definitely."

"Do you prefer a film, or a night at the opera? No, don't answer that. I'm sure you're the same as me there. Do you like loud colors, or subtlety?"

"Subtlety, I suppose."

"Do you wear your heart on your sleeve?"

"I try not to."

"Roses or gardenia?"

"Roses."

"Then what about this one?"

She picked up a crystal decanter with a gold top, and Clara saw that it was engraved again with her initials—*EB*, made into the shape of a butterfly.

"That's pretty."

"Do you like it? It's my personal monogram. I designed it myself, with a little help from Speer. I've always thought of myself as a bit of a butterfly! Now see what you think of this."

The third perfume had voluptuous notes of rose and jasmine, but with a darker heart that seemed to evade definition, a haunting blend of musk and woodsmoke and leather. It hung in the air like strange and evanescent music.

"Oh, I like that. It's mysterious."

"Do you really think so?"

"Yes. It's perfect." Clara dabbed a little behind her ears. "What's in it?"

"Ah!" Eva beamed. "I can't tell you. You should never disclose everything. Always keep a little secret. That's the perfume maker's art. In fact that's what I'm going to call this. The Scent of Secrets. I'll mix a proper bottle for you."

She took out an empty bottle, carefully inscribed a fresh label with the words *Scent of Secrets* in her tiny, meticulous handwriting, and stuck it on. But her pleasure did not last long. The mercurial weather of her moods swiftly swung back to melancholy and her expression grew clouded and brooding.

"Is anything wrong?" Clara asked impulsively.

"Just about everything!" She flung herself down into an armchair, pouted, and gave a shrug.

"Would it help to discuss it?"

Eva glanced up at Clara. A thin sheen of tears glittered in her eyes, but she summoned a smile.

"It's so hard to talk, you see. I'm not supposed to confide in people. I definitely can't speak to the wives of the senior men. But you're not anyone's wife or girlfriend, are you? I mean, not anyone *important*."

For a moment Clara wondered how Eva knew this, until she remembered the stack of film magazines in the sitting room. The celebrity movie magazines of which Eva was such a devoted reader never featured photographs of Clara out with Nazi officials, or even her leading men. She was no Zarah Leander or Kristina Söderbaum, to be found in the daily gossip columns.

Unlike Ursula Schilling, there had never been a story about Clara's dalliance with a costar, or any shots of her staggering out of a National Socialist fund-raiser the worse for wear.

"There must be someone, though. Come on, Clara. I can keep a secret."

Secrets. It would help, Clara decided, to have a secret of her own to share. Even if the secret was not strictly accurate.

"There's a Sturmbannführer I know. Hans Steinbrecher. But I haven't seen him in a while. His work takes him away."

"Poor you." Eva pursed her lips. "I know how that feels. So I can talk to you without worrying that you're going to tell all the senior men, right? Promise?"

"I can absolutely promise you that."

"I really don't want Himmler to know anything about me."

"Why should he?"

"Oh, Himmler likes to know everything about everyone. He's definitely keeping tabs on me. When my sister Ilse had an affair with an Italian officer, Himmler photographed all her letters. Then he produced them for blackmail."

"I would never tell Himmler your secrets."

"Thank you, Clara. I didn't think you would."

She relaxed visibly, drew another cigarette from a silver box, and perched it in her mouth to light. Taking a deep coil of smoke into her lungs, she exhaled and examined her fingernails. Then she turned her hand over and showed Clara the palm.

"When I was young, I went to a fortune-teller. She told me that one day I would become world famous. I used to believe it, but I don't suppose that will ever happen now," she said tonelessly.

She flicked a stray blond curl from her face and pouted.

"I know I'm lucky. There are millions of women who would envy me, and I shouldn't complain, but I just can't *bear* this pretense. I see all those wives laughing, thinking their Führer isn't serious about me, but he is. When I tell him he just smiles and says I'm the most important woman in Germany. The most important woman in Germany? That's a joke. He says when he has achieved all that we need for the Reich, he'll marry me and we'll live in a house he has planned in Linz, where he was born, and he'll write books and I can do whatever I want, but until that time I have to remain a secret. That's what you're looking at, Clara." She spat out the words. "A great big *secret*."

"Surely not." Clara perched on the bed and crossed her legs.

"Yes! And it's all Goebbels's fault." Her face darkened. "Goebbels says the Führer should have no private life. No one's even allowed to know if the Führer has stomach troubles in case it affects his image. *Consider the effect on the German people!*" She mimicked Goebbels's bark with cruel accuracy. "He censors all radio reports, and any journalist who dared to mention my existence would end up in a camp. *The Führer of Germany should have no private life.* That's what Goebbels says. But I'm tired of being Miss No Private Life. If anything happens to Wolf or me, I want them to know that he loved me and was planning to marry me. I'm tired of being a secret. Secrecy is exhausting. You probably don't have many secrets, do you, Clara?"

"Some."

"Not like mine. Anyway, when these international affairs are over, I've arranged to go to Hollywood."

"As an actress?"

"That's right. I want to make a film about our story. How we met. I've already chosen the theme tune. It's *'Blutrote Rosen,'* you know, by Max Mensing's orchestra. 'Blood-red roses speak of happiness to you.'"

As she spoke of her dreams, her eyes lit up with happy anticipation.

"And would you be in this film yourself?" Clara asked.

"Of course. I'd play me. Eva Braun. Little Miss Nobody who fell in love with the Führer of all Germany. It's a marvelous story, isn't it? I'm sure people would be interested. I've told Wolf to hurry up and decide who should play him. I'm thinking of Clark Gable."

The extent of her self-delusion astonished Clara. Of course Eva Braun would never be an actress. Hitler was the actor in their relationship.

"My parents don't like Wolf—they complain he's old enough to be my father and ask when he's going to do the decent thing, and even my own friends I can't trust now." She took a disconsolate drag of her cigarette. "But you don't want to hear all my problems."

Once again, like quicksilver, her face brightened. "I've had a wonderful idea! Frau Goering's giving a party to celebrate the birth of her baby. It's at the Bayerischerhof hotel in the tiki bar. I suppose I'll have to show up, but I can't think of anything worse. I've been dreading it, to tell the truth, but now you can come as my guest. I'd much rather talk to you than those old crows! Will you go?"

Clara shuddered. She had been to enough Nazi receptions to know that they demanded an unusual level of alertness. They weren't her idea of parties, unless *party* implied mingling with people you detested, people who probably wanted you dead. All the same, if she was to find anything to tell the man from London Films, apart from Eva Braun's tastes in perfumery, she could not give up now.

———

A LATE AFTERNOON SUN was slanting down as Clara made her way back through the streets of Munich. She passed a pretzel seller, his wares threaded on a long stick, who smiled at her in a way that his Berlin equivalent would never permit himself, and nodded as a wurst merchant came up beside him, holding boiled sausages in a hot metal container round his neck.

"It's Führerwetter," remarked the pretzel seller, cocking his head at the sky.

"That's because he's in town," said the other, shielding his eyes against the sun.

It was not just the sun that had come out for the Führer. As Clara headed towards Prinzregentenplatz, she saw that a bevy of SS honor guards in black steel helmets and uniforms was positioned outside Hitler's luxurious second-floor apartment. Barriers had been erected all around the square in happy anticipation of the Hitler circus, with its drums and banners and flags, plus its star performer.

She walked resolutely past, heading towards the center of town, but as she approached, she found herself swept up in a larger crowd. Dozens of people thronged joyfully, pouring along the street with a hum of excited anticipation, before slowing to a halt beside the gigantic, neoclassical House of German Art. They stood there, a sea of happy faces pinned behind sleek jacketed troops, as the air rang with shouts and the distant sound of marching boots. Black uniforms moved like an oil slick through the crowd. A man was selling periscopes with mirrors that allowed people at the back to see what was happening, and a detachment of BDM girls with triangular swastika flags were arranged at the front, giggling hysterically.

Suddenly the murmuring intensified to a roar and the people in front of Clara surged forward, arms rising, as a six-wheeled black Mercedes, as sleek and magisterial as a cruise liner, flanked by SS motorcycles, approached, the sun glancing off its chrome hubs. The band was playing the British national anthem, and through the car's window Clara glimpsed a bowler hat and wing collar, the sparkle of a watch chain, and a pair of beady eyes peering out above a toothbrush mustache. A face as ashen as a pine coffin.

"It's Chamberlain!" cried the man next to her. "The British prime minister!"

Bewildered, she turned. "Mr. Chamberlain is *here?*"

"He came by airplane this morning. He's going to meet the Führer at the Berghof!"

Two women edged forward and threw something into the road. A frisson of alarm ran through the crowd until they realized that it was only a scattering of long-stemmed chrysanthemums, their white petals wheeling upwards in a confetti of joy. They sailed into the air before whirling back to the ground again and were crushed by the fat, oblivious tires of the Mercedes, leaving a bruise of flowers in its wake.

15

ROSA WINTER HAD A NEW TYPEWRITER. EVERYONE DID, in fact. All official typewriters throughout the Reich were being replaced with ones that had keys that could spell SS with a Gothic script. Rosa rather liked the look of hers, squared precisely, gleaming and shiny on her orderly desk, alongside the stacked carbons and the official NS Frauenschaft notepaper with its eagle letterhead signifying the offices of the Führerin, and a row of pencils ranked in order of size. Every morning the Führerin glanced at the pencils on Rosa's desk as she passed, as though inspecting a storm trooper honor guard, and that morning she had murmured an approving "Ja," which would have gladdened the heart of any other secretary.

Tidiness was, Rosa knew, the main reason the Führerin liked her. To Gertrud Scholtz-Klink, tidiness was not just a virtue but a political act. In fact, Rosa realized, her habit of putting everything in its correct place was a microcosm of the entire Reich. Nazi Germany was like her own orderly drawers, but on a massive scale. There was a file for every part of society—Mothers, Bund Deutscher Mädel, Hitler Youth. Everything neat and everyone in their place. An identity card for every citizen. A labor service for all ages. A

Party file for every part of society. Germany was like one vast filing system, the kind the Gestapo was said to be assembling, with all citizens noted, annotated, sorted, and accounted for. Every activity categorized and evaluated with a department allocated to it, or an association or a club. *Alles in Ordnung.*

Perhaps that was why Rosa liked keeping her Observations. Journalists looked at the messy parts of life, after all. The bits that didn't fit with the official picture. People who stepped out of line, or slipped through the cracks. People who couldn't be tidied away. She kept her blue leather notebook tucked in the filing cabinet; she couldn't risk leaving it at home. Her mother rifled through her belongings routinely like a domestic branch of the Gestapo, searching for evidence of something she suspected but could not quite pin down, so Rosa brought the notebook to work every day and kept it in her drawer, between the files on childbirth targets in the Brandenburg area and a list of the Frauenschaft leaders in the local districts. It was safer that way.

Rosa didn't mind living with her parents, even if her school friends had long since set up house with office clerks and bank managers and produced families of their own. Anselm and Katrin Winter lived in Bamberger Strasse in Wilmersdorf, a tree-lined street of beautiful, turn-of-the-century houses with elaborate decorative plasterwork and wrought-iron balconies, in an area called the Bayerisches Viertel. Their building had stucco of bone ivory with a pea-green balcony and inside a marbled foyer with a twisty walnut banister and high ceilings, swirled with plaster at the cornices like cake icing. The idea of cake was intensified by the smell of cinnamon and nuts that emanated from the Winters' stove, a marvel of blue and white porcelain tiles, mingling with the aroma of hot cotton from her mother's ironing and the musky smell of Brummer, Rosa's dog.

Brummer was a cross between a schnauzer and a clumsy, anonymous stray, who had contributed melting brown eyes and one folded ear. By some subliminal canine instinct, Brummer knew to the minute when his mistress would be home, and he would stand ready at the door to greet her, whereupon Rosa would bury her face in his neck and inhale his aroma of warm fur, which was to her the loveliest perfume in the world.

Rosa's father worked at the Prussian Academy of Sciences, an imposing building of pale, porticoed stone on Unter den Linden, yet although he was a scientist by profession he was also a great lover of literature. He had schooled Rosa in his beloved Schiller, as well as writers now considered degenerate, like Heine and Mann, and when the Nazis burned these writers' works on the Opernplatz in 1933, Rosa's father had wrapped their books in waxed paper and hidden them in the garden, under the pretense of burying a dead pet rabbit. It was he who had first read Rosa the fairy stories that she now passed on to her nephew, Hans-Otto. Fairy tales teach us what science and philosophy can't, he would insist. They teach us the mystery and the truth of life.

It was possible too, Rosa guessed, that Anselm Winter regarded her continued presence as mitigation against the abrasive personality of his wife, who came from a line of country farmers and considered spinsterhood an anomaly of nature. The Winters were themselves an anomaly in the Bayerisches Viertel, where most of the residents were Jewish, but Rosa's father had been a friend of Albert Einstein's, who'd lived just streets away before he left the country, and he made no distinction between his Jewish neighbors and those who were, in the terminology of the new Reich, genuinely German. Although Herr Doktor Winter endured most of his wife's criticisms with good cheer, his refusal to join the Nazi Party was one shortcom-

ing she knew better than to berate him for—out loud, at any
rate—and she had to content herself with talking wistfully of
the pleasures of various friends whose husbands had been more
politically astute. When Rosa had landed the job at the Frauenschaft, Katrin had been overjoyed.

The great love of Katrin Winter's life was the cinema. She
would spend hours poring over quizzes in the celebrity magazines. *Stern* was her favorite, and she liked to read out items
such as "Could You Be a Star?," which centered on whether
readers were "as photogenic as Brigitte Horney," "as expressive
as Olga Chekhova," or "as disciplined a worker as Marika
Rökk." Rosa's father endured this, but he could not be persuaded to accompany her to the cinema itself, so every week
Rosa would be roped into an outing to watch whatever her
mother chose—usually romantic comedies. The type of story
line Katrin preferred featured young women in reduced circumstances, singers and flower girls, who found themselves un-
expectedly wooed by attractive and wealthy men. Last week's
outing, *Es leuchten die Sterne*, in which a young secretary traveled to Berlin to seek work and was mistaken for a famous
dancer, ending up as the lead in a star-studded musical, conformed precisely to this ideal.

In truth, though Rosa found many of the plots risible and
would have preferred to be at home with a good novel, it was
relaxing to sit there in the flickering dark, watching the actresses with their glamorous costumes and silken skin. They
made such a contrast to the members of the Reichsmütterdienst she saw at the office every day, whose idea of fashion was
flannel coats buttoned to the chin, black fedoras, and clumpy
boots, and for whom a flower on the lapel represented trans-
gressive glamour. Sometimes Rosa wondered what it must be

like to wear a satin dress and feel it move like liquid with your body, rather than riding up and prickling against your skin as her woolen vests and underclothes were wont to do, the garter belt digging into her waist like a medieval instrument of torture.

It was on one of those visits, just the previous day, that it had happened. Katrin Winter had already bought tickets to *Festival of Beauty,* the second half of Leni Riefenstahl's film of the 1936 Olympic Games, which was showing at the Paris Kino on the corner of Uhlandstrasse. The film had been premiered on the Führer's birthday and had tremendous reviews, but Katrin was suffering from a heavy cold, so Rosa called on her sister, Suzi, who was busy with Hans-Otto, and in the end decided to go alone. It had been a tiring day, so she was glad to sink into the warmth of the stalls in a trancelike state, watching the synchronized swimmers sleek as seals in their shiny costumes and the gymnasts like statues from some ancient Greek temple, their skin like luminous carved marble. The audience was overwhelmingly female, so a lone male was noticeable, especially one with a smart gray suit, a sharp face, and a thin pencil mustache, not unlike an American film star himself. She saw him first when they were settling down for the feature, sitting on his own a few rows back and diagonally across from her, brushing a hank of oiled hair out of his eyes. She was aware that throughout the movie he kept shooting her glances. He was there again as the crowd streamed out of the cinema into the street, and when she joined the queue for the tram he came up next to her, tipped his hat, and said, "Lovely film."

He thrust a hand towards her. August Gerlach was his name, and he hoped she wouldn't think him presumptuous if he said she reminded him of Zarah Leander in *Heimat.* He hoped that this didn't sound forward. Did she go to the movies often? What were her favorites? He cupped a cigarette to light it and offered her one too.

Rosa was so startled by these unexpected attentions she hardly knew how to respond. She half wondered if the man was making fun of her, or chatting to her on a bet, but when she glanced around she could see no cohort of sniggering friends behind him, so she carried on the conversation, swapping details of favorite movie stars and recent films, praying for her tram to arrive. When it came, it turned out that Herr Gerlach was traveling in the same direction, so he sat himself comfortably beside her, spreading out on the seat and obliging her to shrink to avoid physical contact. She reasoned that maybe he was lonely. People who weren't used to being on their own did, apparently, find it difficult and would seek out anyone, even strangers, for the sake of human company. Rosa had never remotely felt that way, but she supposed she could sympathize, even if on closer acquaintance Herr Gerlach, with his hard-edged face and loud laugh, looked more at home in a beer cellar than a Hollywood love story.

16

"YOU'VE SEEN THIS, I SUPPOSE."

Ursula was holding a magazine at arm's length, as though it was a piece of litter she had picked off the pavement. It was the current edition of the Nazi women's newspaper, the *NS Frauen Warte*.

"I never miss it."

"Don't joke, Clara. Take a look."

She pointed a disdainful crimson fingertip at a two-page spread of actresses who had appeared in recent films. On one side were vamps and chorus girls, platinum blondes who made up in cosmetics what they lacked in clothing, cavorting in deliberately sleazy poses. On the other side were ranged young women in peasant costumes and braids with faces as blank and clean as starched cotton. Beneath this group a caption read, "You think: boring, we think: healthy and beautiful!"

Clara leaned across and read the accompanying editorial. "Contemporary films do not pay enough attention to idealizing the family, and there are too many childless women featured. The demimonde type, hostile to marriage and family, is the living embodiment of the sterility of the previous epoch of decay."

It was the kind of thing Joseph Goebbels dictated in his sleep.

She shrugged. "We've all heard it before."

"Take a closer look."

Clara did. And on closer inspection she realized the problem. One of the sterile vamps, staring at the camera with smoldering eyes and clad in nothing more than a top hat, black stockings, and a pout, was Ursula herself.

"I can't believe it."

"Nor can I, but that's me done for. It was freezing the day we did that shoot. A studio lot in January. I almost died from pneumonia. If I'd known this was going to happen, I would never have bothered."

Clara took the magazine from her. Ursula Schilling was a rising star of the Reich, a goddess whose picture graced the foyer at Babelsberg and whose voluptuous figure was a staple at every Nazi reception and society party. Her curves, Schwarzkopf-dyed blond hair, and wholesome Aryan looks had made her a natural for the syrupy confections turned out like candy floss by the Ufa studios with the intention of taking the population's mind off butter shortages and war. Ursula had a wardrobe full of mink coats and her photograph in a thousand soldiers' wallets. She had been the ultimate pinup of the Ufa studios, and now she was the poster girl for the scheming vamp.

Ursula gave Clara a look of scrutiny, as if assessing whether she could trust her, exhaled a twisting stream of smoke, and said, "I guessed this was coming. It started around a month ago. I had an unwanted visit. They turned up first thing in the morning, two of them, with faces like a wet Wednesday. I thought they were asking for my autograph, so I slammed the door on them, but it didn't work because they just stood there knocking until I opened up again."

"Police?"

"That was my first thought too. But they described themselves as civil servants. They worked for the government, apparently."

"What did they want?"

Ursula crossed her perfect legs and flicked a languid tower of ash into a nearby hatbox. "They wanted to know if I had ever received a sexual advance from the propaganda minister. What kind of question is that for a girl at six o'clock in the morning?"

"My God. What did you say?"

"What do you think I said? I said of course I have! What girl hasn't?"

"You actually said that?" Whether Ursula was immensely brave, or entirely reckless, Clara couldn't decide, but she couldn't help being impressed.

Ursula sighed and raked her fingers through her ice-blond locks. "I'd only had a couple of hours sleep. I was barely conscious."

"What happened?"

"By the time they'd barged into my apartment and stamped their muddy boots all over my cream carpet, I'd come to my senses. I mean, I'm used to giving interviews, but not the sort that end with a warrant for your arrest. I told them I had nothing more to say."

"Did they accept that?"

"They said if I refused to talk it would constitute a refusal to help the government with its inquiries and I might find my own activities investigated."

"Your activities?"

Ursula fitted another cigarette into her mother-of-pearl holder and raised a pair of exquisitely plucked eyebrows. "Precisely. I have no activities. Not off screen anyway, and now it looks like I'll have precious few on screen either. I knew I should have kept quiet. Remember poor Renate Müller?"

How could Clara forget? Renate Müller was a rising star who'd had the misfortune to come to the attention of the Führer himself. An evening alone at the Reich Chancellery with Herr Hitler had proved so eventful that Renate dined out for months on the eye-popping details, until Goebbels placed her under Gestapo surveillance. Eventually the girl was found dead, having fallen from a window in a clinic where she was being treated for anxiety.

"I don't want to go the way of Renate Müller. Or Helga Schmidt for that matter."

Ursula stared mournfully at the magazine again. "It's a message from Goebbels. He might as well have sent me a postcard."

"I'm sure you're worrying unduly," soothed Clara, who wasn't sure at all. "Goebbels has plenty of other things on his mind at the moment."

"The one thing you can be certain about concerning Goebbels is that women are *always* on his mind."

Ursula was laughing, but there was fear in her eyes.

"It's probably safer being a soldier than an actress these days. Who ever guessed we were signing on for such a dangerous job? If I'd known I'd have gone into something more secure. Stunt flying, perhaps. Or doing the high-wire act."

"What actually happened with Goebbels?"

"Oh, that." Ursula flexed her fingers in front of her like a cat's paw and studied the nails. "The day after our first . . . encounter . . . at the after-party for one of my films, he called me to his office and said he had great plans for me. I was perfect material for the Reich—material, that's what he called me—except that I needed to be 'refashioned.'" A frown snagged her ivory forehead. "It turned out it was my image he wanted to refashion. I was to represent the woman of the new Reich. I was not to resemble a little American vamp anymore. Instead I should say I dreamed of owning a farm in the country and riding horses."

"Horses?"

"Horrible, isn't it? Don't you just *loathe* horses?"

Actually, Clara loved them. She'd had a horse back in Surrey, a dappled bay called Inkerman, a creature of infinite patience and intelligence, and the smell of him, warm leather and horsehair, came back to her in a rush. All the same, it was hard to think of Ursula cantering through the Tiergarten with a flush on her cheeks.

"You could probably get to like them."

"Never. Just think what riding does to the thighs. Besides, darling, horses were only the half of it. Goebbels wanted *Stern* to take pictures of me in the kitchen, whipping up a stew. My dear, can you imagine me with a recipe? I couldn't boil an egg. If I could find an egg to boil, that is."

She shook her head as though Goebbels had asked her to split the atom rather than perform a perfunctory domestic task.

"Besides, I had other plans."

She gave Clara a look, as if assessing whether to trust her, then leaned forward.

"I'd had an approach from Hollywood. A man called Frits Strengholt. The head of MGM, you must have heard of him."

Clara recalled a dough-faced bureaucrat who had been snapped at Hitler's right hand during a number of screenings.

"He's extremely close to Goebbels. He sacked all the Jewish staff in the MGM offices, and he even agreed to divorce his wife because she was Jewish and Goebbels complained. Anyhow, Strengholt said I would be a knockout in the States. I was a second Garbo and had a face to die for. It felt like it was my turn. Everyone's been going to Hollywood and back for the past decade—name me a single star who hasn't been there—Emil Jannings, Lilian Harvey, Olga Chekhova, there's no end of them, so why not me? Only when I applied, the bastards at the Chamber of Culture refused to recommend me for an exit visa."

"On what grounds?"

"Too many actresses are jumping ship. It's bad enough that Marlene Dietrich, the most famous German actress in the world, won't come back. So now they've slapped a ban on other actresses crossing the Atlantic. I'm cursing myself. I would have left last year if it wasn't for . . ."

"Wasn't for what?"

Something in Ursula's face had wilted. Her eyes were huge and woeful, and a dab of wetness smudged her mascara.

"Oh, never mind. I'm pinning my hopes on this evening at the Kunstler Klub that von Arent's invited us to. It's for the benefit of the Americans, to showcase the Ufa stars, and all the big cheeses will be there. I'm going to have another try with my MGM man. See if I can persuade him to sort things out for me."

Turning to the costume girl who had entered the room, she fixed her with a beaming smile and said, "Darling, could you fetch me another coffee? As black as sin and as hot as hell."

Then she tossed her head, dried her eyes, and turned her attention back to Clara. "Enough of my troubles. I hear you're off to a good start with the Führer's girlfriend."

"Shh." Clara looked around her. "Your voice carries, you know."

Ursula laughed. A rich, husky, knowing laugh.

"You imagine they don't know already? They know everything, Clara, and anything they don't already know, they're going to find out. They know everything you think, even before you've thought it. There's no point having secrets here. Secrets in Germany are like butter; they don't keep. You've heard the saying: the only person with a private life in the Reich is the person who's asleep, but that's not enough for them. Goebbels wants to control your dreams."

Ursula shrugged. "What I want to know is how you do it. I've seen the way they hang around you, all the men at the studios, and yet you've managed to keep out of Goebbels's clutches. How've you pulled it off? Are you in love or something?"

The question brought Clara up short. "Why do you ask?"

"You have that look about you just now. As though you're thinking about a man."

"I am. I'm thinking about my godson, Erich. He's fifteen."

Ursula sighed, a long, world-weary sigh. "Fifteen or fifty, men are always a worry."

BACK IN THE PENSION in Maximiliansplatz, Clara sat for some time at the little desk in front of the window, watching a moon of pale bone climbing the sky. It was true that she had been thinking about Erich. She had not seen as much of him recently as she would have liked, and she was dismayed that his first experience of foreign travel had been marred by that incident on the *Wilhelm Gustloff.* Maybe Rupert had made progress in finding out exactly what had happened.

She had meant to write a postcard to Erich, but instead she sat, distracted, making shapes on the letter pad as a tapestry of thoughts wove through her mind. She picked up *Rebecca* and tried to read, but the descriptions of the Cornish landscape only reminded her of Joachim von Ribbentrop saying that Cornwall was his favorite part of England, with the unspoken implication that if ever the Nazis were obliged to invade, Cornwall would be his domain. It was terrible to think of her beloved Cornwall, her childhood holiday home, in his hands.

The thought stirred memories, and on impulse she went over to her suitcase and picked out a locket, all she possessed of her mother's apart from a fox fur coat. The locket was a pretty thing, Victorian probably, with a design of entwined flowers and leaves and a filigree silver clasp. Inside was a photograph of her mother and herself at the age of six—her mother's watchful, luminous eyes and high cheekbones repeated with uncanny precision in the child beside her. Clara dimly remembered that she had been trying to copy her mother's air of reserved self-control, a look that she had eventually perfected. It shocked her to realize that she must be the same age now as her mother was in the picture, and she wondered what her mother would have made of her current situation if she were alive. Would Helene urge Clara to return to the safety of London, as Leo Quinn had? Or would she acknowledge that her daughter had made a new life in a foreign land, just as she herself had done?

For a long time after she died, the image of her mother on her deathbed had been the one that haunted Clara's nightmares—Helene's wasted, bony hand on the eiderdown, her searching brown eyes with violet smudges beneath them, and her long hair, wired with gray and tied in an incongruously girlish plait. But eventually earlier memories returned, many of them bound up with her mother's attempt to re-create her beloved German youth. Though Helene Vine hated it when people noticed her German accent and was always quick to defer to their father, at home she taught her three children to sing *"Stille Nacht"* at Christmastime while she played the piano, and encouraged them to leave their shoes out for presents on St. Nicholas Day, telling them about Black Peter, who beat bad boys and girls with his stick. She baked *Stutenkerl,* little men made of sweet spiced dough, and they ate goose and red cabbage for Christmas lunch. Probably she expected Clara to follow in Angela's footsteps. To be married in England by now, with children perhaps, her acting career long behind her and a dull, domestic life ahead. Would that be so bad?

After Helene Vine died, her two daughters might have grown closer, but instead grief seemed to drive a wedge between them. Angela's politics had veered to the right and she had adopted her father's pro-Nazi sympathies, while Clara came to Berlin. Despite their differences, though, Angela remained an inveterate correspondent, writing punctiliously once a month with news of a world that Clara had long since left behind. How Angela's husband, Gerald, had been put up for White's club by their father and the three of them had been invited to Nancy Astor's place, Cliveden. Frequently she enclosed clippings of herself from *The Tatler,* grouse shooting with the Duke of Sutherland or attending a charity ball with Noël Coward, but while her face may have worn the myopic, glassy expression that had made her such a successful model before her marriage, the mind behind it was as sharp as a whip. Angela prided herself on her ability to tell what her younger sister was thinking—indeed it was probably having Angela as a sister that had honed Clara's ability as an actress.

Angela maintained a relentless campaign to persuade Clara to return to England. "I've never understood why you felt you had to leave us and spend all this time abroad. I know you have your career and everything, but you must miss England, surely? What is it about Germany?"

Clara had been sorely tempted to tell her: of her discovery that their grandmother was Jewish, and that they themselves were a quarter Jewish, a fact that had been kept from them all their lives, as though it was something to be ashamed of. But she could never be truthful with Angela; the intimacy they had once shared was over. Gradually Angela became convinced that Clara's affection for Berlin must be connected to her love life.

"It's a man, isn't it? Anyone special?" Angela had pressed in her knowing, elder sister voice. Then, more softly, "Whoever it is, you want to get a move on, Pidge. Men don't wait around forever."

Pidge was a childhood nickname. A reference to the time when an eight-year-old Clara had found a pigeon with a broken wing, a mess of fright and clotted feathers, and insisted on nursing the bird in a cardboard box until, inevitably, it expired. The memory had stung Clara into denial.

"It isn't a man. There's no one special."

It felt like a lie, but perhaps it was true.

IT WAS HARD TO unwind. Even when she undressed and lay between the cool sheets, Clara couldn't sleep. Angela's question—*Anyone special?*—ran through her brain, along with her advice, so casually dispensed, *Men don't wait around forever.* That was true. The splinter of pain left by Leo was a lingering reminder. Clara recalled what Eva Braun had said about perfume, that sometimes the most unlikely things, when the particles paired and collided, could have a dramatic effect. Then the face of Max Brandt came to her, talking of how perfume stirred olfactory memory—the kind that went to the deep seabed of the brain and unlocked the images buried there. Of the hundreds of strange ingredients in perfume, and the exotic names they had. *They don't work so well in German of course; you have to say them in French.* But Max Brandt was not to be trusted, no matter how attractive he might be. That teasing gaze and seductive smile were concealing something, she was sure, and every instinct Clara possessed warned her to be wary. All the same, when she eventually fell asleep, it was the collision of unlikely particles she dreamed of, and dinner with Max Brandt, speaking softly to her in French.

Rosa Winter reached for Adolf Hitler and idly flicked his right arm up and down in a salute. He looked faintly ridiculous, standing rigidly in his Mercedes 770, with his mustache reduced to a mere dab and cheeks as rosy as those of a person with diphtheria. The Führer figurine was one of several stationed on her desk in preparation for a talk to be given that afternoon to the senior officials of the cultural section of the Reich Mother Service. Already several of the women had begun to arrive, in their frumpy gray coats and flat black boots, notebooks and pens at the ready for the lecture on the importance of promoting the correct German playthings. Toy production in Germany had been severely curtailed in recent years, but the Elastolin company was still doing a roaring trade with its replica soldiers and action figures. As well as Hitler, you could buy Goering, Hess, Goebbels, Himmler, von Schirach, Mussolini, and Franco, though the figurine of SA leader Ernst Röhm had been discreetly discontinued after Hitler had him assassinated in 1934. The figures were made of plastic now because all metal was needed for airplanes, but Joseph Goebbels had recently instructed that the heads of the most important figures should in future be crafted out of porcelain, to look more realistic. Rosa wasn't sure it made much difference. Making Himmler more lifelike was hardly going to persuade children to play with him.

Traditional German toys, preferably made of wood, were essential to convey the correct ideological conditioning, the Führerin believed, so, along with the action figures, Rosa had that morning been sent out to buy puzzle games with pieces of wood that spelled out the name Adolf Hitler, a spelling book—A is for Adolf, B is for Bormann, et cetera—and a mobile with the face of Hitler to hang above a baby's cot. There were card games too, like the one where players competed to collect the top Nazi leaders, with Hitler, of course, worth the maximum number of points. All these toys would be demonstrated to the women's leaders in their session on childhood indoctrination, and everyone would be allowed to examine them more closely, though not, of course, to play with them.

The Führerin had indicated that, as a perk of the job, Rosa might like to take home the Hitler figurine for Suzi's son, Hans-Otto, when they had finished with it. Already Rosa was imagining Hans-Otto's wide face lighting up as he saw it, the vacant blue eyes sparking with delight when she gave it to him that night.

Thursday evenings were when Rosa looked after her nephew while Suzi went to her weekly Reichsmütterdienst meetings and Pauly was off drinking with his friends from work. As soon as she had finished for the day, Rosa took a tram to the dingy, pockmarked block in Moabit where the Kramers had their apartment, and climbed the stone stairs to the fourth floor. But as soon as Suzi opened the door, it was clear she would not be leaving the house. Her eyes were pink and blotchy with crying, and she was wearing her apron. She held a handkerchief up to her face, ushering Rosa inside with a tired wave.

"Is it Pauly again?" During their rows, Pauly was known to resort to physical force to give his argument more emphasis.

"No. But I'm not going out tonight. I have to stay in with Hans-Otto."

"What's wrong?" asked Rosa with a surge of alarm. "Is it another fit?"

"It's worse."

As Suzi shunted her sister into the kitchen, Rosa suppressed a gag. The clammy moisture of a cabbage stew hung in the air, mingled with the heavy damp of drying clothes stacked on an ironing board and underwear soaking in a bucket. Hans-Otto was sitting on the floor, playing lethargically with a cardboard box, still dressed in his school uniform, a short-sleeved shirt buttoned to the neck and tucked into his trousers. His face had a dazed expression, as though he was listening to music that only he could hear, but as soon as he saw Rosa he held out his arms for a hug.

Suzi returned to the sink and resumed savagely scrubbing potatoes. "You know how he is at school. You've seen him, haven't you?"

On the occasions when she had collected him from school, Rosa had watched Hans-Otto among his classmates and winced inwardly at how he hung back while the other boys scampered around the school yard, faces flushed and yelling their lungs out. He didn't properly come alive until they reached the pet shop on the way home. There he would smile at the puppies and place his palms flat on the window as their wet noses nuzzled the glass.

"Well, now we've had this." Suzi fumbled in her apron pocket and thrust a letter towards her sister. It was a thin blue envelope, marked with the official stamp of Hans-Otto's school office, and contained a terse note, outlined in the finest National Socialist officialese.

Dear Herr and Frau Kramer,

I am writing with regard to the episode suffered this week by your son. This episode, as well as difficulties observed by your son's teachers, has alerted us to the possibility of congenital weakness. Under the law for the prevention of geneticically diseased offspring, 1933, I am required to report any signs of weakness or potential disability to the requisite authorities. Please be advised that unless you can provide medical evidence that your son is free from any disease of heredity, the school will report his case for examination by a Hereditary Health Court, who will evaluate his condition. The school awaits your response.

Heil Hitler!

"I don't understand it," muttered Suzi, half despondent, half angry. "All that jargon."

"What are these difficulties they're talking about?"

"You know. It's just Hans-Otto. He's not like other boys. He's slow."

"He's a dreamer. That's what Vati says. Hans-Otto is dreaming up great things. Vati says Einstein didn't talk until he was four."

This remark only seemed to upset Suzi more. "Einstein! He's not Einstein! Look at him!"

Hans-Otto was holding up the figurine of the Führer and

gazing at it with a seraphic air, as though observing the transit of invisible angels.

"You don't know what he's capable of," insisted Rosa stoutly.

"I know what he's *not* capable of! The teachers are supposed to report any child who seems abnormal, and, according to Fräulein Blitzer, that includes not being able to button a coat, doing badly in sports, or failing an exam. Hans-Otto hasn't taken any exams yet, but he certainly can't button his coat, and that fit he had the other day has made everything so much worse. He sits there in a trance. I'm desperate, Rosa."

"What's this Hereditary Health Court they're talking about?"

"A type of health board."

"But what does health have to do with a court? It's nothing to do with the law, is it?"

"I don't really understand it either. Apparently it's a place where they investigate an inherited disease."

"But having a fit isn't inherited."

Suzi's face seemed to contort with suppressed rage and fear. "Pauly's father had fits. Pauly's brother has had them too. It's something called epilepsy. But Pauly absolutely refuses to accept that Hans-Otto is suffering from it. And he insists that his brother's fits were just a consequence of too much beer."

"What about Doktor Eberhardt?" The general practitioner was a kindly man with a practice in Keithstrasse, who had tended the entire Winter family since Rosa and Suzi were children.

"I've seen him, of course. He said he would prefer not to examine Hans-Otto."

"But why?" Rosa was bewildered.

"Because he would be obliged to pass any information about Hans-Otto to a central archive, and he doesn't want to do that."

"Not even to see him, though?"

"I'm glad. I don't want Doktor Eberhardt to write anything about Hans-Otto down. I don't want anything about my son in some file in someone's archive."

"So what can you do?"

Suzi folded her arms defiantly. "It's *you* who needs to do something, Rosa. You understand the way these things work. You talk to these people. You work for the Führerin, after all—the most powerful woman in the land—you must be able to ask her for help."

"But . . ." It was impossible to explain to her elder sister just how adamantly the Führerin was opposed to any form of nepotistic advantage. Giving Rosa the toy that day was the nearest to official corruption that the Führerin had ever come, and Rosa knew she would probably have reimbursed the office later from her own pocket.

"I will. Of course I will. I'll see what I can do."

She cast a glance at Hans-Otto, who was now bashing the Hitler toy with a gentle rhythm, up and down, up and down, on its head.

"Suzi, why don't you go tonight anyway—you need the break. Let me stay with him for a couple of hours."

Once her sister had left, Rosa opened her bag and drew out the book she had plucked from the library before leaving work. The very few children's stories available were all on the recommended list for National Socialist teaching and followed correct ideology. By far the most borrowed was Adolf Holst's *Dragon Slayer*, in which Hitler was pictured as a prince, battling to free the princess who was Germany, but Rosa had chosen a book with a deep burgundy cover and a line drawing of a wizened old dwarf on it, decorated by a title in black Gothic script: *The Household Tales of the Brothers Grimm*. Women on the Mother

Service course were encouraged to read fairy tales to their children on the grounds that they embodied the correct folkish values and the characters in them bravely struggled to find racially pure marriage partners, but Rosa didn't care about any of that, and, obviously, Hans-Otto didn't either. She just loved the stories.

She tickled her nephew's cheek. "Shall I tell you a story?" she asked him.

A dreamy nod.

She settled on the warm chair next to the stove, hauled Hans-Otto onto her lap, and flicked through the book's pages, searching for an appropriate tale as his small body snuggled up to hers. Most of the fairy tales in the NS Frauenschaft version had soldiers in them, like the storm trooper who came to rip open the belly of the wolf who ate Red Riding Hood, or the SS officer who arrested Cinderella's Slavic stepsisters, and there was plenty of violence too. But Rosa disregarded anything too gory—like the story of Snow White, where the Jewish Queen was made to wear red-hot shoes, or "The Jew in the Brambles," in which a magic violin made the merchant dance in a thicket of thorns—and carried on searching until she came to one of her favorites, "Rapunzel."

" 'There was once a man and a woman who had long in vain wished for a child . . .' "

Hans-Otto sucked his thumb and with his other hand pressed the Hitler doll up against his cheek. His eyelids drooped. It was hard to tell if he was listening or not.

18

THE TIKI BAR AT MUNICH'S BAYERISCHERHOF HOTEL WAS AN eccentric testament to the craze for Polynesian culture that had swept Germany a few years earlier. The basement bar was decorated entirely in colorful island fashion, with fishing nets draped from the corners, teak beams decorated with the evil eye supporting the ceiling, and coconut and conch shells studding the bar. The lamps were made from dried blowfish and bamboo, and the cocktails were Bacardis and piña coladas. Island music was piped through the loudspeakers in the wall, and the entrance was flanked by totem poles carved with the grotesque visages of gods and demons. But none of them could compete with the guests of Frau Emmy Goering's soirée.

Clara was dreading the party. She had already walked twice around the center of Munich in an attempt to soothe her nerves. Her relationship with Eva Braun depended on attending this event, yet the prospect of coming face-to-face with Frau von Ribbentrop, who had so recently denounced her as a spy, and Frau Heydrich, who may have repeated that accusation to her husband, was terrifying. It would take every acting skill Clara possessed to retain an outward calm. Might the women take the opportunity to have her arrested there and then? And if so, could Clara count on Eva Braun to vouch for her? Eventually, after attracting the whistles of a pair of storm troopers, who assumed that the attractive lady in high heels and a fox fur coat was parading the streets for their benefit, Clara braced herself and entered the throng.

In the dim and smoky bar, the cream of the master race was out in force: sweaty men with short necks and only a brutal dusting of bristles on their scalps were squeezed into SS dress uniforms that were bursting at the seams. They were loud, competitive, and flushed with drink, and their demeanor was aggressively alert, as if they were assembled for a brawl rather than a high society cocktail party. As was usually the case at Nazi events, male guests vastly outnumbered the female, and the men tended to prioritize the chance of professional advancement over the opportunity to make small talk with other people's wives. In this case they were all vying for the choicer spots next to the more senior officers, jostling for position in the Nazi pecking order.

Swiftly Clara scanned the room, checking which VIPs were present. National Socialist cocktail parties were the opposite of the ordinary kind—you sincerely hoped there would be no one there you knew—and for a moment it seemed she was in luck. She recognized very few people, and no one so much as gave her a glance in return. There was no solitary figure nursing a whiskey and paying her unusual attention. Nor was there any sign of Eva Braun.

Clara edged into a corner, keeping close to the stairway with her back to the wall in case she should need to make a swift exit. The room was packed and oppressively warm, and although she felt a strong temptation to turn tail and slip away, she forced herself to remain. It was essential that she excavate more crucial information from the Führer's girlfriend. Mr.

Churchill and all those people in Whitehall could have no interest at all in Eva Braun's views on perfume, or the fact that she was planning a Hollywood biopic of her love affair with Hitler. They needed concrete insight into the Führer's military plans.

As Clara was thinking this, two things happened. A waiter thrust a vivid green cocktail into her hand, and a large, plump woman elbowed her way through the crowd to greet her. Her hostess, Emmy Goering, the wife of Germany's second most powerful man, was decked in diamond earrings and a matching necklace that cut into her heavy flesh. Just like her husband, whose love of jewelry and outlandish uniforms suggested many happy hours with the dressing up box, Emmy never stinted on extravagant displays of satin, velvet, and lace. This evening bulky Wagnerian braids framed her face and enough taffeta to rig a ship was ruched around her considerable frame, topped with the pelt of a sizable fox. The whole ensemble could not have looked more out of place amid the tropical island décor of the bar. The thicket of SS men parted like the Red Sea as she made her way across the room.

"Clara Vine! Fancy finding you at my little party. Come and talk to me," she commanded imperiously. "I've not seen you since the baby was born."

"I meant to say, Frau Goering, many congratulations."

"Thank you. It's tremendously fulfilling having a child. You should try it. We're holding the baptism next month at Carinhall. The Führer's to be godfather, and I must say he's overjoyed. If he's not to be blessed himself it's the next best thing."

"They say he loves little girls."

For years there had been regular photographs in the papers of the Führer at the Obersalzberg holding the hand of a small blond poppet who shared his birthday and was often invited to tea. Once Martin Bormann's investigations uncovered the child's Jewish grandmother, however, the little girl's invitations dried up and Hitler was advised to take tea with his Alsatian instead.

"You should see the gifts, Clara! Everyone's been so generous."

That was hardly a surprise. The christening of the child who was already being called the Princess of the Reich would almost certainly involve piles of art treasures ransacked from city museums and enough crowned heads of Europe to fill a stamp album.

"The Luftwaffe's promised to build a full-scale replica of Sanssouci palace in the orchard, complete with a little theater for her plays. Isn't that charming?"

"Adorable."

"Though if she's going to be an actress, one does hope she sticks to the stage. The film world these days seems to attract the absolute *dregs* of society, saving your presence, of course, Clara."

Clara summoned a polite smile.

"So what have you been up to? We missed you at the rally."

Yet again, Clara had succeeded in avoiding the annual Nuremberg rally, an affair that actresses as well as international visitors were aggressively encouraged to attend.

"It was such a shame. I was working and I couldn't make it. But I saw the newsreel."

The newsreel was impossible to miss. No one could visit the cinema in September without sitting through a documentary devoted entirely to the Party rally, whose theme this year had been Forward Planning. Goering had focused on "the eternal mask of the Jew devil" and Hitler had followed up with his usual incandescent rant, concluding that the Sudetenland must return to the Reich "no matter what."

Emmy assumed a tone of mock severity. "It's no good saying you've seen the newsreel. The newsreel's no substitute for the real thing, as I hardly need to tell you, dear. It can never capture the atmosphere. It's like film compared to theater." As a stage actress who had never made it into films, Emmy Goering was prone to trumpet the superiority of theatrical performance over all other dramatic work. She was especially given to criticizing Ufa films as lowbrow and lacking in artistic value.

"Anyhow, as we were all down in Nuremberg, it made sense to come on to Munich before heading back to Berlin, which is why I thought it was the perfect opportunity for a party. Though the hotel management has been a frightful bore about security."

Clara glanced around at the flushed faces and the bare shoulders, blazing with jewels. It was true; any assassin planting a bomb in this basement bar would take out most of the top tier of Nazi society. It was little wonder there were six SS guards in the hotel lobby. Yet Emmy Goering's remark only confirmed her alarm.

"So all the top people are here?"

"Apart from the Goebbelses, naturally. But then Magda is in no state, poor woman."

"Is she unwell?"

"Not physically." Emmy Goering gave her a significant look. "Her problem is more of the marital kind. She's not alone, of course."

She nodded towards a dumpy woman standing on her own with an orange juice, whom Clara recognized as Marga Himmler, the former nurse turned chicken farmer, who obeyed the Nazi ordinance against cosmetics like holy writ.

Emmy Goering drew closer. Her dense perfume enveloped them both like a rotting lily.

"Doesn't Marga look miserable? Do you think it's because her husband is off with little Hedwig Pottast, his secretary? Or because she thinks she might have to talk to Lina Heydrich?"

Clara felt her stomach clench; she willed herself not to flinch. "Is Frau Heydrich here too?"

"Yes. I'd introduce you right now but . . ."

Emmy cocked her head towards a patrician ash blonde arguing vigorously with a cowed-looking man whose uniform identified him as an SS Sturmbannführer. It was likely to be a one-way argument—no Sturmbannführer was going to risk disagreeing with the wife of SS Obergruppenführer Reinhard Heydrich.

"She's suffering a lot of stress," Emmy prattled. "Reinhard is drowning in paperwork, they haven't had a holiday for ages, and they have barely any social life in Berlin. She says it's difficult to make new friends because she never knows when her husband might have to arrest them."

Emmy gave a knowing smirk. "To cap it all, she had a frightful falling-out with Marga. Apparently Marga told her husband to persuade Heydrich to divorce Lina."

"Divorce his wife? But why?"

"Marga thinks Lina is unsuitable for someone of Reinhard's stature. Lina was fit to be tied, as you can imagine! And Marga won't give an inch. How difficult for two senior men to have wives that loathe each other. At a time like this, too. Some women are so selfish!"

Clara glanced over at the stout figure of Marga Himmler, nursing her orange juice. Alone among the crowd, she had eschewed evening dress in favor of a dirndl.

"It seems such an unlikely intervention."

"Oh, Marga's like that. She may play the humble hausfrau,

but she can give as good as she gets. She had someone arrested the other day just for overtaking her on the autobahn."

As she spoke, Emmy Goering was eyeing up Clara's pale pink dress with its collar of frosted fur.

"So why are you here in Munich then, if not to attend the rally?"

"I'm making a film at the Geiselgasteig studios. With Ursula Schilling."

"Ursula Schilling?" Emmy took a noisy draw of her cigarette and narrowed her eyes. "From what I'm hearing, the only kind of spotlight that woman will be under in the future is a Gestapo interrogation lamp."

A jolt of anxiety shot through Clara. She forced herself to suppress it. It was always best to affect ignorance when it came to the Gestapo, but Emmy's casual comment made her heart race with alarm. "Why would that be?"

Emmy raised her eyebrows and lowered her voice. "They say she's been consorting with asocial elements."

Clara managed a carefully calibrated expression of surprise—enough to suggest innocence of Ursula Schilling's private life, but not enough to imply that she was in any way close to her fellow actress. That was a familiar demeanor just then. People were as cautious with their expressions as they were with their butter. In Nazi Germany excessive emotion was reserved for marches and party rallies. "Asocial elements? Surely not."

"Let's just say, for the sake of your film I hope she has an understudy."

Privately Clara resolved to find Ursula as soon as possible and warn her.

"Anyhow." Emmy Goering retrieved the maraschino cherry

from the bottom of her glass, speared it on a cocktail stick, and ate it. "You didn't say. Who invited you tonight?"

"Actually, it was Fräulein Braun."

Emmy Goering paused mid-bite, her face a cartoon of astonishment.

"Really? The Führer's . . . I had no idea you two were acquainted."

"Fräulein Braun is very interested in film. She sent a note to me at the studio." Clara glanced around. "But though she invited me, she doesn't seem to have come."

"She's a law unto herself, that girl. She's probably having another photo session." Emmy smiled cruelly. "Eva's always having her portrait taken for him in a white dress—it's a hint Hitler never seems to take."

"The Führer only likes being with her because it means he doesn't need to think," came a familiar voice.

The voice cut through the smoky air like a draft of ice. Clara did not need to turn to know it belonged to her greatest enemy, the person who above all others in Germany regarded her with suspicion and distrust; the wife of the foreign secretary, Annelies von Ribbentrop.

The woman who wanted Clara investigated as an English spy was that evening resplendent in imperial purple, with a frosting of tiny black hairs on her upper lip and blotches of rouge on her cheeks. She took a puff on her gold-tipped Egyptian cigarette and gave Clara a narrow stare.

"If, as you say, she invited you, it seems strange she's not here."

"Good evening, Frau von Ribbentrop."

Annelies gave a wince of acknowledgment.

"Perhaps she's off playing with her perfumes somewhere," suggested Emmy Goering. "That and frivolous films seem to be her only interests. I heard she gets her dressmaker to run up copies of dresses she's seen on screen, so she can feel more like a real actress."

Clara recalled Eva admiring her dress. *I have one just like it!*

"I suppose it gives her something to do," reasoned Frau von Ribbentrop. "Now that she's given up the shop work."

Clara was not surprised to hear Eva Braun subjected to this barrage of scorn. No one would dare disparage Eva in Hitler's presence, so they made up for it when he was not around, and evidently they assumed there was no problem in revealing their feelings in front of Clara. Yet despite the triviality of their conversations, and the torrent of bile they unleashed on the mistress of their beloved Führer, it was important to listen to what they had to say. If the people back in England had identified Eva Braun as a potential clue to Hitler's thinking, there might be a nugget of gold in this river of mudslinging.

"So, Fräulein Vine." Annelies von Ribbentrop folded a canapé into her large jaw like a boa constrictor ingesting a mouse. "It's a surprise to see you here."

What could that mean? Had an order already been put out for her arrest? The foreign minister's wife gave a flicker of a smile. "I suppose you know your prime minister has visited the Berghof?"

It was not the first time Annelies von Ribbentrop had referred to Chamberlain as "your" prime minister, as though Clara were not half German, but she knew better than to rise to it.

"I saw his car go past the other day."

"He only stayed a few hours," Frau von Ribbentrop said coolly. "From what I hear the Führer was not too impressed with his arguments. He says it's time England stopped playing governess to Europe."

Though Frau von Ribbtentrop liked to imply she was confiding a state secret, Clara had managed to gather this much from the copy of *The Times* she'd found at the studios. Chamberlain's mission to Berlin had changed nothing. It was widely reported that Hitler had blackmailed the British prime minister with the threat of immediate war and that the Czechs had been betrayed. One commentator compared Chamberlain to a curate visiting a pub for the first time, imagining all the customers were as decent and honorable as himself.

"I feel sorry for Chamberlain actually," Annelies continued, without a trace of sympathy. "Poor old man. He's very weak and troubled by his health. Did you know that until this week he had never flown in an airplane? Extraordinary, don't you think?"

This was an enjoyable fact. It fitted with the notion of Britain as hopelessly backward-looking in comparison to Germany, with her gleaming Dorniers and Junkers and her ranks of Panzers preparing to roll east. But Emmy Goering was glazing over. Politics bored her. She had once confided to Clara that she wished her husband had made his career on the stage, rather than in the grubby and frankly dangerous world of politics.

"Fräulein Vine was just telling me she's acting with Ursula Schilling," she interrupted.

Annelies von Ribbentrop gave a fastidious little sniff. "That foolish woman! She's probably regretting all that time she spent cultivating Joseph Goebbels now."

Had something happened to Ursula since they had been together last? Clara's alarm was confirmed. She was desperate to know more, but it was impossible to ask.

"How about you, Clara?" Emmy turned to Clara with an air of innocence. "Have you seen Herr Doktor Goebbels recently? In the course of your work, I mean."

There was nothing these two wives would like better than to bracket her with the actresses who were rumored to have slept their way to the top. The best response was an entirely neutral one.

"I saw him and his wife in Berlin the other day."

Frau von Ribbentrop suppressed a snigger. "Not in the same room, surely?"

Emmy Goering shot her a disapproving glance. Goebbels was ridiculous and the public state of the couple's marriage was pitiful, but there were limits.

"Was it about a new film?" she asked primly.

"Yes. The Herr Doktor wants me to voice a documentary about Frau Scholtz-Klink and the place of the German mother."

"That harridan! I can think of one place this German mother would like to put *her*."

HALF AN HOUR LATER Eva Braun still had not appeared. Clara had managed to escape Frau von Ribbentrop, but the strain of avoiding an encounter with Frau Heydrich, plus the gossip about Ursula Schilling and the strength of the Bacardi cocktails, had given her a raging headache. With a swimming head and unsteady feet, she was no longer able to resist the desire to escape. She forced herself to dally another five minutes before slipping out of the bar.

Outside on the hotel's red carpet other women who had enjoyed one cocktail too many were wobbling on their high heels into taxis on the arms of SS officers. The doorkeeper attempted to hail a cab for Clara, but she demurred and turned left, heading not to her pension but to Ursula's hotel. Though she wanted nothing more than to collapse in bed, first she needed to see if Ursula was all right.

Moonlight lent a silvery glamour to the streets, which thanks to the presence of high-ranking international visitors, had been swept until they gleamed. Munich looked as perfect as a film set—for one of the old Expressionist films made by Fritz Lang or Robert Wiene, with shafts of brilliant street light puncturing the blackness of the night and inky alleyways leading off the main streets to small squares glittering with cobbles. As she threaded her way through the side streets, unfamiliar buildings loomed up and faded again like movie scenes, and Clara could not help thinking of what Fritz Guttmann had said about Goebbels: *He sees the whole of the Third Reich as a cinematic event.*

At Ursula's hotel the night receptionist had only just come on duty, so he couldn't vouch for Fräulein Schilling, but he was only too pleased to direct Clara to her room on the second floor. Clara picked her way through the honor guard of jackboots that lined the corridor, waiting outside every room for their nightly polish like a phantom squad of storm troopers on permanent watch. She hoped she would not run into their owners.

She knocked on Ursula's door, but there was no answer.

19

IN A CORNER OF THE PARK, A CLUSTER OF LABOR SERVICE LADS armed with spades were attacking a roped-off area, hacking deep into the turf. They were constructing a bunker in case enemy bombers should fly over Berlin and demolish the houses. If that happened, a siren would sound and everyone would have to go to their nearest shelter or risk certain death as the bombs rained down and fires started. At the same time antiaircraft guns on all the buildings would shoot into the sky, hitting the bombers and bringing them crashing down. The whole city would be lit up by livid flames and the sound of machine guns. It sounded pretty exciting. Like most boys at school, Erich was looking forward to it. He hoped it would happen before he was due to start his own labor service. It would be far more exciting to enroll directly in the air force than to spend six months digging trenches and latrines and draining marshes for the Arbeitsdienst.

Even though his godmother, Clara, was half English, it was plain that Britain needed to be taught a lesson. They had studied it in geography.

"Schmidt, name the chief enemy of the Fatherland!"

"Great Britain, sir."

"Who are the villains of the Versailles Treaty?"

"Britain, France, and America, Herr Kinkel."

"What is the greatest enemy of the civilized world?"

That one was easy. Bolshevism.

Herr Kinkel had told his pupils to draw a large swastika in pencil on the cover of each of their exercise books and write the list of Germany's enemies on the first page. When he discovered that Erich had met Ernst Udet, the air ace, he had been visibly impressed.

Erich rolled over in the warm grass and inhaled the deep green scent. No matter how exciting war was going to be, he didn't mind waiting a bit longer. He loved the Friedrichshain Volkspark. He used to come here a long time ago with his mother when she was alive; on fine days they had sunbathed, and there was a pond with swans and a skating rink and a café. It was a popular place for parents to take children, partly on account of its famous fountain, the Märchenbrunnen, surrounded by stone sculptures representing characters from traditional German fairy tales—Cinderella, Hansel and Gretel, and the rest. The best stories, though, were the ones his mother told him about her film career. Mutti knew all the movie stars, and she'd met a lot of important Party people too. If she'd lived she would have been as famous as Marlene Dietrich. She used to tell him all about the parties and the stars she met—Emil Jannings, Hans Albers, Gustav Fröhlich—with gossipy details of who was in love with whom, though most of them seemed to have been in love with her. Sometimes, if Mutti had been to a party, she would keep a few of the chocolates they served with the coffee for him, and smuggle them back in her handbag. He swiped away a tear. Now all he had was Oma. His grandmother was devoted to him, of course, but she was just a plain old nurse who went off every day to the red-brick Gothic Charité hospital and returned at night stinking of sick and disinfectant and nagging him about school. Oma hated Erich talking about war. There was his godmother, Clara, who had been friends with his mother, only they talked about his mother less and less now. Often he wished they could talk more about her, and that Clara would add to his little stock of memories, which was in danger of dwindling, but he didn't like to bring the subject up in case it upset her.

Normally he saw Clara on a Saturday afternoon, but she was away now, and the day's HJ session had finished, so he had jumped on a tram and come to the park just to get out of the apartment.

A soldier passed, walking arm in arm with his girlfriend. The girl flicked her long, creamy plaits flirtatiously across her shoulder as the man's hand caressed her waist. With a painful stab Erich was reminded yet again of the woman on the ship. Ada. What had really happened to her? He knew she hadn't disembarked at Funchal, whatever the captain insisted. They had talked *after* the ship left Madeira. Oma said he had got muddled, but young people didn't forget things, like adults; their minds were still fresh and sharp. It might be that Ada had gone off with a man—that was obviously what Clara thought— but Erich knew something worse had happened. He knew she was dead, and he guessed that he was the only person in the world who cared.

What would she look like if she had fallen into the sea? Would they even be able to identify her body? He had heard of bodies being pulled out of water—he had even seen one once, a woman being dragged from the Landswehr Canal, shockingly white, with her dress ballooning on the surface of the water. Someone joked that it was the corpse of Rosa Luxemborg, the Communist, who had been shot and dumped in the canal alongside her revolutionary comrade. Erich knew that drowning would disfigure a person—you were bloated beyond recognition and your flesh was eaten away by fish—and he hated to think of that happening to beautiful Ada. He almost felt like praying for her, only he knew praying was wrong.

He wondered if Clara had discovered anything, as she promised, but he guessed she was just fobbing him off. Clara was always too busy acting now to focus on him. Erich was proud, of course, of her acting; it meant he got to meet celebrities like Ernst Udet, which boosted his status at school, but he didn't talk about Clara's acting work too much because actresses were not entirely respectable. He had watched Clara act once, at the studio in a scene with Gustav Fröhlich. It was a love scene, in which Clara had to tell Fröhlich that she was leaving him, and it made Erich squirm. He hadn't realized that film actors had to repeat the same scene over and over again, while the cameras stood just inches from their faces, until the director decided they had got it right. As Erich peered from the shadows of the set, the great hall seemed to shrink so that only Clara and Gustav Fröhlich existed, facing each other in their little pool of light. After each take Clara wiped the emotion from her face and gave him a fresh smile. But when she told Fröhlich the sad news, her face crumpled in the same way, and real tears came to her eyes. Erich wondered how Clara knew what it felt like to tell a man you were leaving him. She didn't have a boyfriend as far as he knew, so did that mean she was making it up? And if she was, how was it possible to look like you meant it each time? How could you summon the emotions and control them, so that your face said only what you wanted it to say?

Sitting up, he felt for the satchel by his side and took out the cigarette card album. All the boys at school collected cigarette cards now. It was the number one craze, and at break time the playground was full of kids trading their cards to get complete sets. The albums came in different colors—gold, red, and blue—and there was a text under the space where each card would be pasted or secured beneath plastic sheets. Erich had completed several albums already, despite the fact that, unlike most of his friends, he didn't even smoke. There were always adults willing to hand out the coupons for the cards, which were high-quality reproductions on a variety of themes from Old Masters to sports cars and castles, and you had to pay extra for an album to collect them in. So far Erich had collected *The Portraiture of Northern Europe*, sports stars, flags, *Germany Awakes*, and most recently, *The Life of Adolf Hitler*. Even though the company that issued them did not make her usual brand, Oma had bought several packets of their cigarettes so they could get the full set.

Now Erich looked down at the cigarette album in front of him: *Stars of the Ufa Studios*. It was a smart, red-and-gold cardboard creation with the title in twirling gilt on the cover and thick leaves inside, with spaces for photographs of forty-eight actors and actresses whose names were inscribed underneath. The album was Ada Freitag's. Ada had the complete series. They must have taken some time to collect, and when she'd taken the album out on the ship he could tell it was a prized possession by the way she handled it, which made it all the more suspicious that she had never come back for it. Erich had gone to Ada's cabin to return it, but by the time he got there the whole place had been cleared, the bunk stripped and the cupboards emptied, and there was a choking smell of disinfectant in the air. So instead he had brought the album back home with him, stashed in the bottom of his bag, along with the green and blue silk scarf she had left. He hadn't told anyone about these items. Flicking through the album, he paused at number thirty-seven. Clara Vine. She looked different in pictures. Smooth and artificial, her pearl-gray skin shimmering and her eyes veiled; nothing like the real Clara, with her quick smile, her eyes sparkling, and her habit of tilting her head to one side when you talked to her. When Clara came back he would show her the album and remind her that Ada Freitag had been one of her biggest fans. Surely that would prompt her to investigate further.

20

H OURS AFTER SHE HAD FALLEN ASLEEP, CLARA WAS JARRED awake with a premonition of doom. Why did Eva ask her to the party at the tiki bar if she was not going to be there? What could have happened to stop her attending? In the gap between sleep and wakefulness, when reasoning took second place to subliminal instinct, Clara realized for certain that something was wrong.

Pulling on the blue dirndl dress Steffi Schaeffer had made, and slipping a trench coat on top, Clara made her way out of the still-sleeping pension. Dawn was breaking, and iridescent clouds streaked the gray sky like mother-of-pearl. For all Clara knew, the Führer may have ordered Eva to Berlin. Or perhaps she had simply felt unable to face the venom of the Nazi wives and girlfriends. That would be perfectly understandable. It was hard to forget the scorn in Frau von Ribbentrop's face as she dismissed the Führer's girlfriend: *Perfume and frivolous films seem to be her only interests.* Yet Clara's instinct persisted. Something had happened to Eva Braun—something terrible.

It took twenty minutes to reach Wasserburgstrasse. As she walked, the sounds of the city waking up filled the air, the screech of trams and the plodding of a milk cart horse, the thumps of newspapermen stacking their kiosks and the clatter of iron shutters as shopkeepers opened up. Nearer Eva's home, in the residential streets, families were waking, making breakfast, children squabbling and preparing for school. At Eva's villa, however, the curtains were drawn. The bell clanged emptily in the hall, provoking the distant barking of the dogs, who were, from the sound of it, confined in the back garden. Clara rang again, received no answer, and stood back to stare up at the shutters.

After what seemed like an age, though it could only have been minutes, a shuffling figure loomed through the glass panels of the door and, following a couple of failed attempts, undid the latch. Eva Braun, wearing a light blue, soiled dressing gown, her face pale and bleary, stood for a moment swaying. Then she staggered back into the living room and half sat, half fell, into an armchair.

"Eva! What happened?"

Following her, Clara surveyed the scene. The room was strewn with discarded clothes, and magazines were scattered on the floor. Cups of coffee littered the table, alongside a bottle of cognac and a small framed photograph of Hitler, the glass cracked. As Clara parted the curtains, allowing a wash of sunlight to penetrate the gloom, Eva winced and turned away. Her skin had the greenish, sickly tinge of drunkenness, and her eyes were half closed. Her dyed hair, showing dark at the roots, hung greasily over her face. Without makeup she looked much younger. Clara unplugged the telephone and shut the front door. Then she knelt down close beside Eva.

"Did you drink too much?" she asked quietly.

Eva groaned.

"Would you like some water?"

Another, softer groan.

"I'll fetch some."

She returned with a cup of water, forcing Eva to sip, but as Clara helped her, balancing the cup on the side of the coffee table, something else caught her eye. An empty bottle of Vanodorm sleeping tablets, with the few remaining tablets scattered across the table.

"My God, Eva! How many have you taken?"

There was a whispered croak. "I didn't count. I took twenty last time and it didn't work . . . so I reckoned I'd take more."

"We need to get you to hospital."

"No!" The force of her own resistance caused Eva to turn greener. She threw up, ejecting a few pills in the process. "Sorry."

Clara found an abandoned cardigan on the floor and wiped the girl's lips with it.

"Don't worry," Clara said. "It's going to be okay."

Eva sank back against the chair. "I'll never be okay. Never again."

"Don't say that, Eva."

"He'll never marry me now."

Her mumble was barely audible, so Clara drew closer. It was vital to prevent the girl lapsing into unconsciousness before she could fetch help.

"You don't know that."

"I do. He told his old girlfriend, and she told me."

"Who is this girlfriend?"

"Mimi. Mimi Reiter. She was his first girlfriend. She was sixteen when she met him and he was thirty-seven. They were walking their dogs in the Kurpark in Berchtesgaden. She said Wolf wanted them to have a host of blond children and she was his ideal woman." Eva gave a choked laugh. "It wasn't true of course."

"Of course not."

Clara reasoned that the best thing was to keep Eva talking. She scrabbled in her bag for a cigarette, lit it, and placed it between the girl's parched lips. Eva inhaled. A flicker of color came back to her pale face.

"They broke up years ago, but she's always showing up at the Berghof as if she owns it. And now they've met up again," she slurred. "She came to his apartment here. In Prinzregentenplatz. She's married now, to an SS officer, Georg Kubisch, so she's Frau Kubisch, but it doesn't seem to have made any difference. She had the nerve to call on Wolf in the hope of staying the night! When I accosted her about it she told me Wolf had said he was not happy with me. He's known from the day we became intimate on that red sofa in his office that it would never last. He's forty-nine now. He thinks he's too old for me."

"She's just jealous, Eva. That's no reason to attempt something silly like this."

Eva groaned again. Fear darkened her eyes. She buried her head in her hands.

"It's not just that," she whimpered. "It's something else. I can't tell you."

"Eva, you must."

"He'll be so angry with me. They all will." She looked up and stared at Clara, then turned dully away. In the sunlight her complexion seemed almost translucent, her lips blue. She dropped the cigarette into an ashtray and slumped down further in her chair.

"It would help to talk," insisted Clara, attempting to prop her up.

"It would help to die."

Eva retched again, and that was when Clara knew. The haggard eyes, the feeling of doom, the illness. They all told the same tale. Eva Braun was pregnant.

With another sigh, Eva's eyes drooped shut and her head fell back. Clara slapped her cheek lightly, but Eva had slipped into unconsciousness. Even a brisk shake of her shoulders failed to rouse her.

Clara knew she needed to act quickly. Easing the sleeping girl onto her side, she plugged the telephone back into its socket and started to dial. But before she did, another thought occurred. An opportunity like this would not come again.

Mounting the stairs swiftly, she headed for Eva's bedroom. She made first for the lingerie drawers, the traditional hiding place for young women's diaries, feeling among neatly folded layers of linen, stockings, and silk knickers for the bulk of a concealed volume. Next she rifled through the ranks of lacy day dresses, embroidered jackets, and gleaming evening gowns hanging impeccably in the wardrobe and opened each of the handbags and evening clutches lined in order of size beneath. Standing on a chair, she ran her hands along the top of the wardrobe, dipping into hatboxes and unsnapping the latches of a suitcase to look inside. Nothing. Urgently she glanced around the room, all too aware that below her the Führer's girlfriend was in dire need of medical help. Recalling where she had concealed her own childhood diary, she crossed to the fireplace. She felt the brickwork of the chimney shaft, fumbling blindly for a cavity where a secret volume might be hidden, but it was fruitless. Turning over the pillows on the bed, Clara probed under the satin eiderdown and beneath the mattress, then dropped to her knees and checked underneath. Nothing but a stack of old film magazines and a neat line of shoes. She shook out the copies of *Stern* and *Die Dame* that lay on the bedside table, but there was no book, pad, or volume to be found. The inventory of the bedroom yielded no secrets about Eva Braun apart from an enthusiasm for Ferragamo shoes and frilly satin underwear.

A similar trawl of the bathroom also drew a blank. Clara's heart sank. Either Eva Braun was far cleverer than she seemed or, as Clara was almost convinced, Guy Hamilton's idea of her diary was nothing more than a spy's fantasy.

She crept downstairs and knelt beside Eva. The girl's face was now chalk white, but the bluish tinge around her lips had deepened. The breath from her slack mouth was coming in jagged gasps.

She had to do something. Clara picked up the telephone and dialed the operator.

"I need to speak to the police."

21

THE MINUTES PASSED AGONIZINGLY AS CLARA PACED THE small living room, watching the rasping breaths of the comatose figure beside her and waiting for the police to arrive. In the apple trees the birds, untroubled by the gravity of the moment, sang their hearts out. The milky morning light had clarified to promise another sunny day, and Stasi and Negus, indignant at being confined to the garden, issued a continual volley of barks to indicate that breakfast was long overdue. It must have been a full five minutes before Clara heard a car screech to a halt outside and footsteps hasten up the path. When she opened the door, however, she repressed a gasp. It was not a policeman on the step but an officer in the formidable black tunic of the SS wearing a cap with a silver death's-head emblem and smartly pressed breeches tucked into glossy jackboots. It took a moment for her to swallow her amazement, because the man standing in front of her, kitted out in the full uniform of Heinrich Himmler's Schutzstaffel, was Max Brandt.

"Herr Brandt?" she stammered.

Ignoring Clara, he pushed past her into the room, taking in the scene in seconds. He marched over to Eva Braun and picked up the bottle of sleeping pills by her side. After a glance at the label he pulled off his gloves, felt Eva's pulse, then let her wrist fall. He strode to the door, turned to Clara, and snapped, "Get in the car right away."

Clara's astonishment at the sight of Max Brandt mutated into an icy apprehension. How was it possible that she had phoned the police and the first person on the scene was Brandt?

"I can't. I've called the police. I'll wait with her——"

"They'll be here in less than three minutes. That's why you need to leave."

"I'm not going. I have to look after Eva."

"If you do, you'll find yourself in custody."

"Custody?"

"They'll arrest you."

"But I was the person who found her!"

"Do you really believe you're going to be congratulated for saving the Führer's girlfriend?"

He strode to the window and yanked the curtains shut. Then he stood in front of her, glaring.

"Don't be a damn little fool, Clara. The eyes of the world are trained on Munich! Negotiations to preserve the peace of Europe are at a delicate stage. Even if you're very lucky and they don't charge you with breaking and entering, there's every chance they'll throw you in prison until the meetings of foreign leaders are passed. Do you have any idea how serious this would look if it gets out? The Führer's mistress attempts suicide for a third time. What does it say about a man, when his girlfriends keep trying to kill themselves? We need to get you out of here."

He held the front door open and gestured to a long, streamlined car with gleaming chrome and white-walled tires. Its engine was still running.

"*Now.*"

Clara cast a reluctant look behind her. Eva sprawled uncon-
scious on the floor. Brandt seized Clara's arm, dragged her out
of the house and into the car. Then he shut the door behind her
with a thunk, jumped behind the wheel and pulled rapidly
away, without a backward glance.

22

CLARA SAT IN STUNNED SILENCE, THE EXPENSIVE ENGINE purring beneath them, desperately trying to assess her situation. How much did Brandt know about her? And why should he want to prevent the police arresting her? Was it because he desired that pleasure for himself? And if so, where the devil was he taking her now?

She glanced around the car in confusion.

"It's an 853A Horch cabriolet," said Brandt tersely. "I borrowed it."

"I wasn't thinking about the car. I was thinking about Eva."

"Eva will be fine."

"What did you mean when you said that his girlfriends keep trying to kill themselves?"

"It's a habit they have. One of his first girlfriends tried to hang herself in the garage. Mimi Reiter. Then his twenty-three-year-old niece, Geli, shot herself in the heart with his Walther pistol. Eva tried to do the same with a gun, although not very convincingly. She had another try with pills a few years ago. The Führer has not been lucky in love. It's one of the perils of mixing with women half your age."

Clara gnawed her lip. She had known Eva Braun for a

matter of days, and what had she deduced? There was a gauche-ness about the girl, and a devastating naïveté. Eva was not like Magda Goebbels, who had become infatuated with the Na-tional Socialist creed, or Annelies von Ribbentrop, who was more of a Nazi than her husband. Least of all like Lina Hey-drich, who shored up the cruelty in her husband's soul. Instead, the woman closest to Germany's Führer seemed to have no po-litical interests whatsoever. Yet how could that be possible?

Clara wondered if Brandt shared her own suspicions about Eva's suicide attempt. That she was pregnant with Hitler's child. "Do you know why she did it?"

"Could be anything. She's unbalanced."

Clara stared out of the window to avoid his eyes. "How did you know where I was this morning?"

"A stroke of luck."

"You can't expect me to believe that. You turned up minutes after I had called the police."

"I happened to be at the police station when you called."

"You happened to be there? Why?"

He shrugged. "Perhaps I lost my dog."

"Don't joke."

"All right. I was on official business."

Official business. What kind of official business did a cul-tural attaché have at a Munich police station? Clara didn't bother wondering because the truth was perfectly evident to her, as sharp as a knife to the heart. Brandt, the man who had danced with her so tenderly in Paris, whose charm had been so seductive, and whose kiss she had dreamed of, was the instru-ment of Heydrich she had been warned of. The man who had been sent to check her movements and build a case against her. Why else should he have appeared, out of the blue, at the home of Eva Braun, ordering her into his car? And, most damning of all, why should he now be wearing the uniform of the SS, when he had told her he was an attaché in the German diplomatic service?

Stealing a glance at him, she saw the tense jut of his jaw, and his eyes, which she had once considered melting, were now steely. Brandt looked old. Perhaps he didn't like what he was doing. What honorable man would? Maybe he regretted deceiving her. Perhaps he hated himself for the task he was carrying out, and for what was about to happen to her. Clara shut her eyes, dreading what lay ahead. A year ago she had been interrogated in Prinz-Albrecht-Strasse, the headquarters of the Gestapo. The memory of that night and day, the casual brutality meted out by Hauptsturmführer Oskar Wengen, a man with the eyes of a snake, still woke her regularly with a racing heart.

Yet the thought of that night also served to focus her. If Max Brandt was Heydrich's man, she was now in his car, powerless, so the best she could do was to give nothing away. He could have no idea that she had been warned of surveillance. She must remain resolutely in character—an actress with no conceivable interest in politics.

She shuffled herself deeper into the cream leather seat, smoothing her dress over her knees and checking her face in the overhead mirror.

Then she stared out the window as the Munich buildings with their cream and gold stone slipped by and the powerful car purred southwards, through the outskirts of the city, until the houses gave way to fields and the autobahn stretched before them. Waves of panic flooded over her, knowing that she was trapped without hope of escape in the custody of Max Brandt. What dreadful fate did he have in mind? And how cynical were his jokes, his smiles, when he must know what lay in store for her. The SS were professionals. Brutality was part of their work. All she could do meanwhile was arm herself with as much information as possible.

"So what's this official business that brings you to Munich?"

"It's to do with a cultural celebration for the SS." Casually, he added, "As it happens, Himmler has awarded me an honorary rank in the SS. I've had to change uniforms."

"I noticed."

"What do you think?"

"I preferred the other one."

The roads had emptied out now and they had passed into the Bavarian countryside. The air was fresh and clean. Pockets of forest were intersected with fields of intense, luminous green, and here and there white-faced houses with painted shutters and red slanting roofs stood, bursts of crimson geraniums frothing at their windows. Cows gazed indifferently at a gate. It was a landscape of idyllic calm, but it was not enough to soothe the anxiety thrumming through Clara's body.

"So where exactly are you taking me?"

"Not far. I found myself invited to a lunch, so you may as well come too."

"And where is this lunch?"

"The Berghof."

The address, uttered so casually, snagged the breath in her throat. The Berghof. Hitler's mountain residence. The heart of his domestic base and the place where, above all others, the Führer felt at home.

Scarcely trusting herself to talk, she persisted. "Do you have any idea who will be at this lunch?"

"Hardly anyone. The Bormanns. Himmler obviously."

"And Heydrich?" she asked, before she could stop herself.

He shot her a quick, curious glance, as if assessing her interest, and replied, "Perhaps. If he's not detained by other business in Munich."

Clara shuddered. The thought of Heydrich's eyes, gray and pitiless as a frozen North Sea, meeting hers across the lunch table terrified her.

Eventually the road began winding upwards and the landscape became mountainous. Ahead, the crags of the Bavarian Alps were silhouetted against the morning sky, lilac and gray, towering into a light net of mist. Snow lay in the folds of their peaks, and, in their valleys, deep silver lakes were captured. Despite her apprehension, Clara was awestruck. These mountains had inspired so many artists, from Caspar David Friedrich to Richard Wagner. They encapsulated the sublime and lent themselves to the wildest flights of fantasy. King Ludwig had built his fairy-tale castle, Neuschwanstein, among their southern foothills, determined to re-create the Germanic legends of Tannhäuser and Lohengrin, and Hitler was merely the latest leader to be transported by their romantic grandeur. This was a landscape that tugged at the heart of the German soul, even if the feelings it aroused were not to be trusted. Something lay deep within these daunting cliffs, something as sharp and unforgiving as the crags themselves, which dwarfed ordinary human beings and made them seem utterly insignificant.

The road narrowed and they passed into a pretty little town, with a sign announcing it as Berchtesgaden. Brandt gestured to a freshly built station, furnished with grand pillars in monumental Third Reich style. It looked freakishly out of place in the quiet alpine surroundings.

"The Führer's architectural tastes always tend towards the grandiose. His offices look like railway stations and his railway stations look like churches."

"What do his churches look like?"

"Heaps of rubble, if our leader has anything to do with it. He doesn't like churches at all. He prefers rally grounds to cathedrals."

Past Berchtesgaden the road began to wind upwards, beneath a banner that read FÜHRER, WIR DANKEN DIR, and out towards more fields. Walkers alongside the road waved and gave the Hitler salute, peering avidly through the windows of the gleaming car on the lookout for celebrities. The men were dressed in traditional leather jackets and Bavarian hats, with knee breeches and socks, the women in starched dirndls, aprons, and white, knitted socks and hobnailed boots. Some carried baskets of flowers.

"They're hoping for a sight of the Führer. He always comes out when he's here. Sometimes the women tear open their blouses as he passes." Brandt grimaced.

"I take it the Führer averts his eyes."

"I'm sure he does. Unfortunately, it's been known for girls to throw themselves at his car in the hope of being injured and then comforted by him."

Eva Braun's pallid face came again into Clara's mind. Once it might have seemed astonishing to her that women would risk physical injury, let alone their lives, for their leader, yet this man carried death around him wherever he went. Suddenly, the thought of where they were headed caused fear like a surge of nausea to catch in her throat and she wound down the window to gulp the fresh air. It was as sharp as diamonds. The bright alpine sun made everything shimmer with iridescence.

"The air's extraordinary here, isn't it?" Brandt commented. "It's to do with the salt deposits in the mountains, apparently. The Führer says it makes him feel well again. Ah, here we are."

They had come to a ten-foot-high double layer of barbed

wire surrounding a roped-off area of the mountainside. The car crunched over the gravel to a stone guardhouse, where the guards stiffened to attention. One ducked his head in, and Clara and Brandt showed their identity cards. Beyond them she glimpsed more guards, patrolling with dogs. They passed a barracks and several parking lots until the road wound round and the house itself came into view.

The Berghof might once have been a charming country home, a white-faced chalet-style construction set into the slope of the hillside, yet now the simple mountain house had been extended to form the hub of an entire Nazi complex, a gated community for the National Socialist elite. All villagers who had lived within sight of the house had been forcibly removed and their chalets and farmhouses transformed into luxury homes for Goering, Goebbels, Hess, and Speer or, if they were too humble, into barracks for soldiers. The entire compound was ringed with antiaircraft guns, and deep underground bomb- and gas-proof bunkers had been built.

The entrance to the house itself was preceded by a steep flight of wide steps. The same steps, Clara remembered, that just a few days ago Neville Chamberlain himself had mounted.

For a moment, as Brandt pulled the Horch to a stop, Clara froze. What was his true motive in bringing her to this place? Being here, in the jaws of the Third Reich, had never seemed so real, or so intimidating. There was no escape here, no refuge from scrutiny. She wasn't in the middle of a city, where she could turn and disappear, or in a film studio, surrounded by people who cared only for their work. She was not among friends but at the beating heart of the Nazi regime, with officers who were trained to look on strangers with particular scrutiny. And she was with Max Brandt, whom she now knew she could never trust. Fear moored her to the seat. She wanted to beg Brandt to turn the car around and drive back fast the way they had come. Then two SS guards leapt forward, black jackets with swastika armbands attached, opened the doors, and gave the Hitler salute. Brandt raised his right hand, turned to Clara, and said softly, "Ready?"

"I'm not sure."

His expression was strange, unreadable. "Relax. You of all people know how to put on a good show."

EVERY CITIZEN OF THE REICH was familiar with the vista from the terrace of the Berghof. Every cinemagoer had seen newsreel film of the Führer, strolling with Himmler or Speer, playing with the flaxen-haired children of his aides, sitting beneath a striped parasol with his loyal dog at his heels while beyond him lay the panoramic vista of Untersberg Mountain with Salzburg Castle in the distance. Some ways away was the Eagle's Nest, Hitler's own teahouse, perched on the summit of Kehlstein Mountain and accessed by an elevator that rose through the granite. Immediately beneath the terrace, meadows rolled into distant forest, above which soared the mountains, veined with snow like a garland of blossom at their peaks. In that mountain range across from the Berghof, Charlemagne was said to sleep, waiting to restore the glory of the German empire. This craggy, romantic landscape could not be less like the military geography of Berlin, with its squares of stone and steel and its ranks of marching soldiers. Yet in different ways both expressed the indomitable ethic of the Nazi soul.

The terrace, which wrapped itself around three sides of the house, was furnished with cane sunloungers, white wooden chairs, and tables. The pale stone shimmered in the sharp alpine air, and lounging against the wall on the far side was a group of men, some in SS uniform, others in field gray, and a couple in suits, chatting to women over pre-lunch drinks. Two little girls in perfectly smocked dresses and braids like chunks of woven corn played with an Alsatian, hanging garlands of daisies around its neck as the dog patiently endured the little fingers digging into its fur. As she watched the knot of people, chatting and laughing, Clara's only consolation was that all the women were wearing dirndls. What luck that in her blind panic that morning she had chosen the dress with puffed sleeves and dirndl neckline to wear. And her silver necklace with the picture of her mother inside. Her clothing, at least, would not give her away.

Brandt strode confidently towards the group. He clicked his heels before dipping his head to hand-kiss the female guests, and then gestured to Clara.

"Fräulein Clara Vine, you may know, from the Ufa studios." His tone implied that even if they had not heard of her, they should have. He introduced the entire group, the men giving Clara a curt bow and clicking heels, the women a handshake. He ended with a buxom blonde.

"And this is Frau Mimi Kubisch."

Kubisch. Clara recognized the name immediately. She knew, as Brandt did, that this was Hitler's first girlfriend, the one who had been Mimi Reiter, yet Clara also knew that this woman had visited Hitler at his apartment just days ago. And if Eva was to be believed, had been told by Hitler that his relationship was ending. Like the others, Mimi wore rustic, Bavarian fashion, which on her translated as a tip-tilted red hat, a puffed-sleeve blouse beneath a black bodice, thick white socks, and brown lace-up brogues. She gave Clara a broad smile.

"Have you been here before, Fräulein Vine?"

"Only in the Ufa newsreel," responded Clara lightly.

"Then you'll be longing to look around! Would you like a tour while the men talk?"

The Berghof might have been inspired by Hitler's passion for Wagner, but there was nothing Wagnerian about the interior. Everywhere stolid bourgeois taste prevailed, with fretted wood, fringed lampshades, and slightly threadbare sofas piled high with embroidered cushions. Mimi followed her gaze.

"There must be fifty cushions with *Ich Liebe Sie* and *Heil Mein Führer!* stitched on them. He won't throw a single one away."

Mimi led the way through a vaulted corridor into a vast room, fit for a medieval banquet, with a gigantic window to one side giving a panoramic view of the mountains. It was more formal here. The walls were covered in Gobelin tapestries and the floor laid with red velvet and Persian carpets. Paintings of nude women hung over the fireplace, and a gigantic eagle crouched above the bronze clock. At one end a grand piano was clustered with silver framed photographs of foreign royalty, including a shot of the Duchess of Windsor, smiling up at Hitler as he took her hand on the steps of the Berghof the previous year. Like so much of Third Reich architecture, the main function of the room was less comfort or convenience, than making everyone feel small.

"This entire place was rebuilt a couple of years ago," Mimi explained. "He's terribly proud of it. All the swastika tiles on the floor are hand-painted, and that tapestry over there lifts up to make way for the movie screen. They show films every evening; several, usually." Mimi smiled merrily. "Nothing's allowed to get in the way of the Führer's screenings. When Mr. Chamberlain came here, the Führer cut the meeting short so he could watch an Ingrid Bergman movie!"

"I heard he liked *The Lives of a Bengal Lancer*."

"Liked it? He's seen it ten times! He's made it compulsory viewing for the SS because it shows how Britain gained her empire. And every night when the movie's finished, he gives his opinion to an adjutant who wires it over to the Propaganda Ministry in Berlin."

"That sounds amazingly efficient."

"It's terribly important, the Führer says. He's been watching a lot of American films recently—Tarzan, Laurel and Hardy, and so on, because he wants to learn about American culture. He loved Laurel and Hardy. Gave them a standing ovation, actually. Oh, here they come . . ."

The door opened at the far end of the room and Clara froze. Five men entered, deep in conversation. Their German was harsh and guttural, and Clara was able to catch only the occasional word or phrase. *Rabble* was one and *essential preparations* was another.

Clara shivered.

"It's always freezing here," said Mimi. "You need to bring a fur coat, even in the warmest weather."

The group at the end of the room erupted in laughter, and Clara nodded at them. "What are they talking about, do you suppose?"

Mimi shrugged. "What do you think? They say Adolf Hitler is the guest at every party. Even when he's not here. Want to go outside? I'm dying for a cigarette."

They lit up and leaned over the balustrade. In the driveway below Clara could see a soldier polishing Brandt's gleaming Horch, buffing its sleek lines as meticulously as if it were one of his own jackboots. The little girls were throwing the Alsatian's ball into the flower beds and watching the animal trample the blooms while a guard, rifle slung over his shoulder, tried ineffectually to prevent them.

"What do you think of the view?"

"It's breathtaking."

"We have Bormann to thank for it."

Mimi pointed behind her to a squat man with a darting, wary gaze. He had no neck and clothes that hung on him like flabby skin.

"Bormann ravaged this place," said Mimi, more softly. "Fifty houses were razed, and a sanitarium. He burned down a farm to make way for a place big enough to accommodate his ten children. It was pretty hard for the families who lived here. My own family knew a lot of them, but even if they'd been here for generations, Bormann wouldn't let them stay. Security reasons."

She turned and rested her elbows on the terrace ledge as she surveyed the men in the hall, pointing at them with the tip of her cigarette.

"I don't suppose you know many of these people. That one's Julius Schaub, the Führer's valet." She indicated a man with bulging eyes. "He limps because several of his toes were amputated for frostbite in the war."

Clara had heard of Schaub. All the actresses knew him. He was in charge of visiting theaters and cabarets to handpick actresses and dancers for quiet evenings with Hitler.

"And that's Albert Bormann, Martin's brother. And my husband, Georg," Mimi added, a trifle dismissively, pointing to a horse-faced man with broken veins spidering his cheeks. "Herr Brandt, of course, you know."

As she looked across, Brandt caught Clara's eye and winked. It was dreadful to think that this man, with his dark jokes and teasing smile, was in Heydrich's pay.

At that moment the doors of the dining room were opened to reveal a phalanx of white-jacketed waiters carrying silver trays.

"At last!" Mimi exclaimed. "Lunch is here. I'm famished! Come on, sit next to me, Clara."

They seated themselves around a long table set with a white linen tablecloth, crystal glasses, and solid gold cutlery, engraved with the initials *AH*. Despite the lavishness of the table settings, there was distinctly little alcohol. No cognac or champagne was in evidence. Instead the men were served beer and the women made do with the Führer's favorite Fachinger mineral water.

The company applied themselves to their meal with zest, but Clara had no appetite. The situation was so bizarre that she felt dazed. She was at the Berghof and sitting at the Führer's dinner table, though fortunately without the host. His seat at the end of the table had been left conspicuously empty.

"Bad luck that he should be away on your first visit," remarked Mimi, following her gaze. "He may come later this evening, though. Are you staying tonight?"

"No," said Clara, a little too quickly.

"That's a shame. But even if you did, you might miss him. He doesn't normally get up till noon." Mimi leaned closer with a smile. "Even then, the servants always have to let us know what mood he's in. And there are some advantages to him not being here." She picked up her fork and turned towards the servant behind her bearing a tray of warm ham. "It means we can eat meat without it being called carrion. And we don't have to listen to endless descriptions of the insides of slaughterhouses. Ugh."

"What does the Führer like to eat?"

"Hardly anything!" Her face mimed disgust. "His favorite dish is Hoppelpoppel, fried eggs with potatoes, but there are so many things he won't eat. Mushrooms, for example, because he's scared of being poisoned. Like a Roman emperor, you know? And of course, he drinks apple peel tea, never alcohol."

A stiff brandy was the only thing Clara longed to consume just then, but Mimi prattled on, seemingly oblivious of her companion's silence.

"Of course, him being away also means we don't have to have any after-lunch entertainment. The Führer likes to get Blondi, his dog, to sing. It's so funny, watching this dog howling away, but we have to keep straight faces. I'm laughing just thinking about it."

Even the image of the Führer's singing dog failed to relax Clara. Any moment she expected the phone would ring, bringing news of Eva's suicide attempt and summoning her in for questioning. Yet there was nothing.

The waiters were just clearing the first course when the conversation suddenly hushed and faces turned towards a door at the back of the room. A slender figure had entered and was surveying the company impassively. He was wearing gray woolen trousers, hanging wide at the thigh and tucked into black jackboots, beneath a gray tunic with a thick black belt. On his collar three silver oak leaves glittered. He seemed, in his uniform, like a dark silence, a hole in the air drawing all the laughter and ease and energy from the room.

Clara realized who she was looking at. Party member number two, SS Reichsführer Heinrich Himmler.

It would be hard to find a more unlikely physical specimen of the Aryan race than Himmler, unless you counted Hitler himself. His blinking eyes behind round wire-rimmed glasses gave him the appearance of a malevolent owl, and only a narrow outcrop of hair survived on his severely shaved skull. The pudgy face and weak, receding chin were in ironic contrast to the stiff silver death's-head gleaming from the cap of his uniform.

Acknowledging the lunch guests with a curt nod, he sat down, calling over a servant who brought him a humidor, shaped like a little hunting chest and decorated with stag horn tips. Removing a Cuban cigar, he lit up with hands that were strikingly delicate.

Himmler's arrival cast a chill over the lunch. Like a sinister, invisible toxin in the air, his presence poisoned the company and changed the tenor of the conversation. The men ignored the women and competed with one another to entertain the SS Reichsführer, while the women censored the gossip from their discussions, as if conscious that they must dwell on more serious matters.

Clara knew she should linger and listen to their chat, but as soon as lunch was over, she escaped back to the Great Hall. The shadow of the mountain had fallen across the house, and the servants had lit a fire to combat the autumnal chill. Trays of coffee and cake were placed on small tables. Clara buried herself in an armchair by the fireplace and stared into the flames, wondering what the next few hours might hold. She felt paralyzed by uncertainty, both about the intentions of Max Brandt and about just how much he knew. She was entirely certain now that Brandt's motivations were not romantic ones. But as to his agenda, and how she should respond, she was frighteningly unclear.

A shadow fell across the fire. She looked up to see a figure gazing speculatively down at her. Clara sat upright and tensed. Heinrich Himmler stood with a cigar in one hand and the other hooked in his pocket, rocking back on his heels, regarding her quizzically.

"Is it true, Fräulein Vine, that the English upper classes always eat porridge for breakfast?"

Of all the things she could have imagined Himmler asking her, this was most certainly the last.

"I don't think it's a hard-and-fast rule, Herr Reichsführer."

"I understand that's the reason for their good figures." He paused, perched on the arm of the chair opposite, and crossed his legs. "I think it's a good idea, actually. I have instructed porridge to be served at every one of my Lebensborn homes."

The Lebensborn institutions were Himmler's pet project. A series of homes where unmarried women who could prove Aryan descent through four generations could bear their babies. After birth they were encouraged to donate them to the SS.

Himmler took a draw on his cigar and exhaled, allowing a miasma of smoke to coil around him. Other guests had gathered, and Clara felt their eyes on her, as if trying to divine how she had drawn Himmler's attention.

"Producing high-quality children is a science, like any other. Nutrition is just one element in a precisely calibrated process. I know this from my own experience. Some years ago I used to breed chickens at my farm in Waldtrudering. It was enlightening matching poultry, mating the correct bloodlines, improving the stock; it taught me a good deal. Sometimes one needed to make firm judgments to attain the highest quality of birds. If one wants to create a pure new strain from a well-tried species that has been exhausted by crossbreeding, then one needs to be selective. Eradicate inferior material that could taint the flock. Pick out the unhealthy ones, the weaklings, those whose diseases render them incurable. Be ruthless in purging the flock of mutant elements. There's no place for bleeding hearts. We can learn a lot from livestock."

He had a low, insidious voice, quite different from the Führer's guttural tones or the harsh scrape of Goebbels's speech. Cruelty came off him in waves, like body heat.

"Or examine, if you will, the actions of a nursery gardener. If he wants to reproduce a strain of plants that has been corrupted, he will weed out all those which are stunted or malformed. And we are grateful to him, because we will all enjoy finer flowers and fruit. It is my conviction that a well-conceived breeding plan must stand at the center of every civilization. Unless one plans a population with scientific exactitude, that population can never be truly, morally pure."

Clara's silver locket, with its photograph of her Jewish mother, burned on her throat. She found her hand gripping the arm of her chair with unnatural rigor and forced herself to relax. It took everything in her to meet that cold, penetrating gaze and hold it.

"This is very interesting, Herr Reichsführer," she managed.

"The biological laws that operate with animal and plant life also apply to humans. Animal breeding and plant cultivation can teach us much about racial hygiene. Nature is perfectly unsentimental. It expels the degenerate and the alien because it understands that they weaken the species." He blinked. There was a dreadful dissonance between his manner and the ugly substance of his speech.

"Sometimes, our human instincts get in the way. Our senses tell us that we should pity the weaklings. Empathize with them. So one of our greatest tasks will be to harden ourselves against the soft language of sentiment and follow what we know to be right. The sentimentalists would argue for sparing the young, but nature knows that it is better to start with them. The earlier that the degenerate young are eliminated, the more resources remain for the healthy stock. And once you have that healthy stock, it becomes imperative to increase it. Childbearing is a woman's highest duty to her Fatherland. It is only when our childbearing is both scientific and sacred that the nation will flourish with eternal life."

He ground out his cigar in a cut-glass ashtray and tucked the stub in his pocket. Outside, the shadow of the mountain crept further across the Berghof, casting the terrace into deeper shade, and inside the glimmer of the fire enclosed the pair of them in its glow.

Himmler's eyes traveled over Clara's breasts and legs, as though assessing her sexual potential.

"You have no children, Fräulein Vine?"

"I'm not married, Herr Reichsführer."

"That need not be an impediment in a woman of good blood."

For an instant she was puzzled. Then she realized. Himmler was suggesting that it was her duty to Germany to bear a child. Husband optional.

"What age are you?"

"Thirty-one."

"And still single." He waved a hand in a slight gesture of concession. "Perhaps you serve the Reich in other ways."

"Thoughts of the Reich are at the very heart of my work."

Himmler gave a colorless smile. "Of course. You are one of Doktor Goebbels's protégées, I understand. I'm sure he appreciates . . . well, everything you do for him."

The only safe response was impassivity.

"The minister has been kind enough to ask me to voice a documentary about Gertrud Scholz-Klink. There's an announcement he wants to make concerning the birth rate and a reward for prolific mothers."

At this, a flicker of irritation crossed Himmler's face. "Does he indeed? That must be my new decoration for kinderreich mothers. I didn't know the Herr Doktor had taken it upon himself to publicize it already."

He turned crossly, knit his hands behind his back, and stared out of the window where the distant mountain loomed purple and indigo in the lengthening shadows. After a few moments, in which he seemed to be collecting his thoughts, he said, "So what do you make of the Berghof, Fräulein Vine?"

"It's very beautiful."

"We made it that way. It was a mess before we took it in hand. Squalid little huts and chalets everywhere. It had to be cleared, but I must say that was no easy task. One resident had the impertinence to approach the Führer himself and hand him a letter begging to be allowed to keep his hut."

"And was he allowed?"

The ghost of a smile twitched Himmler's thin lips. "Let's just say we found him alternative accommodation. Two years in a camp."

Max Brandt had come up to them and was watching Clara. Her eye caught his; she held it without a flicker.

"Ah." Himmler turned. "It seems your Sturmbannführer Brandt is eager to leave, Fräulein Vine."

"So soon?" Clara managed.

Brandt's smile was as jocular as ever, but she noticed that beneath the black tunic, his shoulders were rigid.

"Indeed. Again, my apologies, Herr Reichsführer." He bowed slightly, reached for Clara, and gripped her arm, his fingers digging into the flesh. "You remember, my dear, I have a dinner engagement back in Munich."

He clicked heels to the assembled gathering, and Mimi Kubisch, beaming, grasped Clara's hand in farewell.

The SS valet brought the Horch round to the front. Brandt ushered Clara in and drove sedately down the mountain, but once he had turned the corner out of sight of the Berghof, he sped recklessly along the winding road as if pursued by Valkyries.

23

"SO THIS IS THE DINNER ENGAGEMENT, STURMBANNFÜHRER Brandt?"

He winced at her use of his rank. "Don't call me that. Please call me Max."

They were seated in Max Brandt's fifth-floor suite at the Vier Jahreszeiten hotel. Outside, evening traffic sailed down Maximilianstrasse. Inside the curtains were drawn on an opulent room of brocaded upholstery, walls hung with still lifes of half-peeled fruit, and a vase of lilies with yellow stains at their hearts. Brandt handed Clara a glass of champagne that tasted of vanilla and wet stone.

Brandt's tension had all but disappeared. He smiled and leaned languidly back in his chair. "After all, you made me wait long enough."

Clara sipped her champagne. The cut glass sparkled in the candlelight, and she felt the bubbles tilt at the back of her throat, sharp as diamonds.

He chuckled. "It seems a long time since that night at Chanel's salon. I've looked forward to this ever since. You know, I still can't believe the way you ran rings round me in the streets of Paris. Anyone would think you were practiced in evasion."

"Surely not."

"It's true. And you certainly managed to evade any awkward moments with the Reichsführer too. You handled him extraordinarily well. There are plenty of SS officers who could learn from you. Himmler is not an easy person to make conversation with."

"It seems Himmler likes to make most of the conversation."

"If you can call it conversation. All that stuff about breeding." Brandt shook his head, and the laughter vanished from his eyes.

"I'm sorry you had to accompany me, but there was no other way. I had to get you away from Eva, and there was every danger of your arrest."

"Even so, you might have spared me a trip to the Berghof."

He leaned towards her, suddenly earnest. "Quite the opposite, Clara. What better alibi could you have than a day at the Führer's own home? What better way of ensuring that you were blameless than to have SS Reichsführer Himmler himself vouch for the fact that you spent the day discussing chicken breeding?"

"I thought Wagner was the Führer's special interest?"

"It is. But Teutonic mythology is Himmler's passion. He has a castle in Wewelsburg for his SS leadership dedicated to the Teutonic order. It's a most extraordinary place. It's triangular in shape and full of mosaics decked with mythic significance. All the rooms are named after the Grail legend: King Arthur, Siegfried, Parsifal, and so forth. The crypt is called Valhalla and there are all sorts of stories about what goes on there." He winked. "Don't worry. Women aren't allowed in. Except for SS wedding ceremonies, and I don't imagine you're about to participate in one of those." He paused, and a glimmer of the old, sardonic manner returned. "Unless Sturmbannführer Steinbrecher has plans, of course."

"You really believe they would have arrested me?"

"I didn't tell you this before, but shortly after we arrived at the Berghof a report came through from the police that an intruder had broken into Fräulein Braun's home and attempted to poison her."

"Poison her?"

"That's what they were saying. The security police are obsessed with conspiracies to poison the high command and their families. The police interviewed Eva's neighbors and discovered that a young woman was seen visiting the premises."

"Did they give a description?"

He observed the dread in her eyes and smiled gently. "Only that she was attractive."

Clara took a gulp of her champagne and met his eyes steadily. Had Brandt saved her so that she could demonstrate her gratitude here, in this hotel? Or did he have some other, deeper, motive that she could not as yet fathom?

A sudden knock at the door caused her to freeze, but Brandt smiled.

"Relax." He called, "Komm!" and a waiter entered, wheeling a trolley stacked with dishes. A platter of oysters bedded on ice. Two dishes, topped with silver covers, glasses, and side plates. Delicious smells of rich sauce and meat emanated from the dishes, and the waiter removed the covers with a flourish to reveal golden Wiener schnitzel, crispy fried potatoes, spinach, and carrots. Beside them was a plate piled with grapes and peaches. Clara felt a wave of hunger sweep over her.

"Here, as promised, is dinner! I hope you can manage some after that lunch we had, although I don't think you ate a mouthful. There's something about the Berghof that drives all thought of food from one's mind."

"There are oysters!" she exclaimed.

"They don't look like much, do they?" He picked up a shell and offered it to her with a spritz of lemon. "But they say it's the least distinguished ones that contain the pearls. There. Eat it in one bite."

She felt the oyster slide down her throat, like the purest distilled essence of the sea. She shut her eyes to savor it. When she opened them, he was smiling at her.

"I like watching women eat. It's as if they're devouring life."

"I enjoy eating. Believe me, it was hard to decline dinner with you before. I'm always hungry."

"Good." He lit a pair of candles, and the light flickered in the bowl of Clara's glass. A fire was burning in the grate, and its wavering flames caught in his eyes, illuminating the amber shards in their depths. The light seemed to draw both of them into its soft, enclosed circle, shutting out the shadows beyond, as though they were in one of the paintings on the walls, with the fruit and oyster shells beside them posed like a still life and their own faces lit up from inside with a painterly glow. "I think we should all live more sensuously."

"What does that mean?" she said, taking another oyster and dabbing at her dripping chin.

"We should listen to what our senses tell us. We should be alive to our feelings."

"That's pretty much the opposite of what Reichsführer Himmler was saying."

"Sounds about right then. Although Himmler was correct in one regard."

"Oh yes?"

"It seems curious that a woman like you is still single. May I ask why?"

She fiddled with her glass, then gazed at him directly.

"I suppose because the only man who ever proposed to me

made it a condition of marriage that I move back to England. If I'd done that I would have lost any chance of parts at the Ufa studios. And my work was important to me. *Is* important to me."

"So this man asked you to choose between your work and love?"

"In a way."

"And you chose . . ."

"As you can see, I chose."

"Still." He beamed and crossed his legs. "You don't need to worry about old flames anymore. Not now that you have Sturmbannführer Steinbrecher. Tell me about him. He sounds a nice fellow."

She took another sip and dipped her eyes.

"A good upstanding servant of the Reich?"

"Of course."

"Would you marry him?"

Marry him? Clara wished fervently that she had never invented him. Evasively, she rummaged among the grapes on the tray. "Far too early for that."

Cautiously, she drank her champagne. There was a mystery about Brandt. Something unknowable. She could see why he was in the diplomatic life. Despite the odd glimpses beneath the mask, such as his urgent desire to escape the Berghof, there was a smooth unperturbability to him. His eyes were ranging over the remnants of the dinner tray.

"This fruit is quite something." He sliced a peach into six neat portions, offered her one, and she bit into it. The flesh was sweet and intense, and she felt a pulse of pure pleasure.

"Wonderful, isn't it? I suppose we should make the most of it, in the circumstances."

"The circumstances?"

"Given that we don't know what's coming . . ."

A shadow crossed his eyes. He jumped up, gesturing at the black tunic, with its glistening buttons and silver insignia.

"Would you excuse me? I'd like to change out of this."

"Of course."

He disappeared into the adjacent bedroom, leaving the door ajar, and Clara remembered the image she had conjured back in Berlin, of a half-made bed, with drawn curtains, rumpled sheets, and hot bodies entwined. An anonymous hotel, somewhere like this, closed against the eyes of the world. Why had that image so stubbornly refused to leave her mind? She fortified herself with another glass of champagne, and when she looked up again he was leaning against the doorframe, wearing an open-necked white shirt, which revealed dark curls against a golden skin.

"As far as I'm concerned the less time I spend in uniform, the better."

As he came towards her, he turned off the overhead light, leaving only the glow of a pink fringed lamp. He sat opposite, smelling of eau de cologne and lemon soap, their knees almost touching. As he did, Clara felt a surge of attraction so strong she was almost faint with it, and as an unthinking response to what she was feeling, she said, "Tell me about your wife."

Brandt blinked and stiffened.

"Clara Vine. You have the most extraordinary ability to . . ." He drew a ragged breath. "All right, if that's what you want, we'll talk about my marriage." He leaned forward, his elbows on his knees. "I come from a close family. My father was a lawyer, as I said, and my mother was musical, and they were untypical of their generation in that they loved to spend time with my sisters and brothers and me. We had a family boat, and we would go sailing down the Havel and take holidays on my grandfather's estate outside Potsdam. They were very cultured people. We would stage family concerts, and I suppose I got my love of music from them. Anyhow, I expected that sense of security and predictability to continue when I myself was married. Closeness, loyalty, sharing. Those were my expectations. I thought that was what family was."

Clara couldn't suppress a wry sympathy. Her experience of family had been of bereavement, estrangement, and buttoned-up English unhappiness. She had learned that if you didn't expect much, you wouldn't be disappointed.

"Unfortunately," Brandt continued, "my marriage was not like that at all. Gisela loved the outdoor life, but she disliked music and theater, and most of all she hated traveling. That was, perhaps, the only way in which she was out of step with our leadership. They enjoy the idea of European travel. They've made it their mantra."

"Do you have children?"

His eyes clouded. "I wanted children, but it seemed Gisela couldn't have them. She became pregnant shortly after we married, then lost the child. For years, we tried and nothing happened until one day she told me she was expecting for a second time. I begged her not to go out riding, but she wouldn't listen and she lost that one too. I was still grieving for it when she told me it hadn't been my child anyway. That seemed to seal it."

"So . . . you live in Paris now?"

"Yes. Though I keep an apartment in Charlottenburg. Clausewitzstrasse, just off the Ku'damm, for when I'm in Berlin. It's been in the family for generations. It fell empty after my grandmother died. It was strange, at first, being apart from Gisela, and being back in a place I associated with childhood, but in another way, it has helped clarify my ideas of who I am and what I believe."

"What do you believe?" Clara heard herself ask.

"I have a sense . . . how to describe it? It's like what they call in the Bible 'the end of days.' And if it is the end of days, then perhaps we should, as the Romans say, as *you* once said, carpe diem."

"Seize the day?"

"That's right."

"How gloomy you sound."

"You're right!" His voice had a way of shifting from melancholy to humor in the space of a single sentence. "What kind of man darkens a dinner with a beautiful woman with talk of his ex-wife and the end of days? That's the kind of thing I should reserve for my psychiatrist."

"Do you have a psychiatrist?"

"I did once. I fired him."

"Why?"

"He talked too much."

"What do you mean when you say it's like the end of days?"

"I suppose I mean it may be the end of one era and the beginning of the next."

"You mean war?"

"Perhaps. At times like these everything is changed, isn't it?"

He was staring at her intently. To break the spell Clara got up and went over to the tray to refill her glass. Brandt came up behind her and, very gently, lifted the hair from the nape of her neck, leaned forward, and kissed her there. She felt his breath burn her skin, moving across her hair, and she turned to face him. His eyes were serious and tender, and his thumb moved roughly across her face like the harsh caress of a cat's lick.

He fed her another piece of peach, and her mouth drowned in sweetness. There was a languorous deliberation about him, as though he was prepared to enjoy everything, every sensation and every scent, like a man who might be living his final day.

He cupped her face in his hands.

"Let's not talk about the past. Nothing's predestined. We all have the power to affect our own destiny and make our own choices, don't you agree?"

Why should she not respond to him? At that moment she saw both of them with a sudden vividness as if from above, everything in minute detail, the food on the tray beside them, the shards in his eyes, the delicate powder staining the inside petals of the lily. Suddenly, her situation, and the choice she faced, was cast in intense clarity.

He was right to say people should make their choices, but she had made hers. What was she thinking of, letting her guard down and giving in to the urge for a moment's pleasure? This man wore the uniform of Himmler's SS. He was a member of the regime she had devoted her life to undermining. She broke away and moved across the room.

"Something's the matter," he stated, baldly.

"Of course it is. You're not what you say you are, Max."

"Is that so? What am I then?" He crossed his arms.

"You're in the SS, for a start. That doesn't happen by chance. It takes something to be in the SS."

"Certainly it does. Aryan heritage going back to 1750, at least twenty-three years in age, and five foot six and a half inches in height. Oh, and at some point I'll need to get my blood type tattooed onto my arm. At least that's what it said in the booklet. I didn't read the small print."

"You know that's not what I mean."

"What do you mean?"

"It takes a certain kind of person. Someone who's working for Heydrich."

For a second he stared in amazement. Then he burst out laughing. After a minute he recovered himself and wiped a hand across his eyes. "I shouldn't laugh. It's no laughing matter. But what the hell makes you think that?"

"The rank. The uniform."

"I explained the uniform."

"It's more than that. I have an instinct about you. You've not been honest with me. You're concealing something."

There was another moment of silence. She could see his face calculating, his mind turning before he spoke. He poured himself a shot of brandy and soda, and when he turned back to face her, his eyes had lost their humorous gleam.

"You're right. I've not been honest. But then, my dear Clara, neither have you. You, too, are not what you seem. I've known that for some time. Since the first evening I met you, in fact."

There was a stillness in the room and time seemed to expand, as if the two of them were poised on the threshold of some deeper, more perilous understanding.

"I don't know what you're talking about."

"Don't you? I think you do. I knew there was something about you in Chanel's salon. You confirmed it for me when I followed you back to your hotel. You told me that you're a British agent."

Her entire body became rigid with shock, but she managed a laugh and, to deflect his scrutiny, coolly withdrew a cigarette from her bag.

"What an extraordinary suggestion! I never told you any such thing."

He pulled out his lighter, and the flame leapt up to touch her cigarette.

"Oh, not overtly, of course. You're far too skilled for that. I've seen you check the street around you for shadows. I've noticed the way you assess a situation before you progress. You have that alert intelligence in your eyes: nothing escapes you. You're always listening, even when you seem to be far away. And you speak several languages. To speak another language fluently is to inhabit an entirely different character, don't you think? But the fact is, you told me what you were the instant you mentioned your lover's name. Sturmbannführer Steinbrecher. I recognized that name at once. I know him actually."

"You know him?"

It took every ounce of her acting skill to keep the astonishment from her face.

"Very well."

"Oh. I see."

"I don't think you do. You see, that's my name."

"Steinbrecher?"

"Shall we say my code name. The British gave it to me. When I first made contact with them."

As she stared at him, he sank down into the armchair, gazing into the fire, and then leaned forward, hands clasped together and elbows on his knees. There was no smile in his eyes anymore.

"It was about a year ago when I first made contact with members of the British Foreign Office. I volunteered my services and privileged information to a foreign power. Which is effectively treason, or would be, except that I regard it as pure patriotism. You see, Clara, I no longer recognize the Germany I love. I see these brutes strong-arming a small nation like Austria, and now threatening Czechoslovakia, because they can and because no one will stop them. I see them running riot with the rule of law—Germany, whose legal system is the greatest in the world, which has always stood for justice and right. And when I see this gang of thugs flooding the streets of my beloved country with tides of blood, I feel hatred swelling inside me. Damn Himmler and Heydrich and all the other sadists. I hate this false Germany, as much as I love the real Germany. And I intend to do something about it."

Shock and wonder kept her gaze riveted on him. "What can you do?"

"I'm part of a conspiracy, a plot to overthrow Hitler. We intend to mount a coup."

"A coup?" Even her whisper rang out in the silence of the room.

"More an act of self-defense. Defense of Germany against an aggressive madman."

His face seemed older, anxiety etched into the lines.

"I mean it, Clara. Someone needs to tell the truth about Hitler before it's too late. And now we think the time has come."

"We? Who is *we*?"

"I can't tell you that right now. It would compromise you, as much as them. But one thing is certain, Clara. If Britain believes there's serious opposition to Hitler among the German military, she will be empowered to take a stronger stand against him. Then if this madman attacks Czechoslovakia, he will face an Anglo-French alliance on one side and a Czech force, perhaps allied with Soviet airpower, on the other front."

Clara tried to control her conflicting emotions. Relief, that Brandt was not the tool of Heydrich she had feared, growing admiration for his bravery, and, underlying both, the potent attraction she felt for him.

"Why are you telling me this?"

"I couldn't bear you thinking of me in the same light as them. Some black-shirted gangster who thinks ethics belong in ancient Greece."

He reached forward and brushed a curl of hair from her

cheek. "And there's another reason. There's something you could do for us, Clara."

She had a sinking realization that this was the culmination of what he had been planning since the moment he met her.

"Part of me doesn't want you to be involved with this in any way. I don't want to put you in danger, any more than you might be already. I was already thinking about how you might help us when I met you on the Ku'damm that day . . ."

"Which wasn't a coincidence?"

"No. I went looking for you. Deliberately. Even then, I hadn't quite decided whether to approach you. But when I discovered you'd met the Fuhrer's girlfriend, I realized the opportunity was too good to miss."

"So what do you need me to do?"

"If, as I assume, Eva Braun recovers from her little cry for help, she will be returning to Berlin with the Führer. That's where we'll need you. I can't yet tell you how, or even when, but you'll get adequate warning."

"What sort of warning?"

"I can't tell you that either. Not yet."

He ran a single finger in a curve across her lips.

"Do you know why I chose the name Steinbrecher? It's one of our native flowers—a stone breaker. It grows in the Bavarian Alps. It's nothing much to look at, this little flower, but it's vigorous and strong enough to break paving stones apart. It makes its way up through the cracks in the rocks and fragments them. It's a fragile thing, yet it has the power to tunnel through granite."

"It suits you. You're brave."

"If I were really brave I would pick you up in my arms and carry you through to that bed—it's what I've been planning from the moment we arrived. I would persuade you that it was the right thing to do, even though I know there's something holding you back. And I know it can't be Sturmbahnführer Steinbrecher."

His hand followed the contours of her body as his voice wound through her mind. "Perhaps you can't bear to sleep with a Nazi officer. Even if he detests the Party. Is that it?"

"I've done it before."

"Then you find me too old, too unattractive?"

"No."

"I'm still married. Is that it?"

She shook her head.

"There's someone else?"

"There's no one."

Something yielded in her. She was lonely, wasn't she, and what was the point of refusing the most basic human solace? Whatever her thoughts about Nazi officers, Max Brandt was a decent man. A courageous man. Surely you should cling to the good you found, like a pearl in the harsh rubble of oyster shells? Especially now, when all that was good seemed to be falling away. And he was right. It wasn't as though she was waiting for anyone.

Brandt sensed the change in her and pulled her closer. His hands reached to her shoulders and caressed her arms before his full, soft lips met hers. His strong fingers loosened the buttons at the back of her dress and let it fall, and his hand found its way to her stocking tops, plucking at the garter belt.

"I've taken off my uniform. Why not slip out of yours?"

She arched her body against his chest and felt the warm circle of his arms around her.

From outside came the sharp screech of car tires against the road. Brandt cocked his head and slid his hand over her mouth.

"Hush."

He moved over to the window and lifted a narrow aperture, then let the curtain drop. The lights of a car passing in the street outside reared up, making scissor shapes across the ceiling and picking out his face in the gloom. Clara came up behind him.

"There's a car down there. I saw it this morning when I went to find you. It was already there—before you called the police. Do you have any reason for thinking the Gestapo might be onto you?"

"Frau von Ribbentrop told Lina Heydrich she didn't trust me."

He contemplated this. "That could be it. It never does to underestimate those women. Everyone knows von Ribbentrop's wife is twice as intelligent as him. If the Führer allowed women in his cabinet, he would do well to sack the foreign secretary and instate his wife."

He began to pace the room. "The only thing is . . . if they know you're here, I would expect them to come straight in."

He turned suddenly and took her by the shoulders.

"You need to go back to your hotel and pack. You must leave Munich. There's no alternative."

"There certainly is. I've a part to learn. I've got a film to make. I can't leave Fritz Guttmann in the lurch."

A shadow passed over his eyes. "I'm afraid Fritz Guttmann is in a worse place than that."

"What are you talking about? I saw him only the other day."

"He was arrested yesterday at dawn. He is being questioned on suspicion of assisting foreign powers."

"That's impossible!"

"Remember I mentioned I had a little cultural business to attend to? I went to the studios to warn Guttmann, but it was too late. I blame myself. I got wind of it a couple of days ago, then I was held up in Berlin. I should have left immediately. As soon as I discovered it, I went to the police station. That was how I happened to hear of your call from Fräulein Braun's house. There's nothing I could do to help Guttmann."

"What will they do with him?"

"Work him over first, ask questions later. That's the way they usually operate."

Clara felt the blood drain from her face. What did Fritz Guttmann know? If his association with London Films had been detected, the entire operation was compromised. And even if he did not know exactly what Clara did, he had arranged for her to meet the Führer's girlfriend. If Guttmann talked, there was no telling how many people his knowledge might threaten. Interrogations were like throwing stones in a lake. The consequences of confessions rippled far. And the Gestapo liked throwing stones.

Brandt's face was distracted. Calculating.

"I've changed my mind. You can't go back to your hotel. We have to catch the first available train."

"But . . ."

"There isn't any time to lose, Clara. You're coming back with me to Berlin."

24

VILLAGES AND TOWNS SPED PAST AS THE TRAIN MADE ITS way north in the six-hour journey to the Anhalter Bahnhof. Dawn was lightening the fields and forests, and in the farmsteads, cherry, apple, and nut trees were in fruit. Mist rose from the grass as it was warmed by a low morning sun.

They had taken window seats in a second-class compartment. Around the carriage, photographs of the Bavarian countryside were framed on the walls alongside a sign decreeing NICHT RAUCHER. Max Brandt sat opposite her in his foreign service uniform. Clara still had on the blue dress she had worn the previous day. The only other occupants of the compartment were a kindly looking elderly couple in Bavarian costume unwrapping hot bacon rolls, whose smell quickly filled the carriage and piqued Clara's senses.

Clara occupied herself by gazing out of the window at the fields, the clusters of farmhouses, and the occasional small church. They passed a youth camp, with its scattering of little wooden huts, and a banner over the entrance stating WIR SIND ZUM STERBEN FÜR DEUTSCHLAND GEBOREN— "We were born to die for Germany." Looking out at the fat, uniform squares of corn rolling into the distance, Clara couldn't help thinking of footage of the Nuremberg rally, with hundreds of thousands of people ranked in the rally ground, stretching as far as the eye could see.

At one stop, a young man entered the carriage, hauled a heavy suitcase up onto the baggage rack, and settled himself in a corner. In sharp contrast to the traditional costumes of the old couple, he wore a floppy cravat and a suit with a wide stripe. The savory fragrance of the bacon rolls caused him to dab his mustache fastidiously with a handkerchief before he extracted a newspaper and fenced himself off.

Brandt sat with his jackboots stretched out. Occasionally his leg touched Clara's. When a tunnel plunged them momentarily into darkness, he reached over and felt for her hand, only to withdraw his hand as daylight flooded back.

The train clattered and groaned. The gentle swaying on the tracks was soothing, yet Clara's thoughts churned. She was still reeling from Brandt's revelation: a plot to oust the Führer. The coup would take place very soon, within days perhaps, and they—the plotters—wanted her involvement too, though they would not yet explain how. She was also shaken by his casual comment that she was being followed. That meant Sabine's warning was justified and her instincts, as she moved around Munich, had been entirely correct.

They had made their arrangements hastily on the way to the station. It was Thursday. Clara would go to Brandt's Berlin apartment the following Sunday. Only then would he explain precisely what they wanted of her. He made her memorize his address in Clausewitzstrasse—*named after Prussia's greatest military strategist, appropriate in the circumstances, don't you think?*—then warned her not to utter another word, not on any subject, not even the movies. Yet although they had agreed not to talk, she continually caught Brandt's glance on her, his eyes probing, and, despite her anxiety about the plot, another question kept running through her mind. Why had she rejected his advances? What instinct had caused her to draw away from him?

If you're not waiting for someone, then it's only your past that's stopping you.

Every so often the train halted at a platform long enough for her to glimpse newsstands hung with bright magazines and newspapers. WITH HITLER AND CHAMBERLAIN FOR PEACE! Country women stood nearby selling apples, and tubs blazed with scarlet geraniums. Other stations they sped through too fast to catch more than a blur of faces on the platform, and in between them fields unfolded, lakes shimmering like silver lamé, and great tracts of deep German forest, as mysterious and impenetrable as in any fairy tale from the Brothers Grimm. Clara remembered a report about an impassioned farmer who had managed to plant silvery saplings in the shape of an enormous swastika among the pines on his land, so that foreigners arriving in Berlin by plane would see that even the ancient woodland bore Hitler's mark.

Just before Berlin they passed a succession of trains loaded with munitions and artillery, and then an airfield, where a flock of sleek silver planes perched beside their hangars. Shortly afterwards the train's speed began to slacken. Clara's heart quickened: it was an unscheduled stop. Compartment doors banged and boots thudded down the corridor as three men in SS uniforms shouldered their way along the carriages, demanding identity documents. Instantly, a subdued tension pervaded the carriage, as everyone sat up and braced themselves for scrutiny.

A guard slammed open the compartment door with a surly announcement. "Identity check."

He passed his eyes over the old couple's papers so swiftly he could barely have registered their names, then turned to Clara. "Your papers, Fräulein."

Without a word, Clara handed them over, her heart hammering.

The guard looked at the photograph on Clara's red identity document, then at her face, then at the document again. He took his time—twenty, thirty seconds—as a look of blunt puzzlement formed on his florid countenance.

"Can I ask where you boarded this train?"

"Munich."

"And what was your business there?"

"I was making a film."

"A film?"

"At the Geiselgasteig studios. I'm an actress."

That was superfluous. Why had she said that? It was as though she was undermining her own authenticity, inviting him to distrust her.

"What film?"

"It's called *Good King George*."

Why was he asking about the film? God forbid that they knew of Fritz Guttmann's arrest. Would Max intercede if she was detained?

"And you are going all the way to Berlin?"

"That's correct."

The guard grunted. He glanced up at the luggage rack.

"Which are your bags, please?"

Luggage! There had been no time to pack. She had no luggage other than the leather purse she had brought with her to the Berghof. What passenger traveled from one end of the country to the other without a suitcase? Reluctantly, she patted the purse on her lap and answered lightly, "It's a flying visit."

This comment seemed to arouse the guard's suspicions even further. Scowling, he seized her purse and began to paw through the contents. Elizabeth Arden lipstick, Max Factor powder compact, wallet containing a few Reichsmarks, the copy of *Rebecca*. The guard frowned.

"English?"

Clara shuddered. As far as this guard was concerned, a novel in English was probably about as incriminating as a copy of the Communist Manifesto.

"I'm researching a role."

The guard held the book by the spine and shook vigorously, then opened the compact and stared at the mirror image of his red-veined nose.

"We actresses like to look our best," added Clara coyly. "Especially when we are hoping to see Herr Doktor Goebbels for lunch."

The lie made her squirm, but it did the trick. The guard must know, as everyone in Germany knew, of Goebbels's reputation with actresses. He for one was not bold enough to interfere with the minister's casting couch. Snapping the compact closed, he thrust the purse back at her with alacrity.

He turned to Brandt, who handed his own documents over with languid confidence. Noting his rank, the guard clicked his heels. "Thank you, Sturmbannführer Brandt."

The young man with the cravat then furnished his documents. His sallow complexion had paled further, and a line of sweat glistened on his upper lip. The guard read the papers but did not return them. His failure to find fault with Clara seemed to make him more determined.

"You are traveling to Berlin, Herr Honigsbaum?"

"That's what it says on my ticket." The young man was trying to sound authoritative, but he merely sounded arch.

"May I ask what your business is?"

Honigsbaum offered a smile around to his audience—*What kind of question is that?*—but his fellow passengers did not respond.

"I live there."

"So I see. Rykerstrasse, 131. And do you have luggage with you?"

"Certainly." The young man inclined his head towards the luggage rack.

"Open it."

Clara remembered Steffi Schaeffer's comments about Jews being searched on trains, right down to their tubes of toothpaste. Honigsbaum hauled his leather case down from the rack with shaking hands and made several attempts to undo the clasps before he succeeded. The guard rifled through the contents. A bottle of pomade. Underwear. A wrinkled shirt. He seized on a pair of worn brown shoes, tapped the heel, and, reaching inside, peeled back the insole.

"Is there anything I can help you with, Officer?" ventured the young man, unwisely.

The request only spurred the guard to further efforts. He opened the bottle of pomade and shook it, so drops splattered on the floor, then turned a pair of gloves inside out. The young man stood immobile, his face running with sweat. The fat neck of the guard obstructed her view, but Clara saw him withdraw a pocketknife from his tunic and with a swift, practiced movement, slice it through the blue satin lining of the man's case. Cramming his sausage fingers inside, he withdrew something that looked like a deck of greasy cards but on closer sight proved to be a wad of banknotes.

A look of cruel satisfaction broke across his face at this trophy. The guard turned and held the money aloft. "What's this?"

"My savings. Where am I supposed to keep it, with this new ruling about bank accounts? I'm not breaking any law."

"That's for us to say." The guard slammed the case lid shut. "Come with me."

"Why?" The young man's show of indignation entirely failed to mask his fear. He offered an imploring smile round to the rest of the carriage. "I've done nothing wrong . . ."

"That is what we need to establish," said the guard, keeping hold of the suitcase. "Quickly. We don't want to keep these people waiting."

He slid open the door and gripped the young man's elbow. "Heil Hitler!"

Everyone responded.

Clara watched as the guard marched the man out of the train and along the platform, his pallid face mouthing protest, his hands fluttering as other guards came forward to surround them. There was a piercing whistle as the train moved slowly off again. As they passed, the young man glanced directly at Clara, with an expression of imploring anguish.

Brandt did not even look up. His eyes remained trained on his boots as the scent of the spilled pomade rose accusingly from the floor. The elderly woman observed Clara's distress and reached a comforting hand to her arm. "Er war ein Jude," she said. He was a Jew. As if that explained everything.

AT THE ANHALTER BAHNHOF, Clara and Max parted like strangers and she made her way back through the streets to Winterfeldtstrasse. The lift was out of order again and the bulb on the stairwell was broken, so she walked up the seventy-two steps—she knew exactly how many steps to the fifth floor—in semidarkness, listening to the sounds emerging from the closed doors as she ascended. There was a blast of dance music from the schoolteacher on the first floor and querulous voices from the newlywed couple on the second floor. Excitable squabbling from the children in apartment four. But when she reached the top of the stairs next to her own door, an unfamiliar figure loomed in the shadows.

"May I introduce myself? I'm Franz Engel, your new neighbor."

He was a slender man—in his forties perhaps—with a precise, professional demeanor and a gaunt, clean-shaven face that was at once humorless and forgettable. It was the kind of face you might see anywhere, behind a desk or a bank counter, in a school or an office, but never be able to recall. A face that was always going to stick to the rules.

"I just wanted to say hello."

"Do you know what happened to Herr Kaufmann? Is anything wrong?"

He shrugged. "I'm afraid I don't know. The lease of this apartment has been assigned to me."

Through his opened door she caught a glimpse of the apartment behind him. Drab gray paint, cheap, practical wooden furniture.

Herr Engel gave a bureaucratic smile, and although instinct told Clara she should engage him in conversation and inquire after his job, perhaps, or where he had last lived, or at the very least comment on the weather, for once her Englishness failed her and she remained silent.

In a clipped voice Engel said, "Anyhow, I just wanted to let you know I had moved in."

He vanished quickly into his apartment and shut the door.

Perhaps it was fatigue, or the alarming events of the past twenty-four hours, but as Clara unlocked her door and entered her own apartment she was trembling. Who was Franz Engel? A teacher or a civil servant or a clerk? He could be any of those and still be a Gestapo spy. That was the genius of the Gestapo— its strength lay almost entirely in its network of informers. Its spies fanned out through Berlin like a malevolent spider's web, connecting every strand of society. If, as Sabine said, the order had gone out that Clara must be watched, what better method than to take the empty lease on the adjacent apartment and install a man within? Listening for whether Clara tuned to foreign radio stations, watching who visited, how long they stayed, observing her daily routine, and eavesdropping through the wall on her conversations.

She went to her window and looked out across the rooftops to the arched dome of Nollendorfplatz U-Bahn. How she loved this place, the vibrant hub of Weimar Berlin, packed with nightclubs and cabarets at the time that the Nazis came to power! Even though they had closed down the clubs and replaced the Expressionist repertoire of the famous Metropol Theater with operettas and light revues, it was still possible to feel the old racy pulse of the city. The buildings with their scrollwork and plaster ornamentation bore witness to a lingering Weimar charm, and the crash of bottles collected from bars in the small hours suggested that some traditions hadn't changed.

This was her home, but for the first time since she moved in, she realized she might soon have to leave.

CHAPTER

25

T HE SECOND MOST IMPORTANT WOMAN IN GERMANY, GERtrud Scholtz-Klink, was in a filthy mood. She was engaged in a battle over territory—not quite as frenetic or bloody as that over the Sudetenland, but just as heartfelt. The Führer, she had told Bormann, despite his fulsome tributes at the Nuremberg rally, was simply not sparing time to meet her. There had now been 300,000 applications from women in the Sudetenland to join the organization, and that was on top of 470,000 from Austria. Yet she was still not getting the official recognition or encouragement that she deserved.

As the Führerin paused for breath, Rosa looked around her boss's office—a place of utilitarian drabness that seemed the perfect outward expression of Frau Scholtz-Klink's personality. There was no mirror, there being no need for cosmetic adjustments, and the sole touch of luxury Gertrud Scholtz-Klink allowed herself was a row of leather-bound speeches of Adolf Hitler with lettering picked out in gilt. On the wall, by way of decoration, was a tapestry bearing a pronouncement from the Führer, stitched in elaborate Gothic letters in black thread:

WOMAN'S WORLD IS HER HUSBAND, HER FAMILY,

HER CHILDREN, AND HER HOME.

WE DO NOT FIND IT RIGHT

WHEN SHE PRESSES INTO THE WORLD OF MEN.

When eventually the Führerin finished dictating the letter to Reichsführer Himmler and flounced out for a meeting with the Faith and Beauty League, Rosa moved swiftly. Her boss would not be back for a good hour, giving Rosa the chance to attend to the matter that was preoccupying her.

The light in the windowless library was dim, and the air smelled musty and unused, reflecting how few visitors it received. This was not a place people came to browse. The shelves of books were far outnumbered by rows of tall steel racks crammed with thousands of files, organized under sections including Family Policy, Marriage, and Race Hygiene. Rosa gave a quick smile to the librarian, a mountainous woman whose job afforded very little exercise, and received a sour nod in return. Rosa's position as secretary to the Führerin lent her a certain status, but the librarian was underemployed and liked to flex what little authority she possessed to the full.

"Can I help you, Fräulein Winter?"

"I'm just looking in the files for something on racial science."

The librarian inclined her head towards the shelves beside the chart explaining differences between the Nordic, Alpine, and Baltic races and the inheritance of tainted blood through the generations. The chart was a baleful thing, illustrating the progress of the bad blood with crimson arrows pointing in various directions, like a diagram on a detective's wall to follow the movements of a heinous crime.

"Anything particular you need?"

The woman was more like a guard than a librarian, as though, if not vigilantly protected, her files might be accessed by any passerby in search of light reading.

"It's fine. I'll just have a quick look."

Rosa needed to find what happened when children were reported to something called a Reich Health Board, but she had absolutely no idea where to start. She leafed through the files at random, her fingers trembling, the contents blurring before her eyes. Tiny puffs of dust rose up as she browsed, suggesting that no one had felt the need to access any of this information since the day it was stored.

She withdrew a pamphlet entitled "Mate Selection Guidelines," with section headings like "You and the Question of Blood" and "What Is Race?" She skimmed a little:

> Since normal and sick hereditary factors are passed on equally to the offspring, the knowledge of hereditary factors and the duty to intervene—to restrict and to promote them for the formation of coming generations—are of enormous importance. At conception, the essence and worth of a person for his folk and his race are already determined. Hence the responsibility for the next generation lies with us.

The page concluded with the triumphant announcement:

> Everything weak or inferior is annihilated.

It read like gibberish. Sickened, Rosa couldn't see how any of this rhetoric could possibly apply to Hans-Otto, but she sensed the librarian peering suspiciously in her direction and knew she would have to offer more information.

"We just needed to clarify an item of law. About Reich Health Boards."

"Why didn't you say so, then? It will be Hereditary Health you need."

The librarian heaved herself to her feet and progressed along the length of another shelf, her fat fingers flicking expertly through the files. "Better let me help you. I don't want anything getting out of alphabetical order."

She pulled open a drawer and plucked out a pamphlet. "You'll need to start with this."

The brochure was entitled "Law for the Prevention of Genetically Diseased Offspring, 1933." Rosa read it through. The law concerned anyone who suffered from any of nine conditions assumed to be hereditary: feeblemindedness, schizophrenia, manic-depressive disorder, Huntington's chorea, genetic blindness, genetic deafness, severe physical deformity, chronic alcoholism, and epilepsy.

Epilepsy.

The pamphlet was illustrated. Rosa gazed appalled at the grisly portraits of the mentally weak, easily identified by their slack, empty expressions and lolling tongues. They reminded her of a newsreel she had once seen in the cinema—a documentary screened before the main feature which argued that some people led "a life unworthy of life" and were doomed to rot in institutions. The Fatherland should be rid of such "burdens on the German worker."

None of this, though, surely, had any connection to the note from Hans-Otto's school. She felt sweat prickling under her blouse and sensed the librarian's eyes boring into her, as though this was the most interesting thing that had happened all day. Once again, Rosa was compelled to explain.

"I'm just trying to remind myself of the details of the Hereditary Health boards for children."

"Oh, those. They're new. You need to look under Proposals for Registration of Diseased Offspring."

"If you could show me . . ."

"They've just come through. A letter's been sent out to all the schools, so I filed it under Education."

The woman heaved her way across the room and extracted a piece of paper, stamped with the crest of the Reich Interior Ministry.

A decree has been enacted compelling all physicians, nurses, midwives, and other professionals involved in the care of children to report infants and children who show signs of mental and physical disability. The prescribed registration form is designed with the intention of giving increased medical care. District doctors will send the completed form to the National Committee for Observation.

The aim is to prevent the neglect of healthy children in a family through excessive care of the sick. Details of any child who might warrant registration under the scheme will be forwarded to the Health Board unless sufficient authority is given for such registration to be suspended.

The letter finished with the touch that was the hallmark of all Nazi bureaucracy, a combination of promise and threat.

A reward of two Reichsmarks will be given to the teacher or health administrator who forwards a name to the register. Failure to register any such infant will be subject to investigation.

The final salutation, however, was unambiguous.

Heil Hitler!

Rosa thanked the librarian and made her way blindly back to her desk. She had a stack of typing to complete, but although her fingers flitted across the keys mechanically, her mind was full of the letter, with its ominous circumlocution and evasive terminology. *Disability. Registration. Increased medical care. Excessive care of the sick.*

Each one was a dagger of ice to the heart.

Rosa had a special reverence for words. She had always believed that they were instruments of enlightenment and that if you chose the correct words in the right order they would help you to see the world in a more beautiful and perfect light. That was why she had wanted to be a writer. It was why she worked away at her Observations in the privacy of her bedroom every night, struggling to recapture the things she had seen that day in precisely the right language. Finding words that would make her experiences leap off the page. But now, for the first time, she understood that words could be used to obscure as much as elucidate. Abstract words and ugly official phrases grew up like a thicket of thorns around an idea. Walls of bland bureaucratic jargon could hide horror. Rosa saw now that words were dangerous, and powerful. If you used the right words, you could do anything.

F OR DAYS NOW THE CITY HAD BEEN ALIVE WITH POLITICIANS.
Hurrying down the Wilhelmstrasse, burning the midnight
oil in the embassies. Making so many foreign calls it was
almost impossible for the wiretappers to keep up. At street
level the bars and cafés buzzed with rumors, and all night
the dull rumble of convoys, lorries, tractors, and tanks kept
people awake in their beds. Police car sirens wailed through
the streets. Prime Minister Chamberlain had met with Hitler twice now, yet the stalemate persisted. Berlin felt like a
city teetering on the edge of something, uncertain whether
the speeches of politicians represented the wind of change
or mere bluster. History hung in the balance like a charge of
cordite in the air.

Clara hesitated for a moment outside the doors of the
Casino Club in Bendlerstrasse, her eye caught by a solitary
figure across the road. A short, white-haired man was leaving the granite-faced headquarters of the Wehrmacht directly opposite, a wire-haired dachshund tucked under each
arm. The sight would have been entirely unexceptional had
Clara not known that the man was Admiral Wilhelm Canaris, head of German Military Intelligence and the only man
in the German high command who rivaled Hitler in his

devotion to dogs. Canaris's dachshunds traveled with him everywhere; he would book twin-bedded hotel rooms so that the dogs could sleep beside him, they spent all day in his office, and in the evening he carried them tenderly home in his black government Mercedes. As Clara turned away, she wondered whatever had possessed Rupert to suggest meeting up so close to the nerve center of the German Wehrmacht. Except, knowing Rupert, that was probably the point.

Checking her reflection in the revolving brass doors, she searched for anything that might betray the tension of the last few days. Her figure was flattered by the same green silk suit she had worn to Coco Chanel's salon, although that evening now seemed a lifetime away. Her hair was freshly styled, and the dark smudges of fatigue around her eyes might just as well have been the results of a particularly riotous movie afterparty.

She found Rupert sitting at a corner table, downing a vodka and tonic.

"I've never been to this place before," she told him as she took a swift, instinctive look around the room. "Isn't it full of army officers?"

"That's why I come here. They're some of my best contacts." He slid another glass across the table to her, and she found herself drinking it down gratefully. "To what do I owe the pleasure?"

"Actually, Rupert, I had a little request to make."

"I suspected you wanted something more than the sheer enjoyment of seeing me."

"I need to place an advertisement in the *Chronicle*."

"For a friend, I take it?"

"That's right."

It was not a surprising request. The Situations Wanted columns of the *Daily Chronicle* were full of appeals from German Jews for any work, in exchange for the guarantee of fifty pounds sponsorship to cover the passage to England. "German couple need position, preferably together, all housekeeping and gardening possible." "Hanover family seek work, anything considered." "Young lady, modest, hard worker, urgently looks for position with English family."

"It's to go in next week. Wednesday's edition."

"I could get it in sooner."

"No. That's the day they want. There's a lot of readers for the Wednesday edition, apparently."

Rupert extracted his notebook. "Do you have the wording?"

"Berlin lady seeks London employer. German and Latin tuition possible. Tel: Berlin 1845."

"Latin? Really? So she's an intellectual, this friend of yours."

"She's a keen learner."

"And no name?"

"She prefers it that way."

"Probably wise. I wish her luck. They're all trying to make it to England now. It's hard enough even to get to the coast. The stations in Paris are crammed. It's impossible to get a ticket on the boat train."

"It's going to be worse for those who stay."

"I don't doubt it. I heard that the Berlin police chief wants to create a ghetto for wealthy Jews in Berlin, charging the Jews themselves to construct it."

"What do you think will happen, Rupert?"

The revolving doors ushered in a blast of chill air and a detachment of Wehrmacht officers, prompting Rupert to fold some bills beneath the ashtray and get to his feet.

"Fancy a little fresh air?" he asked.

They walked up Bendlerstrasse, past the army headquarters,

and round the corner along the Landswehr Canal, a swollen channel of khaki with a rainbow of oil shimmering on its surface.

Rupert dug his hands in his pockets and stared ahead.

"You asked me what I think will happen. I heard some interesting information the other day from an army contact of mine. There's a stirring of something in the Wehrmacht. Some kind of protest. A lot of the army are made up of Prussian aristocracy who regard Himmler and Heydrich as despicable thugs, and they're extremely exercised about the idea that Hitler might take the Sudetenland by force. They're planning something."

Clara forced herself to stay silent.

"My guess is, whatever they're planning, it will be too late. Hitler has had two flak wagons attached to his special train and arms stationed on the carriage roof. And Goebbels has called a major rally at the Sportpalast to prepare the Party faithful for war."

He turned towards her. "It's looking grim, Clara. In London the schoolchildren are being evacuated. They've mobilized the fleet. They've handed out gas masks. My mother had to stop her cook from testing her mask by putting her head in the oven."

Clara couldn't suppress a smile at the idea of the formidable Lady Allingham in a gas mask.

"I know, it sounds funny, but it's serious, sweetheart. All the parks are being dug up. Hyde Park is bristling with antiaircraft guns. The hospitals are being emptied so they can accept war casualties, and the Archbishop of Canterbury has called the nation to prayer."

"I've heard nothing about that here."

"Are you surprised? Goebbels is doing a miraculous job of keeping it out of the press. Unfortunately, my editor has the same idea."

"Oh, Rupert. Is Winstanley still spiking your pieces?"

"The idiot's convinced that Hitler has no aggressive intentions beyond the Sudetenland. He won't listen to anyone saying that the Führer has designs on the whole of Czechoslovakia. He sneers at me. Where is the proof? No one has ever managed to find a document with Hitler's signature on it that suggests the bastard has any aggressive plans at all. Until you find that, there's no persuading them. If I were you I'd be thinking about leaving."

Clara longed to confide in Rupert about the plot. It pained her that this man to whom she felt so close, the person who had first suggested she come and try a career in Berlin, knew barely anything of her private life, nor she of his. They shared so much, after all—an English childhood, mutual friends, and Leo Quinn. Leo most of all. Leo had been Rupert's closest friend. His shadow seemed to walk between them—never mentioned, always there.

"Nothing's going to happen, I feel sure of it."

How insanely optimistic her voice sounded. She looked at the windows they passed. How long before they were covered with Herr Feinmann's blackout cardboard?

"And there was me thinking you wanted to check my progress on the cruise ship girl."

"Oh, I did. I'm seeing Erich tomorrow and he's sure to ask me."

"Well, it turns out your Erich was right. A woman *did* disappear off that ship. I've a friend in the Kriminalpolizei, so I called him and he agreed to do some digging at police HQ at

Alexanderplatz. He found a missing person's file. Ada Freitag, aged twenty-three, reported by her parents, Viktor and Hilde Freitag of Wedding, on August twenty-ninth. Ada never returned from a cruise on the *Wilhelm Gustloff*. She was their only daughter and she'd never been in any trouble before. High-spirited is what I think they called her, but no reason to think she would abandon her old parents without a word, even if, as the captain insisted, she disembarked at Madeira."

"So if there's a missing person's file, that means they're looking for her?"

"That's the intriguing thing. My man promised to show me the file, but when he went back to collect it, it had vanished. He asked around, and his superiors told him there was no record of it. It had never existed."

"So the case is not being investigated?"

"There is no case."

"But they can't just leave it at that!"

"Can't they? Shall I tell you what my Kripo friend said to me? He said the girl is missing, her file is missing, and in his professional opinion, unless I want my journalistic visa to go missing too, I should not ask another question about it." He frowned and shook his head.

"But why should anyone want to keep her disappearance a secret? Can it be just because of the bad publicity for the Kraft durch Freude?"

"Perhaps. But I can't help suspecting something more. Straight after I asked a question about your Ada Freitag in a press conference at the Promi, Goebbels sought me out and offered me an exclusive story. That's not like him. I'm certain he was trying to distract me. And when I told my man at the Kripo that I'd raised it with Goebbels, he nearly had a heart attack.

He advised me to stick to questions on international affairs. But why should it be more dangerous to ask questions about a girl on a cruise than about the advance on the Sudetenland? It makes no sense at all. Erich was right, sweetheart. There is something very odd going on here."

27

ROSA WAS FINDING IT IMPOSSIBLE TO CONCENTRATE ON HER work. Every time she started a letter, her thoughts would return to the telephone call she had received earlier that day. She'd recognized the brash, confident voice at once, and had almost dropped the phone in shock.

"Is that my favorite Zarah Leander look-alike?"

It was Herr August Gerlach, the man from the cinema; and he wondered if Rosa would like to meet up.

How had he managed to track her down? She must have told him she worked at the Führerin's office, though she didn't recall it. His request took her so much by surprise that she didn't know what to say. She didn't really want to meet him, but nor was she quick enough to refuse. Stepping into the silence, Gerlach suggested a wine restaurant called the Ganymed on the banks of the Spree near Friedrichstrasse and gave her the address. He would be there at seven o'clock that evening if she was free.

At the end of the afternoon she escaped to the lavatory and stared at the peeling poster on the wall.

**THOUGH WOMEN ARE ARMED ONLY WITH
THE SOUP LADLE AND THE BROOM, OUR IMPACT
MUST BE AS GREAT AS OTHER WEAPONS.**

No opportunity for propaganda must be lost. Even in the lavatory.

Regarding herself in the tiny mirror, she twisted her hair savagely back into its braid. When she was young her father had teasingly called her a stork, because she was tall and skinny, and although she still practiced the gymnastic exercises she had learned in the Bund Deutscher Mädel, she remained as storklike as ever, only now she had thick glasses too. There was a gap between her teeth, and her clothes felt dull and frumpy. Freckles were scattered liverishly across her pale face. Yet this man had seemed keen to meet up, so there must be something about her that he liked. She checked her stockings for runs, glad that she had worn her best pair that morning, then mortified at what such thoughts implied. She drew out of her bag a tin of Khasana cheek color and lipstick, and applied them surreptitiously, praying that she would not encounter the Führerin on the way out. If the Führerin saw a staff member wearing cosmetics, she would stop the worker on the spot, whip out a handkerchief, and wipe it off there and then.

In truth Rosa had simply no idea how the encounter tonight would turn out because it was her first proper date. There had been occasional outings when she was much younger with the cousin of a friend, but they had always been with a group, and Adam was a nervy, religious boy, far too inhibited to seek intimacy. Since then Rosa rarely met any men, unless they were Party functionaries visiting the Frauenschaft on business, or friends of her father's who were ancient and interested only in chess. Although the BDM was nicknamed the League of German Mattresses for the frequency with which girls found themselves pregnant after social outings with the HJ, Rosa's experience had been one of excessive athletics and blameless chastity. Her Arbeit service had been spent with a gaggle of other girls on a potato farm north of Berlin, and now she found herself at the Frauenschaft, in a world run for women by women, and despite everything the Führerin said about raising the birth rate, Rosa could think of no way that she was ever going to meet a man. Sometimes in Germany it was as though politicians wanted to keep men and women in entirely separate compartments, like sugar and flour, or dynamite and matches, not to be mixed.

As she hurried down Derfflingerstrasse towards the Kurfürstenstrasse U-Bahn, Rosa wondered what Herr Gerlach would talk about. Suzi had led her to understand that men mostly wanted to talk about themselves, which was fine by her, but she worried that she might need a few conversational topics just in case. Not politics, obviously, and not work either. Gerlach didn't look like a man who was too keen on literature, and she didn't want to risk discussing an author who might turn out to be degenerate. It would have to be movies. That, or dogs.

With a shudder she remembered the motto of the Love and Marriage talk. *Keep your body pure! Do not remain single! Choose a spouse of similar blood! Hope for as many children as possible!* They didn't seem to be very specific guidelines for a dating situation. She wished she had taken some tips from Suzi, but hadn't her sister always said Rosa was immature—that she saw the world in terms of fairy tales and lived a kind of fantasy life, which prevented her from viewing the world as it really was—"one long disappointment"? Rosa needed to grow up, Suzi insisted, or she'd never find a man.

In the U-Bahn a wave of nausea engulfed Rosa. The smells of sweat, old cooking oil, and worse reeked pungently from the crowds on the platform. That was the worst thing about the shortage of soap. Strap-hanging on the train, up close to your fellow citizens, you could not forget that Berliners were now forced to wash their clothes in plain water, if they bothered at all. Rosa wanted to press a handkerchief to her nose, but she was far too polite, so she took out a copy of *NS Frauen Warte* and tried to focus on an article about Marlene Dietrich in a velvet trouser suit in Hollywood. Rosa wondered what America was really like. Everything she knew about that distant country came from the movies and Karl May's westerns, mostly involving deserts, red Indians, and bears. May's cowboy adventures were the Führer's favorites; he had spoken about them on the wireless. The stories gave him courage, and he recommended them to all his top men.

Gerlach was leaning against a lamppost outside the restaurant. Recognizing Rosa, he straightened and flicked away the butt of his cigarette, a slow smile spreading across his thin lips. "I hoped you'd come."

Why was she there? She felt no excitement or pleasure at seeing August Gerlach. Instead, all she felt was a vague pang of disappointment. He looked older than he had at the cinema, at least thirty-five, she guessed, and the film-star glamour he had possessed beneath the cinema's neon lights had faded to a scrappy mustache and wolfishly prominent canines. He wore a sharp gray suit, a slightly grubby fedora, and his sleek, oiled hair glistened in the lamplight. She fortified herself by thinking how pleased her mother would be if she said she'd had a drink with a man. Perhaps it was normal to want to walk away again as fast as possible.

Gerlach took her elbow, and she tried to stop herself flinching at the unexpected touch as he led her to one of the outside tables that lined the Spree facing the street. Dusk was falling, and bright, arterial pulses of neon rippled on the water. On the S-Bahn arch opposite, a train tore through the air heading into the suburbs. Rosa looked up at the faces in the lighted windows, wishing she was among them.

August Gerlach spread his body out, elbows on the table and, as anticipated, began talking about himself. The company he worked for was being Aryanized and the Jewish owners were leaving, meaning that there were plenty of job opportunities coming up.

"It's all about being in the right place at the right time, but I'm sure you know all about that," he declared, favoring Rosa with a broad smile. "You're a clever girl, getting yourself a job in the Frauenschaft. You're obviously going places."

She smiled back, awkwardly.

He leaned towards her encouragingly. "You've really got under my skin, you know, Fräulein Winter. Rosa. As soon as I saw you at the cinema I thought you looked very . . ." He searched for the correct adjective. "Intelligent."

"Thank you." Being called intelligent was not exactly a compliment in the Reich, not for a woman, but Rosa took it as one, and she liked the fact that he seemed to think it was one too.

"You're quite a looker as well. That's a lovely suntan you have. Been somewhere nice recently?"

"I went on a cruise on the *Wilhelm Gustloff.* To Madeira and Portugal."

He blew out his cheeks in an impressed sigh. "Aren't you the lucky one!"

"I suppose so." In an instant Rosa was transported back to the spray-lashed deck, smoking a cigarette and enjoying the bracing feeling of the water needling her face. Then, through the rain-drenched air, the sight of the girl's corpse pulled from the sea, her bright sundress clinging to her icy flesh.

"Bet you enjoyed yourself. I've heard those cruises are for the big shots. The VIPs."

Stung by this suggestion, she frowned. "Not exactly. There were all sorts on board."

"Not the likes of me, I'll bet. More the teachers' pets."

"No, really, that's the thing about the KdF cruises. They're for everyone."

"If you say so, sweetie. Wish I could have been there with you. It sounds fabulous."

"It was. I would have enjoyed it more, only . . ."

"Only what?"

"There was an accident on the ship. It rather spoiled the trip for me."

He was scouring the drinks menu. "Say, that's a shame. What happened?"

Rosa hadn't really wanted to tell Herr Gerlach what she'd seen. It was bad enough to be sitting there in the company of a man with whom, she swiftly realized, she had absolutely nothing in common, let alone to sully it further with talk of dead bodies and the terrible sight that had haunted her for weeks. Yet, she reasoned, she had already decided that she was going to tell somebody, and she didn't have much else to talk about. Besides, Gerlach was paying for her drink.

"All right, I'll tell you, if you really want to know. It was an awful accident. A girl died. She fell into the sea."

"My God. That's hard." Gerlach gave a shrug that conveyed his absolute disregard for dead girls. "Accidents can happen anywhere, though. Even on cruise liners. People drown."

"I know. But the thing is . . ." Rosa leaned across the table, even though no one was listening. "The more I think about it, the more I believe . . ." The girl's white face came back to her, the bloody mess of her head. She took a determined breath. "The more I believe that she didn't just fall."

He looked up. "What are you saying?"

"I think someone pushed her."

"Pushed her?" Gerlach exhaled a stream of smoke, a little smile dancing on his lips. "You sound like a girl with a vivid imagination."

A vivid imagination. That was what her father always said. But when her father said it, he meant it as a compliment. Gerlach made it sound like a crime.

"I'm not imagining it. I'm absolutely sure of it."

"This isn't some fantasy that's got into your pretty little head? Not been watching too many movies?"

"Not at all," she retorted. "I saw the body with my own eyes."

That made him sit up. He ground out his cigarette, then steepled his fingers. "You saw it?"

"Yes. When she was taken out of the water."

"And you saw her being pushed in too?"

"Not exactly."

"What's that supposed to mean?"

"I think she *was* pushed. Or worse. But . . ."

"But what?"

Rosa was beginning to deeply regret ever mentioning the topic.

"I probably shouldn't tell you any more. In fact, the captain came to see me. He advised me not to talk at all about what I'd seen."

Gerlach raised his eyebrows.

"Exactly," said Rosa. "But . . . why would he do that, if he wasn't trying to cover something up?"

"Wait a minute, let's get this straight."

Gerlach lit himself another cigarette and flicked the match over the railing to immediate extinction in the Spree.

"You saw a dead body and you think this girl was murdered? And you think the captain of the *Wilhelm Gustloff* was involved in a conspiracy to cover it up?"

Rosa was now bitterly wishing she had never brought the subject up with August Gerlach, who obviously thought she was some kind of fantasist. When he put it like that, it did sound melodramatic. She felt compelled to convince him that she was not crazy.

"I'm not making this up. It's a feeling I have. Anyway, I'm trying to decide if I should tell anyone . . ."

"How many people have you told so far?"

"None."

"Well, that's not true, is it? You told me quite happily. And we've only met twice."

"I said, I've told no one." She looked sideways, towards the sluggish waters of the canal, and couldn't help thinking of the bodies that they said were found floating there too, mushrooming up from the gloomy depths. Miserable relicts of humanity reduced to puffy white flesh, scooped up by the bargemen at dawn.

"You don't seem that bothered about what the captain said."

A spark of alarm flickered through her.

"What are you? A policeman or something? Obviously the captain had a reason for asking me not to discuss it, and it might have been simply that he didn't want to alarm the other passengers. But it could have been something else."

"Which is why you're going to discuss it with all your friends."

Rosa was not about to mention that she had very few friends. The women at work tended to avoid her, wrongly believing that she would repeat their gossip to the Führerin.

"I would never do that."

"Perhaps not." He was cool now, rolling his cigarette between his fingers, scrutinizing her. "But how about your parents?"

"It would scare them."

"The rest of the family?"

"We don't really have that kind of conversation."

"You told *me*, though. Despite the fact that the captain specifically asked you to keep it confidential."

Rosa felt a hot rush of indignation rising within her. Who was August Gerlach to lecture her?

"Well, I'm sorry. You seemed like the kind of person I could confide in." He didn't, of course, but she could hardly say that.

This remark made him smile. He looked out across the canal, as though contemplating her conundrum, and exhaled a stream of smoke, watching it curl up into the air.

"Want to know what I think, Rosa? I think you're a nice girl. Perhaps you watch too many detective movies, but you're a bright lady and you have good prospects. You should keep your nose out of this business."

The waitress brought their drinks, and Rosa took a huge gulp of her beer, in the interest of finishing it quickly. Gerlach's eyes followed the tight skirt and shapely legs of the waitress as she retreated, then turned back to Rosa.

"So are you going to follow my advice?"

She nodded. She was desperate to let the subject drop. She had no idea how long she would have to sit here before she could get away. When a man invited you for a drink, did it actually mean just a single drink?

Gerlach reached across to her hand and patted it. "Don't look so worried, sweetie. I'm just looking out for you. Let's not spoil any more of our evening talking about dead bodies. Not when there are movies to talk about. On the subject of which, I took the liberty of getting tickets for *The Divine Jetta*. It stars Grethe Weiser as a cabaret singer wooed by a Tyrolean count. Next week at the Kino Sportpalast. How about it?"

28

I T WOULD BE A RELIEF, IN A WAY, TO SEE ERICH.

He had called the day before, and although Clara always did her best to keep telephone conversations from her apartment to a minimum, nothing that Erich ever said could possibly arouse the suspicion of the hidden army at the telephone exchange who eavesdropped on the calls of every foreigner, or even half foreigner, in Berlin. Erich wanted to give her something, apparently. Perhaps a gift that he had forgotten from his holiday. They arranged to take advantage of the last vestiges of warm weather and go to the Strandbad at Wannsee.

The beach at the Wannsee lake was an old favorite of the boy's. A short walk from Nikolassee station on the S-Bahn down a sandy, pine-fringed lane, the beach, lapped by the shallow fresh waters of the lake, was a welcome relief from the dusty heat of the city. Jetties protruded into the Wannsee, and yachts could usually be seen tacking in the distance, framed against the gloomy pine fringes of the eastern shore. Bathers could hire deck chairs or hooded seats in white wicker. With its sausage and beer stalls, the Strandbad offered an entirely egalitarian experience for Berliners, unless, of course, they happened to be Jewish. As Clara and

Erich made their way down the steps to the beach, they passed a sign announcing BADEVERBOT FÜR JUDEN AM STRANDBAD WANNSEE. Jews should not even think about using the beach. Clara, of course, thought about that sign every time she passed it, but on this day she had more on her mind than the possibility that her Jewish self should be discovered defiling Aryan sand.

ERICH, AS HE ALWAYS DID, plunged straight into the water and swam a strong circuit while Clara queued for bottles of lemonade. As this was likely to be the last opportunity to enjoy the water and sunshine before the approach of a Berlin winter made such diversions impossible, the beach was thronged with groups of Hitler Youth and Bund Deutscher Mädel flirting and showing off, families commandeering rings of deck chairs, and lovers admiring the caramel smoothness of each other's bodies. Loudspeakers lashed to the lampposts broadcast a medley of light and military music, interspersed with the odd homily from Joseph Goebbels. As she waited, Clara noticed a man buying a copy of the *Völkischer Beobachter* at the kiosk. She thought he was staring at her, before he glanced down and she realized that his gaze might just have more to do with her tanned legs in her bathing costume.

She returned to her spot on the beach and sat looking out at the sparkling lake and the dark fringe of the Grunewald beyond. How incredible it was that she should be sitting in this lovely place, surrounded by the carefree laughter of Berliners relaxing, while back in the city a cabal of plotters were preparing to overthrow the Reich Chancellery. Clara was glad she was wearing sunglasses. Surely her face would betray the anxiety that was thrumming through her brain and Erich would ask her what was wrong. Some secrets were too heavy for a boy his age to bear, and besides, Erich's sense of duty and patriotism were bolstered daily by his sessions with the Hitler Youth.

That was just how it was for boys now. The speeches and slogans and marching songs they learned at the age of ten in the Pimpf were repeated for all their formative years in the HJ, followed by the service year and then the armed forces beyond. Everyone knew Hitler's motto: "The weak must be chiseled away. A young German must be as swift as a greyhound, as tough as leather, and as hard as Krupp's steel." Children were no different from cars or airplanes on the Führer's production line. If it came to a conflict between his beloved godmother and his adored Hitler Jugend, who knew what Erich would say or do?

He flung himself on the sand beside her, scattering icy drops of water like a dog.

"Nothing's as good as swimming in the Wannsee," he declared.

"Not even the Atlantic Ocean?"

"No. There were pools on the cruise ship, but I prefer our lakes."

He rolled over, propped himself on his elbows, then squinted up at her with his mother's dark, quizzical eyes.

"Clara . . . Did you find anything out about her? Ada. Like you said you would?"

How could she tell him that her inquiries about Ada Freitag had reached a dead end? What had Rupert said? *Someone had seemed very keen to keep her disappearance a secret.* Keen enough to alter the ship's log to suggest that the woman had left the *Wilhelm Gustloff* rather than fallen overboard. Keen enough that the Kriminalpolizei's own missing person's file on her had been disposed of. Was that merely an instance of traditional Reich paranoia, mounting a cover-up to conceal an official mistake? To avoid any stain on the glamorous reputation of Strength Through Joy, which was right up there with the Luftwaffe as a source of Nazi pride? Or was it something more? Either way, telling Erich the truth would prompt an avalanche of questions, and right now she had more pressing things on her mind.

"I did ask a few questions, Erich. I asked a journalist contact of mine to make some inquiries at the police station, and I saw him yesterday to follow it up. But so far there's not much . . ." In the circumstances a lie couldn't hurt. "Obviously they're investigating the situation."

"Good. Because I was meaning to tell you, she left some things."

Erich sat up and reached for his knapsack. "Remember I said Ada was a fan of yours? And she had a complete collection of the Ufa stars series? Well, the last time I saw her, when she said she had to go off for a few minutes, she asked me to look after her things."

Out of the knapsack he drew a silk scarf, patterned with distinctive green and blue rhombuses that contained within them an interlocking double C, and a large, scarlet book.

"She left this."

"It's lovely."

Clara examined the scarf closely, looking at the hand stitching and the rolled edges. What kind of young German woman could buy an expensive silk Chanel scarf?

"And this." He handed her the book. "If you're going to be finding out about it, perhaps you should have them. They could help the police investigation."

He tucked the scarf into Clara's bag and opened the gilt and scarlet album. Clara turned the pages dutifully.

"You're Number Thirty-seven."

She smiled. That made sense. Everyone in Germany had a number.

It was a wistful shot of herself gazing skywards as Gretchen, the part she had played the previous year in *The Pilot's Wife*. She remembered so vividly the day it had been taken. It had been easy to look sad, because she had just learned of the death of a Luftwaffe pilot who had become a friend. Indeed it was a miracle she wasn't crying.

"Ada said she was a fan of yours, Clara. Will it help the investigation, do you think?"

"It might. You never know."

A bank of cloud passed over the sun and the bathers gave a collective shiver. Faces turned upwards and bodies tensed, assessing whether it was a passing chill or if the darkened sky meant this long spell of fine weather was finally shattered.

"Fancy a Wurstsemmel?" Clara asked.

Erich nodded, and she headed back along the beach towards the concrete parade where a line of booths sold beer and snacks and ice cream. Lining up for a couple of sausage rolls, she glanced around her, and as she did the feeling resurfaced, the one she knew so well, that warned someone was watching her. She looked about carefully, studying the faces of the people, and that was when she noticed him. The man whom she had seen buying the *Völkischer Beobachter* at a newspaper kiosk earlier—the one who had stared at her legs. There he was again, standing with his back to her as he chatted to the girl behind the counter. There was something wrong about him, but what? He was in his thirties, wearing shirtsleeves and braces, a jacket dangling over his arm. He had a deep tan, but there was no sign of sand on his trousers or his lace-up shoes. What kind of man came to the beach in office clothes? As he handed over his change, tucked the paper beneath his arm, and sauntered off down the parade, Clara realized suddenly what it was that disturbed her. The newspaper. No matter how exciting the news from the continent, what man bought *two* copies of the same paper on the same day?

Alarm washed over her. Max Brandt was right. There was a shadow after her and she had finally set eyes on him. She walked casually back to Erich on the beach, gave him his sausage roll, and said, "It's getting cold now. I think it's time to leave."

THEY TOOK THE S-BAHN back to Friedrichstrasse. Clara chose the seat in the corner with a view of the entire carriage, and Erich, buoyed by his swim, sprawled across the seat, chatting constantly. A few minutes into the ride the connecting door of the carriage clanged and a man entered, taking up a seat as far as possible from her own. The wire-rimmed glasses were unmistakable. She glanced across at him a couple of times, but his gaze didn't move from the window. Was he one of Heydrich's men? Were they about to arrest her?

At Friedrichstrasse station she parted from Erich, made her way down to Leipziger Strasse, and crossed the green slug of the canal, heading for Nollendorfplatz. Then she paused. There was no point leading her pursuer straight to her apartment. She turned resolutely on her heel and headed north instead.

Potsdamer Platz was its usual tumult of traffic. Clara halted on the pavement, as though waiting to cross, while she took stock. Her pulse was racing. Bicycles wove in and out of the tram tracks, and pedestrians swirled around the green clock tower at the center of the square. Neon advertising slogans shouted at one another above people's heads, and late Saturday shoppers poured into Wertheim's department store. On impulse she slipped into a doorway of the cast-iron octagonal lavatories, known as Café Achteck in Berlin vernacular, pulled from her bag the Chanel scarf, and tied it round her hair. When she emerged she jumped on the first tram.

The tram took her to the far east of the city, to areas she rarely visited, past tenements with dank courtyards where hawkers and vegetable sellers parked their carts. She glimpsed the insides of the blocks with dingy whitewash and peeling plaster, occupied by the type of family where the men would spend their wages drinking and fighting before coming home for a repeat performance. Disembarking, she walked along. Everywhere little notices were pasted onto gates and doors. TO BE SOLD. CARPETS IN GOOD CONDITION, FURNITURE, OTHER ITEMS. UTENSILS. Jews who fled—or "evacuated," in the official terminology— were obliged to leave all their possessions behind, and these belongings, everything from china to sheets and armchairs, were itemized and listed and passed to the state, so it made sense to sell as much as possible before you left. How dispensable people were, Clara realized, and how trifling the possessions they had spent a lifetime acquiring.

She continued at a purposeful pace, intensely aware of the sounds and sights around her, stilling her own suspicions to register every sensation that occurred—the screech of a train running above the buildings out to the suburbs, blue electricity flashing in the dusk. A man pouring a zinc bucket of water into a drain, a child hauling her toy pram up some steps. At one point a cat approached, rubbing against her legs, and she stooped to caress it. As she stroked it, she glanced around, but there was nothing behind her, no one out of the ordinary, no figure slipping from the edges of her vision like a predatory shadow.

On the corner of Knaackstrasse she stopped in a café, choosing a table in the way that Leo had taught her—halfway along the room with her back to the wall and clear sight of the exits—and ordered a pot of coffee. The window afforded a view across a wide intersection. Another instruction of Leo's came into her head.

Examine the territory.

It was a lesson he had drawn from bird watching. Most people see only a fraction of what they look at, he'd explained, but the spy must look for what she is not expecting to see. Like the dappled feathers of a bird that have been designed through aeons of evolution to blend precisely into a tree trunk, or the speckles on its breast that match the flinty texture of a plowed field. Because it will be there that the anomaly lurks.

Once she started looking, it was easy to spot him. He stood directly opposite her on the other side of the street, lost in a crowd of people at a stand-up noodle bar. A poultry truck momentarily obscured her view. When it had passed, he had disappeared.

She stared blindly at the menu. Then, she half turned her back on the window, took out her compact, and applied a layer of Velvet Red, watching the street behind her in the mirror. She repeated the action regularly over the next half hour, revealing nothing, but a man at the table next to her—perhaps assuming her regular cosmetic checks were for his benefit—grinned over the top of his newspaper. He was reading about the failure of the Hitler-Chamberlain talks at Bad Godesberg, and seeing her glance flicker over the headlines, he commented softly, "We have rotten luck in our leaders."

Clara didn't reply. If the man was genuine, he would soon find himself arrested for remarks like that. And if he was a

plant and she responded, she would be the one arrested for trea-
sonous comments. It was safer to say nothing. She gathered her
things and left the café.

By the time she made her way back up Leipziger Strasse, she
was exhausted. She had walked miles. Her feet hurt, and she
was shivering in the flimsy dress and cardigan she had worn for
the beach. Approaching Potsdamer Strasse, she became aware
of something strange—a distant rumble in the air—and tilting
her head she detected a muted din from the direction of Unter
den Linden. The sound rose, and others began to turn towards
it. There was nothing unusual about a rally in Berlin—they
were almost daily occurrences—yet it seemed odd that one
should take place so late in the evening. As the shoal of curious
people surged forward, she allowed herself to drift in their
wake.

The sight that greeted her, as she rounded the corner of Wilhelmstrasse, was astonishing even by the standards of war-
ready Berlin. Rank upon rank of soldiers marched down the
avenue in a seemingly endless line, field guns mounted on
motor trucks. They were followed by motorcycle outliers and
heavy motor-drawn cannons. Rows of Panzer tanks, engines
roaring and tracks clattering on the asphalt, growled their way
up past the British embassy to the spot where hundreds of people were gathered in the square. Outside the Reich Chancellery,
its boxy frontage lit up with spotlights, swastika banners fluttered like standards at some medieval tournament. The soldiers' faces were white blurs against their black and field-gray
tunics. Burying herself in the crowd Clara watched as the endless parade rolled by, a frank propagandist statement of a regime boldly readying itself for war, brashly illuminated by arc
lights from an Ufa-Tonwoche crew. The sky darkened, and in
deafening counterpoint squadrons of Luftwaffe planes were

roaring above them, causing heads to crane up at the sky and a shudder to pass through the crowd like wind through the leaves of a tree. Staring at the tanks, imagining the contrast between their steel and iron and the fragility of the human lives inside them, Clara pictured the troops in their helmets and the planes overhead spreading through Germany in a vast wall of men and metal, gravitating inexorably towards war.

Crowds in Berlin were usually pumped up and feverishly excited, but this one was dejected, mutinous even, like a football crowd whose team is losing, and whose supporters begin to slink away early. If this display was designed to intimidate the populace, or prepare them for an imminent war, she decided, then it was failing miserably.

Once the troops had passed, leaving only a ghost of exhaust fumes in their wake, the crowd began to break up. But Clara remained, watching the last vestiges of the motorcade disappear down the street. Beside her two drunks who had stumbled out of a bar to see what all the commotion was about stared openmouthed at the vanishing parade, then shook their heads. Behind them, a man with a pot of glue was posting up an advertisement for the Winterhilfswerk, the winter relief charity. It was the usual kind of picture, plump, smiling children at their mother's knee and a slogan reading, "No one will feel hunger or cold."

"So even that's verboten now," quipped one drunk.

The poster painter ignored him.

"Call it relief?" the drunk's friend jeered. "The only people relieved are us. And we only get relieved of our money."

A few people around them exchanged glances, as if daring one another to say something, but no one had the inclination, and within minutes everyone had drifted away.

29

A RATTLE AT CLARA'S DOOR REVEALED THE PRESENCE of a small girl with a red bucket and a tray of Nazi Party lapel pins. Every Sunday householders could expect youthful callers asking for a "voluntary" contribution to Party funds. The children would have the names of all the occupants of an apartment block and beside each name the sums that each had given on previous occasions. Often the sheet of paper would be proffered so that you could compare how much you gave in comparison with your neighbors. The youth leaders chose Sunday for these collections because this meant the children would be too busy to attend church. Christianity was not approved of—Erich had quite earnestly advised Clara several times that Christ was a Jew— and now only a trickle of elderly people attended services while children were sent on marches or collecting missions. Yet the strange thing was, Clara thought, that their earnest, shining-eyed insistence on the HJ gospel, and their unrelenting commitment to proselytizing it, was identical to that of those missionaries who once used to knock on apartment doors, Bibles in hand, in an effort to save your eternal soul.

On that day the girl's tray held small round wooden pins of the Reichsmütterdienst, formed in the shape of an alpine flower. Clara chose one, gave the girl a mark for it, and watched as the child moved on to the next door to rouse Herr Engel.

Anxiety had dulled her appetite, so after drinking a quick cup of tea—black because she had forgotten to buy milk—Clara headed out. In the streets, sandbags had been piled up, and children were playing with one that had split, scooping handfuls of the sand into their own little fortresses. The metal railings alongside had been removed, for melting down into airplanes.

The city seemed at its most beautiful that day—the trees were flushed with gold and the first true autumnal edge had entered the air—but beneath Berlin's distinctive smell of buses and trams, asphalt and pine, there was another scent now: the smell of fear. It was pressed into the walls and trapped in the streets, lurking behind the impassive faces. Even though the Ku'damm still hummed with the bustle of those out on a Sunday stroll, girls window-shopping the smart stores, ancient men with cracked leathery faces and fur rugs over their knees sipping steaming coffee with pursed lips, sparrows bobbing on and off the tables, bicycle bells ringing, and Zoo station, rearing like a great botanical greenhouse, behind them. The fear was there in Clara herself as she forced herself to walk at the same unhurried pace as the Sunday strollers, praying that yesterday's shadow had not resumed his task.

As she walked, Clara thought about the message she had sent to London Films and calculated what she had achieved in the past few weeks. She had done what they asked her to do. She had got close to Eva Braun. She had learned that Hitler was intemperate, likely to wage war at any moment, but other than that, she had uncovered no valuable detail. Now she was about to be drawn into a plot against Hitler staged by Germans themselves. What would the men back in London make of that?

CLAUSEWITZSTRASSE WAS A tree-lined street leading off the smartest end of the Ku'damm in Charlottenburg. The expensive, nineteenth-century buildings with their white stucco faces and mahogany-paneled halls housed doctors and lawyers, many of them Jewish, judging by the Meyers and Grossmans on the brass nameplates by the bell that Clara rang. At the top of the block a curtain twitched at a window.

Max Brandt opened the door, but he was no longer the passionate, seductive figure who had wooed her with oysters and champagne in his Munich hotel room. His eyes were bloodshot, and a bluish tinge of stubble darkened his cheeks. He wore a crumpled, open-necked shirt and suspenders, and smelled of alcohol and cigarette smoke. For a moment he hesitated and she thought he would embrace her, but instead he waved her inside to the drawing room, where a man in an immaculate field-gray uniform stood in the center of the room.

"Ulrich Welzer. Clara Vine."

Welzer stiffened with Prussian instinct and clicked his heels. He must have been around forty. His features were finely chiseled by generations of breeding, and he had a wave of immaculate blond hair.

"Ulrich wanted to meet you briefly."

Welzer grasped Clara's hand and fixed her with a penetrating stare. His eyes swept over her cotton blouse and tweed skirt, noting the cut of her hair, the color of her eyes. He even glanced down at her shoes—black leather T-bar—and then up again to the silver locket at her throat. She had the impression that he was committing every part of her to memory. She returned his gaze unwaveringly.

"Fräulein Vine." He spoke with precise, upper-class diction. "I'm due to drive out to the country for lunch with my mother today, and she will not look kindly on me if I'm late. But believe me when I say, I am very pleased to make your acquaintance."

"And I yours."

"Ulrich works at the Abwehr, with Colonel Oster," said Brandt.

Clara frowned, confused.

"I'm sorry, Clara. We've been up half the night talking. I forgot that you know nothing of this. I'll explain."

"And perhaps we can make a better acquaintance when this enterprise is over," suggested Welzer. "I have seen many of your films, Fräulein Vine. In happier times. I would far prefer to discuss movies than army maneuvers."

With a nod at Brandt, he crossed to the door and was gone.

"Did I interrupt something?" asked Clara.

"He just wanted to get a good look at you."

"So he'll recognize me when he sees me again?"

Instead of replying, Brandt turned on the wireless—an act that had become automatic for any Berliner planning a private conversation. It was one of the "People's" sets, the Volksempfänger, which were universally dubbed Goebbels's snout. Dance music drifted out.

"In England they have a record label called His Master's Voice. I suppose the Goebbels's snout must be Our Master's Voice."

The orchestra was playing the sweet, lyrical ballad called "Adolf Hitler's Lieblingsblume," which was wildly popular just then. Adolf Hitler's favorite flower. The song had the tendency, once heard, to embed itself in the listener's mind for hours.

High on steep cliffs blooms a flower,
To which the Chancellor turns his thoughts.
Adolf Hitler's favorite flower
Is the simple Eidelweiss.

Brandt listened for a moment. "Do you like this one?"

"No. It's dreadful."

"You're wrong, my dear. It's brilliant. Goebbels thought of it. Adolf Hitler's favorite flower. Hitler doesn't give a damn about flowers, of course, I know for a fact, but Goebbels thinks of everything. Whatever else you say about him, Goebbels is a tailor. He tailors people to be the way he wants them. Sit down or take a look around while I fix you some coffee."

Clara walked thoughtfully round the apartment. It was luxuriously equipped, the antique furniture burnished and gleaming, the walls covered in artworks she could tell were valuable: an engraving of a hare, a still life of flowers, and one of a dead partridge. Another wall was devoted to bookcases, and the floor was covered in deep Persian rugs. A bronze copy of the Brandenburg Gate's quadriga stood on the mantelpiece, and a low Chinese lacquered table was piled with yet more books. In a corner, a cabinet of burled walnut held a cluster of bottles—brandy, cognac, vodka—and a cocktail shaker, and above it hung watercolors of a German lake. Beside it was a glass bottle containing a ship in full rig spreading its sails. Clara bent to inspect the meticulous modeling of the decks and the steelwork. Tiny passengers could be seen on deck and through the windows of the cabins. Like all German products, it was engineered to a high standard, a perfectly reproduced nineteenth-century sailing ship. Behind the radio on a chest of drawers stood a photograph of two small boys in sailor suits, accompanied by a young woman in white lace, whose dark curls and jovial smile marked her as Brandt's mother.

Brandt returned with two cups of steaming coffee. It was the real thing, Clara could tell from its aroma. He set them down, then flung himself onto the sofa and spread his arms across the back.

"That's my mother you were looking at. I miss her every day. Do you miss yours?"

"It's been more than ten years since she died, but yes, I do."

"Were you alike?"

"Physically very much, and I think in some aspects of character too, but my mother kept her cards close to her chest and I never really felt I knew her. The reason I came to Berlin originally was because I wanted to understand the country she'd grown up in and feel closer to her, but . . ." Clara scratched a pensive fingernail along the sofa's arm. "Though I miss her, it sounds wrong, I feel angry at her too."

"For dying?"

"Her death left me feeling abandoned." Clara had never told anyone this, not even her sister. "That sounds monstrous, I know, but her dying when I was so young left me with a sense that you can't ever rely on anyone. Or that anyone you do love will desert you. In some ways, that's been true in my life."

Brandt was gazing at her fixedly. "It will only be true if you allow it to be. You can protect yourself from love, Clara, or you can take a chance and risk being hurt." He touched her hand fleetingly. "Everything I know about you tells me you're brave enough to take risks."

She blinked and turned away, fixing her attention on the ship in its bottle. Brandt leaned forward grave-faced, suddenly businesslike. "We need to talk. Things are moving fast. Remember when we last spoke I told you that it was crucial for us that Chamberlain take a strong stand against Hitler's threats to the Sudetenland? Well, Chamberlain's back in London and it seems Hitler has no intention of backing down from his scheme. Welzer has just informed me that Hitler has secretly moved his troops into attack formation along the Czech border. The resistance has decided it's now or never."

Clara replaced her coffee untouched. She repressed a shiver. "What does that mean?"

"It means I need to give you a little more information about our plans.

"This has been a long time in the preparation, but our plans have only firmed up in the last few weeks. Last month Ludwig Beck, the chief of staff, resigned as a Wehrmacht officer in protest at Hitler's plans to take Czechoslovakia by force. Since then, an entire provisional government has been drawn up. Under the plan, Beck will be regent in the post-Hitler regime. The plotters will arrest Hitler and bring him to trial."

Shock ran through Clara like an electric charge. "They would really put Hitler on trial?"

"They've gathered a file of Hitler's crimes and will prosecute him in a people's court. They've lined up a neurologist to testify that he's insane, and they've found that he and his parents are descended from a line of highly psychotic people. The plot goes right up to Canaris, the head of the Abwehr."

"Admiral Canaris?" Clara thought of the white-haired figure she had seen carrying his beloved dachshunds. "You mean German military intelligence is behind this plot?" She stared at Brandt, struggling to grasp the magnitude of the endeavor. And its courageousness.

"Canaris has all the files on the Nazi leaders, he knows everything, but it's too risky for him to play a leading part. So he's promoted a young colonel, Hans Oster, to mastermind our coup. Colonel Oster is a devout Christian. He hates the SS. He has long been obsessed with getting rid of Hitler."

"How will it happen?"

"As I said, we've been planning this for a long time. We have a string of safe houses around the Reich Chancellery stashed with arms and ammunition. We'll occupy the government quarter, take over the government communication centers, and neutralize the Gestapo and the SS. The Gestapo has camouflaged its buildings well—they're mainly quite innocuous outposts, but Arthur Nebe, the Gestapo's head of criminal investigation, has provided a map of all the Gestapo bases in Berlin. Count von Helldorf, the head of the Berlin police, is also one of us."

Canaris? Arthur Nebe? And the head of the Berlin police? Clara was stunned at the level of the people involved.

"The idea is, if we raid the Gestapo, SD, and SS offices, we should turn up enough evidence to try all the key players and provide legitimacy for our coup to the rest of the world. At the same time we'll have a ready-made list of names and addresses of Gestapo informers to be rounded up and arrested."

Brandt's voice was utterly calm, but his hands were tightly clenched and their knuckles white. "We've decided that tomorrow's the time to strike."

"Tomorrow!"

"It has to be. The country must be on the brink of war for a coup like this to succeed. That's the only circumstance in which army officers could be persuaded to rise up against Hitler. Only a lunatic would underestimate the force he exerts on the minds of the people. The only way they will accept their Führer's arrest is if they see it as an alternative to dragging us into a senseless war. And it looks very much as though that is exactly what Hitler has in mind."

"So what will happen?" Her thoughts were roiling.

"Captain Friedrich Heinz, a colleague of Oster's, has a commando unit of twenty men. They will assemble at dawn at army headquarters in Bendlerstrasse. They will be issued with grenades and guns with instructions to take the Chancellery by force. The commander of the Berlin military district, General von Witzleben, will be escorted to the Chancellery by a unit of thirty active army officers. Then we will arrest Hitler."

Clara thought of the impenetrable wall of black-suited SS who formed around the Führer at all times.

"But surely Hitler's protected by his own bodyguard? They'll die before they give him up."

"The Leibstandarte SS Adolf Hitler consists of thirty-nine men and three officers. Each member of his bodyguard is specially selected and personally approved by the Führer himself. Only twelve are on duty at any moment. There is one security guard at the main entrance of Wilhelmstrasse 78, and one at Hitler's residence, at number 77. There are other armed guards around the Chancellery and special security officers who work at reception. They look like ordinary reception officers but they are trained to recognize people of interest. Potential assassins. However, that number of guards is not an overwhelming security force. A commando raid of twenty would certainly be able to overcome them."

"And what then?"

"The Twenty-third Infantry Division is based in Potsdam. They will be ordered to march on Berlin and occupy all key ministries, radio stations, and police, Gestapo, and SS installations. They'll seize Himmler, Goering, and Goebbels. We will need to occupy all the transport and communications centers in

Berlin. For the purposes of this operation, Oster's code name is Uncle Whitsun. Hitler is Emil, the Reich Chancellery is Mount Olympus."

Brandt's eyes rested on her, tender and probing, and suddenly he clattered his cup down on its saucer and got to his feet. "Forget this damn coffee."

He strode over to the decanter and filled a glass, gave it a squirt of soda, then turned to face her.

"This is where you come in."

Until this moment, Clara was too astonished and overwhelmed to question why she was receiving all this detail. Now she felt a frisson of alarm. Her role in this audacious attempt had already been decided.

"The coup is timed for eleven o'clock. We have a civil servant from the Foreign Ministry who will unlock the double doors of the Chancellery from the inside so we can get to Hitler's quarters. Welzer will be inside already, but he's leading a squad of men who will come through the private entrance to the Reich Chancellery. You probably didn't know about the private entrance."

Clara recalled Eva Braun's complaint. *I have to go in and out through a private entrance, in case anyone sees me.*

"Go on," she urged.

"It's a side door that scarcely anyone knows about. It was put in in 'thirty-five, at the same time that they built the bunker under the ballroom. It's accessed through a concealed door in the ballroom wall. You go down some steps, but instead of entering the shelter, you turn right, up another flight of steps, and the door is there. It opens onto the Chancellery garden. From there, there's an entrance onto the Wilhelmstrasse, just between the Agriculture Ministry and the old presidential palace. It was put in place in case Hitler ever needed to make a quick exit. The private entrance is always kept locked. Only a few people have the key, and one of them is Fräulein Braun. We need you to go to the Chancellery in the morning. Find some pretext to encourage Fräulein Braun to open that entrance. Although preferably you'll obtain the key from her and unlock it yourself."

"What if she's not in?"

"She will be. Hitler and Eva arrived on the Führer's train last night. You need to be at the main entrance of the Chancellery at ten o'clock. Say you're visiting Fräulein Braun."

"And if I find her? What then?"

"Get the key from her and take it down to the entrance. Make sure the door is unlocked by eleven o'clock. Then leave. Nothing else."

"What will happen to Eva?"

"Initially, she'll be arrested." His attitude had changed now. He was no longer protective but intensely focused.

"And then what?"

"Precisely what the Nazis do with their enemies. Shoot her, most probably."

Clara recoiled. Eva was a young woman, as girlish and naïve as the perfume she wore, violets and vanilla shot through with a touch of steel and self-pity. She was privy to the secrets of a monstrous dictator. But did she deserve to die for it? *A bit of a butterfly.* That was how she described herself. Who broke a butterfly on a wheel?

"It's the only way, Clara. This is no time for sentimentality."

"Eva Braun's guilty of no crime! You can't visit the sins of the men on their women. She isn't part of what he does."

"She's part of his game."

A sudden, inexplicable surge of anger rose in Clara. The

thought that Eva—silly, gullible Eva—should be punished so savagely for her delusions revolted her.

"But life's not a game! It's not like chess. It's not all about black and white. There are gray figures too."

He sat down beside her and took her hands. Gazing at her searchingly, he said, "There's no room for gray figures now. It must be black or white. You're either for us or against us. These people would kill you at the drop of a hat. If you're going to be able to fight them, you need to be prepared to kill too."

"You and I are fighting for a state that upholds the rule of law. A state that doesn't execute people without trial. Promise me, Max, if you have any influence, you'll prevent them harming her."

He rose abruptly. Walking back to the cocktail table, he poured another draft of whiskey. Then he turned.

"All right. I give you my word. You'll need this."

He passed her a flimsy piece of tracing paper, the size of a playing card.

"What is it?"

"A floor plan of the Chancellery. I've marked the location of the private entrance and of Eva Braun's room."

Clara took out a bullet-shaped tube of Elizabeth Arden Velvet Red lipstick from her bag. "It's almost finished, unfortunately," she said, ruefully. "Lord knows when I'll get another one." She folded the paper and rolled it tightly into the nearly empty tube.

Brandt smiled grimly as she returned the lipstick to her bag. He reached over and his fingertips brushed her cheek. His gaze was intense.

"Clara. It's very possible we could fail."

For the first time she heard fear in his voice. She felt a corresponding spark of terror leap inside her.

"If you don't want to take the risk, just say so. No one would blame you."

"I do want to. I'll do it."

ON THE KU'DAMM, the last vestiges of warmth had vanished. As Clara threaded through the crowds, the weight of the secret she possessed pressed down on her. By this time tomorrow, if all went well, the horror that engulfed everyone in Germany could be over. The arrests and persecution would come to an end. She passed a news cabinet housing the latest editions of *Der Stürmer*, which on that day, as so often, bore the banner headline GERMANY AWAKE! THE JEWS ARE OUR MISFORTUNE, and she imagined Steffi Schaeffer's daughter, Nina, kicking it until it shattered—and then kicking in every *Stürmer* cabinet in Berlin, so that a crystal carpet of glass spilled across the streets. The graffiti and Party slogans would be washed away, along with the fear and apprehension in people's eyes. The Hitler Youth would disband, and she could make a visit to England with Erich. She would take him to see the sights—the Houses of Parliament, the Tower of London, a play in the West End. Even introduce him to her family. England and Germany—the two countries she loved. Germany would awake, as if from a bad dream. It would be a fresh beginning.

Back in her apartment, she slid the flimsy floor plan of the Reich Chancellery out of her lipstick tube and pored over it, trying to fix in her brain the route from Eva Braun's bedroom to the private entrance. Along the corridor, turn left, down two flights of stairs, cross the ballroom to a door in the paneling three-quarters of the way along the right-hand wall, then through an underground corridor to the private entrance. She ran and reran the route in her head. Something about it reminded her of one of those Greek myths Leo loved—Ariadne, who used a piece of string to find a way out of the maze. Suddenly Clara was no longer able to stem the tides of memory. What was Leo doing back in England? Was he in an office somewhere, or digging an air-raid shelter in his garden? Trying on a gas mask? Might he even, at that moment, be wondering about her?

When she was satisfied that she had imprinted the twists and turns of the Reich Chancellery interior in her mind, she took the map to the stove in the kitchen. Adding some charcoal, she watched the flames leap up and consume it.

Then she made herself some toast and black tea, put a Bach symphony on the record player, and twiddled the dials of her radio until she found the BBC, keeping the volume set to low and pressing her ear against the set. Through the ether came a sepulchral voice, at once solemn and regretful, like that of a professional undertaker. Prime Minister Neville Chamberlain was broadcasting to the British empire.

How horrible, fantastic, incredible it is that we should be digging trenches and trying on gas masks here because of a quarrel in a faraway country between people of whom we know nothing.

His polite curate's voice ran on, incapable of believing any ill of other human beings.

I have realized vividly how Herr Hitler feels that he must champion other Germans.... He told me privately ... that after this Sudeten German question is settled, that is the end of Germany's territorial claims in Europe.

How gullible the man was! Could he honestly believe that Hitler had no intention of going further?

Mr. Chamberlain wanted Britain to know that he would not rush to war for the sake of the Czech nation.

*However much we may sympathize with a small nation con-
fronted by a big and powerful neighbor, we cannot in all circumstances undertake to involve the whole British empire in war
simply on her account.... War is a fearful thing, and we must be
very clear, before we embark on it.*

Clara felt the sour taste of dismay. If Chamberlain wanted
to signal to Hitler that there would be no British opposition to
his seizure of the Sudetenland, he could not have done it more
clearly.

Eventually, she took a bath, trying to relax. She lay in bed,
waiting for sleep to come, but when it did it was torn by dreams.
Of Leo and Ariadne and herself, hopelessly lost in the maze,
desperate to find the way out.

30

ROSA WAITED UNTIL LUNCH HOUR, WHEN THE FÜHRERIN had left. Then she felt in her pocket again for the card she had kept there.

Rupert Allingham
BUREAU CHIEF
THE DAILY CHRONICLE
KOCHSTRASSE, 50
BERLIN-KREUZBERG

She had liked the English journalist. Apart from their brief exchange, she knew nothing at all about Herr Allingham, but the Führerin had been much taken with him, perhaps because of his handsome blond looks, and he was a journalist, which gave Rosa a kind of fellow feeling. Moreover he was the only person in Berlin—apart from August Gerlach—who had shown the slightest interest in what she had experienced.

There was a dejected air on the streets. The newsstands carried reports of the latest atrocities perpetrated against Germans in the Sudetenland. People seemed to avert their eyes from the grim headlines as they walked, as though

seeking to insulate themselves from the world and all the bad
news it contained. But no matter what was happening beyond
the country's borders, in Berlin, Hitler's building jag continued
unabated. As Rosa skirted the rubble of a construction site, she
looked down at the card in her hand to check the address once
more.

The newspaper district in Kreuzberg was familiar from her
days of applying for journalistic jobs. It was a small grid of
streets, yet it housed the offices of hundreds of enterprises, from
the giant Ullstein and Mosse publishers to the Scherl publishing
empire, as well as the offices of countless printing companies
and photographic agencies. For a long time Rosa had deliberately avoided this part of town, but the sight of Mossehaus,
Erich Mendelsohn's striking, modernist building constructed
for the *Berliner Tageblatt*, sent a fresh thrill through her. With
its sensuous curves of aluminum and glass, as though a space-
ship had landed in the midst of the city, it seemed like a taste of
the future, even if the *Tageblatt* itself, hated by Goebbels, was
rapidly becoming part of the past. Mossehaus was so much more
exciting than Angriff Haus, the dour headquarters of the Nazi
propaganda sheet, with its billowing black banner outside.

She found Rupert Allingham at his desk, eating a bread roll
and sausages. When she knocked on his office door, he looked
up eagerly, as though he was expecting someone else, but when
he saw it was her, his face fell. His eyes were bloodshot and his
face speckled with stubble, and she sensed he had no recollec-
tion of her at all. Her heart sank. Still, she flourished his card
to jog his memory.

"Thank you for seeing me, Herr Allingham. I feel a bit of a
fool. Taking up your time when you could be doing something
more important . . ."

"Not at all."

He gestured towards a chair, and she had to brush cigarette ash from the worn plush before sitting. The office was nothing like any of the places Rosa had visited in her earlier pilgrimages around the newspaper district. It was far dingier and more chaotic. It contained only two chairs, a cheap-looking desk, and a filing cabinet sagging half open like a broken jaw, spilling its contents. A tower of yellowing papers tilted drunkenly against the wall beneath a calendar featuring Brandenburg scenes, and manila files stuffed with cuttings were scattered everywhere. The mantelpiece was stacked with cards and invitations, and in a bookcase she noticed books by authors she was sure had been ruled degenerate.

He gave the décor a desultory wave. "I'm afraid my office assistant has abandoned me to enjoy connubial bliss. Hence" —he nodded weakly at the chaos—"all this. Entropy, I think Mr. Einstein called it, though I doubt even he could make sense of what I find in these papers. Do you read many newspapers? You wouldn't believe how many I have to plow through, though frankly I prefer the arts pages. They're so much less depressing, especially since our farsighted propaganda minister banned negative reviews. However, if you know any fine young woman who would enjoy running a newspaper office, let me know, won't you?"

"I will."

"Though God knows how long I'll be here for. If Winstanley proves awkward, I might be off to Prague. Damn."

He flicked away the trail of ash that Rosa had already noticed on the tweedy lapel of his suit. "Savile Row, though you wouldn't know it."

Rosa smiled nervously. She had no idea what Savile Row was, but she could see that the suit, though decrepit, was beautifully cut.

"I've given up sending my clothes to the cleaners. They're always out of laundry soap, and once they go I never know if I'll see them again. But then that's a common problem in this city, isn't it? Unexplained disappearances."

This rambling discourse, which seemed to be directed at himself as much as at her, was interrupted by a spasm of coughing sounding like a motorcycle engine that had failed to start. Once he had finished, Rupert reached across for a cigarette, tilted his chair back, and regarded her quizzically.

"So. The lady from the Führerin's office. I hope your boss hasn't sent you to check up on me."

"Of course not!"

"Not trying to get me on the books of her marriage bureau?"

"I don't think so."

"I wish I had something to offer you but . . ." He tilted the sausage carton towards her. "We're all out of coffee. And I don't suppose you fancy a brandy?"

She shook her head.

"It's a little early, perhaps, but I won't tell if you don't."

"Really. No. I'm fine, Herr Allingham."

"Then . . ." He gazed at her helplessly. She realized he was genuinely at a loss over why she was there.

Falteringly she began. "When you visited our office the other day, you asked me about the cruise ship I was on this summer. The *Wilhelm Gustloff.* You asked if I enjoyed it, and I told you I didn't. But I want to explain to someone why that was. You see . . . something happened on that ship, and I saw it, but the captain warned me that if I told a single soul, I would never again be permitted on a KdF cruise. I would probably lose my job too. So I did nothing."

His posture remained languid, but his blue eyes had come alive with interest.

"Something happened, you say." He flicked a pen between his fingers.

"Yes. A bad thing. And I think something should be done about it."

Absently, Rupert began cleaning the barrel of his pen with the silk lining of his tie.

"And what exactly should be done?"

"It's been weeks and I can't stop thinking about it. So at the very least I've decided I just have to tell someone. Who do you think I should tell?"

"Why don't you start with me?"

31

CLARA OPENED HER EYES WARILY, LETTING THE SOFT GRAY dawn seep into her soul. Then she sat bolt upright. The apartment was awash with pale morning light. From outside came the customary rattle of shops running up their shutters, trams clattering, and pedestrians disembarking at Nollendorfplatz. Everywhere people were waking, dressing, and preparing for another, ordinary working day, with no hint of the shattering events that were shortly to unfold. Across Berlin, the raiding party would have been issued their arms and grenades, ammunition would have been loaded into automatic weapons, and final preparations for the coup put in place. She imagined the click of guns quietly being loaded in rooms and apartments around the Reich Chancellery, the shuffling of boots, the final cigarettes and the last nervous coughs among the plotters. While Hitler and Eva Braun slept on unawares.

Her head was throbbing from stress and lack of sleep. She went into the bathroom, blinked in the harsh light at the pallid face staring back at her from the mirror, then swallowed a couple of aspirin. She dressed quickly in a burgundy wool skirt and jacket, a look that felt smart but unostentatious, and made herself up more fully than usual, brushing a hint of rouge across the apples of her cheeks and applying a quick spritz of Soir de Paris. One never knew when feminine persuasion would be needed. She chose small pearl earrings and fastened her silver locket at her throat. Picking up her coat, she checked the pockets for anything that might incriminate her, gave a final glance in the mirror, and closed the door behind her.

At precisely three minutes to ten she was crossing Wilhelmplatz, past the Kaiserhof hotel, and facing the entrance to the Reich Chancellery, a blaze of banners spilled like scarlet ink across its somber limestone façade. She paused at the U-Bahn entrance next to a kiosk, pretending to consult that morning's edition of the *Berliner Tageblatt* while she battled overwhelming stage fright. She repeated her plans in her head, the way she rehearsed her lines while standing in the wings on set. *Go directly to Eva's room. Get the key. Open the private door beneath the ballroom. Exit through the Chancellery garden.* Yet, for a few seconds, fear at the scale of the task ahead, and at the penalty she would face if she failed, left her paralyzed to the spot.

Here, so close to the seat of power, the tension felt palpable. In front of the enormous double doors, cars were already drawing up at the steps, disgorging Wehrmacht officers, foreign diplomats, and their entourages. Ministers and Party officials were passing through with reflexive salutes to the waiting sentries, preparing for a day of crisis meetings and military discussions. The feverish atmosphere coming from the Chancellery transmitted itself to passing pedestrians, who glanced across apprehensively as they hurried by. Even the breeze seemed nervous, chivvying the leaves along the gutters and buffeting the papers on the news vendor's kiosk.

The eighteenth-century Reich Chancellery, once occupied by Bismarck, was in the process of being rebuilt. Hitler despised the Wilhelmstrasse extension, declaring its dingy gray frontage fit "only for a soap company" rather than the headquarters of a greater German Reich. He wanted a stage set of imperial majesty. A building vast enough to intimidate visitors and reduce foreign diplomats to a panic of impotence and awe. A personal office the size of a football field to match the dimensions of his ego. All the buildings on the northern side of Voss Strasse had been ruthlessly demolished to make way for a monumental, modernist block designed by Albert Speer, with a courtyard and Ionic columns hung with iron lanterns and a gigantic golden eagle. Six thousand workers had labored day and night for a year. The enormity of the still unfinished enterprise was clearly visible, rising from the last vestiges of scaffolding like a great warship, its granite façade the color of dull steel. As with everything in the Reich, overwhelming ambition was wedded to a breathtaking attention to detail. An immense gallery modeled on Versailles was hung with Gobelin tapestries, beyond which stretched a Great Mosaic Hall, a kind of pagan chapel for the Nazi regime, resembling a glowing cliff of blood-red marble inlaid with glass and gold. Everything about the severe architecture and seemingly endless corridors was designed to intimidate. And to disorientate.

Repressing a shiver, Clara crossed the street, passed through the heavy bronze doors, and entered the Ehrenhof, the Hall of Honor. The vast courtyard, flanked by stone pillars, led to a gateway, guarded by massive twin statues, representing the Party and the Army. Her heels echoed on the stone flags as she made her way to the reception area, where a black-tunicked guard waited behind a glass-partitioned desk. There was no going back now. Her part in this life-or-death enterprise had begun.

"I'm visiting Fräulein Braun."

He extended a hand for her documents, then another guard leaned over. Both wore black uniforms set off by white belts and scarlet Party armbands. They must be, she recalled, the SS special guard. What had Brandt said? *They look like ordinary reception officers, but they are trained to recognize people of interest.* She fixed her attention on the man in front of her, focusing on the gleam of his head through the shaved prickles of his scalp.

"One moment, Fräulein."

He picked up a telephone, closing the glass partition so that she could not hear the conversation. Clara's pulse sounded so loudly in her ears she could swear it was audible.

A few moments later, the guard replaced the receiver. He continued to scrutinize her papers with a furrowed brow.

"What is your relationship with Fräulein Braun?"

"I'm a friend."

"Is this your first visit?"

"Here, yes." She tried a broad smile. He ignored it.

"And what is the nature of the visit?"

A lighthearted shrug. "What do most women do when they get together?"

The guard didn't know, or if he did, he wasn't letting on, so she added, "We gossip! We always have so much to talk about. And she likes to ask me about my films." Was that reckless? Did it identify her as a member of the cultural elite, perhaps one of those dangerous freethinkers who might pose a danger to the Führer's innocent girlfriend? There was a glimmer of suspicion in the officer's eyes and he seemed poised to question her further, but at that moment a detachment of officers and politicians arrived and he gave Clara a curt nod.

"This officer will escort you."

It would be hard to find a greater contrast to the rustic simplicity of the Berghof than the severe classicism of the new Reich Chancellery. It was like being in a great, marble-lined cathedral to some austere god. The cavernous recesses of the hall bounced the echoes of her footsteps back at her like rifle shots. They passed bronzes of athletes rippling with muscles and vases two feet high overflowing with chrysanthemums. Grand pianos and candelabras groaning with crystal. Everything was finished in minute detail, from the mosaic inlaid floors, the gilded pillars, and the lintels with sculptures to the wrough-iron medieval sconces. At the far side of the hall Clara glimpsed a lavish ballroom abutted by a winter garden, a fixture in every grand German edifice, with tropical leaves crowding the glass.

Yet nothing, that day, was quite routine. The chilly front hall was as crowded as the Anhalter Bahnhof at rush hour. Knots of diplomats and ministers milled in the corridors, and army officers with braided uniforms bustled swiftly past as Clara and the guard went up a wide staircase. As they crossed the gleaming halls, she craned her head to see into the rooms. She glimpsed a dining room, being set with cutlery and white napkins, and protected by an SS adjutant who stood vigilantly on a mat so his boots and rifle butt would not scuff the pristine marble floor.

At the end of the corridor a sleek cluster of officers stood chatting. As she approached, Clara saw with a jolt that at the center of the group was Ulrich Welzer. Their eyes locked for an instant and she discerned in his face an animal fear, that the plot would be discovered, that before the day had passed they would find themselves chained in the bowels of Prinz-Albrecht-Strasse, before an ignominious end at the guillotine at Plötzensee prison. Another second and Welzer had turned on his heel and was gone.

Her guide led her up another flight of stairs and turned right into the upper floor of the Old Chancellery. In this wing, Clara knew from the floor plan, lay the Führer's private domain. Here his bedroom, private study, and bathroom, as well as Eva Braun's own suite, were located. Here the corridors were fustily carpeted and the dark green wallpaper gave off the faded grandeur of an expensive hotel long past its prime. The walls were hung with dull, gold-framed still lifes of fruit, half-peeled oranges, or blowsy roses, and landscapes of valleys and village churches.

At the end of the corridor, the guard stopped at a heavy wooden door and rapped sharply.

"A visitor, Fräulein Braun."

Eva Braun loved to dress in bold colors, and the patterned tea dress in vivid yellow and blue she wore that morning was no exception. But it was the only lively thing about her. Her face, beneath freshly bleached hair, was pale and her eyes puffy, as though she had been recently crying. She looked little better than the last time Clara had seen her, slumped in her Munich apartment with half a bottle of sleeping tablets inside her.

The guard clicked his heels. Eva nodded listlessly and closed the door behind Clara.

"This is a surprise."

Clara smiled and clasped her hands. "I'm so sorry, Eva. I should probably have telephoned first. But I wanted to see how you were . . . after the other day."

"Then I suppose I should thank you."

Eva led the way into her quarters. "See what I mean about this place?" she asked.

It was easy to see how this room might have suited its earlier occupant, the former president of Germany, the octogenarian Hindenburg. Everything in the décor, from the heavy, gilded oil paintings and dull curtains to the massive furniture, was eighty years out of date. This was an old man's domain, dominated by a giant portrait of the man himself, with baggy poached-egg eyes, handlebar mustache, and chest groaning with medals. Eva's makeup and hairbrushes, scattered carelessly across the Biedermeier dressing table, looked like a doll's things, and her clothes were a colorful jumble inside Hindenburg's vast wardrobe. Even her perfume smelled sweetly incongruous in that gloomy air. The bed, its clammy sheets topped with a canopy of tasseled emerald damask, looked about as inviting as a funeral bier. The only thing not out of the nineteenth century was the light dance music issuing from the wireless.

Eva clicked off the music. She reached for a packet of cigarettes, pausing to light one and offering it to Clara.

"Sorry. I didn't mean to sound rude. Actually, I'm terribly glad to have someone to talk to. You've no idea how awful it's been since we arrived."

She curled up in an armchair, tucked her feet beneath her, and motioned to Clara to sit beside her.

"I *hate* it here. He wouldn't let me bring my friend Herta, so I'm all alone. It's bad enough being in this horrible room and never seeing Wolf, but I can't even go out when I please. He says it's a difficult time and that I need to be invisible. Imagine that, I can't even walk out of the door!" She pouted mutinously. "He got his aide to tell me I had to stay in my room all day today. Cooped up all day! Because there was important political business going on. Anyone would think I was a schoolgirl sent to her room! I feel like Rapunzel in the tower. I wouldn't be surprised if I *died* here. I tell you, I used to go to boarding school—it was a horrible Catholic place outside Munich and I loathed it—but this is far worse."

"Perhaps you should have stayed in Munich."

"He insisted I come. I don't know why. Because when I get here it's always the same story. I sit here *waiting* while my whole life slips by." She ran her fingers through her hair defiantly. "I've a good mind to march downstairs and start playing the piano in front of the lot of them."

Clara knew she would do no such thing. The fires of rebellion burned weakly in Eva, and any act of mutiny would most probably be visited on herself. No doubt that was why Hitler had brought her here—to keep an eye on her. Just in case she was tempted to have another episode with the sleeping pills.

"There's almost nothing I'm allowed to do anymore. Would you believe Bormann even stopped me writing a diary?"

This remark, uttered so casually, struck Clara like a hammer blow.

"So you don't . . . ?"

"I had a lovely green leather book I'd kept since I was a girl. I'd note down all my thoughts and plans and dreams, you know, as well as everything that happened to me. But a few years ago someone got hold of a few pages of it and Bormann went *crazy*. *Never* write anything down, that's what he told me. *Don't* leave a trail. Memorize. That's what you actresses do, isn't it? You just remember things?"

Clara reached over and touched Eva lightly. "I've been worried about you, Eva. After the other day."

"I was silly. I shouldn't have."

"You said something had happened. That people would be angry with you."

Eva picked at the hem of her skirt.

"I wonder," persisted Clara. "I mean, I think I've guessed what the problem is."

Eva looked up, startled.

"You're pregnant, aren't you?"

A jolt of horror crossed Eva's pale features. Then she laughed, a wild, hysterical laugh, which eventually caught in her throat and made her choke.

"I shouldn't laugh . . ." She wiped her eyes as she recovered herself. "You don't know how funny that is. Except it's not funny at all."

She took a deep drag of her cigarette and exhaled sideways. Then she said: "There's something you don't know about me. I have no womb. I was born without one. It's called Mayer-Rokitansky syndrome. So I couldn't get pregnant if I tried." Her voice wobbled. "I can *never* have children."

"Oh, Eva, I'm so sorry!"

"I've hardly told anyone." She sniffed and blinked away the glittering tears in her eyes. "I take . . . you know . . . precautions like any other woman, and I swore my mother to secrecy. But I *love* children."

"What does the Führer say about this?"

"He doesn't know."

"So if he doesn't know . . ."

"Goebbels found out," Eva said flatly.

"You told Goebbels?"

"Don't be insane! I wouldn't tell Goebbels the time of day! I've no idea how he found out. Perhaps Dr. Morell told him." Eva dragged a handkerchief from her sleeve and sniffed. "Now I'm *terrified* he'll tell Himmler."

"Why would he do that?"

"Maybe Himmler has a secret on him, so he gives Himmler my secret in return."

"Would that really matter?"

Tears gleamed on the girl's pallid cheeks like rain on wet stone.

Though Clara's nerves were straining for sounds of activity

in the building below, she found herself transfixed by the younger woman's predicament. Marooned in her private misery, the Führer's girlfriend seemed entirely impervious to a world in deadly, escalating crisis around her.

"Wolf is always talking about what women are for. And Himmler says childbearing is the *only* purpose of women. Women are about safeguarding racial purity and providing the next generation. The other day at the Berghof he told me his latest idea is that women who can't bear children should never be allowed to marry. And men who are married to barren women should be permitted to divorce them immediately. What would that mean for me and Wolf?"

Gently, Clara said, "But you're not married to the Führer."

"Not now. But Wolf has said he will marry me. I finally got him to promise and he said he would after . . . well, after . . ."

"After what?"

Eva shrugged. "After some time has passed."

Clara checked her watch. Ten forty. Very soon she was going to have to persuade the unhappy girl in front of her to hand over the key to the private entrance. Pulling aside the heavy damask curtain, she glanced out at the Wilhelmstrasse below. Just yards from here, in a string of secret apartments and houses, men were preparing to launch an audacious coup. Officers were readying weapons and grenades. Colonel Oster, Ulrich Welzer, and Max Brandt were gathering the surge of courage they needed to make their daring move.

Eva sprang up skittishly, joining Clara at the window and squeezing her arm. "I'm so glad you're here, Clara! It's wonderful to have company."

"Doesn't anyone else visit?"

"Hardly. Wolf suggested I read, but there's nothing to read here except great dusty old tomes about . . . I don't know, Bismarck and people. And no one ever visits me here except the girl from Ludwig Scherk's. I had her come over a few months ago because I wanted a fragrance for Wolf and I needed her to bring some samples, and we got quite friendly. She told me some really fascinating things about perfume. But I haven't seen her for ages."

The clock outside chimed. Fifteen minutes to go. Beneath them, cars were still drawing up at the Chancellery entrance. The distinctive figure of the French ambassador, François-Poncet, in homburg and spotted bow tie, hurried from his limousine.

Eva's eyes followed Clara's.

"It's busy today."

"It seems so."

"It's something to do with the Czech crisis. That's why he's put me in Schutzhaft." She meant it ironically. *Schutzhaft*, "protective custody," was the term the Gestapo used for brutal detention without trial.

"You won't tell anyone, will you, Clara? About my problem?"

"I promise. I won't tell anyone, Eva." Clara took Eva's hands in hers. "On one condition."

Eva reeled away from her. Dismay and incomprehension clouded her eyes.

"What do you mean? I thought I could trust you!"

"You can, I promise."

"You're one of Goebbels's spies, aren't you? One of those actresses he sleeps with? You must be, you've had so many roles. They say all the most successful actresses have to sleep with him. Is that why you made friends with me? Is that why you came to the house when I'd taken the pills?"

"Of course not! Don't be absurd." Clara was soothing, terrified that Eva's raised voice might attract the attention of the guards. "I'm not Goebbels's spy. I came to your house that day because I had a feeling."

"People don't have *feelings*!"

"Some of us do," Clara said. "Don't worry, Eva. I'm asking only a little thing. Just between us women. You remember that man I was talking about? That sturmbannführer?"

"Steinbrecher? The one who's sweet on you?"

"That's him. He's in the lobby downstairs. And to be honest, it's a bit awkward." She gave a wry smile. "I don't want to encounter him again. For personal reasons." She paused to let the feminine implications sink in. "And I remember you saying you use a private entrance to the Reich Chancellery."

"I have to. In case anyone sees me." Eva grimaced. "In case Magda Goebbels or that bitch Emmy Goering or any of the other wives discover that little Miss No Private Life is in town."

"So would you mind if I borrowed the key? So I could avoid him?"

Eva frowned.

"The entrance is rather awkward to find. You have to cross the ballroom and find a door set into the paneling, but I can't show you the way. I don't dare. Wolf has absolutely banned me from leaving this room."

Clara shook her head. The route to the private entrance was seared into her mind. "Don't worry. I can always ask—"

"No! You mustn't do that! The private entrance is confidential. Almost no one knows it exists! Hardly anyone has a key. If you said you were going there it would cause all sorts of fuss. They'd probably arrest you. Wolf would be furious. It's a security issue."

"I'll be very discreet."

Eva frowned at her doubtfully. Then, to Clara's relief, she shrugged.

"Okay. It's a door set into the paneling exactly two-thirds of the way down on the right-hand side of the ballroom. There's no handle. You have to know exactly which panel it is and push it. Then it leads out into the garden. You can borrow the key. I'm not going anywhere today. But you must return it later. Mark it for me and leave it with the guard at reception. And seal the envelope tight!"

Clara wondered what the next hour would bring for Eva Braun. Arrest, almost certainly. And terror. Perhaps pain. She felt a stab of guilt at her role in the young woman's fate. Then she reminded herself of Steffi Schaeffer and her daughter, Nina, and everyone else who had suffered or was suffering under the regime of Eva's beloved Wolf.

"I promise."

"Don't bother to promise. I've learned not to believe anyone's promises."

Nonetheless, she gave Clara the key.

CLARA MOVED SWIFTLY ALONG the corridor, her footsteps drowned in the deep carpet. The floor plan seared into her mind told her that she needed to pass the library and descend two floors by the main staircase, then turn left and thread back through the ballroom. The little brass key weighed in her pocket. By her reckoning she had precisely seven minutes to find the hidden door and open it. Even now, the infantry would be making their way from Potsdam and the chief of staff would be escorted from the Bendlerstrasse to arrest Hitler himself.

She descended the first set of stairs and saw, immediately opposite, a sentry guarding a door framed by a pair of caryatids. On the sleeve of his black uniform was embroidered in silver ADOLF HITLER, identifying him as a select Leibstandarte bodyguard. He stiffened as she passed, and she felt fear pushing against the inside of her skin like something alive. But he didn't challenge her, so she continued quickly along the corridor until she reached the second set of stairs. As she stood at the top of the steps, she became aware of a new level of frenetic activity, like a hive that has been stirred, an angry mixture of adrenaline and excitement. All around the marble hall were echoing voices, slamming doors, the bleat of telephones in distant rooms.

She took a ragged breath, then crossed the cavernous hall with confidence, making for the corridor that led north, towards the ballroom. From up ahead came the sound of hurried footsteps, and she saw officers approaching. At their center walked Goering and von Ribbentrop.

Fighting a powerful urge to retreat, Clara attempted to slow her racing heart. What if she was recognized? It could not be more terrifying to enter Hades and meet the god of the underworld than to encounter von Ribbentrop, the man who suspected her of being a spy. The advancing men occupied the entire width of the corridor, their conversation a harsh jangle, which resounded off the stone walls. There was no chance she could avoid them.

Opening the door immediately beside her, Clara stepped inside.

The room she now stood in was dominated by a massive table, set as if for a meeting, with paper pads, ink, blotters, and ashtrays. Each chair showcased an eagle and swastika on its back. This had to be Hitler's cabinet room. The place where his inner circle met to debate, in the days when there was still any semblance of debate about the Führer's aggressive plans.

Clara reminded herself that, if she were caught, Eva Braun would vouch for her presence in the Chancellery. She was just making a friendly visit. It was all perfectly plausible. But why would a casual friend be hiding in the cabinet room?

The footsteps halted outside the half-opened door. From her vantage point Clara could see a slice of Goering, his vast bulk swathed in Luftwaffe gray, his huge feet in gleaming shoes, and beside him von Ribbentrop, with his back to her. The swell of voices grew louder. They were talking about war. And they were about to enter the room.

Every fiber in her body froze, except for the tiny twitching muscle next to her left eye. As she shrank behind the door, she realized that Goering and von Ribbentrop were arguing. She caught only broken phrases: "Luftwaffe power . . . entirely inadequate to destroy London" and then, "There's no money for war."

Suddenly, Goering's voice rose to a bellow. "You're a warmonger and a criminal fool, von Ribbentrop. I know what war is, and I don't want to go through it again! I tell you, if war breaks out, you can sit beside me in the first bomber!"

His footsteps echoed off down the corridor, forcing his followers to keep pace. Von Ribbentrop, too, strode away. Clara realized that she had been holding her breath and, after they passed, let it out in a great sigh.

IN ONLY A FEW more minutes she needed to reach the private entrance or the raiding party waiting for access would be halted in the garden. She slipped out of the cabinet room and kept walking down the hall to the ballroom, but as soon as she entered she saw her task would be more difficult than she had imagined.

The ballroom was a relatively recent addition—created to accommodate the increasing numbers of visitors invited for

Nazi receptions. Grand chandeliers hung from the ceiling, and its walls were bare and white as an iced wedding cake. Great pillars of red marble flanked each side of the room, and in between the pillars were blanks of ivory paneling, as pristine and untrammeled as a sheet of snow. The door was, according to Eva, set two-thirds of the way down on the right. Or was it three-quarters? Clara searched the length of the wall for anything that might stand out. It took several scans before she saw it. A slightly thicker panel, with the shadow of a dark slit at the top. Swiftly, she crossed the room, pushed the panel, and a door opened.

The contrast between the ballroom she had just left and the corridor she found herself in could not have been more stark. It was pitch-dark and icy cold. The trademark cast-iron wall sconces Hitler favored in his nostalgia for some medieval Germanic past were unlit. The brickwork was as damp as a dungeon; the sour smell of wet concrete hung in the air. Fumbling along, Clara almost tripped when she reached the first in the flight of ten steps that led steeply down towards a heavy steel door. That had to be the air-raid shelter. Turning blindly right, she fumbled for a second door. Grappling in the dark, she found a chilly steel handle and with her fingers located the keyhole.

She took the key from her pocket, turned it in the lock, and walked up another ten steps into the light.

CLARA MUST HAVE PASSED the Reich Chancellery in Wilhelmstrasse a hundred times, yet it was still a revelation to find several acres of garden behind its high walls. The garden was designed on the same monumental scale as the Chancellery itself. Spacious lawns were bisected by graveled paths, and roses bloomed the length of the block from Wilhelmstrasse right through to Hermann-Goering-Strasse. On the far side a barracks had been built to house Hitler's personal guard, and flanking the terrace were two giant bronze horses. Directly opposite them, facing Hitler's study, was an orangery—more of a small glass palace—dedicated to the cultivation of the Führer's vegetables. The only actual gardening was being performed by a young man about a hundred yards away, hoeing a bed of roses around the base of an ornamental pool. Of the conspirators, there was no sign.

Slipping the key back in her pocket, Clara stepped into the garden, leaving the door ajar. Her pulse was racing. She had not thought properly about what she should do at this point. She had simply assumed that Welzer's party of soldiers would be ready and waiting for her.

She threaded her way along a gravel walk skirting the back of the old presidential palace, directly beneath what she knew was Hitler's bedroom and private study. She compelled herself to walk calmly, as though she had every reason to be strolling in Hitler's private garden on a busy weekday morning. God forbid she should encounter the Führer himself, hands clasped behind his back, in his habitual stroll. Nerves jangling, she detected, at the far side of the garden, a sentry emerging from the guardhouse with a black dog tugging on its tight leash, its long pink tongue lolling. The animal had not noticed her, and the pair seemed to be heading away from her, but how long would it be before that dog scented her presence, and alerted its keeper to an intruder?

Then she saw it. A narrow aperture that formed a claustrophobic alley, barely two feet wide, running along the side of the Agricultural Ministry building. It extended more than a hundred feet between the two buildings, culminating in a wrought-iron gate. Trying not to betray her fear by running, she pushed the gate open, to find herself back in the bustle of dizzying pedestrians and traffic on the Wilhelmstrasse.

She hesitated as the sounds of the city rose up around her, and glanced swiftly down the street, her nerves thrumming, scanning for any signal that could signify the approach of the conspirators. At that moment a man exited the bronze double doors of the Chancellery to her right and strode purposefully towards her.

Ulrich Welzer's chiseled face was an impenetrable mask. Terror was coming off him like an electric current as he neared Clara.

"Thank God," he muttered, under his breath. He avoided her eyes.

She glanced behind him in bewilderment. "What's going on?"

"It's off."

"Off? Has something happened?"

Suddenly his face shuttered, and Clara turned her head to see another uniform approaching. It took less than a second to recognize the razor-blade cheekbones and the aquiline profile. Obergruppenführer Reinhard Heydrich.

Fear insinuated itself, trailing down her spine, nearly buckling her knees.

"Well? Don't keep us all waiting, Colonel Welzer. Has something happened?" Heydrich's narrow eyes ranged over her.

Welzer jerked himself to attention, clicking his heels and giving a knife-sharp salute.

"Wonderful news, Herr Obergruppenführer! News has come from Britain. Chamberlain has agreed to fly to Germany. Herr Mussolini wants Hitler to postpone mobilization for twenty-four hours and the Führer has agreed. The British ambassador, Nevile Henderson, has just arrived at the Reich Chancellery.

The conference will be held tomorrow morning in Munich. The Führer is heading down to meet Mussolini tonight."

"To Munich?" Heydrich repeated, his face alive with calculating tension, his eyes already scanning the Chancellery doors as if eager to insert himself at the center of events.

"Herr Mussolini won't come to Berlin. The Führer will leave from the Anhalter Bahnhof within hours."

Heydrich pivoted and marched off towards the Chancellery without a word. Welzer turned stiffly to Clara.

"And now I should let you leave, Fräulein." His gaze locked on hers. "It's indeed wonderful news, isn't it?"

"Yes," she repeated numbly. "Wonderful news."

WHEN CLARA CLOSED THE DOOR OF HER APARTMENT behind her and looked at herself in the mirror, a ghost stared back at her. Her lips were bloodless, and, as a delayed reaction to the tension, a violent shaking ran through her body.

So Chamberlain was making an eleventh-hour trip to dissuade Hitler from military action. How could he be so blind as to believe that Hitler posed no further threat to Europe?

Inside her pocket the key to the Reich Chancellery private entrance weighed heavily. How long would it be before Eva guilelessly mentioned that she had given away her key to the private door? And even if she didn't, what would happen when some part of the plot was inevitably exposed? Everyone who had been in the Reich Chancellery that day would be arrested and interrogated. She prayed Max was lying low somewhere.

She paced around the apartment, unable to settle. It was only a matter of time before the actions of that morning caught up with her. It could be days, but it was more likely hours. Her only hope was that in the rush to board the Führer's special train to Munich, Eva would be too preoccupied to worry about the missing key. Too busy joyfully packing up her clothes and perfume samples, delighted to escape her Berlin prison. The thought of Eva's perfume samples recalled something else—a remark that had been hammering at the doors of Clara's mind since she heard it. Eva's comment about her only acquaintance in Berlin. *The girl from Ludwig Scherk's.*

Scherk's was one of the biggest cosmetic companies in Berlin. Everything about it was enormously successful; even its headquarters—a red-brick modernist building in Steglitz—had won a clutch of architectural prizes. Advertisements for bestselling Scherk products like Arabian Nights perfume, a concoction of sandalwood and amber, or the Mystikum powder compact, could be found in every glossy magazine. But its cosmetics weren't limited to women. Scherk's Tarr pomade was Goebbels's favorite and, according to Magda, revealed in one of her periodic fits of jealousy, he had selected an especially pretty salesgirl to bring his personalized supplies to the Propaganda Ministry. Could that be a coincidence, or might Goebbels have recommended his own salesgirl to Eva? What better way to spy on the Führer's girlfriend than to have a young woman befriend her and report back, with all the snippets of gossip and the confidences that such a relationship involved? Wasn't that exactly what Clara was doing herself?

This was Eva's life. Spied on from every quarter. Unable to bear children for her Führer. Befriended on all sides by people who would happily betray her.

Clara took up the bottle of Scent of Secrets that Eva Braun had made for her, inhaling the deep, voluptuous scent. Perfume was Eva's small act of mutiny against a lover who despised cosmetics of any kind. But her mutiny was nothing compared to the real dissent that existed beneath the surface of this country. All over Germany people were carrying out their own individual acts of resistance against the regime, from the citizens who avoided the Hitler salute to Helga Schmidt, who had loved repeating jokes about the Führer until she was silenced. Even little Nina Schaeffer, kicking down the cabinets of *Der Stürmer*. But what did any of those acts of defiance amount to, when men as powerful as Admiral Canaris, the head of the Abwehr, and Arthur Nebe, the chief of police, had failed to topple Hitler? All resistance was destined to be crushed like flowers in the path of a Panzer tank.

If Hitler was to be stopped, force would have to come from further afield. From England or France. From the men at their desks in Whitehall, with their calm assumption that Clara would carry out whatever task they asked of her, no matter what the risk to her personal safety.

It's what you do, isn't it?

Instantly her thoughts turned to the meeting she had set up through the advertisement she'd persuaded Rupert to place in his newspaper. "Berlin lady seeks London employer. German and Latin tuition possible. Tel: Berlin 1845."

If London Films had found her message and interpreted it correctly, the contact should be waiting at the Siegessäule at 6:45 P.M. tomorrow to learn the results of her encounter with Eva Braun. Yet what would Clara be able to tell them? Her heart sank. Apart from the facts that Eva had tried to kill herself and was unable to have children and was more interested in the affairs of film stars than in her lover's lethal intentions in Europe, Clara had uncovered nothing. Her mission had failed.

A knock on the door caused her to gasp. Had a security check identified her as a visitor to the Reich Chancellery? Had Eva already mentioned that the actress Clara Vine had borrowed her private key? She gave a frantic glance in the mirror, readying herself like the actress she was, and braced herself to find out.

She opened the door to find the lean figure of her new neighbor, Herr Engel, rimless glasses glinting and a smile on his smooth, thin-lipped face. Faint strains of Baroque music, which Clara recognized as Telemann's Piano Suite in A Major, issued from his opened door. He cast a curious glance past Clara, into her apartment.

"I hope I'm not interrupting."

Clara wedged herself in the doorway to block his view. "Do you need something, Herr Engel?"

Her hostility disconcerted him. He frowned. "Some visitors called for you earlier. I thought I should let you know."

"Visitors? Did they say what they wanted?"

"I didn't think it was my business to ask." A small wince of elaboration. "I think they may have been policemen."

"Oh? Did they say so?"

"No."

"Then what gave you that impression?"

"Just something about them."

Clara was silent.

He bent towards her, lowering his voice.

"Forgive me, Fräulein Vine, for presuming, but I told them you were out. I explained you were probably away filming and I wasn't sure when you would return. I advised them not to bother coming back for the next few days."

Why had Herr Engel said that? Why had he vouched for her?

"I said if I saw you I'd let you know someone had called. I asked if they wanted to leave a message, but they said it wouldn't be necessary."

Clara's heart plummeted, but she maintained an air of polite curiosity.

"So when exactly was this?"

"It must have been about ten this morning."

Ten o'clock? That was impossible. It was before she had even set foot in the Chancellery. An hour before the coup attempt.

"Are you certain?"

"I was listening to the wireless. I would normally be at work, but my rounds don't start today until one."

"Your rounds?"

"I'm a doctor."

"A doctor?" she repeated dumbly.

"Yes. Doktor Franz Engel. I work in the children's department of the Charité."

Looking at the gaunt figure more carefully now, she suddenly realized that she had been entirely mistaken about him. She had taken the severe-looking stranger for an informer, and assumed that his arrival in the neighboring apartment was just another hazard to be wary of. Instead, he was merely another good citizen, a doctor who worked with children, who played Telemann on his gramophone, who was going about his business like everyone else, trying to keep a low profile.

Relief and the stress of the day came together. To her horror, Clara felt tears sting her eyes. Politely, the doctor looked away.

Gently he asked, "Is there anything wrong, Fräulein Vine?"

"Nothing. I've been working a lot recently. I'm just tired . . ."

His eyes studied her. Then he said, "I mustn't disturb you then. I simply wanted to let you—and only you—know."

"Thank you Herr—Doktor—Engel. I'm very grateful."

"Not at all. Just being a good neighbor."

He smiled kindly and disappeared. That was the thing about this new Berlin. Everyone in the city was an actor. Everyone was playing a part, but it was impossible sometimes to know what parts they were playing.

33

C LARA APPROACHED BERLIN'S VICTORY COLUMN, THE Siegessäule, at twenty minutes to seven, her coat belted tightly and her hair twisted up beneath an anonymous gray trilby. Under one arm she carried a copy of *Berlin Illustrated*, and in her pocket was her fallback, a ticket to a KdF concert at the Volkstheater Berlin on Kant Strasse. She had never felt so tired. Yet the events of the previous day and the last-minute failure of the coup had left her in a sickening state of perpetual alert.

That morning the conference had been held in the Führer's apartment in Prinzregentenplatz. The *Berlin Illustrated* carried pictures of Hitler, a red carpet rolling out from the steps of the Führerbau for the signing of the Munich agreement, and Daladier, Mussolini, and Chamberlain sitting on the same scarlet sofa where Hitler and Eva Braun first became lovers. The leaders agreed that Hitler's annexation of the Sudetenland should be permitted. Within ten days, Czech troops would evacuate the Sudetenland.

The photograph of Chamberlain waving the paper in the air at Heston Airport had gone round the world. Chamberlain and Hitler had signed an agreement "never to go to war again." The prime minister's triumphant gesture reminded Clara of the autograph hunters who congregated outside the Ufa Palast after a premiere, gleefully waving their books with the signature of their favorite star. Chamberlain and his wife had appeared on the balcony of Buckingham Palace with George VI and Queen Elizabeth, and outside, the palace crowds had cheered. Three van loads of flowers had been delivered to Number Ten.

Hitler's popularity had never been greater.

The Siegessäule was a popular meeting spot and had a special place in the affections of Berliners. They joked that the golden angel on its two-hundred-foot-high peak was the only virgin left in Berlin, because she was the only one safely out of Goebbels's reach.

That evening there were several people milling around the base of the tower, but no sign of anyone who might be from London Films. Clara scanned the faces, focusing on single men who might possibly be her contact, and fixed on a man with a briefcase looking twitchy, until he was joined by a woman in a trench coat and swung his arm jubilantly round her shoulder. Although the night was drawing in and the light falling, there were still plenty of people taking an evening constitutional with their dogs among the Tiergarten's winding gravel paths, but she identified no remotely likely candidate. No solitary figure, hesitating in the shadows.

As the traffic swirled round the roundabout, Clara made a couple of circuits of the monument and checked her watch. 6:45 P.M. She would give it another few minutes and then leave. She was about to pivot away when a drift of air from behind caused her to look around.

Her heart turned over.

"Max?" she said, astonished.

The vigor had left him, and he seemed tense and drained. An errant lock of hair fell into his eyes.

"What are you doing here?"

"Clara, I need to speak to you."

"Why are you here?"

"I wanted to see you. It might be the last time. Come."

He drew her away, crossing the road and leading her into the shelter of the trees. Clara cast a swift glance back at the Siegessäule and decided that the contact from London Films would have to wait.

"Let's walk quickly. The place is teeming with agents."

"My God, why?"

"Heydrich's men, the SD, have an operation on this evening—they're aiming to catch a Czech agent who has a rendezvous in the Tiergarten—so all the agents have been dressed as gardeners and equipped with rakes."

Shocked, Clara scanned the park looking for the blur of a face or the glint of metal under the canopy of trees. How could her own surveillance have been so careless?

Some distance into the park, a rose garden was laid out— a souvenir of the original eighteenth-century French-style modeling of the Tiergarten—and as they passed, the pale blur of roses stood out in the gloom, their fragrance swallowed up in the chill evening air. Still gripping her arm, Max led her along an avenue flanked by bronze statues of Prussian statesmen and mythological creatures.

"I don't have much time." His tone was low and urgent. "I need to leave Germany. The Gestapo is on my heels. I'll be given a safe berth in England, of course, just so long as I can get past the border, but they've put an alert out to arrest me on sight." He laughed bitterly. "They say Hitler is Europe's greatest travel agent because he has everyone on the move. That's certainly the case for me."

Alarm cascaded through her. "Has something leaked?"

"I'm glad for your sake, Clara, that this has nothing to do with the plot."

"But then . . . what?" She was bewildered.

"I have Madame Chanel to thank for my situation."

"Chanel?"

"Remember that evening in Chanel's salon? There was a man there. You asked about him."

Clara pictured the salon again and tried, through the dancing couples and the dazzle of jewels, to visualize the person she had vaguely recognized, a handsome officer with thick hair brushed back from a broad forehead and wide-set eyes. "Walter Schellenberg. That's what you said."

"SS Oberführer Walter Schellenberg. A very charming diplomatic intelligence officer. He's just been promoted, actually. He works in the Sicherheitsdienst. He's Heydrich's number two. It seems Chanel reported her suspicions of me to Schellenberg. He took them back to his boss."

"He came all the way to Paris to check you out?"

"Oh no. I was just unlucky. Schellenberg was not in Paris to expose a treacherous cultural attaché—he was on an entirely different mission. A very specific request for Coco Chanel. Heydrich had overheard Fräulein Braun talking at a dinner about her plan to create a cologne for Hitler."

"That's right. She told me about it too. And Heydrich wanted to help?"

"How sweet you are, Clara! Heydrich's motives are never the kindly ones that people like you imagine. No, Heydrich became aware that Eva Braun had asked a young woman to bring samples of perfume into the Reich Chancellery."

"I know about that. It was a girl from Ludwig Scherk's. I think Goebbels may have recommended her."

"Well, Heydrich didn't think her motives were so innocent. He got the idea that perfume would be an ideal method of poisoning the Führer."

"Poisoning him?"

"Exactly. What could be better? A perfume that was also a poison. Something so innocent, yet so intimate. Heydrich knew nothing about this young woman except that she was turning up regularly at the Reich Chancellery with samples and bottles for the Führer's mistress, so the paranoid bastard immediately suspected a plot to kill the Führer. Extraordinary, isn't it, that he should see plots where there were none, but miss the one that was going on under his nose?"

"Is it possible to poison someone with perfume?"

"That's precisely what Schellenberg was sent to find out. He was to ask Chanel if a perfume could also be a poison."

Clara's thoughts were racing. She recalled Eva's words. *You'd never think perfume would contain strange, synthetic molecules, would you?*

"And what did Chanel say?" she asked urgently.

"Chanel assured him there was no better thing than perfume to get under a person's skin."

"Did you know all about this that night in Paris?"

"No. Not until much later. It was Canaris who told me. When I first heard rumors of a plan to unseat Hitler, in late August, I made straight for Berlin and sought him out. Canaris welcomed my involvement and announced he was bringing me into the Abwehr, claiming my contacts in France would be useful to military intelligence, but in reality, it was so that he could afford me some protection. He introduced me to the officers here who were preparing the coup."

"But this woman with the perfume? Was she really planning to poison Hitler?"

"Heydrich installed a man in her workplace to watch her. This man got friendly with her and reported back her gossip. Apparently she told him she had some great scheme concerning the Führer's girlfriend."

"A scheme?"

"That's all she said, according to Heydrich's spy. When he pressed her, she clammed up. Went all secretive on him. But what would she have to be secretive about, if it wasn't some plot against the Führer?"

"So why didn't Heydrich arrest her at once?"

"He ordered her arrest, but she left town in a hurry. She disappeared on a cruise ship and hasn't been heard of since."

A cruise ship. The invisible pattern that Clara's mind had been searching for leapt out vividly before her, like a tapestry with its last stitch in place. She finally understood.

"Heydrich had his man follow her," continued Max. "But nothing came of it."

Nothing came of it, because the girl from Ludwig Scherk's was Ada Freitag, the girl Erich had met on the *Wilhelm Gustloff* and whose disappearance had caused him such anxiety. That was why Rupert had been warned not to pursue the story any further. That was why her file had vanished. It explained why the Kriminalpolizei said the missing girl should stay missing.

"I just . . ."

"What?" He leaned closer in the dark.

Clara didn't reply. The more you knew the more risk you ran, especially when Heydrich was on your tail.

"It seems wild to imagine this woman might have actually thought she could poison Hitler."

"Does it? She had some ulterior motive, Canaris said. No one makes friends with Fräulein Braun for the sake of her company. You of all people should know that."

They had reached the fringes of the Königsplatz, where the smoke-blackened Reichstag building, which had never been fully repaired since the fire five years previously, gleamed like a dirty fossil in the lamplight.

"As it happens, I did learn something that evening in Paris," Max continued. "Walter Schellenberg had a secondary purpose for being there. It hasn't escaped the Nazis' notice that Chanel is supremely well connected with the British establishment. Before I met you that evening, Schellenberg had had a quiet talk with me. He wanted to know if I thought Chanel would be useful as a go-between for the German and English ruling classes."

"Coco Chanel?"

"Strange, isn't it, the power of fashion? Chanel is a small woman, but her influence is enormous. She knows Churchill, the Mitfords, the Duke of Westminster, perhaps even your father."

Clara remembered the chill, appraising glance that Chanel had cast over her. Had she been assessing exactly how much Clara knew, and how useful she might be to the Nazi cause?

"Now Schellenberg is planning a different kind of talk with me. And he won't be using any diplomatic charm."

She pressed his arm closer. "Perhaps you're worrying unduly—"

"I don't think so. I met my housekeeper in the KaDeWe food hall today and she mentioned that she had noticed my door needed mending. I understood immediately what she meant—someone had entered my apartment when I wasn't there. It was all I needed to know; I realized at once that I can't go back there."

"Where will you go?"

"I don't know. Canaris can't help me—he's warned me not even to contact him. I can't go crawling to my ex-wife or my former in-laws. It would only put them in danger. And besides, I'm not sure Gisela wouldn't seize the opportunity to denounce me herself. Ulrich Welzer's elderly mother offered to hide me at her country estate, but if anyone got wind of that, it would only attract attention to Ulrich. I need to get to Switzerland or Holland as soon as possible, but I don't know how the hell I'm going to do that. Schellenberg has supplied my name to the border points and put a watch on the stations."

"I think . . . I might know someone who can help you."

Steffi Schaeffer.

"She's a dressmaker. She works out of the Scheunenviertel. She knows groups with safe houses all over Berlin and exit routes too. She's part of the resistance, Max. She'll help you disappear."

"And where would I find this miraculous dressmaker?"

Clara made him memorize the address.

He gave a weary smile. "Does she welcome in every Nazi officer who turns up at her door?"

"She'll trust you if you tell her I sent you."

"That would be foolish of her. I'm not sure I'd want to rely on security like that."

"Ask her how her little girl, Nina, is doing. Ask if Nina's been kicking any *Stürmer* cabinets recently. Steffi will know what that means."

He stopped and looked down at her. "You need to be thinking about your own future."

"Don't worry about me."

He reached a hand to her cheek. "Why wouldn't I? This isn't the kind of ending I imagined for us."

"So you did imagine something for us then?" she asked impulsively.

"Something like this."

He bent to kiss her. For the first time she reciprocated, surrendering at last to the impulse she had first felt that night in Paris, pressing tightly against his chest and yielding to his deep, lingering embrace. Yet even as she did, a part of her still held back. Sensing it, he drew away.

"Max . . ."

He put a finger on her lips. "Don't. You had the opportunity in Paris, even in Munich, but you stopped yourself. I assume there's someone else . . ."

"There's no one."

"Perhaps. I believe you, of course, and maybe we'll see each other again—in England, I hope. Although I still think we should have taken our chances in Paris. We might have visited the Mona Lisa and that artistic ape. We could have spent a whole day seeing the sights, and a whole night forgetting them."

She saw the sorrow in his eyes, and to distract him she said, "That ape—the one that makes his own drawings? What on earth does he draw?"

Brandt recovered himself and stood upright, bracing his shoulders. "It's rather sad really," he replied, wryly. "This poor animal draws so beautifully, but he only draws one thing. He draws the bars of his own cage."

He kissed her again and pulled away.

"Goodbye, my dearest Clara."

With that, he strode swiftly away.

Clara stood motionless, still as the statues around her. The Tiergarten might have been full of agents that evening, but her heart was too full to care who might be watching.

34

I N THE DAYS THAT FOLLOWED, CLARA COULD DO LITTLE
more than go through the motions of her own life. Yet no
matter how numb she felt, she knew better than to turn
down Benno von Arent's invitation to the Kunstler Klub.
The club was based in a stately villa on Skagerrak-Platz.
Light bloomed through the windows, and the glare of flashbulbs from waiting photographers dazzled the arriving
guests as SS guards in rubberized capes held open umbrellas
against the patter of rain. A cluster of celebrity spotters
looked on avidly as a line of gleaming cars streamed into
the driveway, their headlights slicing through the wet darkness, and disgorged a succession of actresses, perched on the
arms of their consorts like beautiful, jeweled birds of prey.
All the major actresses of the Reich were there that night—
Lilian Harvey, Brigitte Horney, Kristina Söderbaum, Lil
Dagover, and Zarah Leander. The moguls of Hollywood
were being wooed by Goebbels's own galaxy, his very own
stable of stars.

Inside, the curved wooden paneling of the building, pink
rosewood inlaid with mahogany, seemed to emulate the
curves of the female clientele. Intricately carved mirrors reflected the soft glow of candelabras. Beyond the entrance

lay a winter garden, a dance floor, and a beer cellar. In the corner a jazz band played. Waiters slid through the throng bearing trays with Sekt and bowls of nuts and olives for the men from Twentieth Century–Fox, Paramount, and MGM. Gossip journalists circulated with their notebooks, and bare-shouldered actresses with reddened lips swapped air kisses. The entire scene was like Erich's cigarette album come to life.

Clara took a glass of Sekt and stepped into the throng. Goebbels certainly knew how to host a celebration. For his Olympics party two years earlier, he had taken over an entire island in the Wannsee, sprinkled the bushes with butterfly lights, and spread sumptuous tables out beneath the trees. This evening he had again spared no expense. Although his new emphasis on family values obliged him to bring Magda, who was touring the room shaking hands with an expression of frigid misery more appropriate to a disaster zone than a celebrity gathering, Berlin's best-known singers and musical acts had also been summoned, and to complement the magic of the movies, Goebbels had hired Alois Kassner, the top illusionist of the day.

Clara surveyed the room and lit on a man with a humorless, pudgy face and hair shaved two inches above his ears whom she recognized as Frits Strengholt, the head of MGM. This was the man who was supposed to be sorting things out for Ursula. Quickly she scanned the throng for her friend, yet she could see no sign of her. Had Ursula's invitation been withdrawn at Goebbels's request? Or did Emmy Goering's remarks presage something more serious?

A fusillade of paparazzi shots sparked at the entrance of Olga Chekhova, a regally beautiful star who was one of the regime's most famous actresses. With her ivory complexion and hooded eyes heavy with kohl, she slid through the phosphorescence of the flashbulbs like a glamorous ghost. La Chekhova was half Russian and the niece of Anton Chekhov, which meant that rumors circled constantly about her Bolshevik sympathies, but Hitler was a big fan of her films, and that was better security than an SS bodyguard and a golden Party medal. Despite her A-list status, she had proved remarkably friendly on the shoot for *Bel Ami* in Paris that summer, and now she came straight over to Clara's side.

"If I have to spend this evening listening to Hollywood producers telling me Doktor Goebbels is the greatest cultural champion the world has seen, I'm going to scream. How are you, Clara? You're looking very lovely."

"Olga. I wonder, have you by any chance seen Ursula Schilling?"

The diva's creamy face darkened, and instinctively she lowered her voice.

"Clara, my dear, I thought you knew. When did you last go to Babelsberg?"

"I've been in Munich. Why?"

Olga grimaced. "It's all round the Ufa studios. No one can talk of anything else. Ursula was taken in for questioning a few days ago. They brought her up from Munich to Prinz-Albrecht-Strasse."

Clara felt a sinking dread. "Questioning? About what?"

"She's being investigated for allegations of sleeping with a Jew."

Clara recalled Ursula's face in the studio canteen. *I would have left last year if it wasn't for...*

"Contrary to the Nuremberg laws, as I don't need to remind you," Olga added softly. "Maximum sentence several years in jail."

"Who is he?"

"Quite a surprise actually. Not what you would expect at all.

His name is Joachim Haber. Terrifically good looking and a little younger than her. He's a sound engineer."

"A sound engineer!"

"I know. Really an ordinary sort of fellow. He worked at the studios before the Aryanization, and since he lost his job he's been making ends meet with all sorts of low-paid electrical jobs, nothing remotely grand. They had a plan to leave Germany and settle in California, but until then he was living in Ursula's home in Neubabelsberg doing all her washing and cooking. He's not at all what you'd expect for a girl like her."

She paused and studied Clara musingly. "But then people can be so mysterious, can't they? You never know what's going on underneath. And we actresses are especially good at that, I suppose."

Clara repressed a shiver. "Who denounced her?"

Olga shrugged, causing her jewels to sparkle in the light. "Her cleaner reported her. But it could have been anyone, darling, couldn't it?"

She laid a white-gloved hand on Clara's arm, and that single satin touch seemed to communicate something important.

"I'm never surprised when I discover an actor has a secret, are you? We so love to be in the spotlight, but where there are spotlights, there will always be darkness too."

Was Olga Chekhova suggesting that she knew the truth about Clara? Or that she herself had something to hide?

Parting from the beautiful star with a quick smile, Clara moved towards the stage, where Alois Kassner was performing. She recognized him from the poster pasted outside her block in Winterfeldtstrasse: "Kassner makes a girl vanish!"

Magicians were everywhere in Berlin just then, from chancers performing the three-card trick on street corners to celebrated variety artists on the bill at the Wintergarten. Like those of acrobats, contortionists, and escape artists, magicians' acts had taken over from the political songs and risqué humor of the cabarets. Those had been swept away in the early days of the regime. Perhaps, at a time when people were disappearing daily, it was a relief to focus on fantasy, on women who vanished from wooden cabinets and rabbits that emerged from hats.

That evening Kassner was performing some kind of card trick. He had laid a deck of cards out in lines in front of him on a table covered in crimson velvet and was moving them faster than the eye could follow, flipping and whirring, spinning them into a hundred different positions.

"Fräulein, can I ask your assistance?" the magician called out to her. "Would you please pick a card?"

She complied.

"The king of diamonds. An excellent choice for a beautiful queen! Would you replace it please, Fräulein?"

Clara gave the card back and watched Kassner rotate it around the table as people gathered round.

"Now could you remind me, Fräulein, which card was yours?" said Kassner, expecting her to fail. Before she could stop herself, Clara had pointed it out.

"A remarkable guess. Perhaps you would try again."

She picked the ten of diamonds from the deck, and again the cards whirred in his hands as he shuffled them around the table. Again, she managed to follow its progress and identify it with ease. Murmurs of admiration came from those who had gathered to watch.

"What an eye you have, Fräulein."

"Again!" demanded the onlookers.

"Perhaps a different trick this time," decreed Kassner, sensing competition. "The beautiful lady has an excellent eye, but memory is another matter. In a moment, I will show the audience my ability to memorize an entire deck of cards in any order. Maybe"—he smiled, holding out a hand of cards to Clara—"you would like a try at that?"

Clara was about to demur, but the sight of the cards brought back her rainy teenage holidays, when her family whiled away the hours as the rain hammered down on the Cornish fields outside. One of Clara's diversions had been to memorize cards by using pictures from her own life. The Germans had a word for this memory trick, *Eselsbrücke*, because it was a technique that made a bridge between one part of the mind and another.

"All right." She nodded and smiled.

Kassner fanned out ten cards on the velvet. "An easy start. I will give the lady thirty seconds to commit just ten cards, in order, to memory."

Clara looked down and saw her childhood open out before her. First came the three of clubs, and she saw the three of them—Angela, Kenneth, and herself—as children, with the queen of hearts, their mother, picnicking in the avenue of tall trees in their Surrey garden. The trees resembled the ten of spades, alongside the jack of diamonds, who looked mischievously like their dog, Jip. The nine of clubs was the muddy prints of Kenneth's boots when they came in from outside. Then came the four of diamonds, four hearts shattering into jagged pieces when her mother's illness was diagnosed, and the ace of spades, which was the darkness that descended over their lives.

She carried on the story in her head until Kassner swept the cards up and fixed her with his challenging stare.

"Enough time, Fräulein?"

"The three of clubs, the queen of hearts, the ten of spades, the jack of diamonds, the nine of clubs, the four of diamonds, the ace of spades, the two of diamonds, the king of clubs, the ace of diamonds."

People clapped, and the magician's eyes hardened.

"Bravo, Fräulein. Shall we try with a few more cards?"

Clara was about to agree, but she had glimpsed a figure standing to her left.

"I'd rather not, thank you."

"Go on!" The crowd thought she was teasing. Kassner raised an eyebrow.

"Fifteen cards this time. Surely, you could manage that?" he wheedled.

"Fifteen cards!" demanded the audience.

"I couldn't possibly."

Kassner mimed a courtly bow. "Thank you, then, for your participation. Perhaps you would do me the honor of accepting a ticket to my next performance?"

As Clara took the proffered envelope, a voice came in her ear. "But you were doing so well!"

The voice was sinuous but brimming with malice, like a razor blade dipped in honey. It belonged to the scrawny, pin-striped figure of Joseph Goebbels.

"You have an excellent memory, Fräulein Vine."

"No better than any actress, Herr Doktor."

"I beg to differ. And I think you are far more than an actress, Fräulein."

Goebbels was exceptionally dapper that evening, in an evening suit with an orchid in the buttonhole and his handmade, platform patent leather shoes polished to a high shine. He dipped his head to kiss her hand. In contrast to their previous meeting, he was cordial, if not jubilant.

"How charming to see you again, Fräulein Vine. Don't get too thin, will you? It's not good for an actress's image."

He seemed gleeful. As though something more that the Munich triumph was motivating him.

"I understand you were obliged to leave Munich early."

"Unfortunately, yes."

"No matter. As it happens, your film has been canceled. Herr Guttmann is currently residing in Dachau."

Clara willed her face to remain expressionless. She saw Goebbels searching her features for a reaction.

"I'm sorry to hear it."

"He was found to be consorting with undesirables." For a moment Goebbels left the ambiguity lingering in the air. Then he said, "He's also charged with exchanging information with the Führer's adversaries abroad. So far he's not been especially forthcoming in explaining himself, but, as I told them, that's just like his films! Completely unintelligible!"

He chuckled a little at his own wit.

"Still, I'm sure they'll come up with something to make him more . . . loquacious."

Clara felt a wrenching pang of sorrow for Guttmann, and a hope that his cadaverous frame and narrow shoulders would withstand what his interrogators had to offer him.

Goebbels took a languid sip of Sekt. "Herr Guttmann introduced you to Fräulein Braun, I think?"

"Yes, he did. She had written me a letter, actually."

"Of course. A fan letter, I'm sure. But it intrigued me. Why a man like that should involve himself by introducing an actress to the Führer's girlfriend. What did you make of her?"

"I thought she was charming."

"I think so too, though many would disagree. You know, I wonder sometimes whether the Führer is too insistent on his plan to be married to Germany. I've begun to think that Fräulein Braun might make a more satisfactory spouse in some regards. At the very least, she should receive more public recognition."

Surely this was the opposite of what Goebbels actually believed? Clara was at a loss for how to respond, but the minister removed a silver cigarette case from his jacket, offered her one, then lit it with his special lighter, which bore Hitler's initials.

"I know what you're thinking, Fräulein, and indeed, until quite recently, I would have agreed with you. I was the first to say that our leader should be regarded as a man with no private life. The adulation of the public stage is enough. He needs to devote himself to his destiny and so forth." He waved his palm to indicate the platitudinous waffle the public was obliged to endure. "Yet now I realize there's a lot to be said for the family man. Perhaps we do need to see our Führer in human terms, as well as a great leader."

What was it Brandt had said about Goebbels? *He's a tailor. He tailors people to be the way he wants them.* Looking at Goebbels's clever, calculating face, she understood his motivation. If Hitler had ordered Goebbels to behave more like a family man, then shouldn't Hitler, too, be seen in more human terms? And Eva Braun was his raw material. Like some grotesque Pygmalion, Goebbels was planning to fashion Eva to be the human side of Hitler.

"Remember how your British press made no mention of the touching love story between the Duke and Duchess of Windsor? What did that avail?" he mused. "They still married, happily, but in the process England lost a great monarch. No, I think it's a shame our little Eva needs to remain a secret."

He tilted his head and exhaled a stream of smoke. "Still. We all have our secrets, don't we, Fräulein Vine?"

"If you say so, Herr Doktor."

From the direction of the band rose the plangent voice of the Marlene Dietrich classic.

Falling in love again. Never wanted to. What am I to do? I can't help it.

Goebbels winced. "We can't talk with this racket. Come with me."

He stalked briskly across the room, opened a door that gave onto a small dressing room, and gestured for Clara to close the door behind her.

"There is another matter that has been on my mind. A delicate matter."

"Herr Doktor?"

His eyes never left her face. "I heard that you may have been on the end of some unwanted attention."

Clara remained impassive, waiting for him to elaborate. Her heart was hammering.

"I understand you've suffered some unnecessary official interest."

"Forgive me, Herr Doktor . . ."

"Don't be dense, woman. Someone's been following you."

"I'm not sure I understand."

Goebbels rolled his eyes. "Really? Don't you? Then let me explain. I've heard that you, quite wrongly, have been the target of some official interest from the officers of the SS Reichsführer."

Himmler?

"What would the SS Reichsführer want with me?" she asked evenly. Her hands were trembling, so she clasped them casually behind her back.

"It's a case of misplaced innuendo. Coarse minds. It's quite revolting what filth some imaginations can conjure."

"But I'm not sure precisely what they think—"

"It doesn't matter *precisely what they think*," he interrupted. "The fact is that a rogue section of our security forces has been assembled for a quite outrageous task. They've been involved in wiretapping my hotel rooms and so on, intent on laying spurious allegations against me, which could only be of help to our enemies. They've been selecting certain innocent women and following them, then inviting those women to be interviewed at the Lichterfelde barracks. I wanted to know if you had received a visit."

"What kind of visit?"

"An early morning one."

Understanding was dawning on Clara with a great, exhilarating rush of relief. The people who had followed her for the best part of the month—who had come to her apartment just the other day—were not Heydrich's men suspecting her of espionage. They were a special division of the Gestapo, commissioned by Heinrich Himmler, and the crime they suspected her of was adultery. Adultery with the minister of propaganda, Joseph Goebbels. Clara almost laughed out loud. It must have been the first time anyone had been relieved to be followed by the Gestapo.

"As a matter of fact, Herr Doktor, I did have a visit the other day. Two men called for me, but I was out."

Goebbels's relief was visible.

"I'm pleased you were spared the trouble. And don't worry about a repeat visit—it won't happen. I've taken action to prevent this nonsense. You should find yourself free from bother, but if anything does happen, I shall take it as a personal affront. I want you to contact me instantly."

"Of course."

His face twisted with anger. "It's monstrous that members

of the Reich Chamber of Culture should be interrogated about their every move. I, and no one else, am in charge of the lives of artists in the Reich."

"I assure you, Herr Doktor, if I get any more calls, you'll be the first to know."

His anger abated. He flashed his wide smile. "You've done well, Fräulein Vine."

He looked her up and down. "When we first encountered you in—when was it, 1933?—we worried that your looks might be a little . . . *dark* for a National Socialist actress. You seemed, if you'll forgive the slur, a touch non-Aryan, not to mention half English, which is hardly something to boast about. Yet your performances have won us over."

"Thank you, Herr Doktor. You are too kind."

"And I've not forgotten that documentary you're to voice about the Frauenschaft. The film will be ready to dub at the Ufa sound studio anytime now. I shall have them call you to discuss it."

He straightened his lapels and brushed some invisible dust from his jacket.

Clara braced herself. "Herr Doktor . . . there is another member of the Reich Chamber of Culture who would very much benefit from your help."

"Oh yes?"

"Ursula Schilling."

Goebbels's eyes flickered over her, but he remained silent.

"She's been a victim of that misplaced innuendo you talked about, and, even worse, I've heard she's been arrested," Clara persisted. "I think she's in great need of your protection."

Goebbels gave her a dyspeptic look. "Fräulein Schilling is accused of consorting with a Jew."

"Yet her enemies are suggesting so much more."

Her heart was in her mouth. How had she dared to allude to Ursula's harassment by Goebbels? In the Reich minister's scrawny face, conflicting imperatives were at war. Goebbels's hatred of Jews was competing with his fury over Himmler's interference in his affairs. Which would win out?

He rubbed his hands together and shrugged. "I'll look into it."

"She'd be extremely grateful."

"As I said, I'll have a look. But I take a dim view of artists who are known to have prostituted themselves with Jews."

"I wondered . . ."

He sighed and drummed his fingers on the dressing table. She was trying his patience now.

"What did you wonder, Fräulein? I do have a houseful of Hollywood executives waiting for me outside."

"That's just the thing. As it happens, Ursula Schilling has been approached to work in Hollywood, and I know the Chamber of Culture is generally against our actresses leaving to work abroad at a time of national unity. Yet I wondered, perhaps, whether it might be worth making an exception in this case? The British have a saying, 'Out of sight, out of mind.' Maybe if Ursula went to America she would be out of everyone's mind?"

His dark eyes flickered suspiciously over her. Then he grunted.

"Perhaps you're right. The Reich would do well without a Jew-lover like her. You can tell Fräulein Schilling that an exit visa will be available at the Propaganda Ministry for her immediate departure. And good riddance."

He made for the door. "I have to leave now—I need to be away by eleven. In such momentous times it is more vital than ever that I complete my diary. Did you know I keep a diary?"

"The Frau Doktor mentioned it."

"Did she? Well, I'm proud of it. I write it every evening. It's a document of immense historical value. I keep the past volumes photographed on Agfa glass plates and stored in a special underground vault at the Reichsbank because if, God forbid, war should come, they're far too valuable to be allowed to fall victim to an air raid. My diaries provide a record of my entire life and times, and if fate allows me a few years for the task, I intend to edit them for the sake of future generations."

"I'm sure your diaries would be of great interest to a lot of people."

"Exactly. It takes a certain skill to write a diary. I treat mine as a work of literary art—I like to include observations, detail, and color. They give texture to history, I think."

Sometimes, his ambition still amazed her. Not content with directing the thoughts of an entire nation through their newspapers and radio programs and horoscopes, Goebbels wanted to direct posterity too. His unseen editorial hand would live on through his diary, editing history the way he wanted it.

"Some people see a diary as a kind of sniveling receptacle for every little woe, but that never reads well. Posterity doesn't want to know about that. I always think there are some diaries that should be preserved in a vault and others that should never see the light of day." He nodded briefly. "I'll say good night, Fräulein."

IN THE CLUBROOM THE PARTY was in full swing. Clara threaded her way through the celebrity throng, slipping past dinner-jacketed executives, uniformed officers, and glittering actresses with her head down. She dodged the waiters bearing trays of sparkling wine and the girls circulating with complimentary cigarettes. Twice she heard her name called, but she did not respond. Her mind was reeling. She needed time to process all that had happened.

As she left the club, the band struck up a familiar tune. It was the same sweet, melancholy song that she had heard in Paris.

J'attendrai, le jour et la nuit, j'attendrai toujours ton retour.

Day and night I shall wait for your return. Sometimes, Clara felt as though she had been waiting for something for years, yet she was still not quite certain what it was.

THE SPORTPALAST ON POTSDAMER STRASSE WAS AN IM-
mense white barracks of a place, built in the early years of
the century with an ice rink and shops and a stadium capable of holding fourteen thousand people. It was a popular
venue for boxing matches—the cream of society turned out
for fights featuring the celebrated heavyweight Max
Schmeling—as well as beer festivals, concerts, and cycle
races. But in the past five years it had become the venue for
an even more popular form of entertainment: Nazi Party
rallies. Perhaps because only the Party faithful were invited,
the Hitler Youth leaders and the local Party divisions, these
tended to be lively affairs, one of which had taken place just
a few days ago according to tattered remains of a flyer on
the wall: "For one night only: The Führer: A Man of Peace!"

Rosa wished she had never mentioned meeting a man to
her mother. Already Katrin Winter was making preparations in her head while Rosa's father had an edge of worry
in his eyes when his daughter explained that she had no
idea where the man lived, who his family was, or exactly
what he did. But Anselm Winter had faith in his daughter's
good sense, and, besides, it was very difficult to tell a twenty-
five-year-old woman whom she could and could not meet

for a date at the cinema. To disguise her trepidation as she waited, Rosa watched the people around her, thinking that they might make one of her Observations. There was a couple next to her, obviously married from the tone of their conversation, which was an argument about their chances of ever owning a new Volkswagen. Two elderly ladies, one large and one thin, walked past, exercising dogs that were the precise mirrors of their owners. Across the forecourt a pair of workmen were attempting to free a swastika banner that had become entangled in a streetlamp. One man held the ladder while the other lunged fruitlessly at the rope before abandoning the attempt and leaving the banner hanging limply, like a noose. The couple next to her began laughing at his efforts, but it still wasn't enough to distract Rosa from the meeting with August Gerlach.

She saw Gerlach before he saw her, heading across the road with a determined hunch to his shoulders, wearing the same grubby fedora and natty gray suit he'd worn both times she saw him before. His jocular demeanor was nowhere to be seen. Instead, his narrow blade of a mouth was a grimace and the bristles on his jaw cast a blue shadow on his face. Rosa had a tendency to see the animal characteristics in human beings, and she often privately entertained herself by attributing the appropriate creature to each person she met. Everything about August Gerlach, from his purposeful stalk, looking neither left nor right, to his lean frame and sharp nose, had a lupine quality. There was something of the wolf about Gerlach—he had that beast's clever eyes and alert, predatory air. Yet even as she thought this, Rosa reprimanded herself for being what Suzi would call immature and summoned an enthusiastic smile.

"Hello, sweetheart. Pfennig for your thoughts."

"I was just thinking of a story."

"A story you know? Or one you made up?"

"Just something I wrote."

Gerlach led the way to the bar area, where he bought a cup of hot chocolate for her and a glass of beer for himself. He took off his hat and looked around.

"I was here, actually, the other night. The Führer was in magnificent form. You should have heard him. He went on for hours. He's very angry about the Czechs."

"Why are they always so hysterical at the Sportpalast?"

"Hysterical?" He sounded testy. "Why do you say that?"

It was the word Rosa's father used. Whenever the speeches came on the radio at home, Anselm Winter would turn them off and put music on the gramophone instead, but sometimes, from another room, she would hear him listening to the Führer's shriek, when he thought no one else could hear.

"Overexcited, I suppose is what I mean."

"There's plenty to get excited about."

"Is there? I don't feel excited. But perhaps I don't read the papers enough."

"Good thing." Gerlach smiled. "Pretty ladies shouldn't discuss politics. Anyway, I'm looking forward to this movie. Grethe Weiser's a real piece of work."

A piece of work. What did that mean?

He gave Rosa's drab, olive-green suit an appraising look. She had come straight from work, though she was wearing lipstick, and had stuck a pink carnation in her hat in honor of the occasion.

"Ever thought of letting your hair down?"

Rosa blushed. She was entirely unused to direct comments on her looks or being called a pretty lady or having a man rake his eyes over her with such merciless attention. She wasn't going to tell him that it had never occurred to her to wear her hair in anything but braids.

"Sometimes."

"You should. Ditch the spectacles too. It would suit you."

He rattled the ice round in his glass, like a gambler rolling a die. "So you do that then? Think up stories?"

"Just fragments really. Impressions."

"Clever girl."

"I've always liked writing, you see. I used to want to be a writer, when I was younger, and I read somewhere that the place to start would be to record the details of what you see in everyday life. Even quite ordinary things. They don't have to be dramatic or important. It makes you notice more, you see, and it trains you to describe—"

"Because . . ." Gerlach interrupted, shaking his head. "It's beginning to make sense to me now. It was a story, wasn't it? Your tale about the lady on the *Wilhelm Gustloff.*"

"Not at all."

His odd, sharp smile curled across his thin lips. "Tell me. I can take a joke. You were just making up . . . what did you call it? . . . an *impression*, to impress me."

Rosa felt the blood rush to her cheeks again, this time in agitation.

"I promise you. It definitely happened. I wouldn't lie. I wasn't trying to impress you. And I don't know why you keep asking about it."

"Why wouldn't I? It's not every day a girl sees a murder."

"I didn't say it was a *murder*!"

"Sounded that way to me. Have you changed your mind, then?"

"I know what I saw."

"Told anyone else about it yet?"

"Of course I haven't! I don't even want to remember it. I don't want to talk about it at all. Though I'm beginning to think I should."

Reaching a hand across, he grabbed her roughly, his fingernails making sharp scarlet crescents in her forearm.

"Now then, sweetie. No need to get upset. People are listening. Don't make a scene."

He looked about him with an explanatory grin, then let her arm go and rubbed the bristles on his jaw.

"Forget I said anything. I shouldn't have mentioned it. How about a smoke before we go in?"

He felt in his pocket and freed a box of cigarettes, extracted one, and clenched it between his lips. Then he felt in his other pocket for a light. And that was when Rosa froze. She had always had a good eye for detail, and the detail that caught her eye now, and made her heart race, was his matchbook. A little fold of white card with gold lettering on it.

WILHELM GUSTLOFF

She remembered the matchbooks clustered on the coffee tables on the ship. She had even thought of bringing one home as a memento, until circumstances had provided other, more horrible memories of her voyage. But how would August Gerlach have come by those matches unless he had been on the *Wilhelm Gustloff* himself? And if he had been on the *Wilhelm Gustloff*, why was he pretending that he hadn't?

Rosa knew there might be an innocent explanation, but innocent explanations were increasingly difficult to come by. She took a deliberate sip of chocolate, hoping that he had not noticed anything amiss, but Gerlach had registered her alarm. He was watching her, she knew it, the smoke of his cigarette pulsing like his own breath.

He leaned towards her, bringing with him a pungent gust of

lemon and vetiver aftershave. His eyes narrowed, as though he was squinting down the barrel of a gun.

"Anything wrong, sweetie?"

"Nothing. I'll just pop into the ladies' before the film starts."

"Don't be long."

She left the café, but instead of turning left, down the steps leading to the Kino, she slipped through the foyer into a narrow tunnel and entered the Sportpalast itself. For a second she halted at the entrance and tried to absorb the sheer scale of it. She had been to the Sportpalast before—she and Suzi had come skating here as girls—but in its deserted state the arena appeared impossibly vast. It was silent and semidark, like some great cathedral, with tiers of balconies rising up to the ceiling and thousands of chairs ranked expectantly before an empty dais. The walls were still decked from Hitler's speech, festooned by banners reading WE FOLLOW OUR FÜHRER, garlanded with ivy wreaths and the obligatory giant eagle with outstretched wings poised above the lectern.

After a second's hesitation, she moved quickly. Even though it would be several minutes before Gerlach came to look for her, she threaded her way urgently along the stalls, making for the far end, where, she guessed, there would be a side exit leading onto Pallasstrasse, through which she could slip away. As she hurried she calculated what to do. She had no idea who August Gerlach was, but she knew that he could find her—he *would* find her—if she didn't act fast. He may not know where she lived, but he had discovered where she worked—she was certain she had never told him—and he would seek her out. In her terror she felt curiously liberated. She realized that Gerlach had answered a question for her, a question she had not even asked herself.

Rosa hastened along Lützowstrasse, hugging the shadows, keeping close to the buildings. Streetlamps inked in the side streets and glanced off the cobbles. A cluster of boys overtook her, laughing, a car blared past, and behind her she heard a man's rapid footsteps growing closer. Seized with alarm, she looked around for somewhere to conceal herself and saw, down a side street, the entrance to a cinema.

The musty, velour-carpeted foyer was deserted. Judging by the music emerging from a curtained entrance, the program had already begun and the ticket clerk had gone off duty. Nor was there anyone waiting behind the coat check counter, so she slipped inside and stood at the back of the stalls in the glimmering light. The stalls were sparsely populated. Only a few people were dotted among the rows as the imperial blare of the Ufa-Tonwoche newsreel announced another military maneuver. The footage showed German army cars roaring into the Sudetenland, and the camera panned along the route, filling up the screen with flowers and right-arm salutes. Children running alongside, town squares decorated with swastikas, and smiling faces everywhere. The camera cut to a newsstand, and the sight of it made Rosa think of Rupert Allingham, wearing his ash-flecked suit and tie at half mast, talking about Prague.

After she had read the report of the dead girl to him from her book of Observations, he had asked her why she wrote. Not presuming to confide her journalistic ambitions, she had answered, "People always want things to be neat, but I like to look at the underside of things, like"—she had searched for an appropriate image—"like turning a carpet over and seeing the pattern beneath."

Rupert's eyes had lit up, like those of a teacher with a good pupil. "That's exactly what journalism is about. Untidying the things that people want tidied, looking at what other people have brushed under the carpet."

"That's journalism?"

"Sure. A better description would be hard to find. Look at things as clearly as you can, and then write about them as clearly as you can. That's journalism. All the rest is entertainment."

Emboldened by this discovery, she had asked, "So what about the lady on the cruise ship? Might you be able to write about what happened to her?"

"Tell you what, you can help me write the story."

She had stared at him, mesmerized, clutching the bag on her lap. "Do you really mean that?"

"I do mean it, Fräulein Winter. You seem a most intelligent young woman and a punctilious writer. It's a shame you're so happily settled with the Führerin. I could do with an office assistant."

Now, standing in the cinema's flickering darkness, she made a decision. She would leave the Führerin's office immediately. She would call first thing tomorrow morning and pretend that she was needed urgently at home, to help with her parents, and give no forwarding address. Then she would collect Hans-Otto from school with Brummer, and let him walk the dog, which was his favorite job in the world, and later she would visit Herr Allingham and apply for the job of office assistant. But before that, there was one last thing she needed to do.

In Derfflingerstrasse, the offices of the Frauenschaft were deserted, but as the Fuhrerin's assistant, Rosa was allowed to keep a key on her ring for emergencies. Though she didn't dare turn on the main lights, it was easy to navigate the darkened corridor to her office and settle in at her desk, where a green-shaded lamp spilled a pool of light onto her new typewriter. Rosa sat for a moment, chewing her nail. She had spent years in this office, at this desk, compiling figures, sorting the names and addresses of women into impersonal columns as though they were some vast mathematical exercise. Filing human beings, diligently, methodically, the way a bookkeeper files his figures or a scientist moves formulae around a board. Typing millions of bland, bureaucratic words in letters and directives and reports. And now, she realized, those bureaucratic words, those directives, that unthinking obedience to authority were the only weapons anyone had.

Decisively she pulled the machine towards her and removed the cover. From the wire basket beside her desk she drew out a sheet of paper with the heavy Gothic letterhead of the Office of the Führerin of the Greater Reich. She wound it into the machine, and began to type.

To whom it may concern,

A medical examination has been carried out on Hans-Otto Kramer at these offices today. I am pleased to tell you that after exhaustive tests, the boy has been found to be normal in all respects and free from congenital disease. After professional consideration of the case of Hans-Otto Kramer, it has been decided that no further action will be taken. Educational authorities are ordered to desist from inquiries forthwith.

An illegible squiggle.

She stamped the bottom of the paper with the official stamp of the Reichsmütterdienst Department of Infant Health, and a second, indigo stamp bearing the swastika and eagle.

Then she typed beneath it, "By order of Gertrud Scholz-Klink, Reich Führerin."

36

I T WAS PAST MIDNIGHT BY THE TIME CLARA GOT BACK TO the apartment, but she was not in the least tired. The discovery that she had been shadowed by Himmler's men, and that Goebbels himself would be forestalling any further surveillance, exhilarated her. And she could scarcely believe her success in persuading Goebbels to provide Ursula with an exit visa. Despite the late hour, the thoughts spinning round her brain meant she would not be able to sleep anytime soon.

She sank down in her armchair with a cup of coffee. Rummaging in a pile of books for a packet of cigarettes, her fingers encountered the album that Ada Freitag had left on the *Wilhelm Gustloff*. The events of the past few days had driven all thought of it from her mind.

She sat back and examined it. It was a beautifully decorated album, about nine inches square, its heavy cardboard covers the plush crimson and gilt of prestige cinema décor. Picked out in embossed, scrolled golden letters on the front was the title *Stars of the Ufa Screen* and underneath the line "Brought to You by Reetsma Cigarettes." Inside was a page fulsomely devoted to the Reetsma brand, "loved around the world for their rich sophistication." Then came tinted photographs presented against a metallic gold background. Each page had a framed space for a single cigarette card, which was secured beneath plastic film, with a name and brief description underneath. Clara turned the pages thoughtfully. All the faces were familiar to her, frozen in the studio's artificial glare, their smiles pearly and their skin shimmering under the lights. There was Hans Albers, Zarah Leander, Gustav Fröhlich, Emil Jannings, and Kirsten Söderbaum. It was like looking at a montage of her own life over the past five years, or the public side of it at least. Clara had worked with all of these actors at some point, in a stream of mostly forgettable romantic comedies, spy capers, and historical biopics, and she had enjoyed it too—the actors' talent was usually in inverse proportion to the quality of the scripts they were obliged to perform. Unconsciously she smiled as she flicked through the album. Everyone was there, even Ursula Schilling, pouting distantly, and, on one of the last pages, there was a picture of Clara herself. The photograph had been taken to publicize her film the previous year with the air ace Ernst Udet, who was now head of the Luftwaffe's technical division. The picture looked both like and unlike her, dressed in a gingham dirndl, her hair braided, gazing raptly at the sky above. Clara marveled at the silky shimmer of her skin. She looked for all the world like a confident, happy woman, gazing expectantly into the distance, "a flower of German womanhood," as one of the reviews had called her. Though *Der Angriff*, more snidely, had reminded readers of her foreign blood by referring to her as an "English rose."

As she looked at the card, something curious occurred to Clara. Spies, Leo had once told her, use all of their senses. Sight, touch, hearing, taste, and even smell. The smell of earth recently disturbed, of cooking on a man's clothes, of a gun that has been discharged—all were invisible clues that were hard to disguise. The scent she detected now was sweet and powdery, a complex mix of narcissus, violet, and hyacinth that struck a chord in her memory. Je Reviens. The legendary perfume from the House of Worth.

Eva Braun's favorite perfume.

Peeling back the plastic and slipping the card out of its sleeve to examine it more closely, she turned it over. For an instant she was perplexed, then astonished. The back of the card was covered in fine rounded letters, minutely compressed, with a date at the top. Where had she seen that handwriting before?

> *July 5. A red letter day. Hairdresser and seamstress.*
> *Tonight, after three weeks, I will finally see my man!*

It came to Clara. The same handwriting was on the perfume bottle that Eva Braun had given her.

She ran her fingers over the card for a while, as if it were braille, as its implications sank in. She had in her hand the ultimate card trick. A diary hidden on cigarette cards.

Clara thought of Eva's words as she lay on the floor of her villa, sleeping pills scattered across the floor. *It's not just that. It's something else. I can't tell you.*

It was not the fact that Eva's infertility had been discovered. Nor was it her terror of being abandoned by Hitler that had produced such suicidal despair. It was the realization that the diary she had secretly kept had been stolen.

Eva must have cast around for a way to keep her diary without it being discovered, and resolved to hide it in plain sight. Everyone knew she was a film fan. Eva's cigarette album went everywhere with her. The album was proof, if proof were needed, of the essential frivolity of her nature. Eva collected cigarette cards like a child, she was as starstruck as a teenager, so where better to keep her confessions until the time came to reveal them to the world? Yet somehow Eva's diary ended up on a cruise ship in the middle of the Atlantic. And the woman who stole it, Ada Freitag, was almost certainly killed for it.

Ada Freitag needed to leave Germany in a hurry not because she had any interest in poisoning the Führer but because she had discovered Eva Braun's diary, and understood its implications. She was planning to sell it on a stop-off during her cruise, in Lisbon perhaps, only Heydrich's man had got there first. He had ruthlessly disposed of Ada Freitag and searched her cabin, but had found no poison. Because it was not poison that was to damage Hitler; it was a far more intimate weapon.

Hastily Clara went through the album, peeling back the plastic and slipping out each of the cards. On the back of a picture of Hans Albers was an account of a day at the Berghof.

> *Our perfect day ended with a western. Those cowboy films bore me stiff but Wolf loves them. He says the American conquest of the Red Indian lands is like the German search for Lebensraum.*

Clara skimmed quickly, the letters blurring beneath her eyes as she read through the gossip and heartache and female longing. Behind a picture of Brigitte Horney, Eva had written,

> *How many times have I heard him talk about after the war? It's always after the war! Now I don't think there will ever be an after the war. Once Himmler finds out, that will be an end of me, so I may as well take the initiative and end myself!*

Another entry, on a photograph of Lida Baarová, dated July 1938, read,

> *Mimi Reiter came last night. Mimi says she visited*
> *Wolf in his apartment and he told her everything.*
> *She was telling me because he was too weak to tell me*
> *himself. I'm too young for him. He wants to end it.*
> *My God, I want to die.*

Clara's eyes flickered over the entry on Marika Rökk's card.

> *He says the Poles are more like animals than human*
> *beings. Completely stupid and primitive, and their*
> *ruling class is degraded by lower races. They deserve*
> *elimination, not assimilation.*

Elimination?
On the back of Olga Chekhova's card, Eva had written,

> *Wolf calls his plan the Plan Green. It starts with*
> *Czechoslovakia, and then Poland.*

Clara's heart was pounding as she struggled to assimilate the meaning of the lines she was reading. Picking out the card with her own picture on it, she read:

> *Last night Wolf said that after the war he would*
> *marry me! When is after the war? I asked. When*
> *Poland is subjugated, he explained. Very soon, he told*
> *me, Poland will cease to exist.*

Clara gasped. This more than anything was what the British government needed to see. *Poland will cease to exist.* It put the lie to any hope that Hitler would end his conquests with the Sudetenland. The people in London needed to know, as they cast around desperately for an alternative to war, that the Führer's true ambition was not a small, disputed portion of southern Czechoslovakia. He intended to wipe out an entire nation, and then another, in his monstrous quest for a greater Reich.

Her mind reeling, she laid the diary down on her lap and read no more. Finally she took it up again and turned to the entry on Ursula Schilling's card. It was dated August 15. Six weeks ago. And what she read there, in Eva's tiny, precise handwriting, chilled her to the bone.

> *Today at lunch Wolf was talking about the Jews.*
> *Everyone was arguing, discussing different methods*
> *of transporting them. But Wolf said that was the*
> *wrong way to tackle the Jewish problem. Deportation*
> *was a half measure. It would solve nothing. The final*
> *solution to the Jewish race must be their entire*
> *extermination.*

The final solution? Clara felt the nausea rise within her. She snapped the album shut, as if it was possible to contain within its crimson covers all the horrors it revealed. Eva Braun's perfume was not lethal, but her diary was. Written so artlessly, and hidden so artfully, it laid bare the murderous mind of the Führer like nothing else.

I N THE CORNER OF THE FRIEDRICHSHAIN VOLKSPARK, BEYOND
the bunkers lying like open graves in the bleached grass,
workers were raking dead leaves into a bonfire, as though
burning the last of summer itself. The first heavy drops of
rain, foreshadowing a storm, dappled the dusty pavements,
and the prospect of a Berlin autumn brought a chill to the
bones.

As Clara walked she thought of Max. Had Steffi Schaeffer managed to hide him? Berlin had become a city of the
hidden. Of refugees, their jewels stitched against their skin
in heavy, invisible seams, their lives in their linings, carrying their secrets close. Of U-boats, concealed in back rooms
and attics, with forged papers and desperate plans, and of
plotters hidden in safe houses, waiting for the moment to
strike. Of food, secreted in bags, smuggled to those who
were hiding, and of secrets concealed on cards, telling the
truths that no one dared speak.

Clara had attempted her own form of concealment.

That morning she had taken her copy of *Mein Kampf,* a
smart edition bound in wine-red leather that had been a
personal gift from the Führer to all cast members of *The
Pilot's Wife*—a film he was said to have especially enjoyed.

Turning to Chapter Five, "The World War," she took a sharp knife and carved a rectangle down through the center of the block of pages. Then she collected the deck of cigarette cards that constituted Eva Braun's diary and placed them in the space she had created, before covering them by sticking the first page of Chapter Six to the previous page. As she looked around her apartment, wondering where to conceal the book, inspiration struck her. She slid the volume beneath the wobbly leg of her desk. A copy of *Mein Kampf* was part of the furniture in most German homes, so when one part of the furniture was being used to prop up another, what intruder would give it a second glance?

In her bag she carried a purse, identity documents, and a packet of cigarettes, in one of which the tobacco had been replaced with a rolled cigarette paper, bearing the next day's date. A veneer of tobacco had been reinserted at the tip. She also had her fallback, the ticket Alois Kassner had given her to his cabaret on Friedrichstrasse. As cover stories went, an invitation to the theater from the great Kassner himself would surely dazzle the most suspicious of policemen.

Missing the meeting at the Siegessäule had been unavoidable, but the plan had always been that she could communicate through a message in the dead letter box, which, Hamilton promised, was checked regularly. With the Munich agreement signed, and so many convinced war had been averted, it was more crucial than ever that the people back in London hear what Eva Braun had to say.

Clara slid her hand into her coat pocket, where a single card remained: the one with her own photograph on it.

Last night Wolf said that after the war he would marry me! When is after the war? I asked. When Poland is

*subjugated, he explained. Very soon, he told me, Poland
will cease to exist.*

The Märchenbrunnen, the fairy-tale fountain, was a piece
of Baroque whimsy crafted for the children of Berlin in the
days when family promenades on Sunday afternoons were routine and children considerably easier to enchant. Situated on
the northwestern end of the Volkspark and accessed through a
pair of arches, it was flanked by two long stone benches and
fenced off from the rest of the park by a parade of pillars. Marble versions of the fairy-tale characters posed joylessly around
the water as though some wintry magician had turned them to
stone. The tortoises, designed to issue jets of water into the air,
were turned off and the tiered pools lay stagnant. Clara waited
as an old lady, bundled up spherically against the chill, with an
equally rotund poodle on a leash, made a leisurely progress
around the fountain before turning out of the gate towards
Friedenstrasse. There was no one else in sight, apart from a leaf
raker about a hundred yards away, focusing on the grass beneath a group of lime trees. Resolutely, Clara approached the
bench on the left-hand side, closest to the pillar, sat down, and
let one hand drop. There was the cavity, exactly as Guy Hamilton had described, a six-inch indentation large enough, she
hoped, to conceal a packet of Reetsma cigarettes.

She sat for a moment. In the stillness of the park, the noise
of the distant traffic was muted like the faint roar of the sea.
Taking out her compact, she could see that there was no one
behind her and that the leaf raker, having completed his pile of
leaves, was moving away. She was about to extract the cigarette
packet from her bag when she remembered something that
Leo had taught her.

If time allows, perform a trial run.

After rising smartly, she walked back through the stone arch and along a mossy graveled path, fringed with evergreen shrubs. The vegetation was damp from the recent shower, with silver beads of rain trapped in the clefts of the leaves and a dank, loamy smell rising from the earth. She performed a loop of the park, walking at a measured pace right around a small lake, before returning along a different path and reentering the arch. When she did, she discovered that the stone bench was now occupied by a man in a sage-green loden overcoat. He stood as she approached.

She had not seen him in five years, but he had barely changed. He was tall and sinewy, leaner, perhaps, than ever, with the same high cheekbones and strong jaw, but a few more lines around his eyes. His face, though she had half forgotten it, was instantly familiar; that demeanor, so valuable in a spy, that seemed to register expressions with only a flicker before they were suppressed. The delicate Irish coloring, fine red-gold stubble on his chin, and the brush of hair resistant to pomade. The firm mouth, whose lines appeared to be compressing some intense emotion. The shock of seeing Leo Quinn knocked the breath out of her. The noise drained from the world and every lineament of her body quivered, like an instrument touched by a bow. After a few seconds she managed to say, "I might have guessed it would be you, after that message you sent."

"I didn't send any message."

"You must have. Ovid? The man from London Films quoted a line of Ovid. I assumed it was a message from you."

"It wasn't."

Her heart plummeted.

"Shall we walk?" Leo said.

They headed out of the park and turned left, in the direction of Alexanderplatz. He kept his hands jammed in his pockets, eyes straight ahead. He must have seen her approach the DLB the first time and then waited—knowing she would make a trial run, because that was what he had taught her.

"What did it say? This line that wasn't a message?"

"Good manners and a fine disposition are the best beauty treatments."

He smiled tightly. "I see."

"What do you see?" she challenged, almost stepping off the curb into the path of a tram, and feeling his hand lightly restraining her.

"It's an exercise I set."

"You set it? Are you a teacher now?"

"In a manner of speaking."

"Oh. I didn't know."

He fell silent again. There was so much Clara wanted to say, but she could see no way to breach this wall of awkwardness that had grown up between them, consigning them to an icy formality. All the times she had dreamed of being reunited with him. How often she had lain in bed remembering the ecstasy of their love affair, retracing the contours of his body, the feel of his lips against hers. How often in her mind she had replayed their conversations, the poems he had read to her.

And now this.

His eyes avoided her. All the questions she had yearned to ask him over the years hovered unspoken as chill courtesy imprisoned them. Was he married now? In love with someone else? Was he happy to see her, or did the terrible manner of their parting darken his memories, the way it did hers?

Where were they heading? Leo kept his hands deep in his pockets, his steps matching her own in the way she remembered, as though they shared a purpose. As they progressed northwards, through the fringes of Friedrichshain towards Prenzlauer Berg, she realized that their path was taking them down a street that would lead straight past the former SIS safe house—the yellow-painted, turn-of-the-century block with white scrolled detail above the entrance, where, five years ago, he had asked her to marry him. Leo must have recalled it too, because a wince went through him and without looking up at it he turned, sharply, to cross the road.

When they were safely past the block and had rounded the corner, he finally spoke.

"I should apologize. I'm here because of a last-minute change of circumstances. The man who should have been here was diverted. So please forgive me if it seems inappropriate."

"It doesn't."

"Good." His mouth was still taut, as though he was holding everything back.

"I did go yesterday, to the Siegessäule. But I got waylaid," she said. "There was no way to warn you."

"Of course. It doesn't matter. You found the DLB. I assume you were about to set up another meeting."

"Yes. There are things I need to communicate. I need to talk to you, Leo."

"By all means."

"Not here."

"Where?"

"My apartment."

"And that is . . . ?"

"Winterfeldtstrasse. Number 35. Apartment six."

"I'll be there in an hour."

He made an abrupt turn, rounded a corner, and disappeared from sight.

———

BY THE TIME HE knocked at her door, Clara was still in a daze. As she let him in, Leo took a quick, hungry look around the room, as if he wanted to absorb everything in it at a single glance, because of what it might reveal about her. The photographs on the mantelpiece, the potted geranium on the kitchen table, the oil painting of a saxophone player in jagged grays and browns by the artist Bruno Weiss.

"You said you had something to show me."

She went across the drawing room, and his eyes followed, taking in the small, blue-covered copy of Rilke's poems on the desk as she removed the leather-bound *Mein Kampf* from beneath its wobbly leg.

"I found these." She pried the page open and took out the stack of cards. He frowned.

"Eva Braun was banned from keeping a diary by Martin Bormann, but Eva couldn't stop herself. Her diary was important to her—it was the only place she could talk about her real feelings—so she found a way to hide it. All her fears about Hitler, everything he confided to her about his plans. All in her own handwriting. See?"

She handed the cards to Leo, who shuffled through them with growing amazement.

"How did you get these?"

"The album was stolen from Eva, and the woman who took it must have been planning to sell it but she disappeared on a cruise. It was my godson who found it . . ."

"Your godson?"

"Erich Schmidt. Remember?"

It was the first time she had referred to their shared past. He nodded, head bent, still scrutinizing the cards.

"There's this one too."

From her pocket she withdrew the card bearing the portrait of herself. Leo hesitated, squinted at the picture, then turned it over.

> *Last night Wolf said that after the war he would marry me! When is after the war? I asked. When Poland is subjugated, he explained. Very soon, he told me, Poland will cease to exist.*

"This is astonishing," he murmured.

"There's more. And so much worse. Hitler talks about the extermination of the entire Jewish race. It's written proof, Leo. That's what they need. You must take these back to London. I'll give you other examples of her handwriting, to verify it. We can't let the politicians think it's all over, that Hitler's demands have been met and he's no longer a threat. I heard Richard Dimbleby on the wireless saying Chamberlain's achievement was a triumph. It's dangerous to assume that Hitler has no aggressive intentions. He intends to destroy Europe. To exterminate the Jews. The idea that people think he will stop at the Sudetenland terrifies me."

"Don't be terrified, Clara. No one I know believes any such thing."

It was the first time he had used her name and the first time she had heard a note of anything in his voice that was like concern. He stood there, in his coat, while his sea-green eyes, unreadable as ever, pulled her in like a tide. The stillness between them was tangible.

She said, "Why did you not come to the Siegessäule?"

"I did. I was right there. You didn't see me. You were with a man."

"That was Max Brandt. He's one of ours. Code name Steinbrecher. I wasn't expecting him there. He surprised me."

"You had your arm in his."

"That was . . . work."

"It didn't look like work"—his voice was bureaucratically flat—"when you kissed him."

"I was saying goodbye. Max is a good man, Leo, and he's in terrible danger. He needed to leave Berlin and he wanted to see me before he did. If you were there, you should have come and spoken to me."

"Should I?"

"Yes. You should. If you were that close, the least you could do was make contact."

They stood, separated by only a narrow, trembling distance, and he was so quiet that she feared for a moment he was angry. When he did speak, however, his voice was low and level.

"Is that what you think, Clara? The *least* I could do? I watched the only woman I have ever loved arm in arm with another man. I watched you kiss him. And you think I should have made contact? It was all I could do to walk away."

She was trying to frame a reply. The words took shape in her mouth, but they died on her lips.

"Are you free, Leo?"

"I haven't been free since the day I met you."

When he reached out she felt the tensions of her dangerous existence fall from her like chains. She stepped towards him and ran her hand across his face, discovering the feel of it still inside her fingers, imprinted there. Her body fitted into his perfectly, as though they had been designed for each other.

She wanted to talk, but knew that if she began, she would not stop. Leo was shrugging off his coat and jacket, easing his braces, while their mouths met.

She pulled away. "Wait."

She undressed, peeling off the layers of clothing and lifting her arms to free the clasp of her silver locket. He took the locket from her, set it down, tenderly kissed her naked neck, and encircled her trembling body with his own.

MUCH LATER, WHEN THE evening sun was a faint glow and a few stars already glimmered in the sky, she brought him coffee and toast and sat naked in bed beside him. He was smiling at her, as though he would never stop. He looked around the room as if every item in it, from the desk, to the red armchair, to the pictures on the wall filled him with indescribable tenderness, because they belonged to her.

Downstairs someone was banging away at a piano, and the dusky light filtering through the leaves of the tree outside cast the room in a greenish tint. Clara felt as though they were suspended in that aqueous light, inviolate from everything around them, and she had the momentary bliss of satisfaction, as when every piece of a puzzle has finally fallen into place.

"I thought about you all the time. I had no idea where you were."

"I tried to forget you. I deliberately attempted to block Germany from my mind. I involved myself in other areas."

"And other women?"

His only answer was a shrug, a gesture that seemed to dismiss every woman he had met since she had last seen him, and expressed the absolute irrelevance of her question.

"I tried different ways of thinking about us," he said. "All sorts of metaphors. I had an image of us as two planets, circling each other from afar but never actually leaving each other's orbit. Pulled by such gravitational attraction that our paths would always be joined."

"Did you worry about me?"

"Of course."

She laid her head on his chest, so his voice was a low rumble, reverberating through his flesh and entering hers.

"Why did you never contact me?"

"I wrote to you. I must have written a hundred letters. But I never sent them."

"I often thought of telephoning. Just to hear your voice."

He traced a curl of hair around her ear. "You probably couldn't have found me if you'd tried. It's an odd, transient place, the intelligence service. People disappear without a trace, and you don't know whether they've been sacked, or found out, or simply posted elsewhere. That happened to me, until I was approached by a man called Dansey . . ."

She sat up.

"Colonel Dansey?"

"You've heard of him?"

"Guy Hamilton told me about him. What's he like?"

"I think he's very astute. Hamilton probably told you Dansey has firm ideas about the security of our network in Europe. And he's working on alternatives. He's looking for people who will be able to move around the continent fairly easily, if circumstances arise. Who are fluent in several languages. With a valid reason to travel."

"People like me."

"Yes. He mentioned you specifically."

"Is that why you're here then? Because Dansey sent you?"

"It might be why he approached me, but it's not why I came. I came because war could break out at any time, and I needed to know what you planned to do."

"If that was all, you could have asked Rupert."

His eyes gleamed. He caught her in his arms again and kissed her, burying his face in her flesh and inhaling the deep, warm scent of her.

"I came, Clara, because every day away from you convinced me that I shouldn't live a second more of my life without you. When I insisted on you leaving Berlin if we were to be married, I was a fearful, anxious fool. All I could see was you being arrested, or suffering, and I wanted to save you from that. I thought the prospect of you risking your life was more than I could bear. But being without you entirely was far, far worse."

She pulled away and regarded him soberly.

"What did Dansey want of me?"

"His idea is to establish an outfit inside Germany who could play an important part when war comes. He's keen to recruit women because he thinks they have more patience. They pay closer attention to detail. They can read relationships and human motivations better than men, he believes. I suppose that's true. I was never good at judging *you*. He wants to know what you might do, if war comes. Whether you would agree to stay here."

"I see."

Suddenly she didn't want to think about the future, or not that part of it. She lay back in his arms, remembering the time they had first met, when he told her about his hobby, translating classical literature.

"Are you still doing your translations?"

"I'm working on Rilke's *Sonnets to Orpheus* right now. Rilke has a wonderful way of making the German language sound soft and fluid."

"Orpheus was the musician, wasn't he?"

"Yes, he was a beautiful singer—his music transfixed the whole of nature. Animals would come and kneel before him when he sang. He could coax the rocks and stones to dance. And through his music he was able to cross the boundary between life and death to fetch his wife from the underworld. Ovid wrote about him too."

That reminded her. "What did you mean when you said you set that piece of Ovid as an exercise? A teaching exercise? You're not a schoolteacher, are you? I assumed you were working for the film company."

"I am, some of the time. The teaching is part of my other work. I'm training people how to use codes. Anyone who works with us will need to understand codes, ciphers, and all sorts of secret communication techniques. At the moment the outfit I work with is still pretty new. You won't find us in the telephone directory."

"So what exactly do you do?"

"I can't tell you, Clara, not until you need to know. But trust me, we're soon going to need more secure methods of communication. And codes will be an essential part of that. It seemed important to me that agents have something that would be easily memorized, yet individual. Poems are a common device, but everyone chooses 'Ozymandias' or 'The Charge of the Light Brigade' —poems that are easily recognized, even by foreigners. We wanted something entirely unpublished that could never be found in a reference book, so I suggested my translations of Ovid."

She made a wry face. "Which have still not been published?"

He laughed. "Perhaps someday. But they're serving a more important function right now."

He ran a finger down her neck and kissed the hollow at the base of her throat. "What's this perfume?"

She reached over to the bedside table and showed him the flask with Eva Braun's meticulous handwriting on the label.

"It's called Scent of Secrets."

"It's lovely."

Leo removed the stopper, gently anointing her wrist.

"You should let me have the bottle when it's done. Then wherever I go I can smell the last few drops and remember this moment."

Clara smiled. How was it possible to feel so happy with all the agony and anxiety that was going on in the city? War might come soon, and what would that mean for Erich, who was so keen to fight for his country? And all the friends she had here in Berlin? Five years ago, Leo had wanted her to leave Germany. Now, it seemed, he was asking her to stay. Perhaps she would not, after all, need to choose between love and duty.

"Your Orpheus. Did his wife ever leave the underworld?"

"She was permitted to follow her husband, unless he looked back."

"What happened if he looked back?"

"She stayed there."

He leaned over and kissed her again, deep and lingering.

"It's a story, Clara."

She looked out at the dusk. Beyond the window a swirl of migrating birds was massing, wheeling, and turning in the darkening sky. A susurration of starlings, that's what it was called, she remembered suddenly, a perfect aerial formation, tilting and diving through the early evening mist, changing direction abruptly like the whisk of a living cloak, narrowing to a twisting ribbon, then bulging into a cloud. More and more birds joined the flock so that eventually a great throng bloomed in the sky, massing above the city rooftops, scattering and rejoining, soaring up into the vault of clouds.

Clara tried to picture where the birds were heading. Another continent, it must be, Africa perhaps; some latitude that would provide sanctuary from the gathering winter storms. And she wondered if she and Leo would ever know such an escape. What did the future hold for them? In that moment she had an image of them properly together, without the need for caution or subterfuge, moving out of the shadows and into the pure light of day. She imagined how it might feel, to live in the warmth of a southern sun, and see its colors and flowers. To walk in distant streets and gardens without fear. To breathe the jasmine and smell the soft air of safety on the breeze.

T HE OSTER CONSPIRACY WAS A WIDE-RANGING MILITARY PLOT TO oust Hitler in September 1938. The planned coup involved senior German military and intelligence leaders, members of the Berlin police, and many other individuals. The plan was to mount a raid on the Reich Chancellery. But it failed at the eleventh hour, stymied by Chamberlain's decision to appease Hitler.

EVA BRAUN did keep a diary. Some entries, up to 1935, have been published, but after that her writing has gone missing. One document, published in 1949, purported to be her vanished diary but was widely dismissed as a fake.

In 1939, *Time* magazine published an article about the relationship between Eva Braun and Hitler, saying that Hitler had "at least partly supported" Eva for several years and that she had confided to intimates that she expected to marry him within a year. Her suicide attempts are documented. Many of the women associated with Hitler attempted or committed suicide, and Eva Braun made her first attempt in 1931 and another in 1935.

THE CRUISE LINER *WILHELM GUSTLOFF* may have started out in the service of pleasure, but it became a byword for tragedy in maritime history. When war broke out, in 1939, the *Wilhelm Gustloff* was converted by the military into a hospital ship and U-boat training school and remained as such until January 30, 1945, when the captain was ordered to evacuate German refugees and soldiers fleeing the Red Army from the East Prussian port of Gotenhafen. The ship was torpedoed by a Soviet submarine. More than nine thousand people died in the freezing Baltic waters, making it the worst shipping disaster in history. The sinking of the pride of the Strength Through Joy program, twelve years to the day since Hitler seized power, seemed to symbolize the destruction of the Thousand Year Reich.

COCO CHANEL remained in Paris after it was occupied by German forces and kept her own suite at the Ritz. At the end of the war she fled to Switzerland, so was spared from being put on trial for collaboration, but her association with Nazi officers has come under intense scrutiny, especially since the declassification of military archives revealing that the French Préfecture de Police had a document on Chanel, describing her as "Couturier and perfumer. Pseudonym: Westminster. Agent reference: F 7124." In 1943, Chanel traveled to Berlin with "Spatz" Dincklage to meet Heinrich Himmler, and in late 1943 or early 1944, Chanel and Walter Schellenberg devised a plan to press Britain to end hostilities with Germany. Schellenberg was sentenced at Nuremberg for war crimes but released when he was diagnosed with liver disease. Chanel paid for his medical care and living expenses until he died in 1952.

ON NOVEMBER 9, 1938, at the goading of Goebbels, a wave of violence against Jews and Jewish property was unleashed throughout Germany in the deadliest pogrom since the Middle Ages. It gained the name Kristallnacht from the amount of broken glass that littered the streets the next morning. The violence shocked the world and convinced many who had previously been complacent about the Nazis' true intentions towards the Jews. It was said that Goebbels planned the violence in order to regain the Führer's favor after the disgrace of his affair.

There were numerous ingenious attempts to assassinate Hitler during the Third Reich, but none, as far as I know, involved the use of perfume.

ACKNOWLEDGMENTS

THE HISTORY OF THE THIRD REICH IS RICHLY DOCUMENTED, but the women's side is less so. Some books, however, provided excellent background for the writing of this novel, including Guido Knopp's *Hitler's Women*, Angela Lambert's *The Lost Life of Eva Braun*, *Eva Braun: Life with Hitler* by Heike B. Gortemaker, and *Women of the Third Reich* by Anna Maria Sigmund.

My huge thanks go to Kate Miciak for her inspired editing and passion for the Clara Vine series. Her warmth and generosity made the editing of this novel a joy. Thanks, too, to Julia Maguire for her help and Nita Pronovost, formerly at Random House Canada, for all her enthusiasm and wise suggestions.

Thank you to my agent, Caradoc King, who was so encouraging when I first mooted the idea of an Anglo-German actress and spy in Nazi Germany and has been tireless in his support. I am deeply grateful to Suzanne Baboneau for first publishing the series in the UK and to my writer friends Amanda Craig, Kate Saunders, Kathy Lette, Liz Jensen, Elizabeth Buchan, and Rachel Kelly for their kindness, interest, and an awful lot of lunch.

From the moment I met Joanna Coles, when we were both young journalists on *The Daily Telegraph* in London, I knew we would be great friends, and her sense of humor, intelligence, and friendship have been priceless to me ever since. Lastly, all my love and gratitude goes to my husband, Philip Kerr. Our ongoing conversation about history, Germany, characters, and writing has been an integral part of my life for the past twenty-five years. To sit around a kitchen table talking about plots—what greater pleasure could there be?

The

SCENT

of

SECRETS

JANE THYNNE

A
READER'S
GUIDE

A FEW STREETS AWAY FROM HARRODS IN LONDON'S KNIGHTS-bridge stands the anonymous, shiny black door of a private members' club. From the outside, you would never know that the club is for agents who served in resistance organizations during WWII and beyond. But when you enter and climb the stairs you pass numerous photographs of female spies who served—and mostly died—in the field. It is deeply inspiring.

When I began writing about a British agent in Germany in the 1930s it was with the bravery of these women in mind. I had always wanted to write a novel set in Berlin. It was a city that went in a matter of months from being the most exciting place in Europe—the center of sexual and cultural freedom, of Expressionist film and Bauhaus art—to the most frightening and repressive. The idea of placing a female British agent not just in Berlin but at the heart of the Nazi regime itself was irresistible.

Having been a journalist, both in TV and newspapers, for most of my career, I was keen on documentary accuracy, so even though I was writing fiction, I spent weeks tramping Berlin's streets, exploring the prewar buildings that remained and picturing those that had been destroyed. It was a strange process in which my imaginary Berlin—the 1930s version—existed like a palimpsest alongside the hastily erected and often ugly postwar buildings. Parts of Goebbels's Propaganda Ministry still stand, and the Babelsberg film studio remains in its entirety, as does Goering's Air Ministry, but we can no longer see Hitler's Reich Chancellery, and the bunker where Hitler and Eva Braun died is buried beneath a parking lot. Yet it wasn't just the official buildings that mattered. Deciding where an actress like Clara Vine might live was just as important. In the end I chose Winterfeldtstrasse, a lovely tree-lined street in Schöneberg just a block away from where Christopher Isherwood wrote the novel that was filmed as *Cabaret*.

The streets of Berlin were the easy bit. The chief challenge of my research was that I was writing about women. There are barely enough libraries in the world to contain the books written about the male side of the Third Reich—the leaders, the politics, the campaigns—but the experience of German women seems to have gone largely unrecorded. What was it like to be in the League of German Girls? To attend a Bride School or a weekly Mother's Course? And in the upper echelons of society, how did it feel to be married to a man who became a monster? Were the Nazi leaders' wives complicit, or did they try to dissuade their men from their crimes?

The answers were not easy to find. No one has wanted to translate the memoirs of women like Lina Heydrich into English, so I brushed up on my German and spent time buried in the London Library, a beautiful Georgian building in St. James's Square. And the information I found provided for me a whole new perspective on the private life of the Third Reich. The domestic details of the women's lives seem so fragile and recognizably ordinary beside the war machine that their husbands were preparing. While I was researching the life of Eva Braun I read a few lines about her love of perfume, how she adored Worth's Je Reviens and liked to create her own concoctions. This was, of course, just another irony of life in Nazi Germany—cosmetics, especially French ones, were frowned on for ordinary women. Yet that detail, like a snatch of perfume itself, lit an idea in my mind. I thought about the power of scent to evoke feelings—not just childhood memories, but unsettling emotions and fear too—and I decided that perfume should be a theme at the heart of my story.

Like the door of that secret agents' club in London, the wartime lives of German women are easy to pass by. But you only understand how a totalitarian society works when you see it on the human scale. To me, glimpsing the personal lives of the senior men through their relationships with their wives and girlfriends only makes their activities more disturbing.

—Jane Thynne

QUESTIONS AND TOPICS
FOR DISCUSSION

1. Who surprised you the most in the novel?

2. Women played a crucial role in Hitler's vision for the future of Germany. Discuss the role of women in German society in the 1930s. How does Hitler want the position of women to change?

3. There are several examples of women who are even more fervently in favor of the Nazi cause than their spouses; did that surprise you? Why or why not? Discuss the relationships between the high-ranking Nazi officials and their wives.

4. What did you think of Rosa's decision to forge her nephew's official medical papers? Were you surprised by her decision? Why or why not?

5. What did you think of Eva Braun? What about her relationship with Hitler? Was she as silly as she sometimes seemed to be, or do you think she understood more about politics than she let on?

6. Discuss the importance of the Nazi youth clubs and the mother schools in implementing the Nazi philosophy.

7. Like most Berliners, Clara grows suspicious of everyone—including her new neighbor, who turns out to be an innocent schoolteacher. Anyone might be a spy, even

young children on their Sunday collection rounds. What means of recourse are there for normal citizens who do not support the Nazi regime?

8.   There seem to be a lot of inconsistencies in the personal, political, and moral philosophies of Hitler and his entourage. Hitler detests makeup yet loves actresses and the cinema. Goebbels champions family values yet is a serial philanderer. Rosa observes that party leaders seem to want to keep men and women separate, like flour and sugar, while at the same time encouraging higher birth rates and more marriage. Can you think of any other examples? How do you rationalize these hypocrisies? How do they?

9.   What surprised you most about Hitler?

10. Compare and contrast the different Nazi wives in the novel.

11. What would your signature scent be?

I f you enjoyed

The SCENT of SECRETS

by Jane Thynne

YOU WON'T WANT TO MISS

The PURSUIT
of PEARLS

Read on for a sneak peek . . .

BERLIN, APRIL 1939

I T IS COLD IN THE DENSE WOODS OF THE GRUNEWALD AT SEVEN on an April morning. Even though spring has dotted the moss with bluebells and wild daffodils and filled the tops of the pines with nesting birds, the temperature is still enough to goose-pimple the arms and cause the hardiest hiker to shiver. It's gloomy, too, even in the glades, where the early sun filtering through the boughs gives only a greenish, watery light and leaves most of the tangled ferns and mulch in darkness. The mist hangs low between the closely packed trees, confusing any traveler unwise enough to stray from the path. The mix of wood here—pine, oak, and birch—has remained unchanged for thousands of years, and wild boar forage for beech mast in the undergrowth as they have always done. Hunters search for deer and pig along dirt tracks that have been trodden since the Middle Ages. Though the city is only a few miles away to the west, the forest could be the same primeval place it was in the Ice Age, when meltwater first created the lakes surrounding Berlin's flat sandy plain and the early German tribes emerged from the boggy swamps.

In the Grunewald, history slips by like a leaf falling to the forest floor.

HEDWIG HOLZ SQUINTED DOWN the barrel of the Walther PPK pistol, released the safety lever, cocked the hammer, took aim, shut her eyes tightly, and squeezed.

Nothing happened.

She dropped the pistol with a sigh, aligned it again, keeping two fingers wrapped around the grip and a little finger curled beneath the magazine the way she had been shown, and aimed again. Despite the freezing air, she could feel a trail of sweat running down her brow and a maddening itch from her woolen vest just below her arm that she longed to scratch. What was more, in her hurry to dress that morning she had chosen the tighter of her two skirts and the waistband was now digging in uncomfortably. Yet she had to stop these trivial bodily sensations from distracting her, just as she must ignore the thrushes flitting between their nests in the high pines, the squirrels scrambling among the branches, and the whole awakening Grunewald around her. She must concentrate. Straighten her arm, feel the cold metal of the pistol burn against her palm, find the target and shoot. Even without her glasses, how hard could that be?

She aimed, shut her eyes again and fired, but although the gun worked this time, the shot veered wildly off course, ricocheting around the tranquil woods and provoking a chorus of screeches from the crows overhead. Hedwig flinched, brushed the sweaty trails of hair from her brow with the back of her sleeve, and aimed again. The rustling in the trees above had broken her concentration, and her next shot went even wider, sending a flutter of birds up into the sky and provoking muffled laughs from the gaggle of girls behind her.

They had been there for an hour now, a group of twenty young women, all startlingly alike from a distance, with blue eyes, plaits of various shades of gold pinned up on their heads, and white smocks with neckties over a navy serge pinafore, ankle socks and clumpy black boots. They made a curious sight as they threaded their way along the woodland path behind their leader—an Amazonian figure called Fräulein von Essen, wearing a leather jerkin and carrying a satchel of ammunition and a target which she established a hundred meters away from the firing site. They could expect to be there for another hour at least, Hedwig thought despondently, until Fräulein von Essen was satisfied that every girl among them could shoot a man at a hundred paces.

Shooting was the last activity Hedwig expected when she joined the Faith and Beauty society. Far from shooting a man, all most girls wanted was to capture one. The Glaube und Schönheit society was, after all, the Third Reich's elite finishing school for young women. Its girls were the pearls of the Reich and the plan was to equip them with the poise, polish, and talent required to marry into the top ranks of the Nazi hierarchy.

To this end, every weekend, and several evenings in the week, a select group of girls would gather at the Faith and Beauty community house in the picturesque woods outside Neubabelsberg to be educated in the finer points of civilization: history, the arts, music, dancing, and dinner party conversation. How to discuss Beethoven intelligently and dazzle a man with knowledge of the Franco-Prussian War. How to make tapestries and play chamber music. How to waltz, sketch a head and paint a decent landscape in watercolors. Any old Bride School or Mother Class could teach a girl to cook a herring, the wisdom went, but some German girls should be setting their sights on higher things. That was why Reichsjugendführer Baldur von Schirach, head of all Nazi youth groups, had hit on the idea of a society for the cream of the nation's young women. Faith and Beauty girls were the Third Reich's Vestal Virgins, according to the introductory talk—a comparison that made Hedwig blush profusely when she heard it for the first time.

Every girl applying to the Faith and Beauty society must be blond and blue-eyed—the precise color was measured against an eye chart containing sixty different shades—but there was no actual stipulation that they must also be beautiful, which was fortunate for Hedwig, whose moon-like face was earnest rather than exquisite, and whose mousy hair could only be called blond by a vivid stretch of the imagination. She was tall and bosomy, a born worrier with a perpetually anxious air that vanished only when a good-natured smile lit up her face, exposing her wonky teeth.

Hedwig's appearance was in stark contrast to her only friend in the society, Lottie Franke, a slender beauty with thick, honey-gold hair, a bold gaze, and full mouth. She looked like a girl in a Renaissance portrait, with eyes as blue as gas flames and skin like whipped cream. Although Faith and Beauty girls were encouraged to acquire a suntan, Lottie maintained that sunlight caused wrinkles and insisted on coating herself with Nivea and remaining as pale as wax.

Despite their physical differences, the two had been close since they met on the first day of school, with their satchels on their backs and the traditional cone of sweets in their hands. Frau Mann, the Faith and Beauty principal, never lost a chance to boast that the two girls proved the egalitarian nature of the society. In the Third Reich, elites weren't just for the rich. The other girls may come from middle-class homes with pianos and maids, but Hedwig and Lottie were unambiguously from the wrong side of the tracks. Hedwig and her five brothers inhabited a cramped apartment in Moabit, four rooms with a cuckoo clock in the parlor, a pervasive aroma of pork fat, and a bathroom they shared with another family. Lottie's family was even poorer than Hedwig's. It had been a great sacrifice for the Frankes to find the fees, but Lottie was an only child, and generally Lottie got what Lottie wanted. And what she really wanted was a ticket to a better life. To meet all the right people and leave working-class Berlin behind forever.

Lottie was passionate about fashion, and as part of her Faith and Beauty course she had chosen to study costume design at the nearby Ufa film studios in Babelsberg. She had met any number of film stars—Lilian Harvey, Willi Fritsch, Brigitte Horney, and Marika Rökk—and she was full of snippets of celebrity gossip. Which actor was sleeping with someone else's wife, who had undergone cosmetic surgery, what girl had caught Reichsminister Goebbels's eye. All the Faith and Beauty girls crowded round her. Lottie was the type who knew secrets, and even though she probably made most of them up, hearing about a film star's drug habit was infinitely more diverting than a lecture on Napoleon's retreat from Moscow.

Hedwig braced herself, focused, and took aim again. The gun was heavy—half a kilo of iron that had to be aimed with a straightened right arm. Her next shot went even wider, provoking unrestrained shrieks of laughter from her fellow students. Damn pistol shooting. And archery. What on earth was it for? Fräulein von Essen told them archery would reawaken their sense of the medieval, but Hedwig had a nine-to-five job as a librarian. She had never had a sense of the medieval and didn't want one now. When would she ever need to handle a bow and arrow? Let alone a gun?

As if reading her thoughts, Fräulein von Essen stared at her, flint-eyed, and signaled, with an infinitesimal incline of the head, that she should try again. Hedwig needn't think that mere ineptitude would reprieve her from pistol practice. They could stay there all day, as far as Fräulein von Essen was concerned. Didn't Hedwig remember taking that oath to the Führer about loyalty, sacrifice, and achievement?

Hedwig was distracted—that was the problem—and it was Lottie who was distracting her. She had not turned up for pistol practice that morning, nor had Hedwig seen her at their previous community meeting. She was out during the day, of course, but everyone was supposed to congregate at the community house at six for dinner and evening instruction and Lottie had already missed a two-part talk on medieval tapestries.

Hedwig knew what the problem was, of course. Lottie was in love. When Hedwig asked her who the lucky man was, she had turned secretive, so Hedwig assumed he must be unsuitable. She had no idea who it could be, but Lottie had been making endless outings over recent weeks and refused to tell Hedwig where she had been. God forbid she had eloped. The thought of what that would do to Herr and Frau Franke, who worshipped their clever daughter and had gladly donated their savings for her Faith and Beauty training, made Hedwig wince.

When her next shot veered even further from the target, prompting a further burst of hilarity from the others, Fräulein von Essen put an unexpected end to Hedwig's misery by ordering her to give someone else a try, so she moved gratefully to the back of the group, leaned against the trunk of a tree and miserably surveyed the dank, mushroomy woods around her.

She knew she was supposed to like the forest. They were

constantly sent on hikes with a knapsack and compass, the branches whipping in their face and the undergrowth threatening to trip them up, and besides, true Germans belonged in the woods. They had learned that in the weekly Race Ancestry lessons; according to the Roman author Tacitus, the German race had originated in the forest before giving birth to the whole of human civilization. The original Germans were blue-eyed with golden hair and vigorous bodies, and life in the forest had made them a tough warrior race.

But the silence unnerved her. Berlin was a cacophony of noise, yet here were only pigeons rustling and cooing, the occasional sound of a deer crashing through the undergrowth, and the sporadic crack of the girls' guns.

That morning, though, the silence had been shattered by a bevy of construction workers who had begun work a few hundred meters away, building an air-raid shelter for the film studios. Because of the warmongering of the British, the whole of Berlin was digging air-raid shelters now. Wherever you went in town the rattle of drills and clang of spades could be heard in the background, preparing for the day when British bombers appeared in the skies. Everyone was talking about war, but Hedwig didn't believe it for a second. As far as she was concerned, the chances of any actual fighting were as remote as those ancient battles between the rival tribes of Europe that Tacitus wrote about. No foreign country had stood in the Führer's way before, and there was really no reason to suppose they would now.

On the way back, Fräulein von Essen couldn't resist another dig at Hedwig's hopeless aim.

"Back again tomorrow, ladies. And perhaps this time Hedwig Holz will be able to manage just a single shot on target."

1

BERLIN, IN APRIL 1939, WAS PARTYING LIKE THERE WAS NO tomorrow.

The Führer was fifty and the whole of Germany was in a frenzy. The day itself had been declared a national holiday and the largest military parade ever held—five hours' worth of storm troopers, hurricane troopers, tornado troopers, and every other type of trooper—was proceeding along the new East-West axis, the great triumphal boulevard that ran all the way from Unter den Linden to the Olympic stadium. Guns and tanks glittered in the morning air as the boots of fifty thousand soldiers thudded rhythmically into the ground. One hundred and sixty-two Heinkel bombers, Messerschmitt fighters, and Stuka dive bombers performed flypasts at five-minute intervals, leaving lightning flashes of vapor in the sky. Deputations of the Hitler Youth and League of German Girls had arrived from all over Germany. There were armored cars, cannons, Howitzers, and antiaircraft guns. And more than a million spectators, most of them carrying black bread sandwiches, bottles of beer, and swastika flags.

Clara Vine shuffled her feet and looked down at her glossy Ferragamo leather pumps. They were hand-stitched in Florence, had cost the earth, and they hurt like hell.

Why on earth had she not worn comfortable shoes?

She was hungry and thirsty and longing to sit down. She had been there since nine that morning but had only managed to secure a place three deep opposite the Führer's saluting podium on the Charlottenburger Chaussee. The view to her right was obscured by a large woman with a squashed felt hat, accompanied by two boys of around six and seven. To begin with Clara had pitied the children, doomed to spend the morning fenced in by a forest of legs, but after hours of their relentless wails, inquiring when *exactly* the Führer was coming and how much longer would he be, her sympathy was wearing thin. To her left was a war veteran, medals pinned proudly to his chest, saluting frenetically like someone with uncontrollable muscle spasms. He had come all the way from Saxony and he was not the only one. Thousands of visitors had poured into the city. The stations were teeming and every hotel from the Adlon down was block booked. People who couldn't afford anywhere else had pitched their tents in the parks.

Like all birthdays, Hitler's special day had begun with presents, but that was where the ordinariness ended. Vast marble tables had been assembled in the Reich Chancellery to display Meissen porcelain, silver candlesticks, and Titian paintings, alongside rather more modest gifts from ordinary people, largely made up of swastika cakes and cushions. The Pope, the King of England, and Henry Ford had sent telegrams. The engineer Ferdinand Porsche had presented Hitler with a shiny black convertible VW beetle. Rudolf Hess had acquired a collection of priceless letters written by the Führer's hero, Frederick the Great, and Albert Speer had given him an entire scale model of "Germania"—the new world capital, with buildings made out of balsa wood and glass and a thirteen-foot model of the proposed triumphal arch. This was, without doubt, Hitler's favorite present, and he pored over it like a boy with a train set until he could be persuaded to tear himself away.

On the face of it, Berlin was putting on a magnificent show. Gigantic white pillars had sprouted all the way along major thoroughfares. The newsstands groaned with souvenir birthday issues. Swastikas sprouted from every conceivable surface. Spring was a riot of color in Berlin, so long as the colors were red and black.

Beneath the birthday bunting, however, everything was a little shabbier in Germany's capital. The tablecloths in the restaurants were spotted because there was no detergent, the bread was sawdust, and the Ersatz coffee undrinkable. People looked the other way on the trams because there was no toothpaste, precious few razor blades or shaving foam, and the sour odor of humanity and unwashed clothes hung in the U-Bahn. Even high-class nightclubs like Ciros stank of low-grade cigarettes and taxis home were nonexistent because of the petrol shortage.

After the previous year's Anschluss, when Germany annexed Austria, followed by the bloodless seizure of Czechoslovakia that March, most of Europe guessed a war was on the way. When it happened, it would be Poland's fault, according to the Ministry of Propaganda and Enlightenment, which ensured that newspapers were black with seventy-two-point headlines screaming belligerent revenge on the Poles for their atrocities against Germans in the disputed "Polish corridor." *Poland, Look Out!* There had been murderous attacks on Germans in Danzig. God help any country that stood in Germany's way.

Looking around her, Clara guessed that despite the marching and the machines, no one in this great big birthday pageant really wanted war. The ghost of the last war was still behind their eyes and the thought of what another would do haunted all but the very young. Only the little boys beside her, who now had squeezed between the legs of the storm troopers guarding the route, saw anything thrilling in the inexorable wall of men and tanks rolling past. Everyone else was getting by on an edgy cocktail of hope and denial. Everywhere you went, nerves flashed and shorted, like violet sparks above the tramlines. Tempers frayed. The whole city was as pumped and jittery as a dog being forced to fight.

Above their heads, loudspeakers strung along the street barked out radio broadcasts of Joseph Goebbels between bursts of military music. Goebbels was cheerleading the nation as though the Führer's birthday was synonymous with facing up to the Poles. Enthusiasm for both was compulsory.

"No German at home or anywhere else in the world can fail to take the deepest and heartiest pleasure in participation."

Clara winced. The voice of the short, clubfooted minister for Propaganda and Enlightenment still got under her skin like shards of glass. Even now, after six years in Germany, hearing it daily on the radio and at the film studios where she worked, Joseph Goebbels's wheedling tones could make her flinch like chalk on a blackboard.

Clara was only there because of a solemn promise she had made to her godson Erich Schmidt, who at sixteen had been chosen to lead his battalion of Hitler Youth in the parade. It was a great honor, Erich had impressed on her several times. Only, from where she was standing there seemed little chance of even glimpsing Erich, let alone of him registering her loyal presence.

It didn't have to be that way. As an actress contracted to the Ufa studios, Clara had qualified for a place in the VIP enclosure, alongside prominent personalities in their finery and portly Party dignitaries trussed up in field gray. The viewing stand, garlanded with golden laurels and tented drapes like a marquee at a country wedding, offered a far better view and a gilt chair to sit on. That was why she had risked the Ferragamo shoes, as well as the skirt suit and the tip-tilted hat, which now looked far too smart amid the stolid burghers of the Berlin crowd. Only, when she reached the gates of the VIP enclosure, she realized she couldn't face it. She spent enough of her life in close confines with Nazi officials, without wanting to join them behind a velvet rope with no chance of escape.

A frisson of excitement ran through the crowd. A posse of steel-helmeted, black-jacketed SS officers had appeared and were elbowing their way through, glancing from left to right. Joseph Goebbels, who was recording this extravaganza for posterity, was controlling every aspect down to the last detail. No one was allowed to take their own photographs and police were deputed to arrest anyone in the crowd who wielded a camera or failed to perform the Nazi salute. As the SS men barged past, Clara saw an elderly couple at the back of the crowd, the man a teacher or a pastor, perhaps, and his gray-haired wife beside him, being hustled off to a side street and lined up against a wall to await the police wagon.

Mirror periscopes swiveled like reeds in the wind and the screams around her intensified, rising into a wall of sound. The cordon of SA and SS officers linked arms to prevent the surge of sightseers spilling into the road.

"He's coming!"

The excitement of the moment caused the stolid woman beside her to burst into a cry of joy.

First came a fleet of motorcycle outriders, then Hitler himself, upright at the helm of his seven-liter Mercedes Tourer, with his arm raised in the trademark salute he could apparently hold for two hours straight. His peculiar, impersonal stare traveled like a searchlight across the crowds as his head swiveled intermittently right and left, seemingly seeking out individual faces. Flowers were hurled through the air, hitting the sides of the Mercedes with soft thuds. Surprisingly, only two members of the Adolf Hitler Leibstandarte bodyguard were at his side. The usual car of followers was absent.

How vulnerable he was. All it would take was a single shot and the leader of all Germany, the object of all this adulation, would be extinguished like a lightbulb, along with the fears of an entire continent. Clara wondered if she was the only person in the crowd who had such a thought. German civilians were never told about attempts on the Führer's life, but Clara had heard that in Munich several years ago, during a parade like this, a pistol had been found in a newsreel camera mounted on the roof of a car, the barrel of the gun pointed down the lens. A couple of other attempts had been averted at the last minute. Each lucky escape only served to convince Hitler more firmly of his deepest belief. Destiny was on his side.

As he came parallel a shaft of sun lanced through a rent in the clouds, and a finger of light pointed down towards his car. Hitler's bright blue gaze swiveled in Clara's direction and seemed to penetrate right to where she was standing.

Clara ducked her head, turned sharply, and pushed her way back through the crowd. She had a long day ahead of her and a party to attend that evening. And today of all days she had chosen to move house.

ABOUT THE AUTHOR

JANE THYNNE was born in Venezuela and educated in London. She graduated from Oxford University with a degree in English and joined the BBC as a television director. She has also worked at *The Sunday Times, The Daily Telegraph,* and *The Independent* and appears regularly as a broadcaster on television and radio. She is the author of five previous novels. She is married to the writer Philip Kerr. They have three children and live in London.

www.janethynne.com

Facebook.com/AuthorJaneThynne

@janethynne

ABOUT THE TYPE

This book was set in Walbaum, a typeface designed in 1810 by German punch cutter J. E. (Justus Erich) Walbaum (1768–1839). Walbaum's type is more French than German in appearance. Like Bodoni, it is a classical typeface, yet its openness and slight irregularities give it a human, romantic quality.